TOUCH OF THE DEMON

DIANA ROWLAND

DAW BOOKS, INC.
DONALD A. WOLLHEIM, FOUNDER
375 Hudson Street, New York, NY 10014

ELIZABETH R. WOLLHEIM
SHEILA E. GILBERT
PUBLISHERS

www.dawbooks.com

Cover art by Daniel Dos Santos.

Cover design by G-Force Design.

DAW Book Collectors No. 1611.

DAW Books are distributed by Penguin Group (USA) Inc.

First Printing, January 2013
1 2 3 4 5 6 7 8 9

Raves for Diana Rowland's Kara Gillian Novels:

"A nifty combination of police procedural and urban fantasy. Not too many detectives summon demons in their basement for the fun of it, but Kara Gillian is not your average law enforcement officer."

—Charlaine Harris, *New York Times* bestselling author

"Rowland's world of arcane magic and demons is fresh and original . . . [and her] characters are well-developed and distinct. . . . Dark, fast-paced, and gripping." —SciFiChick

"A fascinating mixture of a hard-boiled police procedural and gritty yet other-worldly urban fantasy. Diana Rowland's professional background as both a street cop and forensic assistant not only shows through but gives the book a realism sadly lacking in all too many urban fantasy 'crime' novels."

—L. E. Modesitt, Jr., author of the *Saga of Recluse*

"Diana Rowland has built a fascinating and compelling urban fantasy series, with main character Kara as tough as she needs to be yet vulnerable enough to be realistic."

—Fresh Fiction

"Rowland once again writes the perfect blend of police procedural and paranormal fantasy."

—Night Owl Paranormal

"Phenomenal world building, a tough yet vulnerable heroine, a captivating love triangle, and an increasingly compelling metanarrative that just gets juicier with each book. . . . Blows most other urban fantasies out of the park."

—All Things Urban Fantasy

"Yet again, Diana Rowland has knocked my socks off with a stellar book that left me positively desperate for more."

—A Book Obsession

"*Mark of the Demon* crosses police procedure with weird magic. Diana Rowland's background makes her an expert in the former, and her writing convinces me she's also an expert in the latter in this fast-paced story that ends with a bang."

—Carrie Vaughn, *New York Times* bestselling author

Also by Diana Rowland:

SECRETS OF THE DEMON
SINS OF THE DEMON
TOUCH OF THE DEMON

****

MY LIFE AS A WHITE TRASH ZOMBIE
EVEN WHITE TRASH ZOMBIES
GET THE BLUES
WHITE TRASH ZOMBIE APOCALYPSE*

* Coming soon from DAW

ACKNOWLEDGMENTS

Huge thanks to Carrie Vaughn, Daniel Abraham, and Paolo Bacigalupi for helping me stay sane-ish during the writing of this. Special thanks to Tara Sullivan Palmer for inviting my kid down the street to play with her kids when I was churning toward my deadline. Enormous thanks to Mary Robinette Kowal, Nina Lourie, Nicole Peeler, and Lindsay Ribar for reading the early drafts and not pulling any punches. Many awesome thanks to Matt Bialer, Joshua Starr, and Betsy Wollheim for doing the behind-the-scenes heavy lifting and support. Sweaty thanks to Robert Butler, J.J. McCleskey, and my sister, Sherry Rowland, for giving me a way to maintain what little sanity I have. And, finally, super duper, smoochy lovey thanks to my husband, Jack, and my daughter, Anna, for putting up with me and for believing in me and for being the Best Family Ever.

Chapter 1

I didn't whimper when the demonic lord placed the collar around my neck and sealed it closed. Didn't curse as it dampened my ability to see the arcane and nullified the chances of anyone's being able to locate me. Didn't cry. Didn't scream. Didn't fall to the floor and curl into the fetal position.

I wanted to. Holy shit, did I ever want to. But in all my years of being a summoner and of being a cop, I knew that if ever I had to appear strong, it was now—when face to face with a demonic lord in the demon realm.

"*Don't you recognize it?*" the lord had asked. "*It's your old summoning chamber.*"

My gaze swept the chamber again. Its dark grey marble floor carved with worn glyphs joined matching walls, so numerous that the room felt circular. No windows, no furnishings, and a massive set of charred double doors ahead of me, one ajar, and two smaller doors to the sides. Arcane light cast by shimmering sigils high above bathed everything in an amber glow and eerie sliding shadows. Wisps of smoke rose from glowing coals in a brazier against the wall, likely the source of the pungent skunk-spray-meets-jasmine odor.

I'd appeared here less than two minutes ago, finally summoned to the demon realm after over a month of dodging the attempts; an evasion aided by wearing an arcane-crippling arm cuff similar to the collar I wore now. Already I could tell that this collar wasn't as brute force crude as the cuff. I wasn't nauseated and could actually see the glimmer of sigils and patterns dancing at the edges of my vision, though I knew without even trying that I wouldn't be able to touch or form them.

The demonic lord stood before me, tall and elegant in what looked like a perfectly tailored charcoal grey Armani suit, complete with crisp white shirt and black tie. Keen silver-grey eyes set in a face with an Asian cast left no doubt that he was thoroughly assessing me on all sorts of levels. Inky black hair entwined with gold cord hung to the small of his back in a heavy intricate braid. Power pulsed from him in such controlled undulations that I got the sense I was only getting a hint of his full aura.

The human—otherwise known as the asshole who summoned me—busied himself at the perimeter of the summoning circle, anchoring the flows and sealing the portal. Though he couldn't have been much more than a teenager, I had to give him some credit. Bare-chested, tall, and lean with a crazy halo of curly blond hair, he dispelled and traced sigils with a confidence that told me he was damned skilled.

I straightened my shoulders. "I've never been here before. What sort of game is this?"

The lord's face grew hard, and when he spoke his voice was a lava flow promising to consume all in its path. "No game, summoner." He seized my chin, looked into my face as though determining my worth. "If you do not know, then you have been kept well hooded by your lord." He released me with a slight shove, and I staggered back a step before recovering. Terror coiled in my gut, but I did my best to put on a sneer.

"This is not my summoning chamber," I said, squaring my shoulders and doing my damnedest to look like I did this sort of thing every day. "I know that much." I scowled and brushed myself off. My pants felt sticky, and when I glanced down at my hands, I realized I was still fairly spattered with atomized bits of Tracy Gordon, the very recently deceased summoner whose collapsing gate got me into this mess. *Gross!* I dragged my gaze back up. "Why have you summoned me?"

The lord's eyes skimmed over me, taking in my general appearance and the spattered bits on my pants and—I knew—in my hair. I had no doubt he knew exactly what it was. But if he thought his summoning of me had disrupted a ritual and shredded a summoner, he sure as shit didn't show a flicker of dismay or remorse. Instead, he turned away, clasped his hands behind his back, and headed for the doors.

"Bring her," he ordered.

A soft scrape of sound from behind alerted me—claws on stone. I turned to see the largest *reyza* I'd ever seen moving my way. Manlike, well-muscled, and more than half again as tall as the lord, he approached, teeth bared in a bestial face, and tail flicking behind. His skin shimmered bronze in the amber light as he spread huge leathery wings. The movement wafted a faint musky, spicy scent toward me that made me wonder if Old Spice was a cheap knockoff of Eau de Reyza.

Gulping, I raised my hands, palms out. "There is no need for force, honored one," I said quickly. "I will offer no resistance."

The reyza growled low in his throat and pointed a clawed hand toward the doors. It was pretty clear what he meant, and I turned quickly to comply. It hadn't been all that long ago that the reyza, Sehkeril, had eviscerated me during the confrontation with the Symbol Man, so I'd pretty much let go of any illusions I might have held about the overall friendliness of demons.

Doing my best impression of a cooperative prisoner, I passed through huge doors of finely carved wood. Twice as tall as me, the heavy doors had definitely been through some shit. Char ate into the wood, in places almost deeply enough to go all the way through the door. A faint acrid odor lingered, though the damage looked smooth, as though from a long time ago, worn down over the years.

I glanced back to see the blond young man following. He pulled on a black silky shirt as he walked, and his expression was an interesting mixture of relief, pride, and delight. I quickly pulled my gaze away before he noticed me looking.

The room beyond the doors mirrored the summoning chamber in size though it had about half as many sides. Two walls opened into corridors, and each of the remaining walls framed alcoves with incredibly lifelike statues of demons and humans.

I kept my cop senses tuned to high alert since information on the people, demons, and layout could be useful later. But mostly I did so because getting into that mindset helped keep me from thinking about how very fucked I was and then melting into a quivering pile of goo. I took in what I could, but with the reyza herding me close behind, I didn't have time to sightsee.

A few steps down the corridor and to the right, we turned and climbed a curving staircase, eventually coming to a room that, judging from distance and direction traveled, was likely directly above the summoning chamber.

A multisided obelisk of polished black stone rose from the center of the chamber, its tip near the high ceiling sputtering a shower of arcane sparks. Ragged fissures radiated from the base in a spoke pattern—eleven of them—each running along the floor toward one of the walls. I was sure there was a name for an eleven-sided figure but had no clue what it might be. Who the hell ever needed to know that?

The whole thing hummed with potency, palpable to me even with the collar on. Odd glyphs sketched in colored chalk marked the tapered tip of each fissure like physical mirrors of the flickering sigils above them. I focused on one of the glyphs and tried to make sense of it. Immediately my heart started pounding inexplicably as if I was waking from a nightmare I couldn't remember. Going back down the stairs seemed like a much better plan than going forward. Except for the big hulking reyza that blocked the way.

On the far side of the chamber, the lord stood on a balcony, facing away, hands clasped behind his back. From where I stood, all I could see of the landscape beyond him were the tops of barren hills, jagged mountains beyond, and an expanse of cloudless sky. Oddly, it was that sky—a rich and deep blue beyond anything seen on Earth—that finally drove it home that I wasn't in Louisiana anymore, Toto. Demons and lords? Pshaw. Those were a dime a dozen back home. Yeah, I was a slow learner sometimes.

I took a couple of steps toward the lord, hugging the wall and putting as much space as I could between me and the Cracks of Doom. Scintillating and raw potency flared from them like angry azure flames, and I froze. The power crackled over me in twisted, disorienting pulses for a few seconds then subsided, leaving my ears ringing and the world tilting. I staggered and set my back against the wall, barely managing to stay upright. In another couple of seconds, it was as if it had never happened, except for me standing drunkenly with my mouth near impossibly dry, as though all of the moisture had been sucked from me. It was small comfort to see that the blond summoner took a step back as well, haughty demeanor gone in a flash, though he recovered within a few heartbeats and regained his stance. He lifted a hand and traced sigils in the air, though, due to the collar, I couldn't see clearly what he was shaping.

I worked spit back into my mouth and shot a look at the lord's back. "What the hell is this place?" I managed, pissed that my voice had a slight quaver.

His only response was to extend his right arm to his side and gesture me to him with a slight movement of index and middle finger, not turning even a millimeter toward me. Clenching my jaw, I moved forward.

When I reached his side he spoke, voice low and disturbingly melodious. "The summoning chamber believes it is yours, whether you do or not."

I flicked my eyes to the fissures. "And how is that even possible?" I asked. "I'm pretty damn sure I've never performed a summoning here."

The lord lifted his chin a fraction. "Idris," he said. I saw the blond summoner straighten. "Go prepare a purification diagram." His voice resonated with intensity. "We will require it shortly."

Yeah, that wasn't ominous or anything. I gulped, working damn hard to maintain a demeanor other than *freaked out.*

He turned to me, face cold and hard, yet with molten, living heat behind his eyes. "Many believe that this grossly apocalyptic landscape—" He gestured toward a jagged range of fractured mountains and a line of hills disturbingly devoid of any hint of vegetation. "—and this—" He gestured to the cracked floor. "—are your doing."

I threw my hands up, utterly frustrated and exasperated. "How?" I demanded. "For fuck's sake, I've never performed a goddamn summoning here! This is only my second time in the demon realm, and the last time I was busy *dying*!" That was after the aforementioned evisceration. Rhyzkahl brought me back to the demon realm to die, allowing me to pass through the void and reform whole and untouched in my own world. But the demonic lord before me now had told me that it might not work a second time. And I wasn't desperate enough to risk suicide. Yet.

He had no reaction to my outburst, unless, perhaps, an even more scary depth to his calm, like a serpent coiled motionless, able to strike in an instant with deadly speed and accuracy.

The lord locked his eyes on mine and spoke a single word.

"Elinor."

I jerked as the name hit me like a spear through my essence. My knees buckled for an instant, and I grabbed for the wall, bizarre and unexpected terror rising through me.

And then it was gone, leaving me gasping raggedly and clutching at the wall. "I don't understand," I said in a hoarse voice, staring at the dark-haired lord.

Did he reach to steady me or anything like that? Hell, no. His eyes remained hard upon mine. "No. I can clearly see that you do not. Rhyzkahl has not told you why he values you."

My balance slowly returned, though I kept my hand on the wall. "I suppose you intend to enlighten me?" I asked, voice still unsteady, to my annoyance.

"No. You bear *his* mark." His eyes dropped to my left forearm where Rhyzkahl had marked me as his sworn summoner. A slight smile touched his mouth. "I simply hold you from him."

I went cold, wondering how far he'd go to keep me from Rhyzkahl. "Then why all this?" I said, gesturing to the room and the landscape. "If your whole intent is to keep me from Rhyzkahl, then why the theatrics and the grand reveal of—" I didn't want to say the name. "—whatever that was?"

He inclined his head toward me, smile increasing a touch, though it only served to make his expression colder. "Because I gleaned *precisely* what I wanted from it." He turned and moved toward the stairs in long smooth strides. "And now, we purify you."

Chapter 2

The reyza shepherded me down the stairs and along the corridor away from the summoning chamber, then down yet more stairs and corridors, and finally into a small bedchamber. From what little I saw in that hurried trek, the place was *gorgeous*. Neglected for sure, but nothing a little cleanup couldn't fix. Glass crunched underfoot near broken windows which had either been patched with a ward or left open to the elements. Dust reigned supreme and minor debris littered most areas. But beyond all that, the absolute beauty of the architecture left me in awe. Spacious and sweeping, stone and wood wound together to form something that felt more like a rugged yet graceful entity than a building. Paintings and statuary lined walls and rested in niches everywhere, and I fretted that I wasn't given the time to stop and look at them.

The reyza continued through the bedchamber and into a room that held a broad stone tub. I would've said it was white marble, but there was a dragonfly-wing iridescence to it that I'd never seen in Earth marble. Demon-marble? Water half-filled the tub and was likely the source of a faint rotten egg smell.

"Time is of the essence," the demon growled. "You must be cleaned and prepared." He reached for me, and I backpedaled to the wall, eyes widening.

"I can do it!" I gasped. "I can wash myself."

His lip curled in a snarl. "You have three hundred heartbeats," he said, flexing clawed hands. He settled into a crouch by the door, eyes never leaving me. "I am counting."

I shucked my nasty clothes off, kicked them aside and

slid into the tepid water. Yep. Sulphur. Much of the well water where I lived had the same odor. I kept a running count while I ducked under and scrubbed at my hair with my fingers. I didn't see anything resembling soap, so I figured that the standard for how clean I needed to be was mostly Without Bits of Body Parts Clinging to Me.

I clambered out of the tub when my own count reached two-sixty and stood, naked, dripping and shivering, before the reyza. My own clothes and possessions were nowhere to be seen, and even though I had no desire to put any of them back on, it still bugged me.

The demon tossed me a towel. "Dry yourself." I quickly complied. "And don this." He passed me a garment—a black knee-length shift that turned out to be little more than a sack with neck and arm holes. No bra, no underwear. To say I felt exposed was an enormous understatement.

The demon snorted, rose from the crouch, gestured to the door. We headed back toward the summoning chamber. Scowling, I picked my way through the glass and debris in the corridors. It had been part of the ambience when I had shoes on, but now, barefoot, it was an up close and personal threat. I had no desire to entertain these motherfuckers with bloody feet and, miraculously, managed the walk without incident.

He opened a door in the corridor near the summoning chamber and waited for me to enter.

I paused in the doorway as an odd feeling of déjà vu swam over me. I'd been in that room before, it told me, dozens of times. In ghostly fragments, I smelled the clean ozone scent of a freshly activated portal, heard snatches of conversation both in demon and what sounded like Italian, felt shivers of excitement, trepidation, and wonder.

A shove in the center of my back dispelled the sensation and reminded me to move.

It wasn't a large room. Maybe five feet by eight, with another door opposite the one I'd stepped through and a single stone bench along one wall. Maybe the purification involved a massage? Hey, a girl could dream.

A large bas-relief reminiscent of da Vinci's Vitruvian Man dominated the wall across from the bench. Around it, dozens of tassels, of what looked a lot like human hair, hung from silken cords looped over pegs along the wall. Sigils, only faintly visible to me due to the collar, flickered around the carving.

The reyza squeezed in, and his massive bulk shifted the feel of the room from small to damn near claustrophobic. When he closed the door, pitch black descended. I could still see the faint wards on the wall, but othersight didn't do shit for real darkness, unless the sigils were ignited or specifically traced for light. My hands clenched into fists as I tried to keep from completely freaking out in the utter darkness. I sank to the bench, listening to the breathing of the reyza.

"Come here often?" I said, managing a cheeky grin in case the reyza could see in the dark. I had no idea.

To my utter surprise he spoke. "On rare occasions," he said with a low snort.

I chuckled, relieved at getting a response. "I'm Kara Gillian," I said, even though I knew perfectly well the demon knew who I was. Names held a lot of power since they were an integral part of summoning, so I figured it would be better to offer mine first than to ask for his.

"Greetings, Kara Gillian," he replied. "I am Gestamar."

Holy shit. I knew that name. Gestamar was mentioned in texts dating back hundreds of years, and was one of the more popular high-level demons to be summoned. I'd never summoned him myself, but only because I was fairly new at summoning reyza, and I tended to be more comfortable with Kehlirik, one of Rhyzkahl's demons and the first twelfth-level demon I'd ever summoned on my own.

"I'm honored to meet you, Gestamar," I said. "The lord who had me summoned, what's his name?"

The demon shifted with a rustle of wings. "Mzatal."

"Never heard of him." Hell, right now my only weapons were Obnoxious and Snark, and I intended to use them whenever possible. Then again, it was true. The only lords I knew of were Rhyzkahl and Szerain. I had a feeling there were many gaps in my knowledge that would soon be filled, whether I wanted it or not.

I started to ask him what the whole damn purification thing was about, but a deep thrum from the direction of the other door interrupted me.

In the next instant Gestamar's hands were around my throat, claws pressing into my skin but not piercing. I bit back a yelp of shock and clutched at his fingers instinctively, but a heartbeat later he pulled his hands away, taking the collar with him. I let out a shaking breath as the arcane leaped into focus around me. Sigils, like strands of intricately woven colored light, pulsed ever so slightly with the thrum from beyond the door. Gestamar lifted a claw and traced a sigil that hung in the air above us and lit the chamber with a golden glow. There'd been one of those in the summoning chamber when I arrived, and some in the room with the fissures, but with the collar on, I'd completely missed their beauty and radiant power. I stared, fascinated and grateful for the brief distraction from my circumstances. On Earth, I traced wards arcanely on surfaces like doors, floors, and walls for specific purposes: protection, aversion, warning, and such. With chalk and blood I crafted floor glyphs for summonings, but I'd never seen a sigil *float* like this in three dimensional vibrant, shifting color.

Gestamar saw the look on my face and snorted. "The sigils of our world. Humans call them floaters."

I exhaled and nodded, sensing the thing as though my *othersight* had developed *otherfeel*. I finally dragged my eyes away from it to take in the rest of the room.

Now I could really see the bas-relief on the wall in front of me. Despite being totally braced for some weird shit to start, I was drawn to this in a more visceral way than to the floater. The stone looked much like the demon marble of the bath, except that it also had fine veins of gold running through it that picked up the sigil's light and brought the surface to life. A life-sized naked man—human or lord, I couldn't tell—faced me in a spread-eagle posture. The full perimeter of the disc writhed with entwined symbols that I couldn't name, yet felt familiar. A bluish arcane glow ran from the top of his head to the edge of the disc in a widening pattern. The alien eyes were what got me though, sculpted into the background texture with such subtle strokes as to be almost overlooked. But once I saw them, I couldn't *not* see them. They fixed me in their gaze, eyes shaped like slanted teardrops with eerie dual pupils and a haunting familiarity. What the hell?

I finally managed to drag my eyes away to the dozens and dozens of tassels. They were most definitely hair, and it sure as hell looked like human hair, at that. Was that part of this ritual? Would this lord cut my hair? *Damn it, I just got it to a decent length!* I thought with a grimace. But at the same time I steeled myself for just that possibility. My fate might very well depend on my ability to roll with weird or unpleasant shit like that. *And I'd rather think that ending up with a bad haircut is the worst it could be.*

"So, uh, if you're going to cut my hair could you comb it out first?" I said, doing my best to keep my tone light and unconcerned, though my heart pounded. "I didn't get a chance after my bath. No conditioner, and it tangles like a bitch," I continued, harnessing the Mighty Power of the Snark to help me get through this.

Gestamar snorted. "No hair will be cut. These are of Szerain—treasured summoners and humans of his."

A weird chill skimmed over me and down my spine. "Is that where we are? Szerain's palace?" Only recently had I found out that my FBI agent friend Ryan Kristoff was actually the demonic lord Szerain, exiled from the demon realm with his memory stripped. I gazed at the collection of mementos and wondered what the oldest was, wondered what sort of people they came from. The demonic lords had been around for a few thousand years, and I sure as hell had trouble getting my head around it. Déjà vu washed over me again, stronger this time, as my eyes rested on one lock of reddish blond hair bound by a green ribbon.

"Yes," the demon replied, voice seeming to lower an octave. "Szerain's palace. In the secondary antechamber of the summoning chamber that birthed the cataclysm."

My breath quickened as memory rose. *Sigils light the chamber with a soft glow. I lift my hair and allow Lord Szerain to neatly slice a lock. He gives me a kind smile and a kiss on the forehead....*

I tensed, and the memory faded as quickly as it had come, leaving me trembling and unsettled. Looking to Gestamar, I struggled for mental balance. "Cataclysm? You mean the fissures and the blasted landscape? That originated here?"

The demon peered at me, pupils narrowing to slits. "Yes. From the chamber to which you were summoned. A horrific event wrought by Szerain. And Elinor."

I struggled to work moisture into my mouth. "What happened?"

He growled low and leaned close, breath hot upon me while I fought the urge to cower back. "Elinor lost control of a powerful ritual—an attempt at a permanent gate." His voice was rich and slow, with ominous overtones that made my gut clench. "It thrashed out of control and she perished." He drew out the last word in a way that sent shivers through me. "And our world broke apart, and the skies wept fire, and the seas lashed the high plains." He tilted his head, eyes on me. "And the ways to Earth slammed shut, trapping humans here to die and severing us from your world for over two hundred years, while this world sought to emulate your vision of hell."

The words tumbled over each other in my head. I squeezed my eyes shut as I struggled to make sense of it. My breath came in shallow pants as a ragged discord seemed to permeate his telling.

I shook my head to try and clear it. Something was wrong with his version, yet I had no idea what it could be. "How—" My voice cracked, and I tried again. "How did she die?"

Gestamar pulled back from me. "She was slain in the midst of the ritual as the gate spiraled out of control."

I fixed my gaze upon him. "But how?" I asked, needing the answer beyond all reason. "What killed her? The gate? What?"

The thrum abruptly increased in tempo. Gestamar stood.

"Wait," I said, pulse pounding. "Do you even know?"

In answer Gestamar bared his teeth, and in a move too swift for me to follow, pulled a thin cloth hood over my head.

My hands balled into fists at my side as he swiftly fastened the hood with arcane bindings. It wasn't tight by any means, and it wasn't difficult to breathe through, but the mere concept of being brought, hooded, into a ritual chamber was enough to give me a mild case of the freakouts. Okay, maybe a major case. Which, I realized a heartbeat later, was very likely this Lord Mzatal's intent.

Anger needled me just enough to counteract the terror, though only a bit. I still had no reason to believe I was going to live through this ritual. I suddenly missed Ryan, even though I knew it had probably been less than half an hour since I'd seen him.

Since we kissed.

We'd worked together for much of the past year and had a good-friends relationship that always seemed to teeter on the edge of something more. In those unnerving seconds when both of us knew we couldn't stop the summoning, he finally kissed me, and damn it I kissed him back. He told me he loved me, and I told him I loved him. And then I was here.

I smiled very slightly beneath the hood. *Well, if I have to die now, at least we got that shit out of the way.*

Gestamar took my left upper arm. "The floor is smooth," he said as he moved me forward and through the door. "Simply walk."

I complied. A few heartbeats later he released me, and someone else took my right arm in a firm but not harsh grip. Not the lord, I decided. This had to be the blond summoner.

The young man slowly led me around the outer perimeter of the ritual circle. Thankfully, the hood did nothing to block my othersight. Brilliantly ignited sigils floated from knee to chest height above the floor in a circle of beautifully interlaced patterns. The only kind of ritual diagram I'd ever drawn was with chalk on the floor, but I could feel the power of this and had no doubt it was the diagram. *Looks like they do things in style in the demon realm.*

A golden glow occupied the far side of the circle. Lord Mzatal. I was certain of it. Under any other circumstances I probably would have thought this was some really cool shit. Actually, I did think it was some cool shit. I simply didn't like the idea that this particular cool shit was about to be used on *me* for who the hell knew what.

The summoner stopped in front of the golden glow, released me and stepped back. Now the lord ran his hands over me in a thorough search that reminded me of a pat-down but without steering clear of any areas. Nor did he feel the need to use any "back of the hand" crap. I remained perfectly still, jaw clenched tight.

The lord finally stood from a crouch after running his hands down each of my legs. "To the center," he said, voice even more intense than before. He said something in demon, and Gestamar gave a rumbled response in kind.

The summoner took my arm again and firmly guided me to the center of the circle, maneuvering between some of the sigils and passing straight through others. Where they touched, my skin tingled, and some tugged at me as if reluctant to let me pass.

"On your back," he said, voice lofty, though it held the faintest touch of a waver that made me think his entire attitude was an act. More games to keep me off balance? If so, the combined effect was certainly working.

Sweat stung my armpits and lower back as I obediently lay supine in the middle of the diagram. The lord approached and crouched, pulled the hood off. I blinked and looked up at him as I tried my damnedest to hide how very scared I was.

He lifted a hand and with a casual flick toward each of my limbs, arcanely bound me spread-eagled, much like the bas-relief. My fear spiked with the sudden restraint, and I bit back a noise of dismay. At least I wasn't naked.

Mzatal looked down at me for a few more heartbeats, then stood and moved to the perimeter of the circle above my head and out of my sight, unless I wanted to do some serious neck-craning. Which I really didn't. I lightly tested the bonds and confirmed that I wasn't getting free of this until the lord released me. Instead, I focused on regulating my breathing and tried, unsuccessfully, to *not* wonder what was about to happen.

The patterns of the diagram brightened even as an intense white light flared into existence above my head. I squeezed my eyes shut as the light seemed to permeate every cell of my being, pulsing with the thrum of the room. It didn't hurt, but it was definitely odd.

After what felt like a few minutes, Mzatal crouched beside me again. His hand trailed from my throat down my torso, in a light probing touch so clinical that it left zero impression of sexual intent. His hand paused at my belly. A slow warmth formed just beneath my skin, almost pleasant at first, but soon progressing to distinctly uncomfortable. I swallowed hard, felt his hand tighten into a fist on my stomach as the warmth shifted to a sensation not unlike a side-stitch, though about three times worse. I tensed as the stitch increased, clenching my teeth against making any sort of *shit that hurts* noise. Right when I was ready to give up on the whole being stoic thing, a flash of heat went through my abdomen and the cramping sensation vanished.

Fear coiled in my gut to replace the cramp-from-hell, and I took several ragged breaths. I badly wanted to ask what the fuck was going on, but I knew he wouldn't answer. Mzatal's hand slid back up to the center of my chest. Once again warmth formed under my skin, followed by a sharp cramp, but this felt much worse than the first. A whimper slid from me despite my best intentions. I kept my hands clenched into fists, shaking as the cramp deepened.

"Hold the flows as they are *without wavering*," Mzatal said to the summoner. I heard the snarl beneath his words and had zero doubt that the blond man paled a bit. I knew I would have.

He splayed his hand hard upon my chest. I opened my eyes to look up at him, nearly regretting it as I saw the dark expression on his face. He flicked his gaze toward Gestamar, said something in demon, lip curled. I heard the name "Rhyzkahl" as he increased the pressure on my chest, and I fought back panic.

"Idris, prepare," he said, voice uncompromising and intense. He lifted his open hand to about six inches above my sternum.

Searing heat ripped through my chest. I screamed, arching my back as I pulled against the arcane bindings. Memory flared of another searing pain driving through my chest, and I screamed again as I fought to get free so I could scrabble at whatever had caused it and save myself.

And then pain and memory were both gone, leaving only echoes behind. I collapsed back, biting my lips against sobs. Tears trickled down the side of my face, and I tried to focus on how annoying it was that I couldn't wipe them away. Anger was better than terror and, at the moment, it wasn't that hard to be pissed off. Except for the part where I got to kiss Ryan, this had been a colossally shitty day from start to finish, and it wasn't even over.

Mzatal's eyes swept over me before they returned to mine. "Now your Lord is stripped of the means to retrieve you," he said, voice dark with a deep vehemence. He slipped the collar back onto my neck before I had time to even flinch. An ache went through me as the arcane faded to a fraction of its fullness.

He stood smoothly, and with an efficient sweep of his arm erased all the patterns and released my bindings. I pulled my limbs in and struggled to sit up, clutching at my chest even though the pain was long gone. I hadn't known that Rhyzkahl had a way to rescue me, but somehow, taking that hope away, even without my previous knowledge of it, cut even more cruelly. I wasn't at all accustomed to feeling helpless and vulnerable, and I deeply despised it.

The lord stepped away from me, looked to Gestamar. "Take her."

To my shock the demon simply scooped me up in his arms. I clung to him, weirdly relieved since I wasn't sure I'd be able to walk. Beyond all the other stresses of this gloriously shitty day, I couldn't remember the last time I'd eaten, and my body was intent on reminding me of that fact. I leaned my head on Gestamar's chest and allowed myself to wallow in misery for awhile, as he passed out of the chamber and down several corridors. He carried me through a musty common area with tables and sofa-like seating and into a small sparse room, maybe eight foot square, furnished with only a narrow bed and a side table with a mug on it. A single tiny window high on the far wall framed a patch of dusk-blue sky and a single winking star. Unlike the room just outside, this one was completely dust-free and the blanket was clean and freshly laid on the bed. A door to the right appeared to lead to a bathroom type of place.

The demon set me down, far more gently than I expected, and guided me to sit on the edge of the bed.

"What happens now?" I asked, too exhausted to hide the quaver in my voice.

He plucked the mug from the table and pressed it into my hands. "You drink," he rumbled.

I didn't know squat about antiques, but I was pretty sure the mug was the real thing. Silver, lined with gold, a vertical ribbed pattern around it and leaves etched on its gracefully curved handle. It sure looked like something from Earth. The murky brown contents weren't nearly as appealing. I lifted the mug dubiously and took a careful sip. It reminded me of liquefied unsalted stew, but with a hint of bitterness that I couldn't identify. My starving body probably wouldn't have cared what it tasted like, but I had to appreciate that it didn't completely suck. I finished the contents, then placed the mug back on the table, hand shaking only slightly. "And now?"

"You sleep," the demon replied.

"And then what?" I asked, meeting his eyes. "What's going to happen to me? Why am I here?"

He snorted. "Because Mzatal wants you here."

I scowled at the non-answer, turned away from him, and curled up on the bed.

"You are not dead," he said. "Consider that, Kara Gillian." I heard him exit and close the door.

And I did. Every moment I continued to draw breath was a moment more to figure out how to get myself out of this shit. I listened carefully but heard no sound of a bolt or lock. I didn't figure it could be that easy, but I had to try. I sat up, padded over to the door and laid my hands flat against it. A faint buzzing sensation cued me that it was likely warded, meaning arcanely locked. I pushed the handle down slowly so as not to make noise, then gave it a tug. It didn't budge. Damn.

I poked around the room for anything of interest or of use, but found nothing pointy, sharp, or weaponizable. I looked up at the high window with its patch of darkening sky and a few stars. I shoved the bed under it, and lifted the table onto the bed, bracing it against the wall. Yep, that did it. I climbed up my makeshift scaffold and got to nose level with the sill, high enough to at least check it out.

I pressed my hand against the glass and found only the barest whisper of arcane. Since it had a latch begging to be tried, I lifted it and pulled. *Holy shit!* The window swung inward with a creak of hinges and a shower of dust. My heart pounded with the possibilities. Judging by what I could see from my position of barely peering over the sill—which was pretty much sky—I figured I was on at least the second story.

Okay, Jill, I'm going to use those muscles you've been trying to get me to build. Exercise and I didn't get along, but somehow Jill—the crime scene technician who'd become my best friend—could get me going. Sometimes. I hauled myself up in a klutzy thrash and wiggle and managed to get a grip on the outside lip with my arms supported on the wide sill, and the rest of me dangling inside. Great. Now what?

I got an answer I didn't want. The stars winked out to pitch black, and a pair of blood red eyes hovered a couple of feet in front of me. The faint scent of sulphur drifted in, and I had no doubt I was face to face with a *zhurn*, a tenth-level demon that was like shadow and night. Crapsticks.

"Greetings, honored one," I said, voice strained as I struggled to maintain the awkward hold. "Nice night." Obviously escape this way wasn't happening tonight.

The zhurn's voice crackled like flames on wet kindling. "No egress this way, summoner."

"Yeah," I said, easing back down to the tabletop. "I kinda get that."

"Sleep," it said, reaching with a shadowy extension to pull the window closed. The red eyes disappeared, but the stars didn't come back. Damn zhurn had closed its eyes and camped over my window.

I climbed down and dragged the table off the bed. Weariness crashed in. It had been a long and particularly shitty day. Sleep wasn't a bad idea. I needed rest to be sharp tomorrow and ready for whatever Lord Asstard had to throw at me. I curled up under the blanket and drifted off immediately, thoughts of Tessa, Jill, Zack . . . and Ryan, swirling.

"I'm coming back, guys, don't worry," I murmured. Even with all the uncertainty and misery, I knew I'd have no trouble getting to sleep. Thankfully, I was right.

Chapter 3

I had no idea how long I slept. The small window high in the wall let sunlight in along with a glimpse of rich blue sky but no other clue as to time of day. It had been twilight when I went to sleep, so apparently it was a full night plus some, give or take a million years. I sat up, absently rubbing my chest, then scowled as I realized I was doing so. The memory of the pain still haunted me.

The adjoining room was, indeed, a bathroom type place, and though the facilities weren't the usual flush-toilet sort, it wasn't difficult to figure out how it worked. A low table held a basin, a cloth, and a jug of water, though nothing as pedestrian as a toothbrush. Still, I washed my face and used a corner of the cloth to scrub the worst of the fuzz from my teeth. I even stripped and washed the parts of me that were stinky. Putting the damn black shift back on wasn't high on my list of favorite things to do, though. What, prisoners of demonic lords weren't allowed underwear?

As I finished and came back out to the bedchamber, the door opened. Gestamar stepped in, carrying two mugs.

"Drink this quickly," he said, holding one out for me. "You have been summoned by Mzatal."

"Can I have some different clothes?" I asked. "A hairbrush? Anything?"

His lip curled, exposing sharp fangs that gleamed white. Apparently *he* had a toothbrush, or the demon equivalent. "No need for different garb," he told me. "What you have is sufficient for now. And if you do not drink, you will go hungry. Your choice."

Scowling, I took the mug and downed the contents. It

wasn't bad, but I definitely wanted solid food sometime soon. This was enough to keep me alive, and that was about it. Then again, my stomach was so queasy from nerves, solid food probably wouldn't stay down for long.

I set the mug aside, and he passed the second one to me, simply saying *chak*, which I assumed to be the name of the beverage. The rich brown liquid steamed with a pleasantly fragrant nutty, earthy scent. I took a sip, then another. It wasn't coffee, but it was hot and pretty damn tasty.

Gestamar pointed toward the door. I took that as my cue to move and, after one last gulp, reluctantly relinquished the mug and its precious contents. Sighing, I dug my fingers through my snarled hair as I exited.

Gestamar directed me to an antechamber, and inside was a set of double doors.

Two life-sized statues of demon-marble flanked the doors. On the left, a woman of mature but indeterminate years stood in tall grace. Though her face was serious, a smile played at the corners of her mouth. A single shoulder strap secured her masterfully carved close-fitting dress, revealing more than it covered. On the right, a young man in a RenFaire outfit stood with his arms folded casually across his chest and a mischievous smile lighting his face.

I peered at them, so exquisitely sculpted I almost swore they were breathing. "Who are they?" I glanced over at the reyza, then back to the statues.

"Nefhotep and Giovanni Racchelli," he said. "Favorites of Szerain. Giovanni died young." He shifted his weight from foot to foot and settled into a crouch. "Nefhotep lived here for over two hundred years."

I blinked in surprise. "Humans?"

"Yes." He adjusted his wings. "From the time long ago when the ways were open," he said, lifting a claw toward the young man then toward the woman. "And fully open, very long ago."

The weird déjà vu feeling crept through me again as I looked at the statue of Giovanni. I knew him, it tried to tell me. Even now I could picture his quick smile and infectious laugh, and for just the briefest instant it was as if the statue moved to turn his teasing grin upon me. My breath caught, my stomach fluttered, my heart pounded, and damn it all, my face heated in—a *blush?* What the hell?

I squeezed my eyes shut to dispel the illusion and turned away. The sensations lingered for another few heartbeats before fading.

"Szerain has always had the gift of capturing the very essence of his subjects," the reyza said, peering at the statues.

"He carved these?" I asked in surprise. Gestamar nodded. Had I ever seen Ryan show any sort of artistic ability? I couldn't think of a single instance, which sent a weird and sad pang through me.

My musing came to an abrupt end as Mzatal strode in, passing me without a glance. He still wore the Armani suit and white shirt, but had changed his tie to one of blood red, and the pattern of his braid seemed different. The double doors swung open before he even reached them, and he entered the room beyond without the slightest hitch in his stride.

Gestamar stood and gestured for me to go in. I did so, jaw tight, hating how grubby and foolish I felt in the damn shift.

With its vaulted ceiling and two huge unbroken windows on the far wall, the room felt spacious despite its small area—not much larger than my living room back home. I couldn't tell what purpose the room had, though, since it was empty of furnishings. The only object remaining was what appeared to be a statue adjacent one of the windows, covered in a white cloth.

Mzatal stood facing the other window, hands behind his back. I stopped a few feet from him.

"So. Great," I said, folding my arms over my chest, and doing my damnedest to marshal something resembling a strong attitude. "You have me. You've made sure that Rhyzkahl can't get me back. I have a comfy cell, and crap food, and no toothbrush. Now what?"

Mzatal slowly turned to face me. His eyes met mine, and I suddenly realized that the absence of a toothbrush really wasn't so bad after all, considering. My mouth went dry as he approached, and I had to steel myself against a shudder as he moved around and behind me. I felt his hands on my shoulders, and then a heartbeat later he lifted the collar from my neck. The arcane clarified and brightened. The room was well-shielded, though I didn't really need to look at the patterns and sigils to know that. There was no way he'd take the collar off me in a room that wasn't, and run the risk that Rhyzkahl could track me.

He remained behind me, unnervingly silent, though I could feel him there, his aura alone near overwhelming. Potency like a wave of nightmare engulfed me as he leaned in closer. "What now, you ask?" he breathed in a quietly menacing voice that sent terror streaking through me. "I decide if you live or die." He paused. "I decide *how* you live, or how you die."

My breath caught in a low sob. I hated him more than anyone or anything at that moment. "Okay, I get it," I managed, nursing what dull anger I could. "You hold full control. You have me scared shitless. You win. Happy now? Whatever this is all about, whether it's me living or dying, fucking do it already."

He continued the circle and stopped in front of me, a faint smile playing at the corners of his mouth. Before I could get pissed at his amusement at my expense, he lifted his hand and looped a softly glowing strand of potency around my throat, then turned, drawing me behind him like a dog on a leash as he approached the covered statue. I seethed, but was nevertheless grateful for the over-the-top display of dominance. I could do anger a lot better than terror.

He stopped a few feet from the statue and moved behind me once again, but this time he gripped my head between his hands, as if to make absolutely certain I couldn't look away.

"Elinor." He spoke the word like an invocation piercing my essence as he stripped the cloth from the statue without touching it. And there she was. Elinor. Youthful. Slight of build with a sweet face that radiated innocence. Sudden swirling dizziness put a stop to my observation.

I jerked, and only the lord's grip on my head kept me from staggering as memories flooded in, memories that I absolutely knew weren't my own. Yet as they poured over me and through me, they drove my own existence and identity before them. The room melted and reformed.

"Come, dear one," Lord Rhyzkahl says, holding his hand out to me, broad expanse of cloudless sky beyond him framed by columns. My stomach flutters, and I feel the blush

rise in my cheeks. I smile and take his hand. Anything for his gaze, his touch. Will he kiss me? Breathless.

The memory shifted dizzyingly.

I wring my hands, banished for the moment to the antechamber. Fear. Uncertainty. I hate it when they argue. I listen to the words though do not understand more than that Lord Rhyzkahl dominates this one and Lord Szerain counters. Do not faint. Do not faint. Do not faint.

Shift.

The ritual seethes around me, tearing at me. Pain blossoms in my chest. Please. Pleeeease. I don't understand. I don't understand!

Shift.

Giovanni places the small cakes one at a time before me, counting. His eyes twinkle, and I cannot concentrate on the numbers. He will surely think me a silly little thing if I cannot even learn to count to ten in Italian. Uno. Due. Tre. Quattro. He touches the back of my hand and smiles. I am undone!

Shift.

Cakes. Cakes. A statue. *Birthday cake. Tessa grinning.*

Pancakes. Lots of pancakes at Lake o' Butter. Jill eating pancakes across the table. Dear One. Cinque. Sei. Sette. Jill. Jill. Otto. Nove. Dieci. Ryan laughing next to me, and Zack rolling his eyes.

Through the maelstrom of memories I became distantly aware of my own whimpering and an increasing grip on my head. My breath hissed through my teeth, and I struggled to focus on the statue as just that—a statue. These weren't my memories. The dreams, the déjà vu, all this . . . This wasn't from me. I was *not* Elinor.

My hands clenched and unclenched as I called up and galvanized my own memories: My mother and father, growing up with Tessa, learning to summon, graduating from the police academy, my first pursuit on foot, the first time I had sex, crawfish and beer, becoming a detective, the pride of putting bad guys in jail, the first time I got punched by a suspect and how I put him in handcuffs, becoming friends with Jill, giggling over reality TV, Christmases and birthdays, Ryan's quick smile and Zack's laugh, Eilahn and Fuzzykins . . .

My breath slowed as the chaos of intruder memories

subsided. I felt the lord behind me, hands still on my head, and I knew in that instant that not only was he deeply reading my thoughts, but also that he was poised to snap my neck depending on his assessment of me.

"Please don't kill me," I said, voice calm and quiet.

His grip eased ever so slightly, though he didn't release me. "Why?"

I didn't hesitate with my reply. "Because I matter."

He held the grip for another three heartbeats, then withdrew his hands and dissipated the strand of potency from around my throat. He replaced the collar, then stepped fully away from me and returned to his former position by the window, looking out, hands behind his back. I closed my eyes for a few seconds as I processed the undeniable fact that I'd been a hair's breadth from death. I knew without a doubt that if I'd been unable to fight my way out of that storm of memories I'd be a twitching corpse on the floor at this moment.

But why?

I wasn't out of the woods yet, but I fully intended to take a bit of ease in this tiny victory. I scrubbed a hand over my face. "Who was she? This Elinor chick."

He surprised me by actually answering the question. "A summoner of adequate aptitude from your seventeenth century, trained by me for a short time, then fostered by Szerain and Rhyzkahl."

"If she was merely adequate," I asked, frowning, "then how the hell did she damn near destroy this world?"

"That, Kara Gillian, remains clouded." He turned back to me, shaking his head. "Something of her nature, of her essence, escalated the ritual beyond recovery, and Szerain remains mute." His eyes narrowed with a touch of what looked like disapproval. "I know it was not within her skills as a summoner to call such power."

I put what few pieces I had together. "I'm not this Elinor, so what's the deal?" I knew I wasn't some sort of reincarnation of her, but I also assumed she and I had a connection. I just didn't know what it was.

"No, upon assessment it is clear that you are not a direct essence transfer," he said, echoing my own thoughts. "Your innate energy signature mirrors hers, but is fully yours." He narrowed his eyes. "But there is another piece of your essence, one that has the feel of an afterthought. This is the part that holds and generates the memories of Elinor and houses a fragment of who she is. Its encapsulation is unconventional, yet it is somehow integral to you."

I blinked and tried to make sense of that but gave up. "I have no idea what you just said."

He leaned toward me a smidge, not seeming at all annoyed by my cluelessness. "An energy signature is much like a fingerprint, though not utterly unique. Close matches are possible. Though, without extraordinary means, the chances of locating a specific signature are infinitesimal given the sheer number of possibilities. I can only speculate at this point. It is as though this fragment of Elinor attached to you, became a part of you, because of the energy signature match. Why or how," he said with a shake of his head, "I do not yet know."

The fact that he took the time to explain it obviously meant something. Too bad I had no idea what.

"Like donating a kidney," I said, folding my arms over my chest.

Mzatal lifted an eyebrow, head tilting a bit. "Perhaps, though with a deeper influence."

Pieces fell into place. "Ah, and that's why I'm so popular—because I have Elinor's magic kidney."

Mzatal's face shifted from the hint of curiosity to the impassive mask. This dude had zero sense of humor. "Yes, it is," he said. "Some seek through speculation, and some through smatterings of knowledge." His eyes were hard upon me. "You are a dangerous unknown, Kara Gillian."

I lifted my chin, mouth tight. "And dangerous things are either used, destroyed, or—" I thought of my bare feet and black shift and obvious prisoner status. "—contained."

"Unless the unknown becomes known," he said. "Then the possibilities shift."

And how the hell was I supposed to make the unknown known in a way that would keep me alive and whole? I sighed inwardly. Right now I wanted coffee and real food, in that order. *Might as well wish for a personal visit from Santa Claus while you're at it,* I chided myself.

He approached me, intense and coiled and calm as he reached and gripped my chin in his hand. His eyes were like ancient pale grey flint shot with silver. A palpable potency radiated from him that sent goosebumps skimming over me. "What is your heart's desire?" he asked, as if my life depended on my answer.

And it most likely did. I returned his gaze as steadily as I could. "To reach my full potential."

He held my chin for several long heartbeats before releasing it, only to seize my left wrist and pull my arm forward. I clenched my teeth as he dropped his eyes to Rhyzkahl's mark and laid a hand over it. He went utterly still for a moment, then drew a deep breath and brought his gaze up to mine.

When the lord spoke it was as if he forced the words out through gritted teeth, though his face betrayed no tension. "This *mark* does nothing to further that desire. Nor does it serve my purposes for you to bear it." Mzatal released my wrist and clasped his hands behind his back. "I will remove Rhyzkahl's stigma and determine what possibilities unfold," he said with icy conviction.

I shook my head in denial at the thought of having the mark removed, an unnamed dread stilling my breath. "Use, destroy, or contain?"

The lord lowered his head. "Your parameters. Use is preferable. Destruction, if use is impractical or impossible. I choose not to maintain a prisoner," he said with a smile that held no comfort.

My throat tightened, and my mouth felt full of sand. As he'd promised, he made the decisions on how I was to live or how I was to die. "And what sort of use would you make of me?"

Mzatal looked upon me as though seeking to determine some unknown. "The destruction aspect is far simpler. Slay and then disperse the essence." He paused. "Use depends upon what remains of you when I remove the stigma," he said, eyes dropping to the mark.

I fought to control the cold panic that thrashed within me. "'What remains'? What the fuck does that mean?"

The skin around his eyes tightened. "Hostile removal of a mark is extremely rare and the process extreme. Madness is a possibility. Removal of this construct of Rhyzkahl's risks essence sheer," he said, with a shake of his head and a touch of a frown. "Nothing of use to either of us would remain."

I stared agape then recovered enough to speak. "Are you fucking kidding me? Then why . . . ?" I shook my head in disbelief that anything could be this convoluted. "You're going to try it anyway, aren't you? You don't give a fuck if I end up broken. It accomplishes the same thing. My destruction. *You* have nothing to lose by trying."

"No, I do not," he said as though my destruction meant nothing. "And much potential to gain. As do you. The risk is worth the consequences to both."

I snorted a laugh at the absurdity. "Oh, sure. A little madness or fucked-up essence is a walk in the park for me and totally worth it for some magic tattoo removal." Sweat trickled down my sides beneath the damn shift.

"Your ignorance in the matter does not change the potentials or the values." He shifted his attention to Gestamar and spoke in demon. I caught the summoner's name twice—Idris—but couldn't get any other sense of what was said. Gestamar grunted and bounded out.

Mzatal drew a deep breath and released it slowly. "Kara Gillian," he said in a potent melodic tone that drove straight through to my core. "You are a dangerous unknown. I prefer you to become a dangerous known with possibilities other than death." He paused and regarded me with keen intensity. "But if deep assessment reveals full essence-binding by Rhyzkahl, then I will have no option but to slay you."

I dragged my hand across my forehead. "Whew! And I thought today wasn't going to be shittier than yesterday!"

"It is in truth a most fortunate day for you," he said as he raked a gaze over me. "Wait here," he ordered, then turned and exited, closing the doors with a flick of his fingers.

Silence descended, broken only by my unsteady breathing. *Dispersal, essence sheer, madness.* Right now the available options were all pretty fucking heinous. Even if I survived the removal fairly whole, I'd be nothing more than a slave. He'd stated quite clearly his desire to use me.

My fear settled into a weird acceptance. There was one other possible out. Mzatal had told me there was less chance of making it through the void a second time. Less chance. Not "no chance." And why would he need to disperse my essence after slaying me if there truly was no chance? *In other words, the available options are "shitty" and "shittier."*

I heard two demons conversing outside the door, and cold slammed through me again. Gestamar back from having Idris prepare some new, horrific ritual? No way was I just going to stand here twiddling my thumbs.

Oddly calm, my gaze swept the room, even though I knew damn well there was no convenient knife or noose. Only the damn statue, and broad thick windows covered in wards. I moved to the window near the statue and put my hand toward it. A tingle of pain shot through it, along with a surge of queasiness. *But I've gone through wards before*, I reminded myself grimly. *I'm wearing the collar. It'll suck, but dying for good or having my essence ripped apart will suck worse.* What choice did I have?

None.

I couldn't let myself think about it anymore. If I did I might lose my nerve and would probably never have another chance to take the plunge. Literally. My heart beat triple time, as if counting off my remaining seconds.

I set my shoulder against Elinor's hip, dug my bare feet into the floor and pushed. She was a heavy bitch, but no match for my desperation. With a creak of stone, the statue slowly tipped, then toppled into the broad window with a satisfying *crash*, creating a sufficiently large hole.

Her head and shoulders protruded from the window into the open air. I clambered onto the statue, hissing as the first wards stung like a thousand bees. I pushed against them, feeling as if I was slogging through goo. A headache spiked as I forced my way forward. Only about a foot more and I could fall. Holy shit, it would suck, but staying here would suck worse. I dimly heard a bellow and the crash of the door being thrown open. Pain and nausea spiraled higher, and I gasped raggedly. I was on her shoulders now. Another inch and—

A different pain speared through my head as a clawed hand tangled in my hair. I let out a cry of pain and scrabbled to grab at the statue's head. So damn close! Gestamar bellowed, pulling at me with a hard grip in my hair and on my thigh. Desperate, I tried to slash my forearm across a shard of glass. Oddly it didn't break the skin any more than a piece of wood might, but the movement caused me to lose my grip on Elinor's head. Pain from the wards seared through me again as the growling demon dragged me bodily back into the room and away from the window.

My knees buckled as the throbbing headache tripled in intensity, but Gestamar shifted his grip to my upper arms and kept me from completely collapsing. Maybe my head would explode and take care of the whole thing. That'd be convenient. Nausea rose, and I tasted bile. I'd almost made it through the wards. Another few seconds . . .

Mzatal entered and stopped before me. I dragged my gaze up to him, but the headache pounded so fiercely there seemed to be three of him. All three Mzatals lowered their heads and regarded me while Gestamar held me firmly before him. "Loss to wandering is a near certainty for death and a second passage through the void," Mzatal told me, mouth pursing in a frown. "A poor choice. A poor option."

Wandering. *Like Tessa*, I realized numbly. Not dispersed but lost in the void. Just as bad. Perhaps even worse.

I opened my mouth to tell him that he hadn't presented any better options, but the nausea rose instead, and I spewed what little was in my gut onto the floor between us. Mzatal took a smooth half-step back to avoid the splatter, more of which ended up on me than him.

"The removal will take place in two days, after we return to my realm," he told me, completely unperturbed, as if I hadn't just tried to jump out of a window and then puked on the floor. "Until then, Safar is your guard and guardian."

My head pounded as I shakily wiped my mouth with the back of my hand. Holy fuck, but I'd never hated anyone as much as I hated this fucking lord at this moment. Misery coiled in my empty stomach as if taunting me that it was there instead of food.

Mzatal regarded me. "It serves your purpose and mine for the unknown to become known, and Szerain's realm holds many keys to unlocking your value. Do not waste the opportunity, Kara Gillian," he said, tone rich and intense. His eyes remained on me for a moment more, then he turned and departed, hands behind his back.

Gestamar released me as another reyza entered, smaller and sharper in features than Gestamar. I swayed and rubbed at my temples, trying hard not to whimper as the two had a brief conversation in demon. I'd never had a migraine before, but I could only imagine this was what one was like.

Safar took hold of my arm in a careful grip, steadying me. "I am Safar, summoner."

"I'm Kara Gillian," I managed.

"Fair greetings, Kara Gillian," he rumbled as he gently moved me toward the door. "Come."

I didn't resist and moved where he directed. A numbness descended on me as he led me through corridors, and my headache receded somewhat as we moved further away from the room and broken window. It still hurt, but now it was more like bad-hangover than alien-about-to-burst-from-my-forehead. Even my nausea retreated. Now I was mostly starving.

"Gestamar is having a draught prepared for your headache," the reyza told me as he maneuvered me through a debris-strewn hallway.

"Oh. Thanks," I said. Not Mzatal. Gestamar. Maybe Mzatal didn't give a fuck how miserable I was. Hell, there was no maybe about it.

My heel came down on a shard of glass as we walked but, to my surprise and relief, no slicing pain came with it. Remembering, I lifted my arm and peered at the long scratch from the window. It was an owie and little more.

"What is this stuff?" I said, nudging a piece with my big toe. "It's not real glass, is it?"

Safar snorted. "It is very real, though not made like the glass of Earth. It is closer to a resin. Stronger, insulates against heat and cold more effectively, and does not cut like your glass."

Without Gestamar breathing down my neck I could slow down enough to take in more of Szerain's palace. I had to wonder how much of a hand he had in its actual creation since the whole thing was like a work of art, mostly curves and graceful arcs—even the doors—with sharp angles kept to a minimum. Portraits, paintings, and statues were ubiquitous—humans, demons, and some—well, I didn't have a clue. Déjà vu integrated like an extra sense. At first it freaked me out; little things like knowing how many windows would be in the next room or which hallway might lead outside. It wasn't always right, but enough for me to have no doubt Elinor had spent some time here.

Safar finally entered a chamber that wasn't my cell. A big window draped in dust-free emerald silk dominated the far wall of a room about the size of my bedroom at home. In other words, not very big. A comfy looking chair of golden velvety stuff nestled by the window. A larger table and matching chair of heavy oak or similar wood dominated the center of the room. Déjà vu reigned supreme in here, and I knew without doubt that a bedchamber was beyond the closed door on the wall to the right.

Safar guided me into the chair at the table and then released me. I sat gratefully, rested my elbows on the table and rubbed at my head, grimacing. He stepped back into the corridor for a brief moment then returned with a mug that he placed before me. "From Gestamar," he stated.

I took the mug and peered briefly at the contents. Couldn't tell a damn thing about it except that it was liquid and it had a weird and tangy scent. Fuck it. It wasn't as if this day could get any worse if the stuff turned out to be foul.

I slugged it down with only a slight grimace. It wasn't vile, though I doubted I'd be asking for seconds.

"Your chambers are here," Safar said as I placed the empty mug on the table. "Bed and bath there." He gestured toward the door with a claw.

"*My* chambers?" I said. "You're not taking me back to that other room?" My spirits dared to rise a few millimeters.

He crouched and shook his head. "*Dahn.*"

I peered at him. "How hard is it to learn y'all's language?" I asked, pretty sure it was hard as hell given the gutturals, stops, and sounds that were just plain weird. *Kri* meant "yes" and *dahn* meant "no." I'd picked that up from my dealings with demons through the years but not a lot else, since the demons I summoned all spoke or at least understood some English.

Safar spread his wings in a bone-popping stretch then settled them again. "Difficult for humans. Most who spend time here learn some words and phrases. Few become conversant. Only three have gained fluency."

Most Who Spend Time Here. *Well, let's just hope I'm not here long enough to learn more than a few phrases.* I grimaced and amended my mental statement. *And not because some asshole lord decides to kill me because he thinks I'm a threat to his world.*

"So, what do I do now?" I asked.

He peered at me. "Eat, bathe, rest, whatever you choose short of killing yourself or leaving the grounds."

"Eat?" I asked as my stomach gave an accompanying growl. "Real food?"

He bared his teeth. "Kri . . . yes. It will be here soon."

I eyed him dubiously. "Not that broth stuff, right? Real, solid food?"

Safar rumbled in what might have been amusement. "Real, solid food."

My spirits rose a couple of inches this time. "Any chance I can get clothing? Underwear? Nifty shit like that?"

"In the bedchamber, awaiting."

Now for the money question. I pursed my lips. "What about a toothbrush?"

"You will find the basics in either the bedchamber or the bath chamber."

Hot damn. I pushed up from the table and headed for the bedroom, along the way realizing that my headache had vanished in the past couple of minutes.

Relief wound through me when I found my own clothing and shoes on the bed, obviously clean. I checked out the bath chamber next and stopped dead in my tracks, eyes fixed on the graceful gold-stone bath tastefully adorned with a pattern of leaves.

"You carved this for me?" I hear myself say, barely able to contain my delight.

Szerain sits on the edge of the tub, fingers idly tracing patterns of light on the surface of the water. He looks over at me, smiles. "Finished only yesterday. You will abide for some time to come. Rhyzkahl and I came to agreement."

"And what of Giovanni?" I ask, barely daring to breathe or hope. He looks away, and my heart sinks. "My Lord?"

And there I was alone in the bath chamber staring at a tub already full of steaming water and no clue what happened to Giovanni. Like a fucking cliffhanger. Gah! I tried to get the image back but no luck.

Well, there was no doubt that Elinor had a thing for this Giovanni. *How did all that turn out?* I wondered. Elinor died. I knew that much. Murdered? Was that it? I couldn't shake the utter certainty that there was something more to her death than simply being consumed in a gate. Not that there was anything simple about that, but still. And then the biggest mystery of them all: How had a slip of a girl with only adequate summoning skills come so close to destroying the world? There was a missing piece to all of this. I *knew* that. Even if no one else knew what had really happened, surely I could figure it out, right? After all, I had the best eyewitness camped out in my head.

And then there was Szerain. I took a step forward and touched the carvings on the lip of the bath where the memory-vision had been. He didn't look anything like Ryan in the face, but his build, green gold eyes and hair were right. Well, Szerain's hair was longer than Ryan's FBI-regulation cut, but the color and texture were a match. What else about him was different? Elinor hadn't been afraid of him. That was some consolation at least.

Every answer seemed to raise two more questions. I gave a mental shrug and dipped my hand in the water. Plush towels, basic toiletry items—including the much-desired toothbrush—and a full hot bath. Looked like just what I needed. Yeah, a nice long soak could make up for a lot.

I stuck my head out of the bedchamber. "I'm going to bathe, okay?"

Safar snorted and crouched, which I took for acknowledgment.

I returned to the bath, stripped quickly, and sank to my neck in the water. For a moment I wondered who the hell filled the damn thing since there was nothing resembling a faucet, but then decided I really didn't care. It was completely awesome. Would've been better if I didn't have a death-or-madness sentence coming up in two days, but what the hell. All the more reason to enjoy the shit while I could.

Chapter 4

After about twenty minutes I felt more human and more certain that I was well clean of any lingering Tracy-bits and my own puke-spatter. I dried and dressed but paused before returning to the main room, taking this chance to peer at the damn collar in the mirror. No seam that I could feel or see. My gaze swept the bathroom and finally rested on the edge of the stone table that held the basin. Crouching awkwardly, I scraped the edge of the collar against the table about half a dozen times then peered at it in the mirror.

Shit. The edge of the table had a long gouge on it, but the stupid collar was as pristine and whole as ever. Not even the slightest mar or scratch. What the hell was this stuff?

Sighing in annoyance and disappointment, I returned to the main room just as a pair of *faas* burst in, one carrying a mug and the other a tray of what I sure hoped was food.

"For you. For youuuuu!" one burbled as they placed tray and mug on the table. With a body about three feet long, a sinuous tail about twice that, and six legs, the faas reminded me of a sleek blue-furred lizard. It peered at me with near comic curiosity, its vertically-slitted bright golden eyes round and shining over a broad snout. Its tail coiled and undulated ceaselessly, and the demon itself vibrated all over as though it could barely contain itself. I'd summoned faas on several occasions to do arcane warding in my house, and I didn't think I'd ever seen one be still. "Jekki! Jekki! I am," it said, vibrating yet more, purple iridescence shimmering over its fur.

I smiled. Couldn't help it. Faas had that effect on me. "Kara Gillian. I'm honored to meet you, Jekki."

The second faas raised up so that it supported itself on the back four legs and had free use of the front two as hands. It traced a quick blue sigil in the air and coalesced it into what looked like a little azure gem which it promptly tossed to Jekki. "Faruk. I am Faruk. Kara Gill Ian," it said, holding its fisted right hand out as though waiting for a fist bump. "Faas of Mzatal say greet to Kara."

I found myself grinning despite the trauma of the past couple of days. I had no idea what the protocol was for this, so I just went with what I knew and gave the faas a fist bump. "Right back atcha, Faruk. Greetings and all that," I said, hoping I hadn't made a social blunder like eating with the wrong fork. Apparently it was okay, because Faruk bared its teeth in a smile and held its hand out toward Jekki, who returned not only the blue gem but two red ones it dug out of a belt pouch. "Eaaaaaaat! Drinnnnnnnnk!" Faruk said, and then both darted out without another word.

Still smiling, I looked over to Safar. "What was that all about?"

Safar rumbled in amusement. "They traded *kek*. Tokens," he said scrunching a soft drawstring pouch that depended from his belt—his only article of clothing. It sounded like a bag of marbles, so I suspected it contained a bunch of these tokens. "Wagers," he said as if that explained everything.

I was about to ask what sort of wager, but a savory scent demanded my attention, and I turned to the table, mouth watering. The faas had brought food—real, solid food—and *that* was the most important thing to me right now. I didn't recognize much of the stuff, but I figured it was safe enough. If Mzatal wanted me dead, it wouldn't be by poisoning.

I broke my liquid diet with gusto, though I stuck mainly to simple, vaguely recognizable things: grape-like fruit that tasted of lemon and melon, potato-y things that tasted like . . . potatoes, which they probably actually were. A creamy sweet cheese that would've gotten a five star rating except for its sickly grey-green color. I only tried it because, unbeknownst to me, some of it was stuck to the bottom of one of the relatively innocuous crackery things. It was so damn good even the color couldn't put me off after that.

The experience should have emboldened me to try some of the other questionable "delicacies," but, um, no. That sort of experimentation would have to wait until I was either hungrier or not so stressed.

I finally wiped my face and hands, dropped the napkin on the table, then looked to Safar. "You said I could do anything as long as I don't try to kill myself or leave the grounds," I said. "Does that mean I'm allowed to explore?"

He stood. "Unless I say you are not to go somewhere, yes."

Bath, food, and a sliver of freedom? My attitude was better already. Might as well find out everything I could before the end, right? I headed out to the hallway, looked up and down. "I've never been in a palace before."

Safar patiently dogged me as I wandered the lower levels of the palace, but after what was probably an hour or so of examining paintings and statues and poking through empty rooms, I found myself in what I knew, with Elinor's help, to be the main entry corridor. I stood near a set of double doors at the end of a broad arched corridor that ran at least twenty-five yards to a matching set of double doors. Judging by the distance, I figured it led to the other side of the palace. One of the doors stood half open, so I headed out to see the sights without bothering to ask Safar for permission. I figured he'd stop me soon enough if I went somewhere I wasn't supposed to go.

The first thing that hit me when I reached the open air was the sense of spaciousness. I mean, I could look up and see sky like this at home, but it just felt *bigger* somehow, as if what I could see was only a small part of what was there.

I stood before the central section of the palace atop a set of three broad steps overlooking a large courtyard. To the left and right, wings of the structure angled out to frame the grounds, the far ends terminating in towers. Déjà vu whispered once again, but this time with a memory of watching the sun set from the tower to the left. Apparently that was west, or whatever the local equivalent was. The west tower rose gracefully above the roof line, but the one to the east was another story. It looked like it had literally melted to half its height, with stone in frozen flows around its base. What the hell could do something like that?

Walkways paved in dirt-stained white stone curved

through ragged grass, sometimes lost in overgrowth. Tangles of weeds flourished in what might have been flowerbeds. In the distance I could see that the courtyard was bounded by what were once likely manicured bushes but were now shaggy lines of wild growth.

I sighed. Much like the interior of the palace, everything suffered from neglect. What a waste. *I guess none of the other lords bother to take care of it with Szerain gone.*

The center of the courtyard was graced by a raised circle of stone approximately twenty feet in diameter surrounded by eleven columns, in an eye-pleasing blend of honey-gold stone and wood, like much of the palace behind me. That was as good a destination as any, so I headed for it. The buzz of insects—or what I assumed were insects—mingled with an intermittent raucous cry that sounded like a cross between a crow and a bullfrog. Untamed vines dripping tiny scarlet flowers snaked up the nearest three columns. As I got closer, I identified them as the source of a pleasant tangy-sweet scent that laced the air.

Peering through the leaves, I saw that the columns bore subtle carvings that had to be sigils, though I didn't recognize a single one of them. The whole place emanated a subtle potency that rippled in goosebumps up my legs, and I had the strange sense that it was asleep and . . . dreaming.

"*Dak bah!*" came a loud shout off to my left. I turned to see a reyza I didn't know and the shadowy form of a zhurn near the wall of the west wing. They were heavily engaged in something that I could only describe as a fast and furious game of rock, paper, scissors, but with a lot more possibilities, and both hands were used. A few minutes of attentive focus taught me not much more, except that the reyza tended to favor a four-fingers-spread configuration, they were pretty damn serious about their fun, and that the kek tokens were passed back and forth periodically.

A rush of air warned me, and I looked up in time to see a *syraza* make a precise and graceful landing in the center of the pavilion, its subtly iridescent-pearl skin catching the sun.

For one brief, heart-stopping moment I thought it was Eilahn, my kickass demon bodyguard. She'd been killed on Earth, which meant that she would, hopefully, return here just as I'd returned to Earth after my death in this world.

But even as my hope flared I realized that it wasn't her. I'd only spent a few minutes with Eilahn in her natural form before she'd shifted into a human guise, but it didn't matter. I knew this was a different demon. It just didn't *feel* like Eilahn.

This demon stood a head taller than me, long of limb, with bird-like delicacy, paper thin wings, and a decidedly feminine cast to its—her?—features. I truly had no idea how gender worked with so many of the demons. Most of the time I simply used whatever pronoun seemed to fit the best. I had no doubt I'd been utterly wrong a time or three, but so far none had taken insult. At least I hoped not.

The syraza looked to me with huge violet eyes set in an almost human face, though broader of forehead and much more elongated. "I am Ilana. Fair greetings," she said in a voice with overtones of delicate chimes and birdsong.

"I'm Kara Gillian," I replied, doing my best to hide my disappointment that she wasn't Eilahn. "Fair greetings. I don't suppose you're here to rescue me from all this?" I gestured to encompass the dingy palace and Safar as well. "Sorry, big guy," I said to him. He merely snorted, but Ilana gave a chiming laugh that wasn't mean or derisive in any way.

"I cannot take you from Mzatal's custody, gentle one, but I would be honored if you would accept my company while you walk Szerain's grounds."

"I would be the one honored," I replied.

She looked to Safar, and a heartbeat later he leaped into the air and winged his way to the central tower of the palace proper, high above the double doors.

The syraza parted her lips and curled them back a smidge in what I interpreted as a syraza smile. She headed for the double doors, and I was about to ask why seeing the grounds entailed going back in, but then decided to go with the flow. It wasn't as if I had any sort of schedule or agenda. We walked the long corridor toward the set of double doors at the far end. Déjà vu familiarity hummed.

"You're with Mzatal?" I asked as we walked. I'd almost asked if she served Mzatal, but somehow that didn't seem quite right.

"I am his *ptarl*. His counselor," she explained. "The lords bear much responsibility, and each has one of the Elder syraza as ptarl, though Rhyzkahl, Szerain, and Kadir are separated from theirs."

Elder syraza. I noted the differences between Ilana and the only other two syraza I'd seen: Eilahn, and Marr, who I'd summoned to pass the eleventh level of summoning. Where the younger syrazas' foreheads were smooth, Ilana's had a subtle vertical ridge from high mid-forehead to the top of her head. She also had prominent ridges in her hide, on her back and lower torso, that were absent in the others. I made mental notes of it all. "How many lords are there?" I asked.

"There are eleven *qaztahl* . . . lords."

Comprehension dawned. Eleven. Eleven walls. Eleven fissures. Eleven columns. These guys sure as hell put a lot of stock in themselves.

"Rhyzkahl, Szerain, and Mzatal you know," she said, and I didn't miss that she obviously knew about Ryan. "The others are Jesral, Amkir, Kadir, Vahl, Seretis and Rayst, Elofir, and Vrizaar."

No way would I remember all of them, but my summoner training had required me to develop pretty good memorization skills that also proved useful in police work. I filed away what I could and figured I'd at least recognize a name if I heard it again.

As we approached a cross-corridor about halfway down, Ilana laid a long, three-fingered hand on my arm to stop me. "Anomaly," she said, gesturing toward the passage ahead. I peered toward where she pointed and could barely see a flicker in the air, like a spark that cast light and sucked it right back in.

"A very minor one," she noted. "Easily dealt with." With astonishing speed, the syraza traced a series of sigils and sent them spinning around the tiny spark. A heartbeat later the sigils flashed and a *crack* echoed down the corridor, not unlike the sound made when I dismissed a demon. "And now it is sealed."

"Um," I said, displaying my amazing intelligence. "What *was* that?"

"A remnant of the cataclysm." She tucked her arm through mine as if it was the most natural act in the world and strolled on. "Left unchecked, rifts in the dimensional fabric can cause much destabilization and damage. Best to seal them quickly, even the very small ones like that, and always the larger ones."

I kept my arm looped through hers. Her touch held a deep comfort and reminded me of what I'd felt from Eilahn, though with Ilana it was much more palpable. Perhaps a syraza characteristic? "What if one of those happens way out in the wilderness where no one sees it forming?"

"Such rarely happens," she said as we came up on the double doors. "And when it does, the *demahnk*, the Elders, feel it. They most often occur in or around the demesnes of the lords because those are the areas of the greatest arcane torsion." Before I could ask even more stupid questions, she said, "Come, I will show you the grove."

The reverence with which she said the word told me that this wasn't going to be a stand of orange trees or anything like that. She opened one of the doors enough for us to slip through. We stepped out into open air again, confirming my déjà vu and observational suspicion that the corridor led from the courtyard all the way through the central palace. Off to the left—east—loomed the barren hills and jagged mountains I'd seen from the Cracks of Doom balcony. I felt as much as saw them, like festering splinters.

Before us, a swath of grass sprinkled with turquoise wildflowers sloped down into a shallow wooded valley with rolling hills that rose to low, forested mountains. Woods in the full leaf of summer dominated the view, but it was a particular stand of trees that captured my attention. Twice the height of the not insubstantial surrounding forest, they stood in a ring near the verge of grass. Two parallel lines of these giants leaned toward one another, forming an inviting, shadowy tunnel from the ring to the edge of the wood. Their leaves shimmered in sparkling amethyst and brilliant green against white trunks, and I had no doubt *this* was the grove. A stone-paved pathway ran from the tree tunnel to where we stood just below the tower that held the summoning chamber—a distance of perhaps a hundred yards.

"That's beautiful," I breathed. "What is it?" It was pretty obvious that this was more than just a bunch of really old and awesome trees.

She cocked her head. "It is difficult to fully explain. At its simplest, it is the locus of an organic network, cultivated and propagated for use by the lords to travel from one to another near instantaneously."

"You mean like teleportation?" I asked.

She spread her wings in an elegant flutter-motion that I had no doubt was a syraza version of a shrug. "The means are far different but the end result is the same. Only the lords and the Elder syraza are able to use them."

"It's beautiful," I repeated. It felt beautiful too, like subtle waves of peace breaking over me with the sigh of wind through the leaves.

"Yes, it is," she replied. "Very beautiful." She stood with her arm still looped through mine. "Each grove has its own caretaker, a *mehnta*. A very special union."

I nodded, considering that. I'd only summoned one of the bizarre tentacle-mouthed mehnta, and that was simply to pass that summoning level. Their saliva had some antibacterial and antiviral properties, but these days it wasn't in as much demand as it would have been even as recently as fifty years ago. "What's it like to travel through a grove?" I asked.

"When we leave here you will experience it."

I tore my eyes from the grove to look at her. "Leave?" Then I realized. "Oh. Right." We were returning to Mzatal's realm so that he could take the mark from me. Cold knotted in my gut as I wondered again what that would entail and what the consequences would be. I hated not knowing what was going on, even in the safest of settings. Here it only served to add another layer to the overall stress and fear.

I lifted my chin toward a cleared area in the forest just this side of the grove. A small stone structure rose from a sea of wildflowers in the clearing. "What's that?"

She bared her teeth lightly in a syraza smile. "It is a place very dear to Szerain. One of his focal points. He spent much time there."

The coil of incessant fear gave way to deep curiosity about Szerain. The memory rose of that one kiss in the last seconds with Ryan before the summoning took me. So much had been said in that kiss. He'd told me he loved me. And I'd told him I loved him. But what did that even mean? It had felt so perfect, so right at that moment.

I found myself walking the path toward the structure

without even consciously deciding to do so. *And how much of Ryan is real?* I asked myself for perhaps the millionth time. *He's a demonic lord and doesn't even know it. How could anything about him be real?*

I was vaguely aware that Ilana had slipped her arm from mine to allow me to continue on my own.

If this place was so special to Szerain I really wanted to see it. I *needed* to see it. There was so much I didn't know. I hurried down the gently sloping path, eager for hints, or answers, or anything else this place might reveal to me.

Chapter 5

Unlike the neglected stone of the courtyard, this path glistened in the sunlight, free of debris or traces of dirt as though carefully tended. Thigh-high wildflowers in vibrant shades of blue and rich golden yellow undulated in the gentle breeze, filling the air with an exotic blend of delicate floral and underlying musk. Smiling, I trailed my hands over the flowers on either side as I walked, enjoying the velvety contact with the petals. Small flying creatures that looked like furry hummingbirds on a bad hair day zipped here and there among the flowers with a shooshing whirr.

The honey-colored stone building ahead was about the size of a two car garage, though lofty, with a peaked roof of overlapping green tiles. Enigmatic carved symbols covered all visible wall surfaces like neat graffiti. *Shrine* was the word that came to mind. Compact and sacred—not in the religious sense but more as if it held deep meaning for somebody.

I tried to imagine Ryan here, imagine him creating this sanctuary, but didn't have much success. I mean, I *knew* Ryan was Szerain, yet I still couldn't really get my head around Szerain-the-demonic-lord being the same as Ryan-the-FBI-agent.

The path led to three steps and a shadowy open doorway that didn't look as if it had ever had a door. As I passed through the doorway, I felt the prickle of warding like I was walking through an invisible barrier. Illusory shadows gave way to clear natural light from a skylight, and my arms rippled in gooseflesh from the arcane "charge" that permeated the place, even with the dampening effect of the collar. Humans and demons regarded me from murals, and water burbled in a stone basin atop a waist-high pedestal in the center of the floor.

The only other furnishings were a low, comfortable looking stone and wood chair with sumptuous green cushions, and an exquisitely carved side table. Definitely a one-lord hang out, I decided. Like the pathways outside, no debris in here either, and not a trace of dust. I wondered if there was some sort of arcane warding to keep it like that. If there was, I sure as hell needed it for my house. I stepped in close to the mini-fountain and turned slowly to take in the murals. The multitude of people and demons depicted came from a wide span of time, judging by the variety of hair and clothing styles.

My breath caught. Elinor. Radiant, she stood against a backdrop of leafy green, hands clasped with the youth from the statue—Giovanni. I half expected the sense of déjà vu to flare, but no. I frowned, wondering again.

The light shifted as something blocked the doorway, and I glanced back, expecting Ilana or Safar.

It wasn't either one of them. A big-ass demon loomed in the entry, flexing its four wickedly clawed hands and hiss-buzzing in a nerve-jangling manner. I thought it was probably a *savik*, a second-level demon, yet I'd never seen one so large. It stood a good seven feet tall, reptilian in overall appearance with inky black skin on its belly and translucent scales like flakes of emerald over the rest of its body. Its head reminded me of a cross between a crocodile and a wolf—with the crocodile winning. Even with its mouth closed, gleaming teeth protruded at varying angles. It stood upright, though it looked as if it could be equally as comfortable on all sixes. In fact, the few times I'd summoned a savik, it had spent most of its time horizontal rather than vertical. And damn . . . not even a quarter of this size.

I went still then very slowly raised my hands, palms out in an It's-cool-I'm-not-doing-anything gesture, but apparently the demon either didn't understand or didn't care. I wasn't really surprised. The savik was only a second-level demon with relatively low intelligence. The ones I'd summoned had been a nightmare to understand or give directions to.

It advanced, opening its mouth in a deep, throbbing

growl, giving me an unwelcome view of even more sharp teeth.

"Shit," I muttered as I backed away. "I don't want any trouble. I'll leave, okay?" Where the hell was Ilana? If I shouted for help, would that simply encourage the demon to attack?

The question became moot as the demon made a leaping lunge at me, jaws wide. I let out a shocked yelp as I backpedaled, picturing those many pointy teeth sinking into my flesh. At the moment of impact, the demon's jaws snapped shut, and it simply barreled into me, sending us both crashing to the floor. I scrambled to remember everything that Eilahn had taught me about fighting and tried to get my feet up and between us so that I could shove the savik off, but the creature was stronger, far more nimble, and fucking *heavy*. In seconds, it pinned me by my shoulders with one pair of hands and gripped my head between the other pair, ignoring my enthusiastic though useless struggles. It lowered its head as it said something in the demon language.

My heart pounded. Where the *fuck* was Ilana or Safar? "I don't speak your language!" I gasped. Maybe this was Mzatal's way of killing me off in an entertaining manner?

"He has touched you," it said in heavily accented English, far better than any savik I'd ever encountered or heard of. "When? How?"

Going still, I stared up at the demon. "Who?" I asked. I was pretty sure I knew who it meant, but I wanted to be certain before revealing anything.

"Szerain," it said, speaking the name with a sibilant intensity that echoed from the walls of the shrine and back to us.

Gulping, I nodded. "Yes," I replied softly. "He's my friend. I care about him very much."

The demon gave an odd whine. "When? Where?" It fixed its gold-flecked, luminescent purple eyes on me.

Keeping my eyes on its, I gave my head a small shake. "I don't dare say it. I don't want Mzatal to know."

"He cannot penetrate *here*. Where? When?" it asked, the intensity in its voice taking on a near desperate edge.

"On Earth," I said. "He doesn't know himself, but he seems content. He's . . ." I groped for a way to explain what an FBI agent was. "He helps protect innocents," I finally said. "We're partners in this."

The savik released my shoulders and head then shifted off to crouch beside me. "Who guards him?"

I pushed myself up to sit. I decided to dub this demon male, since it had that feel about it, though I had no idea if I was even close. "A syraza. At least, I'm pretty sure that's what he is. He goes by Zack."

"Zakaar!" He gave a hiss-growl. "Ptarl of Rhyzkahl." The 'k' sound in his words came out as its own guttural click, giving an unusual cadence to his speech. Zah-KH-aar. Rhyzzz-KH-ahl

So Szerain was being guarded by Rhyzkahl's syraza? "Is that good or bad?" I asked.

The savik snorted. "Good, bad . . . meaningless. It simply is. Zakaar is of the old line. Zakaar will guard him well."

"He does," I said quietly. "He guards him well." I peered at him. "I am Kara Gillian."

The demon dipped his head in acknowledgment. "I am Turek, essence-sworn to Szerain." There was something about the way Turek spoke, a deep resonance in the inflection, that told me he was not only very *very* old, but also that being essence-sworn to a lord was rare and special.

"I am honored to meet you, Turek." I leaned in toward him. "Can you tell me why he was exiled?"

"It was his choice," he replied, eyes luminescent.

"His choice?!" I said, shocked. "But what . . . ? Why would he do that? And why is he called an 'oathbreaker'?"

Turek brought his arms in close. "His actions were judged to violate an ancient oath, and so he is named *ki-raknikahl,* oathbreaker. He holds information he chooses not to reveal concerning the ways and means of his anathema. For this, he is judged to be too dangerous to remain here, and fifteen years, nine months, six days, and two hundred twelve heartbeats ago chose exile over revelation."

I struggled to process that. It was loads more information than I'd ever managed to get up until now, yet at the same time it told me damn near nothing except that the scope of whatever he did was huge. *More data for the mental clue board,* I thought in frustration.

"Is he exiled forever?"

Turek stood and dipped a claw in the water of the pedestal. "It cannot be forever. The balance of potency suffers with the absence of even one qaztahl." After a moment, he lifted his hand and traced a quick amber sigil with a single claw.

I blinked in amazement as a horizontal circle of points of light spun lazily a couple of feet above the basin, making a flat-tire wobble on each revolution. Eleven points. Multiple strands of vari-colored light dropped from each point and twisted together below, like a ring of long fringe with its ends wound into a crazy ball of glowing string. The savik lifted its claw toward the dimmest of the light points that trailed only a single sickly strand. "Szerain. Diminished. Exiled. Vilified. All out of balance."

I scrambled to my feet. "If he's so needed, then why can't he come back now?"

Turek remained silent and made a slashing motion with his hand, dispelling the ring of light. He touched the water again, eerie eyes on the fuzzy image taking shape above the water. I tugged at the collar in annoyance as if tugging could bring sharper focus, but slowly it began to coalesce into an image of the same man I saw in the Elinor bathtub memory, and looking no more like Ryan now than then. *Will his personality be different as well*? I wondered, uncomfortable worry twining through me again.

"The demon council is at an impasse," Turek finally said, again in that resonant tone that felt so powerful and ancient. Perhaps Earth summoners only ever called juvenile savik? They were considered second-level demons, but I had zero doubt that this particular demon was far stronger and had more arcane ability than even a tenth-level zhurn.

"Until resolved, Szerain . . ." Turek paused as if the thought brought pain. "Szerain remains in exile. And it is safer there, safer hidden, than here. Much more challenging for others to reach him. And Zakaar is better able to suppress him should he emerge." His top lip curled back from those razor teeth, and a low growl came from his throat. "He despised being submerged. He will not willingly submit to it again."

Gooseflesh crawled over me. I couldn't even imagine what that would be like. "What happened to Elinor?"

Turek tapped the lip of the basin, claw clicking on the stone, and the image shifted to the sweet-faced young woman. "I cannot speak of what happened to Elinor."

I let out a sigh. Once again with the damn oathbound crap.

But Turek surprised me by continuing. "Szerain asked me to remain silent, and so silent I remain." He shifted the image; Szerain again, but the expression seemed somehow harder.

"What was he like?" I asked, eyes taking in everything about Szerain. "Was he . . . nice?" That wasn't really the word I needed, but I couldn't think of another way to convey what I so desperately wanted to know.

The demon lowered his head and made a sound like a jarful of angry wasps. "Is. Is. What *is* he like." He lifted his head again and punctuated his statement with a harsh snort. "He *is* Szerain," he said as if that explained everything. "He *is* Szerain imprisoned. Rhyzkahl sealed what he could of his arcane potential, overlaid the life of a human." He paused, then lifted his hand from the basin, allowing the image to fade. "He could not change Szerain's core essence, but I do not know how that manifests in a different existence, in a different form."

"He can be very moody," I said softly. "Sometimes he's a real ass, and other times he's gentle and kind. But he . . . cares for me." What could Ryan possibly be going through now, not knowing what was happening to me, not knowing if I was alive or dead? Tears stung my eyes, and I had to blink furiously to hold them back.

"Truly kind, kri. Long, very long ago," Turek said.

Worry nipped at me. "What do you mean 'long ago'?" I asked. "Is he not kind now? I mean, before he was exiled?"

Turek bared his teeth again, but I couldn't tell if it was meant to be a snarl or smile. "Can be kind, kri. But not like during the first age. Not like before the gates collapsed and the potency rebounded. And then the blades brought more shift to all." The savik seemed to droop. "He appeared to be regaining something of his old ways in the years before the cataclysm. Then it was gone."

I frowned. "The what? Blades?"

Turek traced another sigil above the pedestal. "Tools of power for the Three: Rhyzkahl, Mzatal, Szerain. The *Iliok*—the essence blades."

An odd chill crawled down my spine at the name alone. "But what *are* they?"

"Knives, daggers," he said, finishing the sigil. "Each unique. Each shaped from a synthesis of the arcane core and the potency of *iliur*, of the essence." An image coalesced above the pedestal. A simple dagger with a gold-hued blade and a hilt that flared at each end like an elongated apple core. A deep green jewel sparkled in its pommel, winking with amber lights.

I stumbled back, feeling as if my blood had been replaced by ice. Ghostly agony flared throughout me, followed by a confusing maelstrom of horror, grief, terror. I was vaguely aware that I was moaning, *No no no*, yet I didn't know what I was denying, only that I wanted to be away from the terrible image, the beautiful dagger.

My foot caught on a lip of stone, and I nearly fell, but it was enough to pull my gaze away. As if suddenly released, I spun and fled outside, stumbling down the stairs and tripping on the last one. I sprawled onto the walkway, skinning palms and banging my knees harshly. Blood pounded in my ears. A reyza bellowed. Safar landed by the entrance and hissed at the savik. My breath came in short gasps. I had to get away from there. I managed to get back to my feet and hurried away from the shrine in an awkward walk-jog. My knees and palms throbbed and stung, but I didn't care. I simply wanted to be away from that awful image.

Safar bounded up to my side. "Kara Gillian? What has happened?"

I shook my head and struggled to reduce the pace of my flight down to a brisk walk. Was this what a panic attack felt like? "N-nothing's wrong," I said, knowing I wouldn't be able to explain it. "I just need some water."

The reyza gave a worried croon. "This way. Here." He indicated another path, and I gladly followed it since it took me farther away from the shrine.

My pace slowed a bit as we put some distance between us and the clearing. "Where did you and Ilana go, back at the shrine?" I asked, still trying to calm my breathing. "I was lucky Turek didn't kill me." I didn't want to mention that he didn't because the savik had sensed Szerain as Ryan had touched me.

Safar spread his wings and folded them close again. "I heed the wisdom of the Elders. Ilana said to leave you be, and so I did," he said, then snorted. "I doubt your survival had any foundation in luck."

What the hell was that supposed to mean? It was a setup? A thin stream of anger rose, but between the shaking fear that still coursed through me and the realization that I'd obtained a shitload of information on Szerain, it fizzled before it got far. If it was a setup, that meant Ilana wanted me to meet Turek, wanted me to find out more about Szerain. But why? Another note for the mental clue board.

Safar guided me through big double doors at the palace's south face and then into the spacious corridor—the one Ilana had taken me through—that led to the garden with the columned pavilion. He ushered me down a side hallway and into a snug courtyard with a fountain against the far wall. A faas filled an urn from the tumbling miniature waterfall, then hopped through a nearby doorway. The smell of roasting meat clued me in that we were probably near the kitchen. I headed to the fountain and stuck my hands under the cool water, keeping them in long after the dirt was washed clean as I tried unsuccessfully to shake the sense of dread.

"What has disturbed you?"

I nearly jumped out of my skin at the familiar and potent voice behind me. I whirled to see Mzatal regarding me with slightly narrowed eyes, hands behind his back.

"Nothing," I muttered, shaking water from my hands. Maybe that would keep him from noticing that they were trembling.

His eyes narrowed a fraction more as he reached out and took one of my hands. "What has disturbed you?" he repeated as he held it flat between his. A tingle of warmth spread through my hand, and the dull ache from the scrapes faded.

He healed it, I realized with astonishment. What the hell happened to the lord who was about to snap my neck? "I don't know why I freaked out so badly," I said. "In Szerain's shrine place, Turek showed me an image of a knife. A dagger. That's it."

"Szerain's blade, Vsuhl. Hidden, lost." Mzatal released my hand and then took the other. Once again the warm tingle spread through my palm, and to my surprise, in my bruised knees as well. Yet he didn't release my hand after the warmth faded. "And still you tremble," he said.

"Yeah, it . . ." I grimaced and struggled to get my mental equilibrium back. It didn't help that I was reeling a bit from Mzatal's bizarre behavioral shift from "scary motherfucker who will snap your neck" to "oh let me heal those booboos on your hands."

"I guess it was a panic attack," I said, though even as I did so, I frowned. I'd never had a panic attack in my life. "Last couple of days have been a bit stressful."

He continued to hold my hand. "Kara, breathe."

I scowled. "I *am* breathing."

"And *still* you are trembling," he replied, voice persuasive and melodic. "Focus only on the breath. Three breaths. Then call up in your mind's eye the *pygah* sigil."

My brow creased in bafflement. "The what?"

One eyebrow lifted in what might have been surprise before he repeated, "The pygah."

I shrugged. "I have no idea what that is." Was he fucking with me?

Mzatal released my hand and traced a simple, harmonious form in the air, visible to me even with the collar on. He lowered his hand, smiling ever so slightly as it began to tone softly. "The pygah. The balancer. Foundation for breath work for a summoner."

"Show me again how to make it . . . please?" I asked, deeply curious, and at the same time wondering why the hell I didn't know this if it was supposed to be so fundamental.

He flicked his fingers to send the current sigil away, then traced the simple loops again while I watched closely. As he finished, he touched it with potency, an infusion of power to bring it to life, like turning on the electricity. "You followed?" he asked with a questioning tilt of his head.

I nodded. I had no idea how to initiate a floater and knew I couldn't even try while I wore the collar, but I'd memorized the pattern.

"Now, trace it in your mind and breathe," Mzatal said, exuding patience.

A mental tracing? I complied, doing the three breaths thing, oddly surprised to find that it really did help, despite the collar. He nodded, approving. "Now you have the perspective to look at your fear."

"Okay," I said, brow creased in a frown. "Now what?"

"The rest is simple," he said. "You have already, during a most challenging manifestation, recognized that which is you, and that which is Elinor." I realized he was referring to yesterday when he revealed the statue to me. "This is no different."

Of course, I realized. *I* didn't have a panic attack. It was that damn Elinor's freakout.

"Your fear today was acute and so interwoven you could not distinguish yourself from Elinor," Mzatal continued. "Call up the image of Vsuhl again. Call up that which makes you tremble. Trace the sigil, breathe, and seek the boundary between you and the fear. Then expand until it is all of you and none of her."

I met his eyes for several heartbeats as I struggled to fathom whether this was some new game or trickery of his. He returned my gaze evenly, and I finally gave up and did my best to follow his instructions. Closing my eyes, I began the careful breathing and visualized the sigil. Sweat broke out on my upper lip as I cautiously probed the memory, but gradually I could view it without the irrational reaction.

I opened my eyes to see Mzatal watching me closely. "Practice this regularly," he said in a tone that left no doubt that he was accustomed to being obeyed. "Panic *will* destroy you if you do not learn to defuse it efficiently and expeditiously."

He turned and walked away. "If you have not yet taken in the view from the west tower," he said without glancing back or breaking stride, "ask Safar to take you. It is not to be missed, and we depart on the morrow."

I stared after him. Practice regularly and see the sights? Amazingly, I managed to bite down on the urge to shout after him, "Does this mean you're not going to kill me in the morning?" Instead, I turned to Safar: "I guess we're going to the west tower."

Chapter 6

Safar stood, snorted, and bounded down the corridor. At the end he turned back to me and bared his teeth. "Come!"

I smiled and trotted after him, down the central corridor of the west wing and then up a broad spiral stair in the west tower. I knew this stair, or at least Elinor did, but the eerie familiarity surged when we reached the seventh floor, where the chamber spanned the entire floor of the tower with huge windows all around. Eleven of them. I turned slowly, taking it in. Easels. Tables with paints, brushes, and a host of things I couldn't identify. A bench with hammers, mallets, and a variety of chisels. A single wooden stool, unadorned and well-worn.

Several sculptures lay toppled to the floor, broken, and at the base of one wall lay a dusty heap of shredded paintings. The stone above the heap bore a splodge of crimson paint, as though splattered from a container thrown with force. My gut wrenched at the wanton destruction of brilliance.

"Who destroyed all this?"

"Szerain."

My twisting anguish deepened. "Why?"

"After the cataclysm, after the last of the humans died, Szerain started to sculpt and paint but finished nothing. What he began, he destroyed. In time, he did not begin."

A deep sadness tightened my chest. I crouched and picked up a severed stone hand. Slender fingers. A woman. The dream image rose of a shattered statue of Elinor, and I wondered if there was a connection. And if there was, what did that mean? The statues were broken *after* Elinor died so it couldn't be her memory. My breath caught, and cold sank into my bones. From the floor in front of me, the half shattered face of a man stared in horror, mouth twisted in a scream.

I looked around, really seeing the fragments now. Each was as exquisitely crafted as any of the statues in the palace, but every face and twisted limb was the shard of a horrific story. I gingerly placed the hand back on the floor and stood, feeling as though I trespassed on someone else's nightmare. I backed toward the stairs, scrubbing my hands on my jeans. "Let's go."

Safar huffed and bounded up the next curve. I followed, glancing back once at the testament of pain. Was this why I'd never seen Ryan show any sort of artistic ability? Did this agony still grip him? Or was it simply that Szerain couldn't express it through Ryan? I found either possibility equally heartbreaking.

On the next level, Safar disappeared up, but I had to stop and stare. This too was the entire floor of the tower and, judging by the big bed, was likely Szerain's chambers. Hundreds of foot-high statues in wood and stone lined shelves and niches in the walls. Mostly humans with a smattering of demons mixed in.

The tassels of hair, the paintings in the shrine, and now this. Did he grow attached to each and every human only to watch them age and die? How could anyone survive such repeated loss?

A tumble of books and papers overflowed a huge table and littered the floor around it, making Tessa's library look as tidy as an evidence locker. Frowning, I took a step closer. Everything else in the room was in a modicum of order, but the table's disarray had the feel of having been ransacked. I hadn't seen any indication of that anywhere else in the palace despite its being all but abandoned. Not that there was anything I could do about it even if I wanted to. For all I knew it had been like that since his exile. Still, I made a mental note of it.

A draft of fresh air flowed over me, and Safar bellowed from above. I headed up the stairs and found him outside an open door that led to the top of the tower. He bared his teeth at me and bounded to the wall, bellowing again. I closed the door and followed, taking in the sights.

The tower rose above the palace roofline at the end of the west wing. To the west, wooded hills rolled, spiked with random fingers of stone, and mountains hunched on the horizon. To the east lay the courtyard with the columns, the other wing with its melted tower, and beyond that . . . *holy fucking shit.*

My steps slowed, and all sense of déjà vu vanished. Elinor had never seen *this* before, and I'd only had a partial view of it from the balcony on the first day with Mzatal.

In the distance, a crater the size of a small city dominated the utterly barren terrain to the northeast. From it, a great rift sliced across fractured stone, losing itself in a jumble of too-sharp, angular mountains. Gouts of arcane flame leapt and fell from the rift in an eerie dance of chaotic color. Blackened hills devoid of vegetation undulated southward in a widening swath as far as I could see. I had the sneaking suspicion that the odd rock formations in the forest to the west were shards from the disastrous event in the east.

I reached the parapet and spread my hands on the pitted stone. "It looks like a bomb went off," I breathed.

"The cataclysm," Safar said as he hopped onto the wall and crouched. "Very bad. Much destruction."

I struggled to comprehend the forces that could have wrought such devastation. *And I . . . Elinor did this? How is that even possible?* "Is it like this all over the planet?"

"It is most evident near the domain of the Lords, where the ancient valves shattered," he said, "though it is everywhere. The fire rain here was the worst." His wings drooped. "The primeval forest is gone. These woods are young, reestablished only a century ago." He tapped the mottled and pitted stone of the battlement. "Traces yet of the burning."

Nausea roiled my stomach as I ran my fingers over the rough surface. "What about the groves? Were they destroyed as well?" A weird pang gripped me at the thought.

"Dahn. The groves retreated."

"Retreated?" I asked, frowning.

"Retreated into the soil," he clarified. "All survived intact save one that was lost to a chasm, though none could be used for near a hundred years." He huffed. "And the one here closer to a hundred and fifty." Safar gestured toward the crater with a claw. "That was the first valve to go. The rest followed within a day. That was a very bad day."

"Gestamar said that the ways were closed and the humans all died." I looked up into his face. "How many?"

He gazed out over the blasted landscape. "There were near six hundred here with the lords. Most who did not die from cataclysmic events died within a year. A few survived almost two." He shook his large head. "With the ways closed so completely, the humans could not balance the potency within themselves and burned out."

"Wouldn't they go back to Earth? Make it through the void?"

Safar grunted and shook his head. "*Dahn*. No. With the ways closed, there was no passage."

I gripped the stone hard. I knew damn well why Mzatal had suggested I come up here—so that I could feel exactly how I was feeling now. But *why*? What purpose did it serve in his game? I hurriedly wiped away my tears. "How were the ways opened up again?"

The reyza turned on the wall and resettled into a crouch facing me. "Szerain and some of the *demahnk*, the Elder syraza, worked for over two hundred years to correct the inter-dimensional ruptures and arcane distortions enough to reestablish a valve." His eyes slid to mine. "In one nine zero eight on your calendar, in the area you call Siberia."

"Oh . . . wow. So, do you need valves to equalize the arcane pressure or something?" Tessa had a small one of these valve things terminating in her library, and I'd speculated that it functioned as a pressure release valve.

Safar gave a nod. "Simply stated, yes. After that, more were possible, and with less impact." He snorted, lifted his face as if to feel the sun on it fully. "Fifteen years later, at the age of fourteen, Katashi performed the first summoning in centuries."

"Katashi?" I blinked in surprise. Katashi had mentored Tessa in summoning for nearly a decade, and I'd spent a miserable couple of months with him during which I learned zilch except that he was an intolerant, inflexible asshole. I'd assumed he was in his seventies, but if Safar was right, Katashi would actually be over a hundred years old. *Damn*. Well, that explained why so many summoners had been trained by him. I hadn't realized that he was pretty much the grand poobah of modern summoning.

Safar snorted, "Kri, Katashi. He summoned Gestamar in

his near disastrous first summoning. Had he been slain by the recoil rather than merely injured, it is improbable that you would be a summoner now."

Holy crap. Summoning an ancient reyza like Gestamar as an untried and unmentored summoner was a mind-boggling accomplishment. *Katashi must be a fucking genius.* Not that he'd shared any of that with me.

I stared out at the horrific view, skin crawling from the feel of it. Did the demons hate me—Elinor—because of all of this? So far they didn't seem to be holding a grudge, and, for right now, I was okay with not knowing the answer.

For that matter, the demons had been downright accommodating. "Not that I'm complaining, but considering I'm a captive, why are y'all being so nice to me? Apart from Mzatal, who's pretty much a dick."

Safar lowered his head and peered closely at me. "It serves no purpose to cause you unnecessary distress. I have read Earth books, seen Earth captives, so I understand your question, though I do not understand causing distress without purpose."

Earth. I hugged my arms around me, suddenly feeling horribly homesick and isolated. I wanted my own bed, real coffee . . . hell, I'd even take some of Tessa's weird fruity tea at this point. I wondered what "necessary" distress they'd cause if they decided they had a purpose.

The groan of hinges pulled me from my self-pity spiral. I looked back to see the young blond man stepping out through the doorway. He smoothed down the front of a way-cool belted tunic-coat; a faintly Indonesian-looking thing of a color that flowed from purple to green to black as he moved. Definitely not Earth off-the-rack. He ran his hand over his hair with the supposed aim of taming it a bit, though it immediately sprang up again into the unruly blond cloud.

Straightening, I turned to face him. He stepped forward and cleared his throat, fidgeting slightly and not looking at all like the focused summoner of the previous night. I still pegged him at around twenty, but right now he was doing a great impression of a nervous teen. "Greetings," he said with a lift of his chin as he quite obviously fumbled for something resembling poise. "I am Idris Palatino."

I dipped my head in a nod. "I'm Kara." I paused. "But I suppose you already knew that."

He actually blushed. "Yeah," he said, looking down and picking at his sleeve. "I kinda had to know it to . . . y'know."

"To summon me," I finished for him, but I tried to keep the bitterness from my voice. I couldn't find it in me to be obnoxious or snarky to him. It'd be like kicking a puppy.

Idris exhaled, lifted his gaze back up to me. "Yeah, summon you." He smiled nervously. "It was hard."

I leaned back against the stone wall, shrugged. "Well, I don't always come when called."

His smile increased a bit. "I mean, it's not something you do every day—try to summon a human *blind* while they were on the move." He shook his head. "But even when I could find you, I couldn't lock on." His forehead creased. "It was weird."

My own smile spread to a grin. "Yeah, I bet you couldn't." The cuff I'd worn back on Earth was a crude version of the collar and blocked the arcane pretty damn effectively.

"Everything looked okay," he continued. "Even Lord Mzatal said it was good, but then . . . nothing!" An exasperated expression crossed his face, and he shook his head. "I almost didn't believe it when I actually got a lock on you, but then you came through and—" He abruptly paled and drew in a sharp breath. "Holy shit." He paled more.

"Idris?" I pushed off the wall and wondered if he was about to pass out. "You okay, dude?"

"Shit," he breathed. "The blood. You were covered in blood and . . ." He gulped. "Did I screw up a ritual you were working on?" His eyes lifted to mine, pleading. "Did I cause someone to be . . ."

"No," I said emphatically, shaking my head. "No, Idris, I swear that had absolutely *nothing* to do with your summoning of me. That was an entirely different clusterfuck."

He exhaled in profound relief. "Oh. Okay." Some of his color began to return. It was clear he didn't like the image of someone getting shredded, but he was obviously better able to deal with the horror of it if he wasn't the cause. "Sorry," he said, giving me a shaky smile. "Kinda freaked me out."

"Understandable." I liked him a lot more now that I

knew it would affect him so deeply. *So what the hell is he doing here serving this lord?* I wondered.

"It was a gate," I told him. "Or rather, an attempt at one. The summoner who created it—Tracy Gordon—tried to lock me into it." I grimaced. "I got out, but then the guy's partner threw him into the still-active gate." I flicked my fingers out in a "explosion" gesture, winced. "The reason you weren't able to summon me was because I had something a lot like this," I said, tapping the collar around my throat.

Idris began to smile, then grinned as the pieces fell into place for him. "That's why the sliders would just . . . slide! I thought it was a new variance or something and couldn't nail it." Remembered frustration flashed across his face. "The lord said it was something Earth-side and to keep doing what I was doing." He rolled his eyes. "Now I'm glad I didn't start trying new variances. I'd never have—" He winced. "—um, gotten you." A puzzled look came over him. "But, if you had an artifact why didn't you leave it on or stay behind wards?"

I let out a low snort. "After Tracy died it unbalanced the gate. It would have been disastrous, so I took the cuff off to close the gate down properly." I shrugged, spread my hands. "So, for you, patience is a virtue."

"Yeah, for sure in your case," Idris said. "It's not usually possible to summon a human from Earth unless they're at a hotspot—a permanent place that's been amped up for that. Humans simply don't carry enough natural potency for it to work right. Like, when I summon Katashi here, it's from a hotspot at his place." He shrugged.

"How the hell did you get me then?" I held no illusions that I had some sort of mega-potency going on.

He grinned. "It was something the lord figured out and had me work on with him. It took a whole month to get the parameters right," he said with a note of casual pride in his voice. "Lord Mzatal knows his stuff. He had me tap into one of the hotspots here and learn the patterns. It kinda developed from that."

"Is it pretty much the same the other way around? I mean, a summoner on Earth trying to get a human from here?" I continued to hold onto the slim chance that Tessa would get past her summoning block and rescue my ass.

Slim because ever since she'd spent time in the void earlier this year, she'd given no indication that she would ever summon again. She'd always summoned like clockwork before, and I wondered if she even could now. *But surely she would at least try to rescue me, right?*

"Well, the human still needs to be on a hotspot," he said. "But for the most part it's about the same."

My hopes lifted again. "How many hotspots are there here? One on every corner?" Hey, a girl could dream.

"Nooo, not one on every corner." He laughed, though not unkindly. "Not even close. But even so, to get enough power to pull a human, it'd take at least two skilled summoners," Idris said. "Probably three to be sure. All summonings from this end take both a summoner and a lord working together."

Hope dashed. Other than Katashi, I didn't know if Tessa knew any other summoners. And with her avoidance of summoning and summoning topics, there'd been no chance to teach her the nifty storage diagram I'd developed, which might have given her the potency needed to do it alone. Double crap.

Idris seemed pretty cozy, not at all like he was under duress or anything. Here he was talking about doing arcane Research and Development with Mzatal as if it was normal everyday business. What the hell was he doing here with that dickwad? "How long have you been here with Mzatal?"

"Just under four months," he replied. "It goes fast."

"And how long have you been summoning?"

His shoulders lifted in a shrug. "Since I was sixteen. Almost four years now."

I stared at him. "Only four years? Holy shit. I've been doing it close to a decade, and I don't think I know a tenth of what you do."

"Well, I learned a lot from Master Katashi," Idris said. "And now that I'm here," his face filled with awe, "every single day is just . . . wow."

Another summoner trained by Katashi. *So, why the hell didn't I learn anything worth a shit while I was with him?* "Okay, please don't take this the wrong way, but how does your family handle you being *here*?"

He let out a soft chuckle. "Well, they don't know I'm

here," he said, copying my emphasis. "They think I'm in Japan on a special foreign school program. Master Katashi takes care of all that."

"They don't expect emails or phone calls?" I asked somewhat dubiously.

"Yeah, well, Master Katashi told me not to worry about it." He shrugged again, smiled. "He said everything would be taken care of."

Holy crap, but this kid sure seemed way too naïve and trusting to be dealing with demonic lords. "Don't you miss your family?" I hid a grimace, oddly bothered by the idea of him being in the demon realm without his parents' knowledge. Yeah, sure, he was a legal adult, but it still seemed weird.

He exhaled, gave me a smile tinged with sadness. "Don't get me wrong, my family's great. But I've only been with them since I was about fourteen."

"Something happened to your natural family?" I winced and shook my head. "I'm sorry. I have a habit of being too nosy sometimes. It's none of my business."

"Nah, it's okay," he replied. "Actually I was adopted twice. The first couple got me when I was a baby." A fond smile crossed his face, and it was clear that he'd enjoyed a good childhood. But then his smile slipped. "There was a car accident. A truck crossed the center line and they died. I was in the backseat." He exhaled. "I was lucky—I got adopted almost immediately by another really great couple." The smile returned to his face. "Turned out that the guy who lived across the street from my new family was a summoner. One day he caught me peering at his wards, and that was the start of all this." He gestured to encompass the demon realm. Safar gave a low snort from his perch on the wall.

"I'm sorry about your parents," I said quietly. "My mom died of cancer when I was eight, and my dad was killed by a drunk driver three years later. My aunt raised me. She's a summoner," I added. Tracy's comment rose in my mind. *We don't have a choice. They make sure we become summoners.* I pushed it away for now.

"Do you learn a lot with Mzatal?" I asked in a ruthless change of subject. By the relief on his face it was clear he was just as glad of it.

"Yeah," he said, making a face like a glazed-eyed goldfish. "Holy shit, there's always more."

"Do you . . . like him?" I asked doubtfully.

A somewhat pained grimace came over his face. "Well, um, he's an awesome teacher."

"It's cool," I said, grinning. "I get it." *Likeable* wasn't a necessary requirement for a good teacher.

He cocked his head to one side. "I mean, it's hard to explain. He's always about ten steps ahead of me, so I really *really* have to stay on my toes." Then he shrugged. "He always tells me when I'm doing it wrong, but he always tells me when I'm doing it right, too. And he's never stepped outside of our agreement, that's for sure."

I pursed my lips, considering that. He did sound like a good teacher, but I'd probably think more kindly of him if I wasn't constantly worried about him *killing* me. "Agreement? Some sort of official contract?"

Idris nodded. "Yeah. Katashi's already Mzatal's sworn summoner, so anyone else the lord works with would have an official agreement with the terms laid out."

My rising questions derailed as an odd vibration went though the tower. I started to ask Idris if he felt it too, but the frown on his face told me he did.

"Shit," he murmured. His eyes widened as a much stronger vibration shook the tower. "Holy shit!"

I reached for the wall. "What the hell was that?" I asked. "Earthquake?"

In the span of a heartbeat his face shifted from insecure teen to intense and serious arcane practitioner, far closer to how he was in the midst of the purification ritual. "Anomaly," he said, intaking breath at the sharp sound of cracking rock. "Not safe here. Safar! Take her up!"

With that he turned and ran for the door.

Chapter 7

"Wait! Idris!" I yelled. Had he considered that the tower wouldn't be safe for him either? I ran after him, then let out a squawk of surprise as Safar grabbed me around the waist and leaped into the air. I yelped and clutched at his arms as we cleared the tower and gained altitude. "Shiiiiiit!"

"The tower is not safe until they seal the anomaly," Safar said, with a rumble I felt in my bones. "It will not take long."

"Will Idris be all right?" I tightened my grip on his arms as he climbed higher.

"He goes to the summoning chamber to support the syraza," he replied, deep voice calm. "There is a small anomaly within the wall of the tower. They will seal it before anything untoward happens."

A bright flash from above followed closely by a *crack* like thunder pulled my attention. *But there isn't a cloud in the sky.* "Safar? What was that?"

"Another anomaly. Above." He snorted and beat his wings harder, gaining altitude quickly. "And a syraza falls."

I risked a peek down, biting down on a very un-brave whimper upon seeing how *really fucking* high up we were. I looked back up just in time to see Ilana streak by and up.

"Kara Gillian, turn around and hold tightly," Safar said as he continued to climb. With his help, I complied, clinging to the trust that he wouldn't let me slip out of his grasp. As soon as I was fully turned, I wrapped my legs around his waist and my arms around his neck, then hung on for dear life while my heart threatened to pound out of my chest.

Safar abruptly stalled in flight, then did a stomach-churning wingover and began to free fall. "Hold tightly," he repeated. Yeah, no shit, Sherlock. I was pretty darn solid on that point. Out of the corner of my eye, I saw a syraza falling. Ilana and Safar paced him in the fall as they both eased closer.

Safar reached a hand out to the syraza, then jerked as he made contact. His hand dropped away, and a weird dizzying shock passed through me, as if he'd touched a live wire. I nearly lost my grip before recovering and clinging hard again. The reyza shuddered, then went limp, beginning to fall in a very different way.

My gut clenched. "Safar?" I called. I looked up to see him staring and dazed. "Oh, shit. SAFAR!" I gripped as hard as I could with my left arm and my legs, took my right knuckle and twisted it viciously into his sternum. I'd used sternal rubs to wake up drunks before, but it barely made the massive reyza twitch. I reached up and grabbed an ear, twisting hard. "Safar!" I screamed. "Fly, damn it!"

At the ear twist he shuddered and came back to himself, then thrashed to get his wings out to slow our descent and stop the tumbling. He bellowed in pain as his right wing wrenched back, though he managed to get us straightened out. I felt our descent slowing, but a quick glance told me it wasn't going to be enough to keep us from crashing into the trees . . . and not just any trees. The splash of viridian and amethyst identified the grove. At this point the best we could hope for was a crash at slower speed, ending up merely mangled instead of a grease spot. I tucked my head into his neck and wondered if there was any chance I'd make it through the void a second time. Either way, this was going to really suck ass.

We plowed into the densely woven canopy with a shriek of snapping vines and breaking branches. I lost my grip on Safar almost immediately, crashing down through the upper branches, instinctively flailing to check my descent somehow. I remembered how tall these trees were. The ground was a *long* way down. Not that I had much time to think about that. A hundred smaller limbs and vines whipped past me, and a branch smacked me hard on my shoulder. Something caught at my right leg, and I screamed as the twisting snap shot through me. I felt a punch of pain in my left side, then came to a hard stop.

Silence descended, strange after the cacophony of the

fall. It took me a few seconds to catch my breath, but when I did, stabbing pain accompanied each inhalation. I was wedged in a tangle of branches and vines, at least twenty feet above the ground. A few yards to my right I could see the open space of a clearing—the center of the ring of grove trees.

I tried to shift, then let out a breathless scream as pain from my side and leg shot through me. The agony from the leg was simple to figure out. Legs weren't supposed to twist that way, and jagged ends of bone weren't normally visible through the skin. It took me a few more seconds to process the source of the pain in my side. It didn't make sense that the branch would protrude from my body that way. The rivulets of blood tickling my abdomen finally got the message to my screwed up head. *Ah, hell*, I thought dropping my head back against the cluster of vines. *This is bad.*

I heard a bellow and snapping of branches, then a crash of something heavy falling to the ground nearby. Two faas streaked through the clearing and into the trees in the direction of the crash. A moment later they reappeared, supporting a limping Safar. His right wing drooped, and his normally rich bronze skin had a sickly green tinge.

A shudder went through the tangle of branches holding me. Dizzy, I grasped weakly at the mess of vines, fear slicing through me that I'd fall the rest of the way. As badly injured as I was now, I didn't think I'd survive a fall of another twenty feet.

A vine by my hand twitched as a low purring vibration filled the forest. The trees around me gave another shudder, and a heartbeat later vines shifted and slid against me. Okay. Freaky. A deep groaning of movement permeated the grove as leaves and twigs broken by my passage fell from above. A vine as thick as my wrist snaked around my torso just above where the branch had skewered me.

I heard running footsteps in the clearing. Turning my head, I saw Mzatal come to a stop near the treeline, eyes on me, assessing. More vines wrapped around me. I struggled out of panicked instinct, stopping as agony knifed through my side and leg. My eyes met Mzatal's. I tried to call for help, but I could barely get enough breath to *breathe*, much less speak or shout.

Mzatal's eyes narrowed. He stepped forward, then

stopped as if he'd run into a wall. I watched as he raised a hand, testing an unseen barrier. *What the hell?* I wondered in barely controlled panic. Had I managed to fall into some sort of carnivorous plant? Yeah, bleed on the man-eating plant. Always a good plan.

Yet even as I fretted about being eaten, a soft ease stole through me, and my panic faded. I felt oddly relaxed . . . and safe. It occurred to me that if it really was a man-eating plant, it might have released chemicals or pheromones or something to make its prey nice and docile, but I decided it was more comforting to think it was simply a Nice Plant.

Vines continued to shift and move around me. The white trunks and limbs shimmered with heat-wave ripples, though the grove felt cooler than before. The green and violet of the leaves awoke with a luminescent glitter of emerald and amethyst. Mzatal stepped back as the barrier before him took on a barely visible pulsing glow. A wind whispered through the leaves, or maybe the leaves just whispered to me. Mesmerized, I stared up at the shifting beauty.

A leafy tendril touched my face, and the last vestiges of my panic ebbed away. It wasn't going to let me fall. Everything shuddered again and the vines that had wrapped around me began to lift me off the impaling branch. I stared at the leaves above, mind screaming distantly to expect fresh agony, but it was wrong. Only a little tingle. My new Plant Friend wouldn't hurt me. Smiling, I watched the pretty dancing lights.

I relaxed into the cradling hold. Out of the corner of my eye I saw Mzatal pacing along the perimeter, eyes never leaving me. He placed a hand on the barrier and tried to push through, then staggered back a step as it repelled him. His eyes snapped to me as he stood, hands clenched at his sides. Way too tense. He needed a Plant Friend.

Whisper whisper whisper. Sparkly. Everything sparkly.

"Kara, can you hear me?"

Whisper whisper whisper.

Shimmery. Sparkly. Shimmery.

Whisper whisper whisper.

"Kara!"

"No need. To. Shout," I managed, my voice sounding loud and unnatural to me. Vines unwound, pulling away.

The pain returned, and I shuddered and whimpered low. Awareness seeped in: not in the tree anymore, on the ground. "How'd I get here?"

Mzatal crouched at my side, carefully looking me over without touching me. "The grove moved you. It was unprecedented, Kara Gillian," he murmured, gaze flicking from the wound in my side to the mangled mess of my leg. Sudden fear gripped me. Would he even bother trying to heal me?

He looked past me at the retreating vines, then laid a hand in the center of my chest. His jaw clenched and he shook his head, then stripped the collar from me, passed it to Gestamar, and set his hand on my chest again.

"You are badly injured," he said, in what I thought was a keen grasp of the fucking obvious. He looked up and around, expression contemplative. "The grove has stopped the bleeding." Shaking his head, he returned his attention to me. "We will stabilize your leg here, then move you." He pointed to a spot in the center of his forehead. "Focus here," he said, then sketched a quick sigil in the air between us.

I did my best to focus where he indicated, though my vision kept wanting to fuzz in and out. The sigil rotated in a subtly mesmerizing pattern, and gradually it became oddly simple to focus on that and little else. Mzatal set a hand on my thigh, and I felt Gestamar pulling and twisting my leg into a more acceptable configuration, but the agony seemed to be behind a glass wall. Mzatal traced tethers of potency around my leg, then caught the sigil and placed it on my chest. A soothing warmth emanated from it, like a magic pain patch.

"Gestamar will move you now," he told me, speaking in a calm, imperturbable voice. I barely managed a nod, feeling strangely distant from my body.

The reyza lifted me with amazing gentleness. Around me the grove shimmered, and I smiled, feeling its touch like a caress.

I must have drifted off for a few minutes, because the next thing I knew, Gestamar was gently setting me on my bed. Mzatal entered, removing his suit jacket and draping it over the chair before rolling up the sleeves of his pristine white shirt. He moved to my side and ran his hands lightly over my torso.

"How . . . bad?" I asked, the effort of those two words exhausting.

Before Mzatal could respond, Idris entered. He stopped and gave a gasp of shock—inadvertently answering my question of how bad—then flinched at the reproving look from Mzatal. I wanted to laugh, but I knew it would hurt too much.

Mzatal returned his attention to me. "Your right leg is broken. You were impaled through and through on your left side and there is damage within. If you are not healed, you will die."

"Oh . . . okay." Well, he didn't pull any punches. But at least, at this point, I was pretty sure he was going to do what he could to keep me from dying.

Idris audibly gulped and proceeded to edge around the room and out of Mzatal's direct line of sight.

A faas hopped in, and Mzatal took the mug that was offered. In a smooth motion, the lord slid his arm under my shoulders and lifted me to a partial sitting position, supporting me fully. Pain flared behind the shielding wall of the sigil.

"Drink, Kara," he said as he held the mug to my lips.

I suddenly realized how thirsty I was and did my best to drink. It tasted pleasantly sweet and refreshing and felt as if it permeated beyond the physical. It took some doing, but I drained the mug. "What was that?" I managed to whisper.

Mzatal set the mug aside and eased me down to the pillow again. "Tunjen juice. Replenishing both for the physical and the arcane."

The demon realm version of a super sports drink, I thought with detached amusement.

I watched Mzatal as much as I was able, though between the pain and the sigils he was using to dampen it, I tended to drift in and out. He looked seriously fucking intense as he readied himself to work on me.

"What do you know of the groves?" he asked, placing a hand next to the wound in my side.

I frowned. He was going to get blood on a really nice shirt. And how the hell did he get tailored for a suit that nice in the demon realm? And what sort of cuff links did a demonic lord wear? And had he washed his hands?

"Kara," Mzatal said with an undercurrent of command

in his voice, reminding me of the tone cops used when trying to get and keep attention.

Oh, right. He'd asked me a question. "Trees. Lords travel . . ." Muzzily, I realized he wanted me to stay awake and interacting. Likely for my own good or something. Damn it.

Mzatal said a few words in demon to Gestamar. The reyza grunted and bounded out.

He looked back down at me. "You have never been in a grove before." It was a statement, not a question, so I didn't waste energy trying to answer it. He lifted my shirt above the site of the impalement. "Idris, lay support."

The young man jumped at the sound of his name. "Y-yes, my lord," he said, flicking a worried glance my way before beginning to sketch a complex pattern using nothing but shimmering threads of potency. I watched, fascinated, in a dreamy sort of way. This was the first chance I'd had to really see things happening without the collar on.

Idris finished and ignited the pattern. Instantly, I saw it dim as Mzatal drew upon it. A low warmth spread through my side. Now I understood Idris's worried look. If the demonic lord needed a support pattern for additional potency, that meant I was well and truly fucked up. Then again, it wasn't news to me at this point.

I pulled my unsteady attention back to Mzatal. His hair was braided in a complex weave that looked like it needed at least seven or eight strands. Did he do that himself? Or did he have a demon valet do it for him? And where did he get the tie that was currently tucked partially in his shirt to keep it clear of his work? And for that matter, where was I going to get new clothes? Especially bras. I knew the one I had on was pretty well soaked in blood.

"The *zrila* Anak fashioned the tie, and the faas Jekki braids my hair," Mzatal said as he slid a hand beneath me to reach the entry wound. Pain flared at the movement, and I hissed a breath. "When we return to my realm on the morrow," he continued, "the zrila circle will create what garb you require. They are quite skilled."

I managed a slight scowl. "You're reading . . . me."

Mzatal looked from the wound to my face. "Yes, of course."

"Rude." I swallowed, breathing shallowly. "Stop."

"That I cannot do," he replied. "It is as impossible as stopping the taste of wine upon my tongue, or the feel of your skin beneath my hands." In the next instant heat flooded the wound, and I gasped, hands tightening in the sheet. Gradually, it subsided into a warm pulse, spreading in gentle flows from the wound to the rest of my body. I exhaled in relief as the pain faded, noticing that it was already far easier to breathe.

"The sigils fascinate you," Mzatal said almost conversationally, "but it is clear you do not know many of them. What training have you had?"

"My aunt," I replied. It was a lot easier to talk and breathe now, but I was as tired as if I'd run a marathon uphill. Not that I had any intention of ever finding out how tiring a marathon was. "She taught me protocols . . . rituals. I summon demons . . . to learn . . . ask questions." I caught myself drifting and dragged my focus back to him. I didn't want to sleep. Too much chance I might never wake up. "I'm . . . getting better?"

Mzatal drew in a deep breath. He looked damn near as tired as I was. He shifted and placed a hand on my solar plexus. "Yes, better," he said. "Gestamar will splint your leg. I have done much work with the impalement and the internal damage." He gave me the barest ghost of an actual smile. "You will not die this day, Kara Gillian."

I smiled weakly, then slid my hand over his. "Thanks," I mumbled as I allowed my eyes to drift closed.

Chapter 8

I came awake abruptly. "Eilahn?" I called groggily, before realizing where I was and what had happened to her.

"Eilahn is not here, little one," came a rumbled response. I blinked to focus and saw Gestamar crouched beside my bed, carefully knotting a splint around my injured leg.

"You know Eilahn?" I asked.

"Yes."

"She was killed on Earth." My brow furrowed. "Yesterday, I think. Is today the same day as when we fell?"

"Yes, it is the same day," he replied. "You have been asleep for several hours. And yes, she has returned."

"She has?" I exhaled in relief, smiling weakly. "I was so worried."

Gestamar tightened another binding, then shifted and touched my cheek with the back of a claw. "Yes, though Ilana says that she will be in stasis for a time, to recover herself."

"Good . . . good. What about Safar?"

"Mzatal tends Safar's damaged wing now," he replied calmly.

Pain shot through me as Gestamar shifted my leg. And Safar was messed up, too. Wow. Today was turning out to be an even shittier day than the one before. I hadn't thought that was possible. And damn it, the fucking collar was back on. It'd been such a relief to have it off during the healing.

"You roused him," Gestamar said, and it took me a couple of seconds to realize he was referring to Safar. "Neither of you would have survived had you not." He shifted and returned to knotting bindings.

"Good thing he didn't like having his ear twisted," I said with an unsteady smile. The pain was beginning to make its presence known again, pulsing in waves like radio signals from my leg.

Gestamar snorted. "Our ears are quite sensitive. You chose well."

"And what about the syraza?"

"Olihr. Recovered enough to return to Rhyzkahl by midday," Gestamar said casually.

That got my attention. What was one of Rhyzkahl's syraza doing at Szerain's palace? Hope rose. Did Rhyzkahl know I was here?

"What happened?" I asked Gestamar. "I mean, why did we fall?"

"Olihr is young and eager." The reyza gave a low snort. "He sought to close the anomaly above on his own and became incapacitated by the backlash energies," he explained. "When Safar touched Olihr, he received a jolt of it."

Like touching a live wire, I mused.

A scrape of boot on stone gave me enough warning to be prepared as Idris entered and hurried to the side of the bed. It was obvious he was trying hard to not flutter, but the poor kid was clearly way out of his comfort zone. His eyes kept flicking to the swollen mess of my leg and skittering away, face pale and worried.

"Kara, do you need anything?" he asked, practically wringing his hands. "Water? I have water. Or tunjen? Tunjen might be better." His gaze shifted to my leg and away as he gulped. "I'll get you some juice." He wiped his hands on his trousers, scanning the table for anything that resembled juice.

"Painkiller might be better," I said, biting back the urge to tell him to find a Xanax for himself. My voice had an annoying rasp to it, and I grimaced. "Any sort of painkiller. That'd be good."

He stopped fluttering and blinked at me. "Ibuprofen! I have ibuprofen. Be right back!" He turned and headed for the door at a near run, coming to an awkward sliding stop about six inches before barreling into Mzatal.

The lord stood still in the doorway, hands behind his back, as usual, as he gave Idris a hard look. Idris managed to straighten and get fully upright with some semblance of decorum, though the wild mane of his hair ruined the effect a bit. "Sorry, my lord," he said and hurriedly stepped back out of the way.

Mzatal kept his eyes on Idris for another few heartbeats before continuing into the room and allowing the young man to flee. He moved to the other side of the bed from Gestamar, face expressionless and gaze intense as he took in my overall condition. Even through the collar I had the sense he was probing, likely assessing my mental outlook as well as how mangled my physical body was.

I bit back a cry of pain, hands clenching in the sheets as the reyza shifted my leg. Yeah, my mental outlook was just peachy right now.

Mzatal's eyes narrowed a hair. He shifted his attention to Gestamar, said something in demon, and received a deep-voiced answer. Neither's face or manner betrayed the subject, to my deep annoyance.

Mzatal shook his head, spoke again in a slightly more commanding tone. Sick fear pierced through me as the reyza seemed to hesitate. Were they talking about amputating my leg or something extreme like that?

Gestamar gave a huffing snort, replied in demon, then turned and exited the room.

"What's going on?" I asked as I worked on unclenching my hands from the sheet. "Can y'all fix my leg?"

Mzatal slid his gaze to my face. "I have sent Gestamar to create a particular medicinal blend for you."

"Please tell me it's a painkiller," I said, swallowing. "Or at least an antibiotic." I risked another look at my leg. I didn't see any dirt anywhere, so apparently it was cleaned while I slept. "Can't you do one of those sigil things again?"

"You need not worry about infection," he continued, tone unnervingly mild. "And yes, the draught will ease the pain. It is too soon for you to tolerate another analgesic sigil. The bleeding has been stopped and the break set as well as is possible."

As well as is possible? What the hell was that supposed to mean? "Wait . . . you can heal this, right?"

"It is a serious break," he said, clearly watching for my reaction. "I will assess it to see what action will be taken."

I did my damnedest to keep my expression even, but I didn't think I could completely hide the deep fear that took up residence in my gut. "Can't you do some healing now? Or just send me home. Let me go to a hospital. They can fix it back home." I locked eyes with him. "Don't you let me end up a cripple."

His gaze remained steady on me. "I have already done some healing," he stated. "No, I will not send you home or to a hospital. And you will end up as you will end up."

The wash of fury that swept through me helped to drive back some of the pain, but I kept silent and refused to look away. I fucking hated how completely I was at his mercy, and I wanted him to know it.

Out of the corner of my eye I saw Idris come back in. He stopped dead, likely feeling the level of tension in the room, and began to slowly back out, grimacing as the pill bottle rattled. I snapped my gaze to him and held out my hand for the bottle with a give-me-the-goddamn-pills-now expression on my face. He gulped and looked up at Mzatal. He must have received the okay, because he continued to my side.

"Here you go," he said with a wary flick of the eyes at Mzatal before he set the pill bottle in my hand. "Two hundred milligrams."

"Thank you," I managed, fumbling with the top. My hands shook, and I ended up dropping pills on the bed before I managed to get four in my hand. That would bring it up to prescription strength and hopefully put a dent in this pain. "Could I have some water, please?"

"You will not be able to take the draught as well," Mzatal said, calm and conversational, "and the pain relief will be far less with the Earth medication." He lifted one shoulder in a graceful shrug. "It is, however, your choice."

I went still, clutching the pills in one hand. He could have said that before I spent a couple of shaking minutes trying to get the damn pills out of the bottle. *He's fucking with me*, I realized. *Pushing my buttons.* I didn't know if it was to test me or to torment me, but either way, now that I recognized it, I knew how to deal with it. Buttons got pushed all the time when you were a cop, especially as a female.

Sweat trickled down the side of my face from the pain, but I smiled, replaced the pills in the bottle, and snapped the cap back on. This good lord/bad lord game sucked. Wasn't it just a few hours ago he was healing me and telling me about how the zrila made his ties? "That's very kind of you to share that information," I said, voice dripping with honey and false gratitude. "It warms the very cockles of my heart to know that you hold such a deep concern for my well-being."

The lord's face darkened. "You will remember your place, Kara Gillian."

I gave him my best wide-eyed innocent look. "Oh, I know my place, Lord Mzatal," I said, and tapped the collar with my middle finger. A crash to my right told me that Idris had dropped the water glass he was holding, but I kept my smile in place and my finger extended.

He narrowed his eyes but then turned and departed without blasting me into several squishy bits. I exhaled as the door closed behind him and dropped my head back to the pillows. Maybe, *possibly,* I won this round?

"Holy shit," Idris breathed. "Holy shit!"

"First off, try saying 'fuckballs' every now and then for variety," I said, breathing a bit raggedly as the brief adrenaline surge wore off. "Second, could I please have some water?"

"Oh, water." He looked down with dismay at the broken glass at his feet, then swung back to the table. A near-comic sigh of relief escaped him as he found an intact glass. He poured water and brought it back to me. "Fuckballs," he said, trying out the new word. "Fuckballs, Kara, but you're insane."

My hands shook as I took the water, but I managed to drink some before handing it back to him. "Idris, at this point, what do I have to lose? If I roll over, I'm dead. Might as well let him believe I have a spine." I met his eyes. "Remember, fake bravery is better than none at all."

"Yeah, but . . ." He shook his head. "I mean, that's *Mzatal!*"

I let out a breathless laugh. "And I'm *Kara*. And you're *Idris*."

He rolled his eyes. "Whatever. I just don't want to see you get hurt." He glanced at my leg, grimaced. "I mean, more than you already are."

"I'm at his mercy, Idris," I said quietly. "He doesn't need a reason to hurt me. I might as well show that I won't go down without at least the semblance of a fight."

"Yeah. Shit." He sighed. "I don't think I could be like you."

I snorted. "Of course not. You should be like *you*, but the best you you can be." I frowned. "Not sure that made any sense, but hopefully you get the idea."

"It kinda made sense. I guess," he said, though his forehead puckered in mild confusion.

Gestamar returned carrying a mug. He moved to my side and held it out for me. I took it warily and sniffed the watery green contents. It reminded me of freshly mowed grass but didn't smell vile or anything, which surprised me. I was certain Mzatal would find a way to make any meds he gave me utterly nasty.

"Thanks," I said, taking the mug. "I should drink all of this?"

"As much as you can," he rumbled. "Mzatal requested this amount."

I took a deep breath and began to chug it down, then had to stop, nearly gagging. Smell was definitely no way to judge. "Holy . . . gah! That's like drinking a diaper."

The reyza crouched. "If you do not drink it, it will not help with the pain."

I didn't even bother scowling. This was another test or torment, depending on point of view. Steeling myself, I managed to chug the rest of it down. The nasty shit had better kick the pain's ass. Shuddering, I handed the empty mug back to Gestamar. "Idris, water, *please*."

He pressed a glass into my hand. I drank, but it didn't seem to do much good. *Fuck Mzatal*, I thought sourly. What the hell was Idris doing with this asshole?

"If you're here fostering with this lord, then doesn't that mean you're pretty hot shit in some way?" I asked Idris,

He shrugged. "Yeah, I guess I do okay with the summoning stuff."

I took another drink of water in a futile attempt to clear the slimy vile taste from my mouth, then gave Idris a sharp look. "Wait. You do 'okay'? Do you really believe that?" I narrowed my eyes at him. "You summoned *me*, damn it. You're more than 'okay' if you managed that." I sighed, shook my head. "Idris, it's okay to be proud of the shit you can do well. Trust me, there are plenty of people more than ready to tear you down. Why give them a headstart?"

He stared at me, then flushed. "Yeah, I did good with that," he said, smiling with—at last—a touch of pride. "It was hard."

"Yeah, well, I wasn't going down without a fight."

Movement in the doorway caught my eye, and I did a double take as an *ilius* coiled into the room. The waist-high demon curled and spiraled within a haze of confusing multicolored smoke. Flashes of teeth, or an eye, or sinuous body appeared and disappeared seemingly at random. I'd summoned an ilius a few times before, finding them very useful as trackers in my police work, kind of like a demon version of a bloodhound. I didn't know much about them except that they consumed essence as their sustenance and, according to Rhyzkahl, didn't have a taste for humans. I'd always sated them on nutria as payment for their services, and they seemed content enough. Though the thing didn't appear to touch the floor at all, it was definitely more substantial and colorful than the ones I'd summoned to Earth.

"Um . . . Idris? Why is there an ilius in here?" I asked as the demon drift-coiled its way to the balcony.

Idris glanced over at the creature then back to me. "That's just Dakdak looking for Mzatal. Well, not actually looking for him," he said. "Since the ilius is here, it means Mzatal will most likely arrive within a minute or two. I don't mind. It's kinda like an early warning system." He grinned.

That was just too damn funny, and I laughed outright, though it may have had something to do with the shit I just drank. "So you're telling me big bad Mzatal has a pet ilius named Dakdak he hangs with?" I lifted the glass for another cleansing drink of water.

"Yeah. Four close ones actually—Dakdak, Krum, Tata, and Wuki—and a bunch more that just hang out at his place. They're not pets though."

I snorted water out my nose, laughing so hard it hurt. "Tata? And . . . Wuki?" I managed to gasp out. Then the room abruptly tilted. I dropped my head back and clutched at the bed.

"What's wrong?" Idris asked, aflutter again.

"I think—" I shook my head, instantly regretting it. "The green shit works," I slurred, right before the world fell away.

Chapter 9

Morning sun slanted onto the bed through the broad windows, waking me. I groaned and rolled onto my side, then blinked, suddenly fully awake.

That didn't hurt.

Sitting up, I tugged off the blanket to look at my leg—my unsplinted and undamaged leg. Relief flooded me, near dizzying in its intensity. Mzatal must have indeed followed the ilius into the room and completed the healing. Whether he had a change of heart or had simply been fucking with me, at this point I didn't care. The important thing for now was that my leg was still there and, apparently, as good as new.

A quick assessment of the rest of me revealed that not only was everything else healed up, but I was also clean and wearing different clothing.

"Now that's a nice health care plan," I murmured, sliding a hand over the spot on my torso that had so recently housed a tree branch. Not even a scar remained to show it had ever happened.

I startled as Jekki and Faruk burst into the room without knocking, carrying a mug and a plate that they placed on the side table. "Eat! Drink! Leave soon!" they burbled in unison, and then were gone in a swirl of blue fur and tails.

My smile faded and my gut clenched at the thought of going to Mzatal's realm, but I went ahead and drank the chak and ate the—. Okay, I had no idea what it was and thought it might be better that way. It looked like a plate of cat turds drizzled with mustard, but had a texture like biting into a grape and a meaty taste with a zing of sweet spice.

Totally weird but yummy. As soon as I was finished, Gestamar stepped into the room, almost as if he'd been waiting.

"It is time," he said, deep voice resonating. If I hadn't known better, I might have thought he was *trying* to sound ominous. I obediently followed him down to the entry corridor where Mzatal waited. The lord gave me an up and down assessing look but said nothing. I didn't know if he was checking out his healing skills or what. The lord confounded me, running cold to lukewarm, though the undercurrent of I-can-kill-you-any-time-I-want-to sort of put a damper on anything beyond cold.

Gestamar kept a hand on my upper arm as we headed through the south doors and outside. What'd they think I was going to do? Make a break for it? We stopped while Mzatal closed the doors and laid a shitload of wards, then he led the way down the path with long strides. He wasn't wearing the Armani; today the outfit was black pants, black boots, and a crimson knee-length coat, intricately embroidered in gold around the cuffs and hem. The suit was a good look for him, but so was this.

We passed the path to the shrine, and I glanced over to see if I could get a glimpse of Turek, but no luck. I felt the grove before we reached the tree tunnel—a subtle rippling touch like a breeze through leaves. Smiling, I entered the shady passage, and the touch shifted to a welcoming caress. Ahead, Idris, Ilana, Safar, and the two faas waited along with three ilius, and the unknown reyza and zhurn who I'd seen playing the strange rock-paper-scissors in the courtyard. To my relief, Safar seemed well recovered.

Power hummed around us as we stepped farther in. Even though I'd already had the experience of a lifetime in the grove, I looked around in rapt fascination as if I'd been out for a walk and suddenly smelled something amazing and had to stop and find the source. I inhaled as the grove enveloped me; a questing presence that the collar had no power to block.

Anxiety and fear slipped away as I welcomed the touch of the grove and felt the power of it hum through the white trunks around us. I exhaled in wonder, only distantly aware of Mzatal's focus on me. Idris moved to the lord's side and the two exchanged low words, but I was far too entranced by the feel of the grove to pay much attention.

The grove presence retreated as we clustered near the center. Mzatal crouched and placed his hands on a low smooth knob of wood that reminded me of a cypress knee. He channeled a burst of potency into it, and I understood that he wasn't powering the grove as much as he was making an offering to it. Frowning, I wondered how I knew that. It wasn't an Elinor memory or a déjà vu sensation, but I *knew*.

He stood and gestured everyone in close. I caught a glimpse of movement in the trees ahead. I felt a dropping sensation, and then between one blink of an eye and the next, we were in a different grove.

It looked a lot like the one we left, ringed with white trunks, but it was more elongated, had a "flavor" to it that felt different, and the hum resonated lower.

Mzatal started toward the tree tunnel, then paused as a mehnta stepped out from between the trees. Much like a human woman in form, her full breasts were bare and a loose braid of deep violet hung to her feet. Then it got weird. Her back, hard and shiny green, formed a beetle-like carapace that I knew covered wings packed in like a parachute. I had no idea how such light wings could support her heavy, muscled body in flight. Then it got weirder. Instead of a mouth, she had a dozen or so writhing arm-length tentacles, each ending in its own small, toothless mouth complete with lips.

I watched uncertainly as she approached, her mouth tentacles waving in an oddly unnerving fashion. I remained perfectly still as she laid a hand on my arm. At her touch, my uncertainty faded away, to be replaced by a sense of comfort and welcome, as if I'd been away for a long time and was being greeted again.

The mehnta spoke, voice oddly fractured as it came from a dozen sources at once. I struggled to understand, but soon realized she was speaking in the demon tongue.

I looked up to Gestamar. "What is she saying?" I asked, feeling a strange and desperate need to know.

He gave a low rumble before answering. "She has bypassed all protocols and asked for your name."

I smiled in gratitude, then turned my attention back to her. "I am Kara Gillian."

The mehnta kept her touch on my arm and spoke again.

Out of the corner of my eye I could see that Mzatal and Idris had stopped and were now watching our odd exchange.

"She says her name is Lazul," Gestamar said without needing to be asked. The mehnta made an odd whistling sound, then touched my face lightly with her mouth tentacles—soft and warm, like a myriad of little kisses. In any other situation I'd have probably freaked out, but instead, a thrill of delight and acceptance ran through me.

The tentacles lingered for another few seconds, then the mehnta retreated and slipped noiselessly back into the trees.

I exhaled and watched her go, then turned with Gestamar to follow the others up the tree tunnel. The feel of the grove slid away as we exited into the open air, and I swallowed hard against the deep worry that settled back into my gut.

And then . . . wow. We stood upon a clifftop, sea below on the left, dark stony mountains and lush green foliage rising to the right. A warm breeze teased my hair, carrying the pleasant scent of sea and wet earth. The sun hung high in the sky. Midday here. It had been morning at Szerain's.

The ground dropped into a grassy, rock-strewn depression, then rose to the base of Mzatal's palace. The path, cut in the native stone, alternated flat and stairs. The structure itself hugged the cliff face, long and narrow, two levels rising above and more dropping in tiers before the cliff. Glass. Lots and lots of glass. Lots—likely the resinous demonglass. It even comprised the low walls of the long balconies that ran the length of each level and wrapped around the near end of the two above the cliff. Whatever wasn't glass was the ubiquitous dark basalt of the surrounding terrain. A waterfall cascaded from the midst of the structure, plummeting to the sea below. On a verdant sward behind the palace, a thick, flat-topped column about three stories tall and of the same basalt as the palace and cliffs shone as though highly polished. I'd obviously stopped and stared because it took a tug on my arm from Gestamar to get me moving again.

Ahead, Mzatal waited, eyes on me, keen and assessing as I approached. "Your affinity for the grove deepens," he said, as casually as if he'd said, "your hair is brown." But there was a querying penetration to it, a hint that he fully intended to peel back the why of it.

"Yeah, well . . . I like trees," I said, giving a shrug. What the hell was I supposed to say?

He wasn't buying my nonchalance. His eyes remained hard on me for a moment, then he shifted his attention to Idris. "Prepare a trancing diagram." He proceeded to rattle off parameters that I couldn't understand but that apparently made perfect sense to the young summoner. Idris asked for a few clarifications that also sounded like gibberish to me, then took off toward the palace at a light jog.

Mzatal returned his shrewd gaze to me. "We will see if this affinity connects to anything." He lowered his head. "Or anyone," he added, and there was no mistaking the vehemence behind the words.

"It doesn't connect to anything or anyone," I shot back. "It's just bunch of damned trees," I said in a stunning display of brilliance as I jerked my fingers through my hair. "Look, you don't have to do more fucked up ritual crap on me." The purification thing had hurt enough.

"You know—intimately—it is much more than that," he replied, returning to unruffled calm as he pivoted away, clasped his hands behind his back, and headed up the path toward the palace. "I do that which must be done."

"Hurting me?" I demanded, not moving. "You *must* do that?" Gestamar set his hands on my shoulders to move me along but went still as Mzatal opened one hand behind his back.

Cold sliced through me at that simple gesture. I knew in that instant that he could pull power and strike before I'd ever sense it coming.

He faced me. "What I do, I do with purpose." He stepped closer. "Pain is at times a purpose unto itself," he continued, black menace flowing through his voice. "And, at times, a byproduct of a greater purpose."

Instinct screamed at me to back away from the coiled peril before me, but with Gestamar behind me I had no choice but to stand and face it. "Easy for you to say when you're the one dealing it out," I said, even managing to give a lift of my chin.

"It is easy to say because it is truth." He turned and continued up the path. "Bring her if she chooses not to walk on her own."

I snarled at his back. "I can walk," I muttered, and reluctantly did so, though fear of the unknown twisted in my belly. *Asshole*. I hated this. Hated being scared all the time. And I especially hated not knowing what the hell was in store for me. About the only thing I could be sure of was that it would only be harder for me if I resisted. Mzatal didn't need my compliance. He was being damn near generous by allowing me the chance to cooperate and avoid humiliation or discomfort.

With Gestamar's grip firm on my arm, we descended the path from the grove, then climbed the stairs and pathways to the entrance of the palace. Glass from balconies and walls of windows winked above, reflecting the early afternoon sun. The subtle hiss of the waterfall wove a pleasant background to the sweet, throaty songs of what I guessed were birds in the nearby cluster of thick-needled conifers.

The doorway cut directly into the native rock face, and the filigreed stone and glass double doors opened inward to a rough cut grotto with a broad circular staircase going down. And down we went about a billion steps though it was probably more like three stories.

The lord stopped a few steps from the bottom. Gestamar's hand on my arm stopped me as well, but he needn't have bothered. I didn't want to be any closer to Mzatal than I had to be. At first I thought he'd stopped to greet the two ilius that coiled in flashing smoke around him, but a heartbeat later a complex sigil coalesced in front of him, shimmering blue and gold.

I glanced back and up at the reyza. "What is that?"

He let out a low huff. "Message sigil," he replied in what seemed to be his version of a whisper. "From another lord."

Mzatal touched the sigil. A few seconds later flickers of azure-gold potency shimmered around him, and he visibly tensed. Apparently it wasn't a cheery Welcome Home from one of his neighbors.

He pivoted, eyes resting on me for a chilling heartbeat before shifting them to Gestamar. "Leave her with me. Go to Idris. Tell him to abort the trancing and set boundary wards specific to Rhyzkahl on the southern perimeter."

Gestamar released my arm and bounded off. I looked

after his departing form and then back to Mzatal. "What's going on?"

Mzatal closed his eyes and took a deep breath before opening them again. "Rhyzkahl has demanded your release to him."

Hope and relief shot through me. *He knows I'm here. He's going to get me out of this shit.* His syraza Olihr must have confirmed my whereabouts to him. I folded my arms over my chest and glared at Mzatal. "Well, I *am* his summoner. Sounds pretty damn reasonable to me."

"Reasonable to him," he replied. "Unacceptable to me." With a flick of his fingers he wrapped a lasso of potency around my left wrist, then turned and headed down a broad corridor, leaving me no choice but to follow or be dragged. I clenched my jaw tight in fury as he led me past rooms with open doorways; in the rooms beyond, walls of glass looked out over the sea. We reached a central atrium overlooked by mezzanine balconies ringing the five floors above, and he headed up stairs—all the way upstairs, never slowing his pace. By the time we got to the top, I was done, but he was not.

He threw open the doors and proceeded into a stunning hall that *felt* the size of a football field, though I knew that was a gross exaggeration. The walls shone with gold leaf, and inlays of sparkling gems traced graceful patterns overall. Five huge arched alcoves marked each side wall, the eleventh sheltering the door we came through. A myriad of glass panes in the ceiling high above scattered prismatic sunlight over everything. The floor was a wonder in itself, a polished mosaic formed completely of clear crystal-like quartz, translucent and reflecting the sunlight from above in its own dance of color.

With me in tow, Mzatal strode the length of the hall toward a set of doors on the far end. Glimpses into the alcoves revealed sitting areas, doorways, and what I could only describe in the moment as exhibits, not having the luxury to look closer, since Mzatal's pace had me near trotting to keep up. Even under these conditions, I felt like I was moving through a beam of light rather than a room. Four ilius now followed in Mzatal's wake, smokiness reduced to a bare haze in the permeating light, revealing the serpentine coils of colorful, translucent demons that didn't seem to touch the floor at all.

At the far end of the chamber, we passed through double doors into a summoning chamber seemingly identical to Szerain's in size, type of stone, and number of walls. He pulled me to the center and dropped the tether, but before I could so much as twitch, more strands of potency coiled around my feet and legs up to my hips, effectively freezing me in place.

I tightened my hands into fists and glared daggers of white hot hatred at him. He met my eyes, not even a flicker of perturbation in his, as he spoke in demon to the faas Jekki and Faruk, who quickly scurried out. I caught Idris's name in what he said, but there was no way to tell from his tone or demeanor what the context was. This dude could read *Pat the Bunny* and make it terrifying.

My pulse beat a rapid staccato as sick fear clenched my gut. He was going to hurt me again. I had no doubt. I wanted desperately to be tough and strong and not give a crap, but it was pretty fucking difficult considering the circumstances.

He turned to face me, standing about five feet away. "Rhyzkahl will make an attempt to retrieve you," he said. His eyes dropped to the mark on my left forearm. "That must be removed."

The cold fear ratcheted up another notch, and I struggled for something resembling calm. "You can't do that," I said. "You don't have the right." I knew it was an empty protest, but I was sure Rhyzkahl's mark was my only possible lifeline. If Mzatal was truly able to remove it, then how the hell could Rhyzkahl possibly track me and get me out of here? *Unless I find my own way to bust out*, I thought. But how? Ilana had said only the lords and Elders could operate the groves, and I had zero idea where Rhyzkahl's realm was in relation to Mzatal's. I rather doubted it was within easy walking distance.

"Were it a true and complete mark, perhaps not," he said with a shake of his head. "But it is neither. And I will not honor it or him in this."

I scowled down at my mark and then back up to him. "What are you talking about?"

He traced a sigil in the air and floated it toward the perimeter of the circle, then began another. "Key elements are missing, and its full purpose is shrouded."

I watched the sigils as they slowly formed a circle around me. I honestly had no idea if what he said about the mark was true, but I also had no reason to trust or believe him. Not that it made any difference. He was clearly determined to strip it off me. At least he no longer seemed to be quite as eager to kill me, but my essence still clenched at the thought of the mark's removal.

The bindings of potency holding me in place didn't budge as I tested them. "What are you going to do?" I asked, though *How much is this going to suck for me?* was what I really wanted to know.

"Unwind it. Forcibly if necessary," he said, utterly calm as he continued to build the pattern around me. "The components connect him very strongly to you, and you to him. Should he come here," he shook his head, "anything from extrication to your death is possible." His gaze met mine, hard and intense. "And I will not allow it."

I knew damn well that the only possibility of death came from Mzatal, not Rhyzkahl. I resisted the futile urge to struggle against the bindings again. One of the faas returned and set a copper bowl full of steaming liquid on the low table near the perimeter of the diagram. The cloying scent, dense and heavy like a mass of decaying roses, wafted over me.

"Why don't you simply kill me?" I asked with a slight frown. "Why the hell are you going to all this trouble?"

He laid a tracing directly in front of me, then stopped and lifted his eyes to mine. "Because there is yet potential for you to work with me," he said. "And, in this moment, I still have the ability to keep you from him, though as long as the mark is on you, that ability decreases with every heartbeat."

I could only stare at him for several seconds while I processed his statement. "Work with you?" I asked, incredulous. "Like what? Open a fro-yo shop together?"

His expression didn't shift as he placed another beautiful sigil in the inner circle. "I would much prefer to train you and have you work with me as a summoner." He spoke as though having me bound in the center of a ritual was as natural as discussing this over coffee.

"Wow," I said. "That's a tempting offer. And you've been so *nice* in your approach." I loaded my voice with sarcasm. "Gosh. What to do, what to do!" I tipped my eyes upward and pretended to contemplate. "Hmm. I can stay with the lord who's been pretty damn decent to me so far and who swore not to harm me. Or I can go with the one who kidnapped me, hurt me, and now has me tied up inside a ritual diagram." I threw my hands up. "Gosh! It's a motherfucking conundrum!"

I couldn't help but wonder what kind of hold Mzatal had over Idris to get him to cooperate so fully and eagerly. He seemed like a sweet kid. Had the lord messed with his mind somehow? The thought left me cold.

Mzatal released a sigil into the pattern and dropped his hands to his sides as he regarded me with the barest flicker of what might have been anger or annoyance. "Kara Gillian, you are ignorant and naïve in these matters, both of which are correctable. I will help you see things more clearly."

My own anger flared in response. "Y'know, I'm not always the sharpest knife in the drawer, and I'm well aware that there are some serious gaps in my knowledge, but I *do* know that your people skills suck the sweat from a dead dog's balls." I clenched my hands, true fear of mind manipulation thrashing beneath the anger. "Don't you dare fuck with my head. Don't you fucking dare."

"I do what I must," was his infuriating—and terrifying—reply as he began to move around the pattern and behind me. "Proper training and perspective are crucial."

His words dropped like acid into my belly. There was nothing to stop him from stripping my will and personality, and I realized I was far more terrified of that than of dying. "Don't," I said, disheartened to find myself begging. "Please don't take my mind from me."

I felt his presence close in on me from behind and let out a gasp as he took my head between his hands in a disturbing echo of when he'd been on the verge of snapping my neck. "It frightens you to your core," he murmured. "Why?"

I fought to push down the terror with anger. "Because I like me," I snapped. "Because I have goals and dreams, and if I'm not me then I won't ever get there." I swallowed hard. "I won't know to . . . push and strive and learn. If I'm not me

I won't fall in love or help others, and I won't have my friends and Tessa anymore . . . and all that shit *matters* to me and other people. *I* matter!"

He held my head for a heartbeat more. "Then never lose yourself," he said before releasing me and stepping back.

I took several deep breaths, more than a little confused by his mandate, though utterly determined to do just that. I tried to think of some possible way to resist, but my options were pretty damn scant.

Idris entered, silky white shirt stuck to his body with sweat. He looked at me, then his eyes skittered away to Mzatal. "The wards are laid, my lord."

Mzatal moved around in front of me again. "Well done," he told Idris. "I will assess them. While I do so, lay a *hakihn* perimeter here, and I will begin the mark removal upon my return." Clasping his hands behind his back, he strode out, leaving me alone with Idris.

I kept my eyes hard on him as he began to work. "Mzatal's going to hurt me," I said, keeping my voice as even as possible. "You know that, right?"

Idris paled and shook his head. "I . . . No. I mean . . ." He trailed off.

My focus remained locked on him. "Nah, it's cool," I said with a casual shrug I sure as shit didn't feel. "You're just following orders. I get it."

His throat bobbed as he swallowed. "I'm sorry. I gotta . . ." He traced a sigil, then dispersed it as it shimmered unevenly, clearly wrong. "He's . . . well." He scrubbed a hand over his face. "I don't know enough about what's going on."

I wanted to flay him for that, lay him open with a verbal barrage about taking some personal responsibility. But I didn't. I knew it wouldn't make a difference in the end. It was obvious he was already torn and feeling guilty, yet he still continued to work the perimeter. I did take a not-insignificant amount of pleasure in the fact that every third sigil had to be dispersed and reset. Good. At least I was getting to him.

"Maybe it won't hurt," Idris offered. "I mean, the diagram looks like it's more for support and stabilization than anything else."

"Whatever lets you sleep at night," I replied calmly,

pleased when he jerked and had to redo yet another sigil. I stood still with my eyes half-closed as I tried to find some sort of gap or weakness in the diagram. It didn't help that I didn't know what most of the sigils meant, or that I was wearing a fucking anti-arcane collar. My stomach churned with frustration. I wanted to be back in the grove, surrounded by that incredible sense of peace.

My breathing slowed as I focused on that memory, and I clung to it as Mzatal returned. His gaze swept the whole of the chamber, floor to ceiling and back down again as he assessed everything. "Idris, you are not finished," he said. He didn't raise his voice, yet his tone still cut like a knife.

Idris flushed. I allowed myself to enjoy the small victory.

"I . . ." Idris's voice shook, but then he straightened, misery etched on his face as he looked to Mzatal. "I let myself get distracted, my lord."

Mzatal's gaze remained on Idris for several heartbeats. For an instant I almost pitied the kid. But only for an instant. As much as he wanted to deny it, he was a part of what was about to happen to me. I continued to focus on deep breaths while I held the memory of the grove firm in my head.

"Step back," Mzatal said, the intensity of the command palpable. Idris did so, looking more than a little shell-shocked. The lord stepped up to the diagram and finished the perimeter in a matter of seconds, then moved to stand beyond the circle and directly in front of me. "And so we begin."

My calm wavered at his words. I sunk deeper in the memory of the grove while I kept my eyes on Mzatal. *All I want is a way to keep him from hurting me. Is that too much to ask for?*

Apparently so. Mzatal stepped into the diagram and lifted a hand to wrap potency around my right wrist, trapping it to my side. With a sweep of his other hand, he ignited the diagram around us in shimmering beauty that belied its darker purpose. He reached and grasped my left wrist in an uncompromising grip and pulled my arm toward him. Fear rose again, and I clung to the feel of the grove. Its touch enveloped me in comfortable, tangible presence, like a blanket fresh out of the dryer on a frigid day.

He placed a hand over my left forearm, over the mark. I watched warily as he silently assessed it. After a moment he lifted his eyes to mine, a seething mix of anger and disgust backing his gaze. "Tell me how this was made," he said, voice carrying an echo of strain.

I didn't want to tell him a damn thing, but I also knew that he could easily delve and strip the memory out of me if he so desired.

"I was working a case," I told him. "A series of murders that didn't look like murders. I could tell that the essences of the victims were gone. My partner, Ryan, and I found her—the woman who was doing it. But she got the jump on us and managed to get hold of Ryan." I paused, swallowed as the memory of those awful few minutes rose. "She threatened to consume his essence if I didn't open a portal and allow her to have more *hriss*." I took a deep breath and touched the warm-blanket presence for calm.

"I tricked her and summoned Rhyzkahl," I continued. "I told him that if he stopped her and saved Ryan, I'd agree to be his summoner." I searched Mzatal's face for some sort of reaction, but it remained impassive. "We agreed to terms: three years of service, I'd summon him once a month, and he'd answer two questions for me each time. He pulled a knife and cut my arm and his, then pressed them together and said it was done." I exhaled and looked down at the delicately intricate arcane tracings that marked my forearm. Was that only a few months ago? It seemed like forever.

Mzatal shook his head slowly as though trying to process what I said. "A purported mark agreement, under duress, for only three years duration, and an exchange of two questions in return for being *summoned to Earth monthly*." A muscle in his jaw twitched.

I scowled and shrugged. "It worked okay for me. And, anyway, what was I supposed to do? It was that or leave Ryan to have his essence consumed."

Mzatal's mouth tightened as he lifted one hand and touched my temple. "The blade he used—I need to see it."

I debated resisting, but it was too late. Just his suggestion brought the memory to the surface.

A wicked blade shimmers with an oily blue sheen. Its hilt is covered in spikes that thrust between Rhyzkahl's fingers. A dark blue jewel glimmers in the pommel, flickering with dim internal light.

"Enough." He pulled his hand away and shook it as if to rid himself of the feel of the memory. "Rhyzkahl's essence blade—Xhan—tainted with *rakkuhr*," he said, the last word laced with vehemence. He looked down at the mark on my arm, lip curling. "That it was used to forge *this* increases my urgency a hundredfold." He met my eyes again. "How did he fulfill the condition of stopping this woman?"

My unease grew. I had no idea why the blade made a difference, but it obviously meant a hell of a lot to Mzatal. I wasn't thrilled about continuing to feed him information, but I also knew it was that or have him read it from me. "With the same blade," I said. "He stabbed her in the heart and she turned to dust. He said she was a *saarn*."

His grip tightened on my wrist. "This mark will come off, Kara Gillian."

I gulped at the intensity of his words but managed to narrow my eyes in what grim defiance I could muster. "I'd like to get a second opinion."

Mzatal spoke in rapid demon to Gestamar, who growled menacingly. When the lord returned his attention to me again, he spoke through clenched teeth. "Rhyzkahl seeks to regain Szerain's blade. I *will not* allow that to happen."

I ran through possibilities. "You're going to try to get it first, aren't you?" How did I fit into all of this?

"Yes. I *will* find and retrieve Vsuhl." He lifted a hand, and for a bizarre moment I thought he was going to strike me. But in the next instant a knife appeared in his fist, long and narrow with shifting etchings along the blade itself and a silvery grey gem sparkling in the pommel. What I could see of the hilt below his fingers revealed what looked like delicately carved ivory. I had no doubt this was Mzatal's essence blade.

Terror surged through me, and I recoiled as much as I could in the confines of my bindings. I knew, more than anything else in that moment, that I did not want that blade touching me or the mark.

"No!" I struggled against his grip, eyes on the blade. The presence of the grove wrapped around me, but it couldn't dispel this deeper horror. "Please . . . no!"

His grip only tightened. "Kara, I must do this." He

brought the blade close to the mark. I could *feel* the mark recoil from the blade, and I let out a moan.

He bared his teeth as he set the blade flat against my wrist below the mark. Pain like fiery ants flared beneath my skin, and my breath came in shallow pants. I watched in mute horror as the outer coil of the mark twitched and lifted.

Agony seared through me as though part of my essence had been yanked and twisted, and I screamed. An unfamiliar power wound through me, and I seized it, lashing out wildly in my panic and pain. All I knew was that I wanted Mzatal to stop, wanted him *away* from me.

Mzatal staggered back, losing his grip on my arm as the patterns surrounding me shuddered, then fractured, sigils dissipating with whining *cracks*. As quickly as it had come into me, the strange power was gone, leaving me staring in shock at the flickering remnants of the diagram. My arm throbbed in dull pain, and I cradled it to me, wondering if my heart would pound right out of my chest. Mzatal had managed to undo a small part of the mark, but whatever the fuck I'd just done had at least kept him from doing more.

Not that I knew how long that would last. He stood a short distance from me, shoulders rising and falling with heavy breaths. Potency swirled around him like a dark mist as he regarded me, head slightly lowered and blade clenched in his fist.

What the hell did I just do? My mind flailed unsuccessfully for an answer. He was surely going to kill me now.

He stepped in close with impossible speed. I jerked in the bindings, a breathless scream whistling from my throat. A snarl curved his mouth as he leaned close and drew a complex sigil in the air with the point of his blade. I fought back tears, trembling. *What the hell did I do?* I asked myself for what seemed the millionth time. I caught sight of Idris backed against the wall, and I had no doubt that the shock and horror on his face was reflected on my own.

Mzatal lifted his hand and in the next breath the blade was gone. He gripped my wrist again and laid the shimmering sigil upon my mark. "Rhyzkahl felt what was done; I have no doubt. This," he said, stroking the sigil with his forefinger, "will serve as an alarm and deterrent until we resume again."

To my relief the pain eased to nothing beneath the sigil. Gestamar stood. Mzatal spoke to him in demon, then shifted his attention to Idris. "Go with them," he ordered. "Watch the mark. If there is any change in that sigil—even the barest flicker—you will lay an inverse attenuator diagram with my sigil as the focus and . . . Gestamar has his instructions."

Idris paled and looked like he was about to throw up. "Yes, my lord," he replied, voice quavering.

Mzatal looked back to where I stood. His face remained unreadable, but his eyes showed a flicker of . . . worry? Inquiry? It was impossible to tell, and I was far too shaken to be able to puzzle it out. He moved as if he was about to speak, then paused, turned away, and departed instead.

Chapter 10

In dismay, I watched him go, barely even noticing as Gestamar released the bindings and took my arm in a solid grip. "I don't even know what I did," I whispered.

"Come, Kara Gillian." He led me to the doors and out as Idris followed behind.

I stumbled along, not making any attempt to resist. "What happened?"

The reyza turned and entered a cozy room right next to the summoning chamber. "Much," he replied. "The catalyst being that you drew potency from the grove and disrupted the removal." He led me to one of two big cushy chairs and gently pushed me to sit. Fine with me since I wasn't sure I could even stand right now without my knees shaking.

"I had no idea I was drawing *any* kind of potency," I protested. "It . . . hurt. And the blade scared me." I clenched my hands together and dropped my eyes to the mark. With an othersight squint to counter the collar a bit, I focused. Two strands of a tight silvery sigil wound around a loop of it. By Mzatal's mandate the thing held the key to my fate, though the bastard hadn't bothered to share the possibilities with me. Near my wrist, a curve of the mark pulsed bright to dark with a tendril whipping around like a loose fire hose. Yep. Definitely fucked up.

Idris entered and dropped into the chair beside me. He looked shell-shocked as all hell, but he seemed to remember his orders since he glued his attention to the sigil.

Shuddering, I looked back to Gestamar. "What are you supposed to do if the mark changes?"

He crouched. "That is dependent on the outcome of the

diagram Idris lays," he said. "The mark is open. Rhyzkahl will know it has been touched. Risk of his intervention was significant, and now it is greater yet."

I scowled. "Stop talking in circles. Did he tell you to kill me? Is that one of the possible outcomes?"

"Yes," he replied with no hesitation. "It is one of the possibilities."

The color drained from Idris's face. "No," he said, shaking his head. "Wait. . . ."

Gestamar swiveled his head toward Idris. "You will lay the inverse attenuator or her death will be the *only* possibility."

He stood, clenching his hands at his sides, though to his credit he continued to watch the sigil on my arm. "Why? What gives us the right to *kill* her?"

"Because it is the best option," Gestamar stated, as if it was the most logical thing in the world.

Idris glanced at Gestamar and opened his mouth as though to speak, but closed it again and scowled at the mark.

I let out a soft sigh. Idris was as trapped as I was. "Idris." I hesitated. I didn't want to say *It's okay*, because it totally wasn't okay. At all. "It is what it is," I said instead. "Do the attenuator thing. Whatever else happens isn't your fault."

"But it *is*," he shot back. "It's my fault that you're here. Why the hell did I ever think *this*," he made a mock tracing in the air, "was how I wanted to spend my life? I thought I was going to grow up to be a damn vet!"

Despite the entire situation, I had to smile. "Because you're good at it," I said. "You're really damn good."

He tried to run a hand through his hopelessly tangled curls, then gave up. "Yeah, well, I like doing the stuff, y'know? Feels natural. But this?" He gestured toward my arm as he sank back into the chair. "Watching for something that may or may not mean you're about to get wasted by Gestamar? No. Nuh uh."

I bit back a sigh and resisted the urge to rub my arm. I wasn't about to defend the order to kill me, but a part of me ached that Idris was in such a situation. "Well, let's hope that the mark stays nice and quiet." *And let's hope that either Rhyzkahl makes a definitive move, or I find some other way to get the hell away from here.* One thing was for sure—I wasn't going to put up with being hurt anymore.

Mzatal entered. My eyes snapped to him, but he turned to Gestamar, rattling off something in demon. The reyza nodded and departed, and then Mzatal turned to Idris. "We are going to a remote location where we can work with less chance of interference. Prepare a standard research kit with additional stabilizers and go to my grove."

Idris glanced to me and swallowed. "Yes, my lord," he said. He turned and headed out, head bowed.

I scowled at the lord. "So what new delights have you dreamed up for me?"

He sank into the chair vacated by Idris, sat back and regarded me. "I have need to determine what will shield you from reflexively drawing upon the grove energy. Then, I will remove the mark. Rhyzkahl has not only sent a demand but now knows the mark has been touched. He will not delay long. We go to a place where he will not easily track you."

I remained silent for a moment while I processed this, more than a little surprised that he'd bothered to explain this much to me. I finally took a steadying breath. "I know I won't be able to talk you out of this," I said, more calmly than I felt. "But can you please find a way to do it . . . so it doesn't hurt so much?"

"I do not know that such is possible," he replied evenly. "Not with the specialized nature of that mark."

I could feel my mouth tighten. "Well then, why can't you simply knock me out or something?"

"Were it possible to do it with you unconscious, I would," he said in the same calm tone he'd used after I'd broken my leg. "The mark is deeply tied into your consciousness—moreso than a typical mark."

I shoved a hand through my hair, frustrated. "Fine. Whatever." I scowled. "Then let's get this shit over with."

"We wait upon Idris," he replied, unruffled. "It will not be long."

He fell silent, apparently deep in contemplation. My own thoughts drifted, and I leaned back in the chair. Shadow memories and dream fragments flickered at the edge of my mind.

Lord Mzatal approaches! I hurriedly close my journal to hide my folly, more pages filled with doodles than glyph patterning.

"Elinor, stand," he says, holding his hand out. Heart sinking, I give him the journal, tremble as he pages through it.

He looks up, eyes narrowed in . . . anger? Disdain? I cannot tell.

"Why are you here?" he asks.

My breath catches. "To train, my lord." I fight to keep my voice steady. "To learn to be a summoner."

His mouth tightens as he holds the journal up. "This indicates otherwise. Gather your belongings and prepare to travel."

I stare at him, stricken. "No, please, my lord." I cannot breathe, but if I faint it will only make it worse. "Please . . . don't send me away. I'll study harder, I swear it!"

Lord Mzatal tucks the journal under his arm, turns and walks away, hands clasped behind his back. "Go do as you are told, child."

I frowned as the memory faded. Big surprise. Mzatal was a dick to Elinor as well.

Lord Rhyzkahl's arm is around my waist, and I think surely I must be in a dream. "I would have you train with me for a time," he tells me. "And continue with Szerain as well, of course."

"Yes," I breathe. Train with him? Be *with him? How could I possibly say no?*

He strokes the back of his fingers over my cheek and smiles at me. "I will go speak to Szerain of the final arrangements." Then his lips brush mine, and I think I will surely die of pleasure.

I blinked, somewhat off balance by the different feel of the two memories. But it was clear that Rhyzkahl definitely had some sort of interest in her.

"Rhyzkahl and Elinor," I said. "Did they have a relationship?"

Mzatal returned his focus to me. "He favored her."

I waited. "That's all?"

"She held great affection for him," he said. "And he favored her." He shifted, crossed his legs. "She trained with me for a short time, then with Szerain, and finally with Rhyzkahl."

"And she died when the gate collapsed?"

"She died during that ritual, yes," he replied. "In the chamber of your arrival here."

Memories flickered annoyingly, telling me that there had to be more to it. "How could it have gone wrong so badly?"

He shook his head. "I do not know the trigger event, though once it cascaded, it went quickly." A shimmer of anger or frustration passed over his face. "If Szerain knows it, he has kept it well hidden."

I kept my face as composed as possible. "And where is he now?"

He lowered his head and *looked* at me. "I cannot answer that question, as you likely already know."

I chuckled despite myself. Okay, so now I knew for certain that he knew *I* knew about Ryan and Szerain. "Oathbound," I drawled.

"Oathbound," he echoed, with the faint hint of a nod. His mouth tightened. "Complicated and anachronistic. Bound in rhetoric and intrigue."

"Well, I'm pretty good at figuring shit out," I replied. "One pesky oath won't stop me." Assuming I lived long enough to dig into this particular mystery.

His face remained an expressionless mask, silver-grey eyes steady upon me.

"Do you have to leave if *I* talk about it?" I asked. Wouldn't that be fun if I'd discovered lord repellent? Of course the alternative to leaving could be squash-the-human, but since he already had a loaded gun pointed at my head, I had nothing to lose.

He raised an eyebrow. I took that as gushing permission. "Szerain and Elinor had a hand in this big bad cataclysm thing a few hundred years ago," I began. "But nearly destroying the world wasn't enough to get him exiled. Oh, yeah. You guys needed him to fix what he'd broken. Restitution."

Mzatal remained silent, but I thought perhaps a slight spark of interest lit his eyes.

Sitting back, I steepled my fingers as if deep in thought. "So it wasn't until—what? A couple of decades ago or so?—that Szerain did another Bad Thing," I continued. "He got himself into shit so deep there's an Oath from Hell around it, and eventually he got kicked out of here." I tilted my head. "And according to Turek, Szerain *chose* exile instead of handing over information about whatever it was." I tapped my fingertips together. "My question is . . . why did he choose exile? What could possibly be worth it?" Narrowing my eyes, I regarded Mzatal. "Plus I wonder if this Bad Thing had anything to do with the Peter Cerise fiasco." Peter Cerise, whose summoning several decades ago had accidentally called Rhyzkahl instead of Szerain, and resulted in the slaughter of the other five summoners involved. "Is there a connection? And if so, what?"

With the mention of Cerise, a muscle in Mzatal's jaw rippled. I made a note of that sore spot on my mental clue board.

"All must be revealed in time," he said as he rose from the chair.

"But for now you get to torture this mark off of me," I said with a tight smile. "Won't that be fun."

"No, it will not be," he said, face back to the inscrutable mask.

I stood, then gave him a wary look as the hair on my arms lifted. Potency swirled to him like water down a drain in gold and purple flickers on the edge of my othersight. He placed his hands on my shoulders and met my eyes. I found myself wishing I could understand this lord—terrifying and all too ready to kill me one minute, and then almost decent in the next. What the hell was his game?

His gaze bored into me, and I didn't really want to move. The myth surfaced about snakes hypnotizing their prey, but before I could process that, his hands shifted to my face. Not even a heartbeat later his mouth was on mine, kissing me hard and deep, though not at all roughly. Potency crackled through me like a zing of static electricity between my cells and in the next instant he broke the kiss and stood back, hands clasped behind his back, while I struggled for some sort of response.

Un-fucking-readable, he nodded once as if satisfied, then turned toward the door. "Come," he said, though this time it wasn't accompanied by a lasso of power.

I didn't move, could only stare. *What. The. Fuck?*

Mzatal glanced back and saw my awesome statue imitation, took my upper arm and nudged me forward. Blinking, I moved, and he dropped his hand. He led the way out of the room and to his grove, and I followed, keeping a wary eye on him the whole time. My thoughts whirled in uneven loops, but foremost among them was, *I need to get the hell away from Mzatal.*

Gestamar and Idris waited near the entrance to the tree tunnel. Gestamar bellowed a greeting while Idris simply looked nervous and unsettled. Mzatal took my arm as we entered the shadowed tunnel, no doubt to better sense if I should suddenly try and use the power again. I didn't bother to tell him that I had no idea how I'd done it the first time. It didn't matter. As soon as I stepped beneath the sheltering limbs a deep peace descended on me again, and I barely noticed his grip.

He stopped in the center of the grove and passed me over to Gestamar, who wrapped a clawed hand around my arm while the lord crouched and channeled power into the knob of wood in the center of the grove. I remained perfectly still, feeling as if the grove spoke to me in a language beyond words. My eyes slid to Mzatal as he completed the offering of potency and stood. He lifted a hand to initiate the transfer, and in that instant I knew—*knew*—the grove.

The grove shifted around us. We were in the remote location now, wherever that was. Mzatal took my arm again as he greeted the mehnta, but I stayed where I was. Silently, I touched the grove.

"Kara, come," Mzatal said. "There is little time." He began to move but I pulled back against his grip.

"Wait, please." My heart pounded while I hoped to hell and back that the collar would shield my thoughts enough to keep him from realizing what I was about to do.

His grip tightened on my arm, eyes narrowing. "Kara . . . what—" He stopped as the grove began to activate, then cursed, face going intense as he literally dragged me toward the tree tunnel.

I dug my heels in. "No!" *Now*, I silently begged the grove. *Take me now! Take me to Rhyzkahl!*

He stopped as the power rose around us and pivoted to face me. "You will regret this," he said through clenched teeth. "I *will* come for you."

I opened my mouth to say something brilliant like, "Bite me, you lame-ass fuckbrain."

But he was gone before I could even form the words.

Chapter 11

It took me a couple of seconds to realize that Mzatal hadn't simply disappeared. "Holy fuckballs," I breathed, then let out a shaky laugh. *I did it. I used the grove. I escaped!*

The distant bellow of a reyza came to me through the tree tunnel. Rhyzkahl's demons knew I was here, or rather, they knew someone was here. *Nighttime*, I noted instantly. And damn near frigid. The trees of the grove gave off a soft bluish glow, and sigils that reminded me of stick-in-the-ground solar yard lights marked the path of the tree tunnel. Full of triumph and still pumped with adrenaline, I headed for the tunnel and the freedom of Rhyzkahl's realm.

The grove thrummed with a tingle of activation as I reached the arch of trees. I glanced back, and my gut clenched at the sight of Mzatal appearing in the center of the clearing. His face contorted into a snarl of determination as his eyes met mine. My already thudding heart went into hyperdrive. *Shit!* I'd hoped he wouldn't be able to follow so quickly. I broke into a run, heading for the night blackness at the far opening of the tree tunnel. Surely Mzatal wouldn't dare pursue once I was out of the grove and on Rhyzkahl's turf. Or would he? I had no real idea how the dynamics of the lords worked.

I cleared the arched trees, and an instant later a lasso of potency snaked around my right ankle. I yelped and went sprawling, clawing at the ground to try to pull away from him as I kicked and struggled against the damn lasso. *So close . . . so close!* I could see the lights of a palace ahead, and more reyza bellows filled the air.

I risked a glance back at Mzatal, heart dropping at the

black anger on his face. He advanced quickly, keeping the potency rope taut. I continued to struggle, but I knew it was only a matter of seconds before he had me again. *And I'll never have another chance to escape after this.*

Before Mzatal could reach me, a reyza landed beside me with a *whoosh* of air. He bellowed at Mzatal, and I breathed in relief when the lord stopped, though I would've been even more relieved if the reyza had made some sort of effort to disengage the lasso from my foot. The demon's gaze dropped to me. A throbbing growl came from his throat.

I thrust my forearm up at him. "I'm Kara Gillian, sworn summoner of Rhyzkahl," I gasped. "Help me, please!"

The demon took less than a second to assess the mark, then his eyes lifted to Mzatal. He bared his teeth and moved to stand over me protectively.

"Rhyzkahl's marked one in Rhyzkahl's domain," the reyza snarled and pointed at the lasso. "She will not go with you, Mzatal."

My pulse slammed as Mzatal continued to hold the lasso taut. The muscles of his jaw twitched, and the menace of his stare made me wonder if he would actually stop even now.

An eternity later he recalled the lasso with a sharp jerk of his hand. I finally remembered to breathe again

"I *will* retrieve you, Kara," he told me, voice immersing me in threat and promise.

I scrabbled back, hardly daring to believe I was truly free from him. Mzatal didn't move except to lift a hand, gaze locked on me. A cramp-like twinge wavered in my chest, then faded before I even had a chance to fully realize it was there.

Mzatal's expression grew even darker. He clenched his raised hand so hard his knuckles went white. Taking a step back, he slowly lowered his fist, eyes on mine. "I *will* retrieve you," he repeated.

I scrambled to my feet, mouth tight, then gave in to my inner twelve-year old and flipped him off.

He held my gaze for another few nervewracking heartbeats. With a final shake of his head, he turned and strode back down the tree tunnel, hands clenched into fists at his sides as potency that wound through my core like a visceral threat poured from him. It seemed odd to see him *not* walking with his hands clasped behind his back.

The reyza took hold of my upper arm, breath pluming in the chill air as he bellowed after the departing Mzatal. I waited until I felt the grove activate, taking the lord away, and only then let myself slump in relief. Crap, but that had been close.

The cold really hit me now that I could think about it. The light shirt and pants I'd put on this morning were great for the climate in Mzatal's realm, but Rhyzkahl's palace was either much further north, or in an entirely different hemisphere. Of course it didn't take much for me to feel like I was freezing to death. I went to long sleeves anytime the temps dipped below sixty-five, and hat and gloves if they went below forty.

Right now I was seriously ready for hat and gloves. And coat. And boots. And a damn fire.

"Thank you," I said to the reyza, willing my teeth not to chatter. "Will you take me to Rhyzkahl now?" I gently tugged at my arm in the hopes of getting him to release me.

A sigil similar to the message one I'd seen at Mzatal's shimmered into existence in the air in front of the reyza. He touched it with a clawed finger, snorted, and dispersed it, then turned back to me with a soft hiss. To my shock, instead of releasing me, he pulled my arms behind me and bound them with a simple binding ward.

"Hey! Wait!" My heart pounded as I pulled futilely against the binding. "What's going on?" This sure as hell wasn't the reception I'd expected.

"I take you to await the will of Rhyzkahl," the reyza stated, moving me forward and toward the palace with the relentless grip on my upper arm.

My mind whirled. "I don't understand. Why am I bound if I'm his sworn summoner?"

He let out a snort. "Because he has commanded it."

I swallowed hard. Had coming here been a colossal mistake? It wouldn't be the first. I'd sure as hell made some huge ones in my life.

Forcing down the surge of panic, I did my best to pay attention to details around me. The cloudy night closed in as we left the soft glow of the grove area, and I couldn't get a good sense of the layout other than that a massive palace rose ahead, marked by light seeping through windows and a pale blue luminescence to the stone itself.

The reyza moved me through the entrance. I had only the briefest look at a sumptuous and opulent entryway before we passed through and to a door immediately inside. My anxiety rose as the demon continued to escort me down a short hallway and finally through a door into darkness.

With a quick motion, the reyza set a sigil alight above. It bathed the room in a warm golden glow, revealing a small circular chamber devoid of all furnishings. He released my arm in the center, but before I could move, he traced six sigils and spread them to hover a couple of feet from me in each direction. I didn't recognize the sigils, but I had no doubt I didn't want to even try touching them.

"What are you doing?" I asked, seriously freaked out at this point.

"Shielding," the reyza replied with implacable calm. He crouched by the wall and went still, watching me.

The door burst open. I jerked and had to catch myself from taking a step back. Rhyzkahl stood with his left hand on the door, beautiful face hard, radiating intensity like heat from desert stones. His white-blond hair stirred in an unseen wind, and his crystal-blue eyes seemed to bore deep into my essence. He was barefoot, wearing black pants and an unbuttoned black shirt that revealed a well-muscled torso and rock-hard abs.

A smear of blood from his palm marred the pale wood of the door. He lifted his other hand in an upward spinning motion, and an instant later a cylinder of bluish potency sprang into existence around me within the circle of sigils. He moved fully into the room, gaze never wavering from me. The door closed soundly without him touching it.

"Rhyzkahl? What's going on?" I asked, voice shaking. "I escaped Mzatal and came right here—"

"Silence!" he ordered through clenched teeth. Slowly, he circled around, eyes traveling methodically over me. I'd reached one hundred percent freakout at this point, but I did my best to stay as still as possible, though I couldn't keep my knees from shaking.

Rhyzkahl finally completed the circle, keen and inscrutable eyes on my face. He lifted a hand, and the binding on my wrists dissipated. Before I could twitch, he reached through the shield and removed the collar, blue glow coating his arm like a glove. He flicked the collar aside to skitter to the wall, then seized my left wrist and dragged my arm toward him, exposing the mark. He dropped his gaze to it, grip hard.

"Mzatal . . . he tried to get it off," I told him, breath coming raggedly. "I stopped him—"

"I said silence!" He bared his teeth in a feral manner and raised his eyes to mine. I shrank under his hard gaze, a shiver of dread going through me. He was *so* not fucking around. His grip tightened painfully. I clenched my teeth together to stay quiet. He laid his bloody left hand over the mark, and I bit back a whimper as pain seared up my arm, the blood actually sizzling as it touched the tracings. Coming here had been a horrible mistake. Tears sprang to my eyes, and I blinked furiously to hold them back.

Rhyzkahl locked his gaze on the mark for nearly a full minute, still and silent. He finally looked back up to my face, lip curling. "Tell me what he did."

I took a gulping breath. "H-he had me in a diagram—locked me down with potency. He called his essence blade and . . . started to unwind the mark."

"Why did he not finish?"

I sucked my breath in as his eyes penetrated mine. I could *feel* him reading it from me, as if someone was literally moving through my head. It took me a couple of seconds to find my voice before answering. "I pushed him away, scattered the diagram," I managed. "He said I used grove potency."

Rhyzkahl continued to read deeply, eyes narrowing. "How did you get *here*?"

"I asked the grove to bring me here," I told him. And boy, was I ever regretting that decision right now.

He let my wrist drop. The burning eased without the full contact, but the lingering blood still stung, like lemon juice on a sunburn. He began to trace sigils on the cylindrical shield. With the collar off I could see them clearly, but I didn't have the faintest clue as to their meaning or purpose.

A tingling began behind my sternum, in the same place I'd felt the cramping at the grove. I lifted my hand to rub the spot, but Rhyzkahl let out a low hiss and reached toward me. His fingers grazed my skin as he closed his hand into a fist. I sucked in my breath as the strange tingle shifted to a deeply uncomfortable pulling sensation, as if he was tugging at the muscles of my chest. A dim arcane glow seeped from between his fingers, and a thread of potency trailed from his hand to my sternum.

Without warning, he yanked his hand back. Pain ripped through my chest, and I cried out, dropping to my knees within the cylinder. Shaking, I hugged my arms around myself as the pain dulled to a lingering, pulled-muscle discomfort. The whole process reminded me way too much of the horrible purification ritual. *I was supposed to be safe here*, I thought in deep misery.

"He failed to recall you," Rhyzkahl snarled. "And now he has no chance of it." I dragged my gaze up to see him grasping a complex sigil, tendrils twitching as if he held a mass of dying snakes.

He flicked the fingers of his other hand. The potency around me dropped, and the sigils vanished in a brief flare of arcane sparkles. He reached down and grasped my arm to draw me to my feet, then steadied me as I swayed.

"*Mzatal*," he said with venom, "is devious and he is cunning. This—" He held his right hand before me and slowly closed his fist over the twisted, faintly pulsing sigil until there was no more light. "—would have destroyed you within minutes if it had not been extricated." He opened his now empty hand and shook it, as if ridding himself of the detritus. "It had been activated very recently. He was *most* determined that you not come to me."

I tried to work some moisture into my mouth. "Kill me?" I echoed. It didn't surprise me at all that Mzatal would try to do so, but that he'd almost succeeded, even after my escape, was pretty damn unnerving.

Rhyzkahl's expression softened as he pulled me into an embrace. "Yes, dear one. He likely triggered that implant when he pursued you here. It was in the process of unwinding to implode, and was very nearly complete. He . . ." Rhyzkahl hesitated a breath. "He would stop at nothing to use you toward his own ends, and to keep you from being with me." He put a finger under my chin and gently tipped my head up, smiled down at me. "Where you belong."

I put my arms around him, but uncertainty lingered. "Why did you have me tied up?"

He lifted a silky eyebrow. "You, a summoner of some skill, had just come from Mzatal." He stroked the back of his fingers over my cheek, a frown touching his mouth. "Until I made assessments, I could not risk even a single tracing from you, for the welfare of all who reside in my domain."

"Oh. Right." It made perfect sense too, damn it, and annoyance curled through me that I hadn't realized it. That sort of thing was standard procedure for any released hostage. Well, not the arcane assessment part, but the don't-trust-them-until-they're-checked-for-weapons-or traps part.

"You sent him a demand," I said. "What would you have done if I hadn't escaped?"

"I would have come for you, of course," Rhyzkahl replied without hesitation. He lifted his bloody hand. "And was in final preparation to do so."

I didn't know what that meant and, frankly, right then, didn't care. A shiver raced over my skin. "I just want to go home."

"And you will as soon as it is possible," he reassured me. "There is no summoner in my realm to accomplish it. I must confer with others about what method is most feasible."

"All right." I let out a shaky sigh. "I've had an amazingly shitty couple of days. Are you going to keep me locked up in here?"

"Here?" He stepped back and waved a hand dismissively toward the room. "No, you will be taken to chambers I have put at your disposal."

I dared to feel a sliver of relief. "Thanks."

"You need rest," Rhyzkahl said, holding his hand out to the reyza without looking. "We can speak more on the morrow." The reyza pressed something into Rhyzkahl's hand, and a breath later the lord slipped the collar back around my neck and sealed it.

I recoiled in shock. "Wait! Why are you putting this back on me?"

"All is not secure yet," he said in a soothing tone. "It must remain in place for now."

"For how long?" I asked in dismay.

"Until it is safe to remove it." His eyes were steady on mine. "Regrettably, it must chafe a time longer. Go and rest now. Pyrenth will escort you to your chambers."

I couldn't even manage a smile for Rhyzkahl as he leaned in and kissed my forehead. He turned and departed, and as soon as he was gone, the reyza stepped to my side.

"I am Pyrenth, and I greet you anew."

"I am Kara Gillian," I replied numbly.

He inclined his head. "Follow me, Kara Gillian, and I will take you to your resting place."

I did so, thoughts tumbling jaggedly as Rhyzkahl's words settled upon me with crushing weight. Around me, the palace glimmered in white demon-marble, lofty of ceiling and accented with richly colored tapestries and furnishings. We entered a vast great hall with massive twin curving staircases on either side leading up to the next level. The floor contained an intricate mosaic of some sort of blue-gold polished stone that began in the center of the hall with a small and subtle pattern and spread out to the walls in more and more complex forms like a fractal. The walls seemed to be a simple rich blue at first, but as I moved the color very gradually shifted into varying hues of blue, silver, and gold. It rivaled Mzatal's summoning foyer for the award of Most Fucking Impressive Room I've Ever Been In, though I wasn't in the best mood to fully appreciate it.

By the time we got to the top of the stairs, I was completely and utterly done with this day and with mortal danger and with intense, angry demonic lords. Fortunately for all concerned, before I could let loose with a verbal barrage or any other violence, Pyrenth guided me into what were obviously going to be my quarters.

Well, it sure as hell isn't a cell, I thought in stunned silence as Pyrenth gave me the nickel tour. I'd been allotted a luxurious set of rooms that were nicer than the penthouse in a five-star hotel. Not that I'd ever stayed in *any* room in a high-end hotel, much less the penthouse, but I'd watched enough movies to have a decent sense of what it would be like. Opulent main room with couch and fireplace, dining area bigger than my kitchen back home, enormous bedroom containing a massive bed and a wardrobe of dark red wood, a long balcony bounded by a stone parapet with a carved wooden rail on top, and a bath chamber with a tub damn near large enough to swim in.

"The faas have brought a meal for you," Pyrenth said with a gesture to the table as we returned to the main room, where there was enough food of sufficient variety to feed me for a week. At the sight and smell, my stomach woke up and not-so-gently reminded me that I hadn't eaten anything since . . . damn . . . since before we'd left Szerain's palace. No wonder I was cranky.

"There is clothing in the wardrobe in the bedchamber," Pyrenth added. "If you require anything else simply touch the sigil by the door."

I managed a nod and a polite smile, and as soon as the reyza departed I fell upon the food with very unladylike gusto. As my hunger faded, my fatigue increased, but I continued to eat until I realized I was nodding off with my fork halfway to my mouth.

Pushing away from the table, I gave an even more unladylike belch, then tottered into the bedchamber, kicked off my shoes, and barely made it under the covers before collapsing into sleep.

Chapter 12

The mug of chak in my hands steamed in the chill morning air as I stepped out onto the balcony. A chaise lounge upholstered in maroon velvet nestled against the wall, along with a small table of the same dark red wood as my wardrobe. Large stone pots in the corners of the balcony held trees at least ten feet tall with gracefully draping limbs and blue-green leaves as large as my hand. Smaller planters along the wall contained a variety of purple and yellow flowers of varying hues. A gentle scent drifted around me, like vanilla and roses, and I couldn't help but sigh in pleasure at the entire effect, despite being weirded out by everything else going on.

Wards and sigils flickered along the edge of the railing, and I cautiously extended my hand past them. Beyond the parapet frigid air touched my hand, which told me that at least some of the wards were there for climate control. My hand didn't meet any resistance, so apparently none of the wards were meant to contain me. Then again, the three-story drop was probably sufficient for that purpose. I didn't bother trying to get a better look at the wards. With the collar on it was too difficult to see any details, and I knew it would only leave me frustrated and annoyed.

I gazed out toward the grove while I did my best to parse the uneasiness that plagued me. Smaller trees, leafless for winter, clustered around the white trunks of the grove which were crowned in vibrant green and purple leaves as though on a midsummer day. Little bat-bird things fluttered through the canopy, their cries melodically sharp. Craggy, snow-covered mountains rose close beyond—steep and austere, with a beauty of their own, and distinctly different from Mzatal's green realm. To the right, cliffs fell away to a turquoise sea.

I wasn't a prisoner. At least I didn't seem to be one. Not only were my rooms beyond awesome, there'd been enough clothing ready and waiting for me in the large wardrobe—including the fluffy robe and slippers I had on now—to lend plenty of credence to Rhyzkahl's claim that he'd fully expected to retrieve me.

Yet I still had this fucking collar on.

Maybe my problem was that too much had happened too fast? I'd been in the demon realm for less than three full days, and I'd spent most of that time in a constant state of stress and fear—when I wasn't injured, passed out, or asleep, that is. *I haven't had a moment to think*, I realized. And even here, where I'd thought I'd be safe, I remained unsettled.

I knew it was the right decision to escape, to come here. It was pretty obvious I needed to get the hell away from Mzatal, and besides, where else would I go? This was an alien world, likely teeming with all sorts of unknown perils. Going anywhere else would be complete and utter stupidity. *And* I was Rhyzkahl's sworn summoner. This was the most logical place to seek help and sanctuary. Yet, as much as I understood the reasoning behind the way Rhyzkahl treated me last night, I couldn't shake the feeling that something felt off. Then again, I also accepted that my entire state of mind these past few days was pretty much a mess. I didn't know what the hell to feel or believe anymore.

I need some time to think. That's all. In a perfect world I could go spend a few quiet hours in the middle of nowhere with no one around—no humans, no demons, no lords—where I could think about everything that had happened without any fear of distraction, or worry, or concern that a lord was reading my thoughts. So far the *only* advantage of this damn collar was that it seemed to diminish these lords' ability to read me, but that was a nebulous blessing at best.

The pale morning sun slanted through the brilliant colors of the grove, and a light wind stirred the trees to a soft murmur that seemed to speak a message meant only for me. A sensation of comfort and ease crept through me as I watched the mesmerizing flow of leaves.

Light. Air. Spaciousness. Peace. Deep peace.

I took a sip of the chak, surprised to find that it was cold. My bafflement increased when I realized that the sun had shifted position considerably. Apparently I'd been standing out on the balcony for a couple of hours while I contemplated the grove. So much for my plan of considering my options.

Musing on that, I finished off the cold contents of my mug and returned inside. Nearly midday now, and Rhyzkahl still hadn't come to see me. Not that I was pining for him or anything, but it added to the overall feel of weirdness. Still, I was fully able to accept that I was neurotic enough and paranoid enough—especially now—to be blowing his absence way out of proportion. Maybe he was simply enjoying a leisurely breakfast, or working out, or sipping chak over the crossword puzzle in the demon realm newspaper. I grinned at the mental image. *What's a six letter word for 'reyza dung'?*

After a quick bath, I searched through the available clothing and scrounged up a long-sleeved shirt in a purple so rich I could hardly believe it was real and pants that were a lot like jeans but of a softer, somewhat thicker material than denim. I added a hip-length jacket, a light scarf, and knee-high boots, then checked myself out in the floor-to-ceiling mirror. I grinned. Yep, I was as overdressed for the cold as any southerner had a right to be.

I exited my rooms and saw a reyza crouched in the corridor tracing wards and sending them off to places along the hall. He turned his head to me as I exited and bared his teeth in a smile.

"Kehlirik!" I nearly squealed, barely restraining myself from leaping on him and giving him a big hug. I really wasn't sure how he'd react to that, even though it was a weird and huge relief to see a familiar face—even a demon one.

He gave a rumble-snort. "Kara Gillian."

"It's really good to see you," I said fervently. "I was going to take a walk outside. Are you, um, assigned to me?"

He stood, stretched his wings out before settling them again. "Kri . . . yes. Your escort." He began to walk down the corridor. "Outside is this way."

Well, at least he wasn't calling himself my guard. I fell

into step beside him. "I owe you popcorn. I haven't forgotten."

"You may rest assured, summoner, I will not allow you to forget."

I laughed. "I'm sure you won't. And when I get back home I'll have to summon you so that you can see a TV show a friend turned me on to."

Kehlirik gave a heavy snort. "I am not certain of the wisdom of engaging in this tee vee practice."

"Yeah, it totally rots the brain." Then I gave him a sly grin. "I won't make you watch reality TV, but did you know the Harry Potter books have been made into movies?"

That got his attention. He peered at me with interest as we descended the big-ass stairs to the entry area and to the doors leading outside. "That, perhaps, is worth the sacrifice of wisdom."

It wasn't until I got outside and away from the building that I could appreciate the massive grandeur of Rhyzkahl's palace. All that I could see before me, I had seen from my balcony—the surrounding craggy mountains, patches of trees in the grove, the turquoise sea beyond the cliffs—but not the palace itself. Turning, I stared in awe, craning my neck to see its heights. Opulent, imposing, and magnificent, it rose in a symphony of white stone, spires, arched windows, and towers framed by deep blue sky veiled thinly with wisps of winter clouds.

Okay, I thought. *That's a damn nice crib he's got there.* Smiling, I continued to walk with Kehlirik and found myself discussing books and television as I headed down the path. Occasionally, he would pause and point out some feature of the gardens or architecture that he thought I might find interesting: a silvery-leafed tree he claimed was over five hundred years old, a stone arch carved in such delicate filigree I was stunned that it could support its own weight, a translucent boulder the size of my car with ribbons of an amber-colored mineral running through it.

I was mid-sentence when a tone rippled through me, touching my ears and my bones in an oddly pleasant way. I stopped walking, stopped talking, and looked over at Kehlirik. "What the hell was that?"

The reyza rumbled, then rumbled some more, obviously

finding whatever it was highly amusing. "Tones to mark the time. Midday, that was," he said, snorting. "There will also be mid-afternoon, evening, morning, and mid-morning, though only humans need such." He lifted his chin in what looked a lot like pride. "Demons have no need of external reminders."

I considered that. "So, is it a real clock or a magic clock?" I asked, grinning.

"Can it not be both?" he asked.

I opened my mouth to reply, but a zrila darted up to us and stood on its hind legs. A creature the size of a bobcat, it looked like a six-legged newt with skin that shifted in hues of red and blue, although its head was more like that of a hairless koala. It peered at me and gave a series of whistles.

"It wishes to measure you," Kehlirik told me.

"Oh! Sure." Mzatal had said something about how a zrila had made his tie, hadn't he? "They make clothing?"

"The zrila are master textile artisans." His eyes flicked over my current garb. "All of what you wear now was created in a zrila circle."

I blinked in surprise. I'd always assumed that the zrila had fairly low intelligence. "That's pretty awesome. So, uh, what do I have to do to be measured?"

Kehlirik took a step away from me. "Stand still and extend your arms out to your sides."

I did so, then jerked in shock as the zrila leaped up to my shoulder. I began to drop my arms, and the zrila let out a sharp whistle that very clearly meant, "put those arms back out, missy!" I quickly snapped them back out and held them as the zrila proceeded to . . . well, run all over me, from head to toe, winding around my torso and arms and legs and back up again to my shoulder. The whole process took about five seconds, and then it leaped off and was out of sight within about a heartbeat.

I lowered my arms. "Um, that was it?"

Kehlirik gave a snort of what was obviously amusement. "You have now been measured."

Amused and more than a little amazed, I continued walking. Clouds scuttled across the sky as the breeze picked up. I tucked my scarf around my neck, glad that I'd overdressed. Sometimes being a wimpy southerner paid off.

The path forked. I started down the one that headed toward the grove, but Kehlirik paused.

"Where are you going, Kara Gillian?" he asked.

I glanced back at him and smiled. "I want to go sit in the grove for awhile." Already, I could feel a slight touch of its calm as it came into sight. "The past few days have been very shit-tastic. I want to chill for a bit, and it's really lovely and peaceful in there."

He shifted his wings. "Here, there are many places to sit in contemplation," he told me. "And today, for you, this is not one of them."

I blinked at him in surprise, then gave a low chuckle. "Oh, no. I'm not *leaving*. I promise that." I could see how he might have misunderstood my intent, considering how I arrived. "I just really need to go there for a little while and get my head on straight."

"Dahn," he said with quiet insistence. He stepped to me and put a hand on my shoulder. "Not to the grove."

My smile faded, and for several heartbeats I could only stare at him while I tried to process it. "But I'm not trying to leave. I swear." I looked to the grove and then back to him, dismay growing. "Kehlirik, please. I really need this. I give you my word I won't try to leave if you let me go there. Only for a little while. *Please*."

His eyes deepened in what might have been regret or sympathy, but I couldn't really tell for sure. "It is not my decision, Kara Gillian, so I cannot bind you by your word."

"Whose decision is it?" I asked, though I knew damn well whose it was.

"It is the mandate of Rhyzkahl."

Even having guessed it had to be him, it was still a punch in the gut to hear it. "He doesn't trust me?" Why would he think I'd want to run away from him?

Kehlirik shifted his weight from foot to foot. "I can only say that he has forbidden the grove."

I turned toward the trees again, ache of separation like a knot in my chest. The unfairness of it clawed at me. "I only wanted to sit and think," I said as disappointment curdled in my gut.

Kehlirik huffed and resettled his wings. "There is a place that will serve well for this, if you will allow me to show you."

"Sure," I said, throat tight. Apparently I didn't have a choice. Bereft, I turned away from the grove.

"Come," he said. "We will take the path through the gardens."

Annoyed and upset, I followed glumly. Did Rhyzkahl really think I would flee here? And what if I *did* want to leave? Clearly, this option wasn't available to me. *Am I a prisoner again? What the hell is going on?*

An arcane tingle prickled the back of my neck, stopped me in my tracks. *It's the grove*, I realized with astonishment. I could feel when someone was using the grove. How awesome was that? "Someone's coming through the grove," I said. But then worry spasmed through me. What if it was Mzatal trying again to get me back?

But Kehlirik seemed unruffled. "Kri. Qaztahl . . . lords arriving today and tomorrow. Six more."

I stared at him. "Six? Why?"

He snorted. "Because that is the number of those not yet here," he said in a *duh!* tone. "Kadir and Jesral are within the palace already."

"But why are they all coming *here?*" I asked, anxiety flickering. "Is Mzatal coming?"

"It is the time of the conclave," Kehlirik replied calmly. "Should Mzatal choose to participate, he could do so with impunity. It is unlikely he will choose thus. There. Elofir arrives."

Anxiety gave way to curiosity, and I peered toward the tree tunnel. The tingle faded, but not before I noted that it seemed to have a different feel, or resonance, than when it heralded Mzatal. Maybe each lord had his own "signature" when it came to the grove?

A reyza bounded out of the tree tunnel and took flight with a bellow, closely followed into the air by an inky-black shape I knew to be a zhurn. A few seconds later, a man with short, sandy-blond hair and the slim, athletic build of a dancer emerged. Elofir, Kehlirik had said. He wore brown boots and pants paired with a white ruffled shirt that looked like it came out of the Regency era, and he was engaged in an animated discussion with a savik a bit smaller than seven-foot-tall Turek, the one I'd encountered at Szerain's shrine. A syraza trailed a few steps behind. The grove still resonated with Elofir's aura—about as different from Mzatal and Rhyzkahl as night and day. There was nothing of menace or contained danger about him, though he still carried himself with Presence. The power he exuded was gentle and calm, and through my too-fucking-cool connection with the grove, I had the unwavering impression that, if given the choice between losing face or engaging in conflict, he would choose the former, and not because of any sort of cowardice. He simply felt peaceful.

I watched until they disappeared through the archway into the palace, then exhaled and looked over at Kehlirik. "What do they do at this conclave?" I asked. "S'mores? Ghost stories?"

Kehlirik started walking again, and I paced alongside him. "I do not know what this 's'mores' is," he said. "What they do varies, with several elements always being present. Review of agreements, confirmation of the rotations for the next cycle, assessment of anomaly patterning, and a unified rebalance."

"You'd like s'mores," I told him. "Chocolate and melted marshmallow between two graham crackers." I glanced his way. "What are the rotations for?"

"Of the overwatch," he said. "It is critical that each day is covered by at least one lord, though two will be on the rotation. Even a single day unwatched can disastrously unbalance the arcane fields."

I took a few seconds to consider that, remembering Ilana's statement about the lords having much responsibility, and the image of the potency thingy Turek showed me in Szerain's shrine.

"In other words, they maintain this world's arcane power plant and make sure it doesn't overload or have blackouts?" I asked.

"Kri," he said with a twitch of his wings. "It is a simplistic though adequate analogy."

As we rounded a curve in the path, a ruined stone structure came into sight. All thoughts of arcane power plants fled my mind as I took it in. "Oh, wow," I breathed.

The ruins crowned the rise ahead, surrounded by boulders shrugged from the mountainside above. Stairs of white stone climbed toward what had once been a graceful roofed structure of the same pale stone. Only columns and one wall remained standing on its raised foundation, the rest in broken chunks among the tumbled boulders.

Kehlirik followed me up the stairs. Halfway up I *felt* the place. Even broken, it resonated a subtle, permeating potency that made me feel a little floaty in a good way. My steps slowed to a reverent pace as I took it all in. The translucent milky stone of both the remaining structure and the fallen chunks shimmered with a soft bluish glow, and, as I topped the rise, the columns framed the blue-grey sky beyond. Déjà vu kicked in full force. Kehlirik crouched at the edge of the foundation, lifted a claw, and sketched a sigil in the air. I watched in fascination as he sent it spinning to the middle of the ruined pavilion where it flared brightly before fading away.

His eyes went to me. "You may send a . . ." He seemed to be seeking the right word. "Wish," he finally said, though I had the feeling it still wasn't quite what he was trying to convey. "Trace any primary sigil and imbue it with your wish."

I stood silently for a moment, considering, then scowled in annoyance. "I can't," I said, voice loaded with bitterness. "Even without this goddamn collar, I don't know how to do one of those floater sigils."

Kehlirik's eyes went to the collar. He let out a low croon that might have been of sympathy, but it was hard to be sure. "I will trace one for you. It matters not who creates the sigil."

He sketched another sigil, then looked to me, waiting.

Kinda surreal making a wish with a demon, but no point in wasting it. I pursed my lips and considered while a million different things flitted through my mind. Getting home was my top priority, however Rhyzkahl said he was working on that. Then there was protecting myself from Mzatal. But I wasn't going to waste a wish on that fucker. More up close and personal was this elusive crap with Elinor. What the hell. It was only a wish anyway.

I gave Kehlirik a nod. *I want to know what really happened to Elinor.* Just in case, I threw in the post script, *and that means her part in the cataclysm, too*. I snorted. So silly.

Kehlirik sent it to the center where it glowed briefly then dissipated.

"Thanks," I said. "What is this place?"

Crouching, the reyza settled his wings along his back. "It is a very ancient site, a gateway from the time before the Ekiri departed."

"Ekiri? Who were they?" I asked. "And why did they leave?"

A pair of faas hopped to the edge of the pavilion steps and sent in sigils before continuing on in, stopping in the very center where the sigils had disappeared. Kehlirik moved to follow them, and I did likewise.

"They were a race that once lived among us and taught much of the mastery of the arcane," Kehlirik said. "They departed for a new realm many millennia ago."

"That's pretty amazing," I said, slowly looking around. I could spend a lifetime simply learning the history of this world. "Was this damaged during the cataclysm?" I asked.

"Yes," he said, wings drooping slightly. "It had stood unblemished for millennia."

I cautiously put my hand on a stone. It was cool but not as cold as normal stone would have been in this weather. Memories flickered. Her memories.

Cool stone, peace, a smile, ancient blue eyes . . .

I frowned. I wanted more than shadows. Breathing deeply, I sought the deeper memories.

I sketch the sigil and make my wish. Would that I could learn faster. He expects so much of me, and I fear I am a disappointment. In this place I feel whole. Perhaps the ancients can hear me and will touch me from afar. I imagine that the song of the stone is their song, their voices. I have not told Giovanni this for he would surely think me foolish.

Holy crap. Through the memory I could almost *almost* feel how to shape the floater. I tried to call it up again for an instant replay, but nothing. Damn. That could have been useful. Instead, I focused on what I did understand from the memory. "She used to come here a lot," I murmured. It had been whole and untouched in her lifetime, existing in perfection in the shadow of a cliff. Now I could see where the cliff had collapsed, crushing part of the pavilion and creating the tumble of boulders.

Kehlirik dipped his head in a nod. "Elinor. Yes. Alone and with the lord."

I let the memories flicker through my head.

Ancient blue eyes upon me as he approaches. How glori-

ous he is! His smile is like sunshine, and when he touches my cheek I want to melt. He holds me close to his side and strokes my hair. I have no fears here.

"She worshipped him," I said with a soft sigh.

Kehlirik tilted his head, seemed to consider. "Yes, worship. A good choice of word."

"Poor thing," I murmured. So young. Barely old enough to know herself. How could she not adore Rhyzkahl when he extended affection to her? Was this how Rhyzkahl felt about me?

Kehlirik shifted his wings. "She was content."

Could she even conceive of having anything else? I wondered about Giovanni. Maybe in the end she found something else, though since she died so young, it never had a chance to truly blossom.

Sighing, I pulled my hand from the stone. "What about Gio—"

Giovanni's face swam before me, close, pale, and drawn, clearer than memory, more clouded than reality. I couldn't hear him, but his lips formed my name—her name. The discordant whine of a failing ritual enveloped me, setting my teeth on edge, and an instant later was gone. Agony flooded my chest, tearing at me, expanding until there was nothing but pain and silence. Giovanni's face before me, silently saying *Elinor* over and over. Pain. *Elinor, Elinor, Elinor.* Pain. *Elinor, Elinor. Giovanni.*

Shuddering, I sucked breath through my teeth and worked to push away the overwhelming memory that threatened to unbalance me. *These are not my memories*, I fiercely reminded myself. *I can control this.*

Mzatal's advice came back to me, so I drew a deep breath and mentally traced the stupid pygah. Slowly, the disturbing memory retreated back to its lair. It felt different from the other Elinor memories—more isolated, more nightmarish. I lifted my head to see Kehlirik watching me carefully.

I gave him the steadiest smile I could manage. "I'm okay. It was just a strong memory."

He let out a snort and nodded as if satisfied that I unmired myself, then flew up to a shoulder of rock overlooking the ruins.

The two faas abruptly chittered and went still as stone,

including their tails. I'd never, *ever*, seen a faas still. Ever. A heartbeat later they both darted off and through the rocks. I blinked in surprise, about to turn and head back down the hill when I felt it: a lord's aura. And not Rhyzkahl's, I realized with dismay. This aura was cold. No, not just cold. Cold. As. Fuck.

Shit. I so did not want to deal with any lord right now, especially one that even the faas would hide from. What the hell was that all about? But I couldn't see any other way down the hill, and I wasn't small and agile like the faas who'd apparently ducked and hid behind some of the rocks. I finally settled for clambering on a boulder that was partially tucked behind a section of the ruins. Maybe this lord was simply coming up here to do one of those wish-things, and would then leave without bothering to look around. Maybe if I stayed super still he wouldn't notice me.

And maybe I'll sprout wings and fly away, I thought with a scowl. I scuttled back into the shadow and as out of sight as I could get.

I breathed as shallowly as possible, listening to the fall of his footsteps on the stone and peering through a gap in the columns. Blond and androgynous, he sauntered into the center of the ruins, then lifted his head, nostrils flaring as though scenting.

He turned to look directly at me. *Fuck*.

Primal instinct screamed at me to run, but it was all I could do right now to breathe, much less move.

His eyes narrowed. "Come," he said, voice cold and imperiously commanding.

Gulping back the unreasoning terror, I silently cursed. If I refused there was no telling what he'd do. I climbed down and approached, though I took my damn sweet time doing so. My eyes met his, but I quickly yanked my gaze away. Beautiful. A shocking amethyst color that reminded me of the syraza. But I didn't like what was behind those eyes, didn't want to see any more of it. The Symbol Man might have been a ruthless serial killer, but he was a puppy compared to this dude.

I stopped about ten feet away. A smile played on the lord's lips.

"Come," he repeated, indicating a spot directly in front of him.

My skin crawled as I moved forward. His aura flowed over me in an oily wave, sending a shudder of nameless horror through me. It was like being near the creepiest person I'd ever known times a thousand. His lips parted slightly, which only served to increase the ick-factor. A shiver raced over my skin, and I struggled to summon anger instead of the mewling terror that wanted to come out.

He stepped closer so that he was barely a foot in front of me, inhaling deeply as his aura surrounded me, viscous and dark. Slowly he moved around me. My breaths became shallow, and I clenched my hands into fists to keep them from shaking. He stopped behind me, stayed there while I gritted my teeth and fought back a shiver.

The lord took hold of the scarf, wound it back around my throat. He held both ends of it while he stood behind me. He didn't pull, but I knew he wanted me to understand that he could, that he was in control. I swallowed hard, throat moving against the fabric. He gave a light tug, shifting it tighter though nowhere near to the point of choking me. Didn't matter. Totally had me freaked out. My instincts screamed at me to run, but I knew he would enjoy such a chase, knew that it would end badly for me.

A low whimper escaped me as he exerted slow pressure on the scarf to pull me back against him. He inhaled, mouth close to my ear.

"I know your scent, *baztakh*," he murmured, voice resonant with a promise of pain, and terror, and mind-fucking torment.

I squeezed my eyes shut as I sought to tap my anger. He was doing this solely to scare me. And yeah, he was doing a damn good job of it, but that didn't mean it couldn't also piss me off. Taking a deep breath, I focused on the peace and calm of the grove.

Still at my back, he released the scarf and put his hands on my shoulders. The way he slid them down my arms almost made me wish it was a sexual move instead of the unknown that it was.

"Perhaps, when Rhyzkahl has finished using you, he will pass you to me." Dark amusement colored his voice. "I would gladly accept you as partial payment."

I drew a stupid mental pygah and focused on the peace of the grove, slowing my breathing and regaining my composure despite the extreme level of revulsion. "Payment? For what?"

He laughed and set his hands on both sides of my neck, middle fingers tracing over my larynx. "Such matters are not shared with pets."

"I am not, and never will be, a *pet*," I managed to snarl, holding the feel of the grove close to me.

"Ah, you want to play, little pet?" He chuckled low. "I would very much enjoy that."

"You bore me," I said. Play? I had no idea what he was talking about, but I did my damnedest to put as much contempt into my voice as possible. Probably would have been better without the quaver, but I did my best. "I wish no game with you. You're pathetic."

He gave a low laugh, moved languidly around to face me. "You do not smell bored. You do not . . . feel bored." He ran a finger along my clenched jaw, smiled. Hunger danced in his violet eyes. "Subside or rise fully and show me how pathetic I am."

What the hell was he talking about? Rise fully? *He's fucking with me*, I decided. There was no way I could best a lord.

His eyes stayed on my face, amusement flickering in them as he gauged my reaction to his challenge. He let out a low laugh as he reached and shoved me lightly in the chest, still watching as if studying me.

I took a step back. He was definitely goading me, but to what end? Did he truly expect me to strike out at him? I wasn't *that* stupid.

A reyza landed a few feet behind and to the right of the lord. It crouched and bared teeth at me, but this was no reyza smile. As I looked at the demon, recognition tugged, but I couldn't understand why. I'd never summoned this one. I knew that much. Kehlirik was the only reyza I'd ever summoned. And this wasn't one of Mzatal's.

Ice dropped into my belly as the memory struck—my own memory, my own pain: A reyza bellowing as he leaped at me, claws extended. A burning tug at my belly. The sight of my bowels coiled on the floor in front of me. The growing pool of blood.

Sweat stung my armpits despite the chill in the air. This was Sehkeril, the reyza who'd aided the Symbol Man serial killer during his final attempt to summon and bind Rhyzkahl. Sehkeril had eviscerated me, and I had only minutes to live when Rhyzkahl brought me back to the demon realm and allowed me to die here.

The lord closed the gap between us. "I will go now and speak to Rhyzkahl about arrangements," he said, cold amusement in his voice. He leaned in close—far too close—face beside mine as he murmured in my ear. "Sehkeril will keep you company while I am away."

The lord pressed a forefinger into the notch of my throat above my collarbones, just enough to be painful without doing any actual damage. What the *hell?* He smiled as I coughed, looked upon me for another unpleasant moment, then turned and headed away.

Sehkeril growled and clicked his claws together, quite clearly trying to unsettle me. He didn't need to; his creepy lord had taken care of maxing out my freakout, and all I wanted to do right then was to get away from this place. Surely the reyza wouldn't hurt me while I was in Rhyzkahl's realm? Hoping that was true, I turned away from him and hurried back down the stone steps toward the palace, but I heard claws on stone and a near constant growl as he followed. My heart pounded a crazy rhythm as I descended the steps, and my back prickled. I fully expected a shove from behind or some other harassment.

I heard a rush of wings followed by Kehlirik's voice, speaking in demon to Sehkeril, and it definitely wasn't a friendly *How ya doin'?* Glancing back, I saw that Kehlirik was keeping the other reyza occupied. I breathed a silent thanks, but still quickened my pace as soon as I reached the path. I crested the low hill, and the grove came into view. That's where I wanted to be—shielded within the embrace of those living walls. I wasn't safe here, that was for sure.

I'm *not* safe, I realized with sick disappointment. I'd come here—*escaped* to here—assuming I would be safe, that I wouldn't be hurt or harassed or mistreated.

I shot a quick glance behind me as the two reyza took flight, snarling at each other. I wanted to be in the grove, but more than that, I wanted to be away from here.

Why not leave? I suddenly thought. Why *not* find someplace safe and quiet where I could think and ponder and get my head back to where it needed to be. *But I don't know this world, and I really do try not to be extraordinarily stupid.* My gaze went back to the grove, and the familiar calm seeped through me. It *could* take me someplace safe, I realized as clearly as if the grove had spoken to me—and then I somehow knew it had done just that. I didn't know how sentient it was, but I knew, as surely as I'd known that I could use the grove to travel, that it would take me away from Rhyzkahl's realm to someplace safe, with no alien or undue perils, where I could begin to process everything.

Kehlirik and Sehkeril were high and behind me, flying a snarling, hissing aerial dance. If I was going to do this, now was likely my only chance. *No . . . I* am *doing this. I'm leaving.* It was the right move. I knew it. Neither reyza seemed to notice me taking the path toward the grove, but I knew it was only a matter of seconds before they did. I made a quick scan for any other demons nearby and didn't see any. It wasn't very far. I could do this.

I bolted and took off at a dead run for the grove as fast as my not-very-athletic body could manage. If I had any luck at all the two reyza would remain occupied with whatever the hell dominance game they were playing.

Clearly, I had no luck whatsoever, for a bellow sounded not even a heartbeat later. I sprinted all out, eyes on the grove as I gasped for breath. I figured, worst case scenario—meaning Kehlirik broke off immediately—I had about a count of ten to make it to the trees. Once I was within that tree tunnel I was home free. I knew that. The grove wouldn't let anyone pull me away. Five, six, seven; hope rose within me. I was actually going to make it. An exultant smile spread across my face despite the deep burning of my lungs and legs from the sudden exertion. Eight, nine . . .

The mark on my forearm flared white-hot then went utterly cold as a wave of weakness slammed into me. I stumbled, then sprawled to my belly in an awkward slide. I couldn't even get my hands up to break my fall, and pain lanced through my cheek and forehead as the coarse grass scraped my face. I struggled to focus, to get up, to run those last few feet, but my body had zero strength in it. I couldn't even lift my head to look toward the grove, though I could feel it *right there.*

The world dipped and spun. Kehlirik landed beside me

and crouched, crooning softly. *Was this a heart attack?* I wondered, utterly bewildered. So close. I'd been so close. Tears of frustration slid down my cheeks, but I didn't have the strength to sob or scream.

Sehkeril landed near, but Kehlirik warned him off with a roar and a snarl. Kehlirik made a soft ticking sound as he gathered me gently into his arms, my body as limp as if I was unconscious. He shifted so that my head rested against his chest instead of lolling back. The mark on my arm burned with a cold pain, as if ice had been held against it for far too long.

The mark. A shiver went through me. Was that it? Maybe I'd tripped a ward or something. Or maybe Rhyzkahl had somehow zapped me to keep me from leaving. This last thought left me as cold as my mark, yet I had a sickening certainty it was true.

"*Yaghir tahn*, Kara Gillian," he murmured. "Forgive me."

"Wh-what happened?" I slurred, barely able to get the words out and not even sure if he could understand me. I felt like complete shit, utterly weak both inside and out.

Kehlirik stood and began to carry me toward the palace. A *kehza* flew close, curious, but Kehlirik snarled, sending the other demon streaking away. "You were stopped from going to the grove," he told me.

The cold within me seemed to increase. "Mark," I mumbled. Kehlirik merely snorted, which was answer enough for me. Nausea curdled my gut, but I wasn't sure I had even the strength to barf. I wasn't crying anymore—much. I couldn't seem to get a handle on the fear that wanted to take up permanent residence in my chest. *What the fuck do I do now?*

He carried me to my rooms and set me gently on the bed, crooning low in his throat as he pulled a blanket over me. Again he murmured *yaghir tahn*, but I was too demoralized and upset to respond. He crouched beside the bed, massive head lowered toward me, and bestial face contorted with concern. "Rest, Kara Gillian," he said, voice soft and deep.

"I don't want to be here," I whispered, tears still leaking.

He ticked softly as he settled his wings. "There is nowhere for you to go in the moment, so best to abide in peace, though your heart calls you elsewhere."

I didn't want to see his concern, didn't want to hear his comfort. He'd brought me back here to this place where I didn't want to be. Yeah, I'd rest. I didn't really have a choice at the moment, did I? Right now I felt as if I'd had the flu for months, and even blinking required tremendous effort. The only parts of me that actually hurt were the mark and the scrapes on my face, but the rest of me still felt like total shit.

Kehlirik gave a low hiss then rose and exited. I drew a small amount of comfort from the fact that the reyza seemed to be pissed at Rhyzkahl as well.

A few heartbeats later, I felt Rhyzkahl come in. He moved toward the bed. "Dear one," he said, concern on his face.

I wanted to turn away from him, but I didn't have the strength, which pissed me off as much as it scared me. Instead I gave him a *Fuck you* glare with an added touch of *You're a worthless bastard*, then closed my eyes.

The bed shifted as he sat on the edge. A heartbeat later I felt his hand on the scrapes on my cheek. "With Kehlirik distracted, I had no other option but to use the mark to stop you from leaving," he said as a low warmth eased the sting in my face. "There should have been no pain in the mark when I did so. The damage done by Mzatal twisted the connection."

I stayed silent, hurt and pissed.

"I know Kadir frightened you, and I understand your desire to flee," he continued. "I could not allow it as it would take you out of my direct protection." He set his other hand on my forehead, and gradually the horrible-flu sensation faded along with the worst of the crippling weakness.

Kadir. Now the creepshow had a name. Taking a ragged breath, I opened my eyes and looked up at him. "I wouldn't have even encountered him if you'd allowed me to visit the grove," I said, still deeply upset and hurt. "I needed that, and you denied it."

Regret shadowed across his face. "I cannot risk you," he said. "There are many lords arriving, and I cannot adequately protect you in the grove." His eyes met mine. "Even were this not the time of the conclave, Mzatal could arrive at any moment, and he would not leave you sitting peacefully in the grove."

"I can feel before anyone comes through," I muttered, turning my head away. "I needed it."

Rhyzkahl laid a hand over the mark, easing the cold burn and giving me a bit more of my strength back. "And if, in your musings, you again decide you need to depart?" he asked. "What then? I would have no means to recover or rescue you then, and you would be fully at the mercy of others." He paused. "And some know nothing of mercy." He touched my cheek. "Dear one, I sought only to protect you from dangers of which you were unaware."

I had zero doubt he referred to Kadir, and I shivered at the memory. *His* prisoner? I'd take Mzatal's tender care over Lord Creepshow's. "Would it be too fucking hard for you to tell me shit like this?" I turned my head back toward him. "If you're so damn protective, then why did you let that . . . that *freak* paw all over me?"

"He was under guest oath then," Rhyzkahl replied with utter calm. "He is under full oath to me now, and such will not happen again while you're here. As long as you are *here*."

Scowling, I rolled away from him and curled on my side. "I want to go home."

"Yes, I know you do," he said. "And I seek the means. I do not yet have them."

I was still pretty damn tired, but at least I didn't feel like death anymore. Yet I also didn't know if I could believe him. Most confusing was the fact that what he said made sense. Maybe it was simply the fact that I didn't like—and certainly wasn't accustomed to—other people making decisions for me without even the courtesy of explanation or discussion.

"I want to be alone," I said. "Please . . . I need you to go away."

"No." He pulled the covers from me, and then I felt him shift onto the bed. Before I could wonder what the hell he was doing, he lifted me and pulled me into his lap as he sat against the headboard to cradle me close.

I blinked, utterly shocked at the display of tenderness. There'd been times when the demonic lord had shown a measure of what could be construed as affection, but there'd never been anything as overt as this.

And it was exactly what I needed, though I hadn't realized it. Releasing a shuddering breath, I found myself relaxing against him. "Why are you doing this?" I sighed.

He bent his head close to mine, nuzzling gently. "It was not my desire to . . . go away."

I leaned my head against his shoulder, eyes closing. "You always get what you want?" I murmured.

I heard his whispered reply as I drifted off to sleep.

"No."

Chapter 13

I thought it was early evening when I woke. Except that the sun slanted through the windows that faced east, and my bladder was about to damn well burst. *No, not evening*, I realized with a fair amount of dismay. This was the morning of the next day. Holy crap. Even with Rhyzkahl easing a considerable amount of the drain that occurred when he used the mark to stop me, I'd still slept close to a full day. I didn't even want to think about how long I'd be down if he hadn't come and relieved that crushing fatigue.

I rolled over to get out of bed and froze at the sight of a flower on the other pillow—large, fragrant, and as vividly violet as a syraza's eyes. I had zero doubt it was from Rhyzkahl, but . . . wow. He'd cuddled me, and now this. Actual displays of affection. I smiled. It was weird, but also pretty darn cool.

Musing on the entire scenario, I made my way to the bathroom to take care of the most urgent matter, then came back out and nibbled a couple of grapey-blueberry things from the big bowl of fruit on the table to quell the insistent pangs. Other than being hungry, I pretty much felt back to normal, so apparently sleeping for a godawful long time was all I needed. Not that it made any of this easier to figure out.

I stuck the flower in a glass of water and set it on the nightstand. It had an exotic scent that reminded me of the grove. Perhaps that was why he'd left it for me, since I couldn't actually go there.

Sighing, I plopped onto the couch in the main room to brood. Being barred from the grove was definitely upsetting, but it didn't take a lot of navel-gazing to figure out that it wasn't the actual ban that bugged me the most. I mean, sure, that part sucked, but I also understood *why* he'd done the arcane version of tackling me before I walked out into traffic. If I left his realm, then any lord would be free to snatch me up and do whatever they wanted with me.

It was the means that bothered me the most. Great, I had a magic tattoo that could be used to drop me in my tracks. That was fucking wonderful. Plus, the big-strong-man-takes-care-of-helpless-woman vibe wasn't exactly my cup of tea. Why the hell couldn't he have simply told me *why* he didn't want me to go to the grove instead of telling my guardian to not let me near it? Yeah, I could be stubborn, but I usually tried hard to listen to reason. And after my oh-so-pleasant time with Mzatal, I had no desire to go back to being some lord's prisoner.

Two faas burst into the room without knocking, startling me out of my thoughts. They each bore trays of food though, so I decided to forgive them. More hyper than usual, they burbled about visitors and preparations, then slid the food onto the table and were back out the door before I could even thank them.

I grinned and settled down to eat. There were some things I liked about being in the demon realm, and I could definitely get used to nonstop room service. And not having to clean up or do laundry. Yeah, that pretty well rocked.

A tingle at the back of my neck told me that the grove was activated, which meant someone was arriving. More lords. Curious, I quickly yanked on pants and a sweater, grabbed my mug of chak and stepped onto the balcony. This was how I preferred to deal with any other demonic lords, at least for now: three stories up and far out of reach.

A reyza, a kehza, and a pair of faas emerged from the tree tunnel, followed by a dark-skinned lord, bald, with a goatee and no mustache. Gold glinted from his earlobes, and a chain of red-blood gems the size of my thumbnail hung around his neck. Flowing robes of gold and blue swirled about his feet as he walked up the path toward the palace. The grove resonated with calm spiced with a hint of . . . adventure?

I continued to watch with naked interest until the lord

passed out of sight through the main entry below and to the right of my balcony.

Tucking my bare feet underneath me, I sat on the chaise. I'd barely made myself comfortable when I heard the door. A heartbeat later I felt Rhyzkahl's presence. Good. One way or another I was going to get some answers and get my doubts sorted out.

Rhyzkahl's gaze went to me as he stepped out onto the balcony. "You slept deeply."

The look I gave him was uncertain. "Well, you kinda sucked the life out of me."

"I did," he said. "A last resort." He sat beside me on the couch, not quite touching me. His eyes searched my face, assessing. "You are much recovered, though still disturbed."

My mouth twisted. "Yesterday was disturbing on a number of levels." I said. "I didn't know you could do that with the mark. That's pretty frightening."

Rhyzkahl reached out and laid his palm over the mark. "There is a deep connection with the mark, even damaged as it is by Mzatal's interference."

I gave him a wary look. "Could you kill me with it?"

"No," he replied without hesitation. "The mark is not woven for such."

That was certainly a relief, but I wasn't quite ready to fully relax. "Are there any other *features* I don't yet know about that might still bite me in the ass?" I asked, cocking an eyebrow at him.

"No." He traced his fingers along the mark, sending a light shiver through me, though it wasn't completely unpleasant. "I anchored the disrupted strand upon your arrival, but it must be removed and reworked to repair the damage."

Still uneasy, I pulled away from him, stood, and moved to the railing. The grove's trees moved in hypnotic undulations in the low wind. My tension slipped away as I gently touched the grove. I couldn't go out to it, but it was still there for me. The deep calm stole through me like the warmth from a fire, and I exhaled a soft sigh of comfort.

He moved up behind me, put his hands on my shoulders.

"I want to go home," I told him. I knew I sounded like a broken record, but, well, too bad.

"This I know," he said, giving my shoulders a light

squeeze before gently turning me to face him. "It is of your disposition I came to speak." He smiled down at me. "A solution has arisen."

I held back the burst of hope, still cautious. "What sort of solution?"

"It is fortuitous that this is the time of the conclave," he said, taking my hands in his. "There are debts to be paid and agreements to fulfill. With the cooperation of another lord, I can and will prepare a ritual to send you home. I have made arrangements, and it will take place two days hence."

"And I'll go home?" I asked. "That's it? You'll send me home?"

He squeezed my hands. "Yes, I will send you home," he assured me. "You were not brought here by my will. Had it been my desire to do so, I could have taken you at any time."

"You mean, when I summoned you, if you'd wanted to take me back you could have?"

"Yes," he said. "You, dear one, summoned a demonic lord."

"Well, duh," I said. "You were willing." But I realized it made sense that he could bring me back at any time. After all, he'd brought me back with him when I'd been bleeding out and dying. I exhaled in relief. "Home. Wow. Thank you. I miss home so much." I chuckled softly. "And coffee. I *really* miss coffee." Then my smile slipped, and I narrowed my eyes at him. "What did that creepy lord mean about payment?"

A flash of what might have been annoyance lit his eyes for an instant before it was gone. "You experienced Kadir," he said. "You felt him. He chooses words to elicit fear and unease. He cares nothing for the truth."

I peered at him. "So all that stuff about you giving me to him in payment was bullshit?" I asked. "And what would it be payment for, anyway?"

Rhyzkahl shook his head. "The qaztahl have had millennia to forge agreements great and small," he said. "Favors and payments are always owed, but you are *not* slated as payment to Kadir." He scowled as if the mere thought was repulsive. "You have my oath on this."

"Good." I allowed myself to relax a bit. "He's a bad monkey, that one."

"What is the meaning of 'bad monkey'?" he asked with a frown.

I rubbed my arms, chilled at the mere thought of Kadir. "Someone who's not *right*. Someone who doesn't think and feel the way most other folks do." I shook my head. "I've seen it before in sociopaths, but he takes it to a whole other level."

"Yes. He is Kadir," Rhyzkahl said, and I realized that he'd known Kadir for thousands of years. This was nothing new to him. Kadir was simply . . . Kadir; a part of the natural order of things as far as he was concerned. The other lords no doubt handled him with the same sort of care one did with any potentially dangerous creature. They knew what to do and what not to do with him.

Rhyzkahl shifted to face me more fully. "Kadir is one of the reasons I had for halting your departure through the grove," he told me, face serious and intent. "He would have very literally hunted you," he continued, "and had he found you before I did, he would have taken you to his realm without regard for consequences from me."

A sliver of cold terror slid through me at the mere thought. I shuddered, mind shying away from even wondering what would happen to me in such a scenario. "You mentioned an oath last night," I said. "Has he given it to you? Will he harass me again?" I sure as hell didn't want to be stuck inside in order to avoid another encounter with the creepy-as-fuck Kadir.

"Neither he nor Sehkeril will approach or harass you while you are here," he assured me. "I have his oath. He is not one you need fear."

"Okay, then what about the collar?" I asked with a challenging lift of my chin. "If you have his oath then why am I still wearing this fucking thing?"

"Because all those who will be within these walls for the next few days are ruthless and would seek to delve into your being," he replied without hesitation. "The collar offers protection from that."

Anger and frustration flared as my patience with all the shit about my protection evaporated. "Collars are for slaves and pets. So, which am I?" I dropped to my knees before him. "Hell, might as well do this right. Okay, *master*, what's your fucking command?"

Something dark and dangerous flickered over his face. He reached down with both hands to seize me by the upper arms and haul me to my feet, then held me in place, his face inches from mine.

"You are not to kneel to me," he said with an intensity that seared through me and set my heart pounding. "Not as a requirement, nor in jest. You are not now, nor have you ever been my slave." His grip tightened, though not quite to the point of pain. "*You* saw the need to bind me by oath to not bring you harm in your world, nor to challenge the laws of your land, nor bring destruction. Consider well that you are in *my* world now and the wearing of this collar for a short time goes far in protecting not only you but also this realm—and me—from the machinations of unscrupulous qaztahl. I will not remove it prematurely to prove a point." He released his grip and took a step back from me, but his eyes never left mine.

I swallowed hard. "All right," I said reluctantly. "But swear to me that as soon as they're gone, the collar's gone. Please? I hate this thing."

Rhyzkahl stroked the back of his fingers over my cheek. "I swear that, as soon as the conclave is over and the lords have departed, I will remove the collar."

I felt the grove activate again, with yet another, a different, "feel"—confirming my suspicion that each lord had his own signature resonance.

A few heartbeats later Rhyzkahl looked up and lifted his chin toward the grove. "Amkir arrives."

I turned to see three reyza exit the tree tunnel and leap into the air, followed by a pair of faas who immediately darted toward the palace. After another few seconds, a syraza stepped out and took flight, and finally a lord with a faintly olive complexion and short dark hair emerged. His resonance with the grove wasn't calm like the previous lord's or peaceful like Elofir's. This Amkir had a harsh feel that seemed be confirmed by his unsmiling expression and narrowed eyes. He wore a deep green, long-sleeved robe, belted at the waist. The three-quarter sleeves were decorated with bands of gold, and the whole outfit reminded me vaguely of a Russian fresco I'd studied back in college as part of my mostly useless Art History degree.

"Do you expect Mzatal to come?" I asked Rhyzkahl after Amkir disappeared from view.

Rhyzkahl gave a low snort of derision. "I doubt Mzatal has the *tebakh*—" Which I somehow knew meant "balls" or something damn close to it. "—to come to my domain now."

I shivered, remembering Mzatal's face and what he'd said before he'd retreated down the tree tunnel: *I will retrieve you.* I rubbed my arms in an attempt to dispel the memory of his scary-intensity.

Rhyzkahl moved to a place beside me on the rail, watching as Amkir's reyza rose to meet Kehlirik in either greeting or challenge. I couldn't tell the difference.

"Tell me of your time with Mzatal," he said. His eyes were still on Amkir's approach, but I had no doubt his attention was fully on me.

The last thing I wanted to do was go through all of that shit, but at the same time I completely understood Rhyzkahl's desire to know what happened. It was a post-incident debriefing, I figured. Plus, maybe something I'd seen or experienced could give Rhyzkahl an advantage over Mzatal somewhere down the line.

I gave a fairly emotionless recounting of the summoning and the damn purification ceremony. Told him about Idris and his skill, and my exploration of Szerain's palace. I watched him for any reaction when I told him about my connection to Elinor, but his expression remained one of polite interest.

"Did you know about that whole Elinor thing?" I asked.

"Yes, you carry something of her," he replied with complete calm. "It is part of the reason you required extra protection in the form of a syraza guardian."

I straightened, frowning. "Why didn't you ever tell me? I mean, she damn near destroyed this world." I felt the grove activate again, but I resisted the urge to look toward it.

"I did not choose to distress you with unnecessary information," he stated. "It seemed but a mild whisper of memory to you. More awareness, more knowledge on your part, increased the risk of other qaztahl discovering you and seeking you, as occurred with Mzatal." His gaze shifted to the grove as another lord exited. "Vahl," he said with a slight frown.

Vahl's demonic contingent consisted of a reyza, two faas, one kehza, and a graa—a scuttling, crab-spiderish-looking demon that could fly with lightning speed. It had only been a little over a week ago that I'd been attacked by a graa. I knew there was little chance it was the same one, but I couldn't help eyeing it somewhat dubiously as it flew to the top of a squat broad pillar near the grove, already occupied by over a dozen reyza, kehza, and zhurn.

The lord was another matter. Tall, dark-skinned, and broad-shouldered, he wore a close-fitting long-sleeved grey shirt and dark jeans that showed off a build that was muscular in all the right places. His hair was closely shorn, and he sported a perfectly trimmed mustache and beard. His aura was welcoming and dangerous at the same time, and I watched him with avid interest as he approached.

Dark eyes lifted to mine as he strode down the path, and a slight smile touched his mouth. A moment later, the demons on the pillar erupted in an uproar of bellows, snorts, trumpets, and squawks that carried clearly in the crisp air and gave the strong impression of laughter. They engaged in groups of two and three with mega-rock-paper-scissors and other apparent games, lending a party-like atmosphere to the assembly. "They sure like their games," I said.

Rhyzkahl looked over at me with a smile and a raised eyebrow. "Everything is a game to them."

I smiled and continued my tale. Rhyzkahl's eyes narrowed when I told him about the shrine and how I freaked out when I saw the image of the blade. But it was when I told him of falling with Safar and crashing into the grove—and the grove's incredible response—that he truly reacted.

His lips parted slightly, and red-gold potency flickered briefly in his eyes. "And when you passed through the grove after that, was it the same?" he asked, gaze and presence intense. "Did it still respond to you?"

"When we went through the grove to go to Mzatal's realm, it simply felt incredibly peaceful," I told him, smiling a little at the memory. "But the next time we went through, I knew I could use it. That's how I escaped and kept Mzatal from removing your mark."

An unusual, faraway look lit his eyes as he looked out past the rail. "Yes," he said softly. "Clearly you have a very special connection to the groves." A few heartbeats later he returned his focus to me, faraway look gone. "And what of your injuries once Mzatal had you again?"

"He healed me," I replied, then told him of the healing and the return to Mzatal's realm, the attempt to remove the mark and, finally, of his conviction that Rhyzkahl sought Szerain's blade and of Mzatal's drive to get it first.

Rhyzkahl remained silent for a moment after I finished, then turned to face me. "Mzatal is arrogant and knows little of what I want," he said as he stroked the hair back from my face. "That he seeks Vsuhl is valuable information. *Very* valuable." His hand stilled, resting against my cheek. "The *chekkunden* had hopes to make you his own. He did not kill you upon attaining you, and kept you whole." Anger darkened his eyes. "And then he sought to remove my mark," he said, nearly snarling the words. "It is an unforgivable offense."

I rubbed the back of my neck, grimaced. "Well, he came close to killing me more than once."

Rhyzkahl nodded. "And he sought to slay you through the implant." His other hand curled into a fist atop the railing. "He now curses his weakness for not killing you while he had you fully in his control." He sneered. "Foolish that he would think you could ever be *his*."

I smiled tightly. "Yeah, well, I'm not his. I won't *ever* be his."

His eyes shifted to me. "No. No you will not." He pulled me to him before lowering his head and brushing my lips with his. "You belong with me," he said, voice compelling and resolute.

I slowly relaxed against him as he deepened the kiss. This was what I'd been needing all along—the nice, caring, and sensual Rhyzkahl instead of the badass lord. I needed a damn hug, and if a curl-your-toes kiss came along with it, well, that was fine, too. His arms encircled me, holding me close. I slid my hands around his neck and through the white-blond silk of his hair as I eagerly returned the kiss. I'd been way too stressed these past few days, and I knew exactly how I wanted to relieve it.

He slid a hand to the small of my back, pulling me hard against him and showing me his own stress that needed relieving. His other hand tangled in my hair, lightly fisting as he pulled my head back. I groaned as his mouth traveled down over my throat, teeth grazing my skin. I felt the grove activate but I didn't care. I wanted to have sex, not watch lords.

But, Rhyzkahl, damn him, lifted his head and looked out toward the grove. I tried to pull his head back down to mine, but he exhaled and shifted away from me. "The last two, Rayst and," he shook his head slightly, "Seretis."

I did my best to control my pesky libido and looked out at the approaching lords. These two had a scattering of reyza and faas with them, but also at least half a dozen syraza. Rayst had a swarthy complexion and what seemed to be a stocky build beneath nondescript robes, though he moved with a grace and ease that told me the thickness of his body likely wasn't due to being out of shape. Wavy brown hair swept back from his face to the nape of his neck, and the smile on his face was broad and genuine as he conversed with a syraza beside him.

The other lord, Seretis, was tall and rangy, with chiseled cheekbones and dark, wavy hair that brushed his shoulders. He *totally* looked as if he belonged on a Spanish-language soap opera. The fact that he wore a frilly RenFaire type shirt, black breeches, and boots only added to the impression. These two exuded patient kindness and a subtle strength—unless I'd missed something. Why did Rhyzkahl shake his head when he saw them?

I did a mental head count of the lords. Process of elimination meant the first one today had been Vrizaar. At least now I had faces to put with names, except for Jesral.

"So Mzatal won't be coming," I said, relieved.

"He could arrive under protection of the conclave," Rhyzkahl replied, "but he will not. You need not trouble yourself with that." He stepped back, adjusted his clothes with a twitch of his hands, and shook his hair back into perfect place. "There is much I must attend to," he said with a smile, eyes still carrying a hint of a smolder.

Oh, well. So much for de-stressing. I summoned a faint smile in return. He turned to go, then paused and looked back at me. "What of after Mzatal was thrown back, and he failed to remove the mark?" he asked, a frown creasing his forehead. "What happened then?"

I grimaced and ran a hand through my hair. "He wanted to find a way to block my contact with the grove, so he decided to take me to some place in the middle of nowhere so that he could have some time to work without you finding him." I gave a low chuckle. "And that's when I got my ass out of there and used the grove to come here."

"Yes, relocation to a remote grove would have caused delay," Rhyzkahl said, "though I would have found you." He lifted the hand that had been so bloody the night I arrived. "I was in the final preparations for it when you so cleverly escaped." I couldn't be sure, but I thought there was an approving glint in his eye.

"Just in the nick of time, too," I said with a chuckle. "Mzatal was getting . . . um, weird."

Rhyzkahl lowered his hand and frowned. "Weird? What did he do?"

"He kissed me," I said. "But it was *weird* and, I mean . . ." I trailed off, not sure how to explain it.

Red-gold potency abruptly shimmered around him. "Kissed you?" he hissed through clenched teeth. I took a step back in surprise at the vehemence of his reaction. "Mzatal kissed you?" His hands clenched into fists at his sides. "He had no right to touch you thus!"

"Well, yeah, he didn't have the right." I said. "Not without my permission." I frowned and watched him, wary. "Look, it was just a kiss, and an odd one at that. I mean, it lasted a few seconds at most."

The flare of potency faded, but his eyes smoldered again. "Nothing with him is without purpose." He closed the distance between us again, eyes traveling over me. "Nothing."

"I'm starting to realize that," I said with a wry smile.

He moved in and gripped my head firmly in his hands, wound his fingers in my hair.

I laughed low in my throat. "I thought you had lords to attend to?"

"I am unavoidably detained." He tightened his hands in my hair with the perfect amount of intensity to send heat rushing through me. "I have far more pressing business here."

His mouth came down on mine, fierce and possessive, as if to remind me what a *real* kiss was like. His arms came around me, and he lifted and carried me inside before near-throwing me onto the bed. I let out a surprised yelp, then grinned as he took hold of my sweater and pulled it over my head. I hadn't put on a bra earlier, and I was damn glad of it now as he lowered his head to my breasts. He continued to suck and lightly bite as he undid the fastening of my pants, then sat up, grabbed the waistband, and yanked them off me in one fluid motion.

"I do not like that Mzatal touched you," he growled before lowering his head between my legs. I groaned and dropped my head back as he began to work some lordly magic with his tongue. Mzatal certainly hadn't touched me *there*, but I was totally okay with Rhyzkahl doing whatever he felt necessary to fuck the Mzatal off me, so to speak. More than okay. In no time at all I was crying out and clenching in orgasm. *Mzatal who? I don' know any Mzatal. . . .*

Rhyzkahl was far from finished. He straightened up, eyes still lit with a possessive fire that made my loins spasm and shudder in all the right ways. "You are *mine*," he snarled. "*My* summoner." He pushed his pants down only enough to free his erection, which somehow turned me on even more. Yet even with my libido raging like a nuclear reactor in meltdown, I forced myself to hold up a hand. "Wait," I gasped.

To my surprise he went still, though his eyes narrowed in question.

"Swear to me that you won't get me pregnant," I said, still trying to catch my breath. Back at home I was on the pill. Here, I had no such protection, and I did *not* want to take the chance that a lord/human hybrid was possible.

He gave a low snort, though I couldn't tell if it was in amusement or derision. "I have no desire to get you with child," he told me. "I swear I will not do such without your consent." Before I could do more than nod in acceptance, he seized my hips, flipped me onto my stomach, then pulled me up to my hands and knees and entered me in the same movement. With one hand he pushed my head down to the bed as he drove hard into me, wringing low guttural cries from me with every thrust. He knew me so damn well, knew what I wanted—what I *needed* right now. I didn't want love-making. I wanted some hard and mindless fucking, and he was damn well going to give it to me.

His hand tightened in my hair and his other slid around to massage my clit. Before I knew it I climaxed yet again, giving a hoarse scream as I bucked in his grasp. Rhyzkahl continued to thrust deeply as I shuddered, but as soon as I was finished he pulled free and turned me onto my back. He kneed my legs apart and entered me again. His mouth came down on mine as I wrapped my legs around him, yet this time he kept his pace slow, almost teasing as he kissed me. I moaned against his mouth and slid my arms around to stroke the smooth muscles of his back.

He broke the kiss to nuzzle below my ear. "I am deeply pleased you escaped to come here," he murmured.

"You just like staking your claim," I replied with a low laugh.

His teeth grazed my neck. "Dahn. I have no need to claim what is already mine." He began to thrust harder, and my desire for any sort of conversation fled. I lifted my hips to him, already feeling another orgasm building. Was it some sort of demonic lord trick that made that possible? If that was the case, I was totally ruined for human men.

I clutched at him as the pleasure built between us. He came first, with me only a few seconds behind, in a frenzied tangle of limbs and hair and sweat and musk. Eventually he slowed and stopped, still lightly pulsing within me.

"You are *my* summoner," he said, looking into my face.

"No shit, Sherlock," I said with a throaty laugh. I lifted up my arm. "I even have the tat to prove it."

Chapter 14

After Rhyzkahl left to greet the lords, I dozed a bit. Or maybe I was in a post-coital coma. Either way, I lay in languid stupor until well after the midday bell, only dragging myself up and out of bed after a pair of faas entered—again with the no knocking, but bearing food.

After bathing and dressing—and discovering that I was nowhere near as sore as I should have been after the morning's exertions—I headed out to explore more of the palace grounds.

Kehlirik wasn't waiting for me in the corridor, though I had no idea whether it was because Rhyzkahl decided to trust me or because the reyza had been disciplined for my attempted break for the grove. I hoped to hell it wasn't the latter. I liked Kehlirik, and he'd been distracted only because of his efforts to shield me from Sehkeril's harassment.

At the same time, I knew damn well that I was still being watched and guarded, even if I didn't have a giant demon at my side. As I walked down the corridor, I caught flickers of motion in my peripheral vision, and the occasional glint of eyes hidden in shadows. After I stepped outside I peered up at the towers, unsurprised to see Pyrenth and two kehza peering right back at me. Yep, still watched and guarded.

It's for my own protection, I reminded myself, though the thought came with a sour twist of annoyance. The memory of the incident with Kadir rose, and a shiver ran over me that had nothing to do with the chill in the air. Kehlirik hadn't been able to shield me from the creepy lord's attentions. What the hell was I supposed to do if that sort of thing happened again? I scowled as I trudged up the path on the side of the palace away from the grove. I had a hard time believing that an oath would be sufficient protection.

I crested a rise and my scowl faded. The path dropped away to a plot of surprisingly verdant winter grass atop the cliff overlooking the turquoise sea. A light breeze snuck its way through my sweater, and I regretted not bringing a jacket. High clouds streaked the sky, and I wondered if the weather was similar enough to Earth's that fronts could be predicted by how the clouds moved. Not that I knew how to do that. I predicted the weather by calling up the forecast on my smartphone.

On the green stood a gazebo-type thing draped in flowering ivy and surrounded by bushes of brilliant reds and blues. Soft musical tones reached my ears, and as I approached I saw small crystalline ornaments, artfully hung to catch the wind and ringing far more elegantly than the usual wind chimes. A gentle warmth surrounded me as I stepped in, and the flicker of sigils told me that the structure had been warded against wind and cold much like my balcony. The supports of the gazebo rose to delicate filigree arches, the stone translucent and glowing in the sun.

I settled on a bench and let the low melody of the crystal-things soothe me. A faas shimmied up a tree not far away and began to pluck golden winter fruits. Long-winged birds with iridescent green plumage wheeled beyond the lip of the cliff, giving soft cries that sounded more catlike than birdlike. It was all so very close to Earth yet *not*, in a way that was somewhat unnerving, like a doll that was a little too lifelike.

From where I sat I had an excellent view of the sea to my left and the mountains rising behind the palace to my right, and I realized the gazebo had likely been situated for that. My gaze swept over the mountain range and stopped at a section that just looked *wrong*. A chill raced down my spine. I squinted and realized that the dip in that area wasn't a natural valley but a massive crater, large enough to have taken out half a mountain. *More signs of the cataclysm. The decimated location of another ancient valve.*

A scrape of sound on the steps drew my attention. I turned as a woman dressed in a sumptuous, deep turquoise velvet gown and a rich, dark blue, hooded cloak stepped into the gazebo. Probably in her early twenties, she had long and lush chestnut hair and big brown eyes. Her gaze fell on me, and then a huge smile spread across her face.

"Oh my god!" she exclaimed. "Detective Gillian!"

"Ummm," I replied in a remarkable display of intelligence. How the hell did this woman know who I was, and why would she call me *that*? "Yes?"

She moved to the bench near mine, beaming. "You don't remember. It's me . . . Michelle." Apparently I still looked utterly baffled because she added, "Michelle Cleland." She laughed. "I guess I looked pretty shitty the last time you saw me."

My jaw dropped. This was Michelle Cleland? The last time I'd seen her she'd been tied up in the middle of the Symbol Man's summoning circle. A crack addict who'd turned tricks to score more drugs, she'd been an easy target for the serial killer. Now I could see that, yes, the features were the same, but holy crap, the difference! No longer the pinched and gaunt look of an addict, her skin and hair glowed with vibrant health, and she'd filled out to where she was now slender instead of skinny. But more importantly, she looked happy.

"Damn . . . Michelle!" I began to grin. "You look amazing! Wow. I guess things have been okay for you here?"

"It's been awesome," she said with a warm smile as she arranged the cloak around her. "This may sound kinda lame, but thank you. I know you saved me." She dropped her eyes to her hands and then brought them back up to mine. "Coming here saved my life. I know that."

"You have no idea how glad I am to see you're doing so well," I said. "To be honest, I had no idea what really happened to you after the ritual." I grimaced. "For the longest time I thought you were dead."

"I would have been dead pretty damn soon if all that stuff hadn't happened to me," Michelle admitted. "God, I was such a mess." She lifted a hand and brushed a strand of hair back from her face. "I know I'm not perfect now but . . ." She laughed and gestured to herself. "I never even dreamed I could be like this!"

"You look like a damn princess," I said with total approval. "So, tell me what happened. Rhyzkahl took you back, but do you still live with him?" Surely I would have seen her before now, right?

She shook her head, curls bouncing. “Nope. I’m with Lord Vahl. I was a mess when I got here, and it was only a coupla days before Lord Rhyzkahl sent me to Lord Vahl, accompanied by a reyza.” She bit her lip prettily. “He’s taken real good care of me. Got my habit fixed up an’ everything. God, he treats me like a queen. Me!” She laughed. “It’s like a fairy tale.”

I peered at her. “You’re really okay?” I asked. “I mean, you’re not having to do anything you don’t want to, are you?” I narrowed my eyes. “Because if so, you let me know.” Yeah, I was totally in a position to lay down a warning to this Lord Vahl. Riiight.

Her smile widened. “Nope, nothing like that. There’s sex, y’know, but it’s all cool. I’ve never been forced or anything.” Her mouth twitched, and a faint flush crept across her face. “And the sex is damn good, too.”

“I’m really happy for you,” I said sincerely. “That’s the best news I’ve had in a while.”

“So what are you doing here?” Michelle asked, tilting her head. “Back on earth I had nooooo idea you were a summoner.” She laughed. “Or even that there was such a thing, ’cept on TV or something.”

“Yeah, I’m a summoner.” I leaned forward and rested my elbows on my knees. “In fact I’m Lord Rhyzkahl’s summoner, which, um, has made things kind of,” I paused, grimaced, “interesting. I was summoned here against my will, then got away from the lord who did that and came here.” I tugged a hand through my hair. “Honestly, I’m still trying to figure out what’s going on and what to do.”

Her smile slipped, and her forehead puckered in worry. “That sounds scary. I mean, the not knowing part.

“Yeah,” I agreed. “And I miss home.” Two days until Rhyzkahl could send me home. I could last two more days, right?

“Oh . . . oh! You must be ‘the girl’!” At my baffled look she continued. “Right before we left, Vahl said something about coming here because of the conclave and that Lord Rhyzkahl had gotten the girl back.” She shrugged. “No big deal, just realized that had to be you.”

I straightened, doing my best to make it seem casual instead of the somewhat startled reaction that it was. “I can’t imagine there's anyone else it could be." I gave her a look of oh-so-casual query. "Did he say anything else?"

"Not much," she replied. "I asked him what girl, and he laughed and said, 'One that Rhyzkahl really needs.'" She shrugged again. "I guess if you're his sworn summoner that makes a lot of sense."

"Yeah, I suppose so," I replied. *Really needs? For what? To summon him to Earth once a month?*

An oddly familiar discordance, like a high-pitched mental whine, distracted me from my troubled musings. I cast my gaze around but didn't see anything out of the ordinary. Still, I stood up, uneasy.

The shimmer repeated, and this time I remembered where I'd felt it before. "Michelle, I think you need to go find Lord Vahl."

"Is something wrong?" Michelle asked.

"Not sure," I lied. "Best to be safe and find your lord. I need to find Rhyzkahl."

She gave a nervous nod. "Yeah . . . sure. Thanks, Kara." She picked up her skirts and hurried off to the palace. I watched long enough to be sure she was heading back, then took off at a run down the other path.

Once inside, I stopped the first demon I encountered, a faas whose name I couldn't remember. "Where's Rhyzkahl?" I asked, panting for breath. "Something's wrong."

It peered at me. "Wrong what?"

"Anomaly," I told it.

It let out a low squeak. "Rhyzzzzzkahl in plexus!"

"Okay. Where the hell is that?" I had no idea *what* it was either, but that would have to wait.

The demon took off running, and I hurried to follow. I quickly lost track of the various turnings, and ups and downs of stairs, but eventually the faas stopped at the end of a long hall in front of intricately carved double doors. Breathless, I thanked the faas, who dipped its head in acknowledgment before scurrying off. I raised my hand to pound on the door, but Rhyzkahl yanked it open before I could touch it. Behind him I caught a glimpse of shifting globes of light over a stone pedestal and basin much like the one in Szerain's shrine. He leveled a frown at me as he stepped into the hall and grabbed my hand. "Come," he said, closing the door and my view of whatever the orb stuff was.

"You feel it too?" I asked, trotting along as he moved quickly down the corridor.

"Not yet. Olihr notified me. He and the rest of the syraza—" He gave me a sharp look without breaking stride. "You can feel the anomaly?"

"Yeah, I felt it when I was out in the gardens and ran in here to find you."

"How did you feel it?" he asked, near bounding up the stairs and forcing me to break into a jog.

"I, uh, the grove told me," I said, instantly feeling silly for saying it that way, though I didn't know how else to explain it.

His grip tightened on my hand. "The grove told you—*how*?"

I winced at his grip and struggled to keep up. "I don't know. I felt something weird, like an imbalance." I scowled. "It's not like it called me up and said, 'Yo, Kara, some weird shit's going down. Deal with it, girl!'"

We reached a main corridor but by this point I was so hopelessly lost I didn't know if we were on the ground floor or the damn attic. This place really could have used some signs with maps and *You are here* arrows on them.

Rhyzkahl pulled me next to the wall, released my hand, and gave me a hard look. "Stay right here and do not move. The anomaly is within the palace and has the potential for catastrophic damage." He moved off, then stopped and looked back at me. "Stay there," he commanded again, as if suspecting I might have a tendency to do my own thing.

I put my hands on my hips and gave him a sour look.

He narrowed his eyes, perhaps sensing my capacity for obstinance, then turned and headed rapidly off.

A few seconds later I heard voices coming down the corridor behind me, conversing rapidly in demon. I remained where I was at the side of the corridor and folded my hands over my chest as the voices approached. I didn't have long to wait before a pair of lords turned a corner and proceeded toward me. Rayst and Seretis, the last two lords to arrive.

Seretis gave me a quick glance and smile as he moved swiftly past, but Rayst motioned to me.

"Come, it is this way," he said. "You can help lay the structure."

I moved to follow but caught myself just in time, grimacing. "Rhyzkahl told me to stay here."

He stopped. "Here? *Now?*" He shook his head and gave me a smile. "You are needed elsewhere. It will help much to have you anchor the foundation."

I hadn't the faintest clue what he was talking about. I *really* wanted to see what was going on, but at the same time I did try hard not to be extraordinarily stupid. "Rhyzkahl will kick my ass if I move. For real."

Rayst chuckled, then muttered something in demon that had Rhyzkahl's name in it. He flicked a lasso of potency around my wrist and raised an eyebrow. "It is simple. You will tell him I ordered you to come, bound you in potency, and dragged you with me."

"Okay, okay! No dragging necessary." I grinned, but there was a teensy part of me that wondered if he would.

"Excellent. Now come!" He headed off down the corridor, and I followed. He still had the lasso lightly wrapped around my wrist, but he had yet to so much as tug on it.

"I am Rayst," he told me as we walked. "And the one who flew by you, Seretis."

"I'm Kara Gillian," I replied with a smile. "It's an honor to meet you."

"Honor and greetings to you, Kara Gillian." He stopped at a cross corridor, brow creasing as if trying to determine which way to go.

"This way," I said, pointing to the right. I could sense the anomaly, like a knot in an otherwise smooth thread.

Rayst glanced that way, nodded. "You can feel it. Excellent perception."

I led the way now, taking a left at yet another corridor, finally coming out into an indoor courtyard. The ceiling was four stories above, and mezzanines encircled the open space. Half in and half out of a wood-paneled wall, a soccer ball-sized anomaly pulsed and spun. Like the tiny one I'd seen with Ilana at Szerain's place, it alternately radiated and sucked light back into itself, each shift sending a shiver of discordance through me.

Rayst eyed the aberration warily as he recalled the lasso from my wrist. "The syraza are aloft working the vertex. We will construct the binder here." He swept his arm in an arc a few feet from the thing. "Set a quadrant of portal anchors. That will be very useful."

Portal anchors. I could handle that. Maybe. I mean, I was pretty sure I could, though I'd never done them in a quadrant before. I started to turn toward the perimeter, then grimaced. "Wait, I can't." Sighing, I tapped the damn collar. "I can't touch the arcane."

Rayst snorted softly, reached and slid his hands around my neck, then slipped the collar off.

"Thanks," I said, smiling in relief as my sense of the arcane flowed in. "But you know I have to blame that on you as well, right? I'll throw you right under the bus, I'm warning you now."

"Since it is already done, agreed," he replied, eyes flashing with humor.

With the collar off I could see more of the anomaly. In the light phase, brilliant rays flashed from it. In the dark phase, all light sucked into it, and even the room dimmed. I moved to where Rayst had indicated and began to puzzle out how to do a quadrant of anchors. I finally set it up in the way that made the most sense to me, yet after a few minutes I had to wonder if I was doing it wrong. I felt as if I was wrestling six octopuses at once. Was it supposed to be this difficult?

"Ah, Rhyzkahl comes, and he is not pleased," Rayst said, smiling as if that was a good thing. With a few flicks of his hand he set sigils around my quadrant, though I thought I caught a slight frown as his gaze took in how I was holding the anchors. "Now set a basic *ktirem* to hold it stable, and we have our foundation."

"A . . . what?" I could barely hold the anchors. How the hell was I supposed to do something else, assuming I even knew what it was?

"A *ktirem*," he repeated. He quickly traced an unfamiliar pattern and anchored it to the quadrant. "You can hold it, yes?

Gulping, I shook my head, oddly embarrassed at my fumbling efforts. The quadrant had been bad enough, but now I felt like I was trying to sprint while wearing a loaded backpack. "I don't know how," I gasped. "I'm sorry."

Rayst exhaled, brow furrowing as he took in the structure of my anchors. "Why do you have it—" He shook his head, leaving the sentence unfinished, but I had a feeling it was something like "Why do you have it in that godawful fucked up configuration?" or something similar. I had to be doing something wrong. Why else would I already be so wiped out?

But obviously Rayst didn't have time right now to teach me how to do it properly. He quickly laid strands of potency on each of my anchors, then gathered them and passed them to me. "Now hold that like you would a veil for a portal. All you need do is not let go."

I gathered the strands to me, relieved and ashamed, feeling as if I'd just been handed training wheels. Rhyzkahl entered with long strides, angry cast to his face as he took note of my presence. He stopped across from me and began to add to Rayst's pattern. "You were not to move," he said, eyes going from me to Rayst.

"He forced me," I said breathlessly, jerking my chin toward Rayst and giving him a slight wink.

Rhyzkahl began to speak, but Rayst cut him off. "How far along in the *shikvihr* is she, Rhyzkahl?" Even as exhausted as I was, I could tell it was one of those probing questions like "So, what sort of books does your child read?"

Rhyzkahl's face went dark and dangerous. He began to trace fluidly, merging his work with Rayst's, but with a distinctly harsh edge. He lowered his head and spoke in demon to Rayst.

The other lord shook his head and raised an eyebrow as he replied, eyes still on Rhyzkahl. Meanwhile I wondered what the hell a shikvihr was if asking about it could piss off Rhyzkahl so much. And I couldn't even wonder that for long. The two lords were definitely having an effect on the anomaly, but each yank of their pattern sent my own strands wavering. I continued to hold, but I was fast approaching the point of not being able to do much of anything.

Rhyzkahl made a slashing gesture that sent a wave through the pattern, accompanied by a single word that I had a feeling was *Enough*, judging solely by tone and body language.

Rayst replied with two words, and I didn't have to know demon to know it was something awfully close to *Fuck you*.

The two lords worked in tense silence. I wanted to watch, see Rhyzkahl in action, but I didn't dare pull any focus away from my own pattern.

Without any warning, the anomaly disappeared with a *crack*.

My pattern collapsed along with it. I took a staggering step to the wall and slid down it. Sitting felt like a *really* good idea at the moment. How the hell could Idris do all this stuff so easily? *What the hell am I doing wrong?*

Rhyzkahl straightened, gave a slight nod to Rayst in what was probably effusive thanks, considering his current mood, then said a single word and held out his hand, palm up. Rayst pulled the collar out from within his robes. My heart sank at the sight of the damn thing. I hated it. *Hated.* These past few minutes had been glorious, even though I clearly didn't know what the hell I was doing. How could I possibly go back to being so muzzled?

But to my surprise, Rayst paused before setting it in Rhyzkahl's open hand. "Why the need for the collar, Rhyzkahl?"

Rhyzkahl snatched it from Rayst's grasp. "Because there are eight other qaztahl in my domain," he practically snarled. "And I do not care to have her touched."

"Ah, yes," Rayst said. "A valid concern most assuredly. Then why not simply add an addition to the guest oath specifying that she is not to be deeply read?" He smiled. "I will gladly offer mine first."

Well, this was interesting. I stayed very still and quiet and did my best not to draw any attention to myself.

Rhyzkahl's gaze remained intense upon Rayst. "Then offer it," he snapped, followed by a phrase in demon. I frowned. Why couldn't Rhyzkahl have done this from the start so that I didn't have to wear the collar?

Rayst repeated the sentence in demon while swirling the fingers of his right hand against his left palm, coalescing a marble-sized sphere of potency. He offered it to Rhyzkahl with another few words that sounded formulaic. Rhyzkahl took it and said something back, then tightened his hand around the glowing ball. When he opened his hand again the ball was gone.

Apparently satisfied, Rayst glanced back to where I sat oh-so-elegantly against the wall. "Kara, you need rest."

I gave him a weary smile. "Yeah, I'm gonna sit for a bit first." Rayst took a step toward me.

"*I* will tend my summoner," Rhyzkahl nearly snarled as he moved swiftly to my side and crouched.

"Sorry," I said with a grimace. "I guess I overdid it a bit."

"You did well, dear one," he said, touching my cheek before lifting me smoothly in his arms.

I looked over at Rayst with a warm smile. "Thanks," I said, meaning it on several levels.

"Rest well, Kara Gillian," he replied, then turned back to clean up the residuals of the anomaly while Rhyzkahl departed with me.

As the distance from Rayst increased, the tension in Rhyzkahl faded, leaving me wondering if the two had some sort of antagonistic history. Rayst seemed perfectly nice to me, but I'd been fooled by an easy smile before. There was every chance I was only seeing what he wanted me to see.

I leaned my head against his chest, enjoying the warm feeling of being carried and cared for. Rhyzkahl cradled me close, murmuring something in demon as he walked.

"Why didn't you have the lords swear from the beginning not to read me so I wouldn't have to wear that stupid collar?" I asked.

A measure of the tension returned to his neck and shoulders. "The collar was far safer for you and for my interests," he said, then exhaled. "Yet I sensed how deeply you despise it, which is why I accepted Rayst's compromise. The lords will still be able to read your surface thoughts, but none will dare delve once I have secured their oaths."

"Thanks," I said, relieved. I was damn glad to see the last of that stupid thing. "What's a shikvihr?" I asked, unable to hold back the yawn.

He didn't answer for several heartbeats. "A shikvihr is a ritual foundation," he finally said.

"Y'gonna teach me?" I yawned again, eyelids heavy.

"I will teach you many things," he replied as he entered my rooms. He set me on the bed and tugged my boots and pants off, then pulled the covers up over me.

I reached for his hand. "Stay with me."

Rhyzkahl hesitated, then sank to sit on the edge of the bed. A smile touched his mouth, but it seemed somewhat pained. "I will abide for a time."

"Is something wrong?"

He looked away, silent for a moment. "These times are so uncertain and perilous. There is much treachery." He shifted his gaze back to me, gently pushed my hair away from my face and leaned in to kiss me lightly before sitting up again. "I feel it keenly with those who are within these walls."

I gave his hand a light tug. "Then lie down with me and forget all that for a while."

"I cannot. I must secure the oaths of the other lords, and the conclave meets again shortly." His face went unreadable then softened. "I have something I would like to show you tomorrow," he said. "Come to me in the great hall after the midday bell, and I will take you there."

I lifted an eyebrow, intrigued. "What is it?"

"The plexus—where you found me before we dealt with the anomaly. It is where I adjust the planetary flows of the arcane as well as those for my realm."

"I can't wait," I said, fighting to keep my eyes open. Finally, I gave up the struggle and drifted off to the feel of him lightly stroking my hair.

Chapter 15

The next morning the weather confined my explorations to the indoors. Grey and frigid rain sheeted down with possibly some sleet thrown in for good measure, to judge by the hissing patter against the windows. Fortunately there was a shitload of palace to explore, though more than once I wished I had a tour guide to explain some of the features. Demons lurked everywhere I went, and I had no doubt that I was being watched. None, however, approached to offer any sort of guidance.

My wanderings took me past two large kitchens—one dark and quiet, and the other bustling with *luhrek* and faas hard at work—then through a sizable, empty dining hall and into a glassed arboretum, warm and moist despite the chill outside. Butterflies and furry hummingbirds flitted among the flowering trees, and little demon-lizards scurried away here and there. I sat for a while by a burbling pool, contemplating a climb to the snug tree house tucked high into the branches above, before giving up the notion for the moment and heading out again. Eventually, I located the summoning chamber as well as a library that took up several floors. I would have gladly spent the rest of the day there, but the midday bell came before I could even set foot inside.

With a sigh of regret and a mental promise to return, I closed the library door and headed to the great hall, rather proud of myself when I actually managed to find it with only one or two wrong turns—though I ended up coming in through some sort of antechamber instead of the main corridor. My steps slowed as I entered and saw that Rhyzkahl was far from alone. A slim, dark-haired lord who I could only assume was Jesral and, *ugh,* Kadir were at the base of the right staircase, while Rhyzkahl stood in the center of the hall with Amkir, apparently in deep conversation.

I dawdled near the door through which I'd entered, since I didn't want to interrupt, and I sure as hell didn't want to make some sort of stupid social error. I tried to tell myself that this gave me a chance to see what I could of the other lords, but the drawback to that was they could do the same to me. Kadir's violet gaze slid to me like an oily touch, and I carefully avoided any eye contact.

Thankfully it was only a few seconds before Rhyzkahl looked my way and gestured me over. Amkir turned and watched as I approached, dark eyes keen upon me like a hawk on a mouse. His predatory regard unnerved me, but I did my best not to show it.

"Kara Gillian," Rhyzkahl stated in a formal tone. "You are honored by the presence of Lord Amkir."

I turned my attention to Amkir, fairly sure that his eyes hadn't left me this whole time. I had a feeling there was some sort of protocol I was expected to follow, but since I was basically clueless I had to hope I could muddle along and fake it. I gave the lord a slight bow. "It is indeed my honor to meet you, Lord Amkir."

His eyes remained hard upon me, clearly assessing my worth. "Kri," he murmured, then curled his lip and said another word I didn't quite catch, though judging from tone and inflection, it probably wasn't a compliment.

I flicked a glance to Rhyzkahl in hopes that he would either translate or intervene, but he looked away as Jesral called out something to him. He glanced back at Amkir. "I will return." Then he strode off toward Jesral without another word.

Shit. I really didn't want to stay here, but even without knowing specific protocols, I had no doubt that ditching this lord would be considered pretty damn rude. I forced a smile for Amkir, reminding myself that I'd been in plenty of social situations where I had to talk to someone with whom I wasn't totally comfortable. Not that there was much talking going on. He'd yet to say a word to me in English, and I wasn't about to start a conversation.

"Make yourself useful," he abruptly said, eyes fiery and

face hard. "Bring me wine." He flicked his gaze toward a table by the wall. Wine and glasses were there, as well as a faas perfectly ready to serve as needed.

I kept my face as immobile as possible. Rhyzkahl was still deep in conversation with his back to me, so there was no hope of rescue from that quarter. Fine then. I had no desire to make a scene. I could suck up some hazing for a few minutes. I gave Amkir a tight nod and smile, then turned and headed for the wine. I poured quickly and returned at a brisk walk, though not from any desire to leap to his bidding. I simply wanted to get this shit over with.

"Your wine, Lord Amkir," I said, holding the glass out for him.

He made no move to take the glass from me. "You dare offer me that which you have touched?" His lip curled in revulsion. "Pour again and do so properly," he ordered. His right hand twitched as if he was barely holding himself back from striking me for my affront.

I took two steps back from him, just in case, then turned and went back to the damn wine table, mentally tracing the stupid fucking pygah to calm my impulse to tell Amkir where he could shove his wine glass. I poured again, this time holding the glass in a napkin. Rhyzkahl still hadn't glanced my way and seemed intent on his discussion with Jesral, but by this point I'd decided that I'd give Amkir his fucking wine and then go wait somewhere else. Because this was bullshit.

"*Chikdah*," he murmured as I returned, followed by something else that probably was not *Thank you, oh so much!* I didn't need to know the language to know that "chikdah" meant "cunt" or something equally charming. Yeah, this asshole was a regular sweetheart.

Too late, I remembered that the lords could still read surface thoughts. Amkir's eyes blazed with anger as he snatched the glass from my hand. Before I had time to even flinch, he threw the wine in my face, then hurled the glass toward the wall.

I gasped in shock. "Are you *fucking* kidding me? What is your goddamn issue, asshole?" Instantly, I knew my response was a mistake. It was as if I watched the words come out of my mouth in slow motion, completely unable to stop the torrential flow.

Amkir snarled in what could only be satisfaction. With lightning speed he lifted a hand and open-hand slapped me in a strike that sent me staggering. Even as I reeled back he stepped toward me, hand raised for another strike. I lashed out at him with a punch to the chest that sent him stumbling back awkwardly . . .

. . . and I suddenly realized that I hadn't actually touched him.

Grove power thrummed through and over me as I faced Amkir. I was pretty sure I looked awesome as shit, glowy and all, but I wasn't about to stop and check myself out in the nearest mirror.

Black fury filled Amkir's face as he recovered. Strands of potency like long writhing whips coalesced in one fist as he regained his footing, and I had no doubt he intended to put my ass *down*.

I heard Rhyzkahl shout something in demon. I couldn't understand the word, yet I had a sense of the meaning nonetheless—an unexpected benefit of holding the grove power. *Hold* or something close to it. But Amkir either didn't hear or chose to ignore him. Snarling, he drew back his hand and lashed the whips of potency toward me.

Crying out, I threw my hands up while I struggled to form the power I held into some sort of block or shield. Rhyzkahl moved with demonic lord speed, catching Amkir's wrist so that only three of the lashes barely grazed me. Even the light graze stung like crazy. Rhyzkahl snarled something to Amkir, the gist of which seemed to be "stand down."

"Kara Helene Gillian. Subside now," Rhyzkahl said over his shoulder in an *I am SO not fucking around* voice.

I held the power, breath coming raggedly, but I knew there was no way for me to win this. I was going to have to trust Rhyzkahl to keep Amkir from turning me into bloody mist. I released the power and straightened, controlling the shudder as normal sensation returned. I gave Amkir a parting sneer and turned, back prickling as I stalked to the door, absolutely certain that I'd get a ball of power between the shoulder blades any second now. I was almost shocked to reach the door unscathed.

As soon as I ducked through and shut the door behind me I began to tremble. *What the fuck just happened?* I wondered, utterly bewildered and shaken. I began to pace in an attempt to burn off the excess adrenaline. What the hell had I done to warrant that attack?

My steps slowed as I felt a flare of potency beyond the door. I heard and felt a *crack*, and then the potency faded, only to be replaced by voices raised in argument. I wasn't holding the grove power anymore, but some of the sense of the words still came through to me. Something from Amkir about some important thing that had to be completed, and something from Rhyzkahl about getting the fuck out of his fucking palace.

I felt a change of pressure in the air behind me. I spun, expecting another attack, but to my shock it was a syraza, swaying and breathing heavily.

I stared for barely a split second before throwing myself at her and wrapping her in an embrace. I'd only seen her in syraza form for a couple of minutes after I'd summoned her back on Earth, but I knew without a doubt who this was.

"Eilahn," I said, nearly crying in relief at the sight of her. "Holy shit, you're okay. I missed you. Oh, man." Okay, maybe I was really crying.

She chimed in worried tones and wrapped arms around me. "What have you done? What have they done?"

"It's okay, it's okay," I said, gulping back tears of relief and joy. "I didn't grovel when I was supposed to, I guess, and one of those dickwad lords tried to smack me down." I held her close, so insanely glad to have her here. "Rhyzkahl stopped him, but I wasn't going down without a fight." I gave a weak laugh.

She pulled back enough to run hands over me and search my face, as if making absolutely certain I was untouched. "Here is more complicated than Earth because you do not know all the rules," she told me, but her eyes were dark with worry.

I grimaced and nodded. "Yeah, I'm starting to see that." I pushed back the wave of homesickness and hugged her again. "I'm so damn glad to see you." A tremble went through her, and I looked up at her, worried. "Are you all right?" Now I could see that she seemed almost transparent, without the lovely shimmering vibrancy the other syrazas had. "Do you need to sit?"

She folded not very gracefully to a semi cross-legged position, one knee pulled up against her chest. "Better thus, Kara. I left stasis when I felt your distress, but I will be all right for a while. You sit and tell me what happened." Her eyes stayed upon me, assessing.

I sat down beside her, and she curled a wing around me. I gave her a rundown of what happened, trying hard not to leave out any detail in case she could point out something I'd done to set the asshole lord off.

"Amkir most assuredly goaded you," Eilahn said once I'd finished. "Yet I cannot fathom why." She tilted her head and gave me a *look* that told me she knew just how I could be when pushed. She trilled and chimed softly. "To assure that you were not harmed, Lord Rhyzkahl laid hands upon Amkir." She made a sharp little sound. "Intervention by arcane means would have been a much cleaner way. Not as many complications. It would have certainly stopped Amkir, though it may not have done so before he loosed upon you." She shook her head, then let out a soft, trilling laugh. "You do get yourself into trouble when I am not with you, do you not?"

I smiled weakly. "It's my nature." Then I gave a soft sigh. "I'm so glad you're all right." My brow furrowed. "You *are* all right, aren't you?"

"Yes, Kara. Very much so, though I will need to return to stasis soon. Do not worry." She gave me a squeeze with arms and wing.

She felt like barely a wisp in my arms as I hugged her back. Releasing a shuddering breath I stood, worried about her despite her admonition. "I'm okay. I promise," I assured her. "You go back. I'm all right here, and Rhyzkahl's sending me back home tomorrow."

She reached and took hold of my hand, worry in her face seeming to deepen. "If you return to Earth, stay within wards until I can return. I must abide in stasis for a time yet. At least a month of your time most likely. You *must* try to summon me every day until I come to you. No place is truly safe, but there you are terribly exposed." Her hand tightened on mine. "Give me your oath that you will do this—remain behind wards until you summon me."

Nodding, I squeezed her hand. "Eilahn, I give you my oath that I will hunker down in my house and be a regular hermit until you can come back and be my kickass demon bodyguard again."

A small measure of the worry in her expression abated, yet she didn't smile. "Oh, Kara, I must go. Please take care, and look deep into your essence to know who to trust."

And then she was gone. I stood motionless for a moment, while I turned her words over in my head. Who to trust? Frowning, I left the antechamber and headed away from the great hall. Right now, I only trusted the people who didn't want to hurt me. That seemed simple enough.

Alone, I made my way back to the library with the intent of finding something with which to pass the rest of the day and also, hopefully, to avoid contact with any other damn lords. My thigh still stung from Amkir's lash, and I had no doubt that his slap had left a bruise on my cheek. Assholes, all of them. Even Rhyzkahl for not putting a stop to it sooner.

The library held tomes, scrolls, and normal-sized books too, as well as a variety of unknown gadgets and even a section of Earth clocks, most really really old. Paintings hung in alcoves and on the walls, some reminding me of styles I'd seen on Earth. Many, I was sure, were Szerain's work. There were even framed photographs of Earth subjects—the Eiffel Tower, an aerial of the Giza plateau, details of the Great Wall of China, and so much more. But more intriguing were photographs of places, creatures, and demons of the demon realm. That started a whole cascade of speculation on the acquisition of it all. With the mix of books, art, and artifacts, I decided this was a combination library and museum.

I didn't understand how the library was organized, but after a bit of wandering I managed to locate a large section of books that were written in something other than the demon language. Wards flickered along the shelves, and I quickly realized that they were there to protect the books from the various ravages of time. This place was a rare book dealer's wet dream. There were books in damn near every Earth language, including some I wasn't sure even existed anymore, and some ancient, handwritten volumes that I had no doubt predated the invention of the printing press. Many of the English language books were in an old English that proved difficult to read, but I eventually located a section of more modern English, including fiction titles of everything from Harry Potter to John Steinbeck to paperback romances. I grinned at the thought of a zhurn curled up reading a book with Fabio on the cover.

I spied a copy of *The Hobbit* and pulled it off the shelf. Ryan loved this sort of stuff, so maybe it was worth a try. There was a comfy-looking chaise near the end of the stacks, and I headed that way. But an alcove caught my eye before I reached the chaise, and I paused. Like the other alcoves, it held a picture of some sort, though this one was covered, draped in dark red silk.

Curious, I pulled the silk aside and off, revealing the sweet face of Elinor on the painting beneath. The painting exuded *life*, marking it most likely as a work of Szerain. Elinor stood on steps, her hand resting on a luminescent column, and blue sky behind her framed by more columns. *The ruins before they were ruins*, I realized. She wore a simple, pretty dress of rich green that seemed to shimmer though it was only paint. Her eyes reflected life and innocence and wonder, and her mouth curved in a smile that seemed to touch me centuries later.

"It should remain covered," Rhyzkahl said from behind me.

I startled, then turned with a mild scowl. "She was a pretty girl. Why do you hide her away like this?"

Face tight, he passed by me and picked up the red silk. "Because I prefer it that way," he said, reaching high and re-covering the painting.

I folded my arms over my chest. "Why? Because you want to forget all about her?"

He remained with his back to me, hands gripping the sides of the frame. "I cannot forget her," he said, voice low and dark. "And I require no reminder."

I stayed silent for a moment, feeling the pain in his voice. "How did she die?" I finally asked. "I've been told it was because of the gate, but . . ." Flickers of memory stirred in confusing patterns. "But there was more. I *know* it."

Rhyzkahl gripped the frame hard enough to dislodge the cover again. Elinor smiled out as the silk puddled to the floor like a pool of blood. "There was a disruption in the ritual and it spiraled out of control." He seemed to force the words out between his teeth. "She could not stop it. Szerain could not stop it, and she died."

"And you have no idea what that disruption was?" I persisted. "Was it something she did? Or was it Szerain?" I knew I poked at a tender spot, yet my lingering anger about the incident in the main foyer urged me on. "Did you train her? Was she prepared to do this gate? Mzatal said she wasn't much of a summoner, so why was she doing something like this in the first place?"

Rhyzkahl let out a shuddering breath. "Mzatal released her from training." He lifted the cover back over the portrait, then turned to face me. "Szerain and I trained her. She was well enough prepared for her part in the ritual." He paused, anger flashing briefly over his face. "Szerain failed in his support."

My eyes narrowed. "What *was* her part in the ritual?"

"Simply to open the gateway," he said. "Nothing more. Szerain had all other aspects." His right hand clenched into a fist and a muscle leaped in his jaw. "He proceeded without my leave."

I snorted. "Seems a lot of lords do things without your leave." My cheek still ached with the evidence of that.

"Amkir," he murmured, as if only now remembering that I'd been struck. He came closer and laid a hand on my cheek. "They do not do so without reprisal."

"Oh, please," I said, scowling. "What, you'll give him a slap on the wrist? He was a complete *dick* to me, for no reason! He'd have seriously hurt me if you hadn't grabbed his damn arm in time. Then what? 'Oh, Amkir, you naughty boy. You broke my toy!' "

But Rhyzkahl shook his head. "It is not a 'slap on the wrist,' as you phrase it. He suffers my retribution even now."

"And what would that be?" I asked, dubious.

"It involves power flows and is not a matter for humans . . . even you, dear one. He suffers." Anger stirred behind his eyes, and I found myself believing that Rhyzkahl truly had smacked Lord Asshole down.

Sighing, I ran a hand through my hair. "Why did he do that to me?" I asked, still utterly baffled. "I mean . . . it was like he hated me from first sight. Did I do something?"

Rhyzkahl dropped his hand from my cheek then

crouched and ran it over my thigh, easing the sting from the lashes. "Amkir needs no reason," he said, straightening again. "He can most assuredly be harsh with humans."

"Then why did you leave me alone with him?" I asked, annoyed again. "He was hostile from the start, even while you were still there."

"He has been long from humans and overstepped bounds he would never have touched in the past. I misjudged his response." Regret colored his voice. "He will not err thus again, nor will I."

I looked up at him, meeting his eyes. "I need to know I'm safe here," I said. "That's the whole damn reason I came here when I got away from Mzatal."

He caught my face between his hands. "You have nothing to fear now from these visiting lords," he said. "I have seen to it."

"All right," I sighed, then put my arms around him. "I'm trusting you on this."

He tipped my head up and kissed me, a slow and tender show of reassurance that quickly deepened. Whatever the hell kind of relationship Rhyzkahl and I had, even if everything else was weird as shit, this part was pretty damn decent.

He slid his hands beneath my shirt to stroke my back, then broke the kiss to nuzzle my neck. "I once told you I wished to fuck you in every room of my palace," he said, lips moving against my skin. "This one is as yet un-christened."

I laughed low in my throat, already fired by his words. "So you did." I gave a mock sigh. "But I don't know if sex in a library can be all that exciting."

He pulled my shirt down over one shoulder, lowered his head and bit gently. "Then you do not know much and require tutelage."

I dropped my head back. "And I suppose you think you can teach me?" I breathed.

His hand slid up to fondle my breast. He bit again, harder this time, then moved to catch my earlobe in his teeth. "Most definitely," he whispered.

And he did.

Chapter 16

In addition to the library, we ended up christening two more rooms—the tree house of the arboretum and a storage room full of furniture—finally ending up back in my rooms where I eventually fell asleep curled up in his arms, exhausted and sated.

I didn't expect Rhyzkahl to still be there in the morning, and, of course, he wasn't. At first I thought I'd slept a lot later than I'd intended because of the amount of light in the room. It wasn't until I got up and actually looked out the window that I realized why it was so bright.

I let out a squeal. "It snowed!" Not only had it snowed, it *still* snowed, flakes drifting down, adding to the thick layer already on the ground and coating rocks and trees and buildings alike. All but the grove, which shimmered green and purple, untouched by the white blanket.

I tore through the available clothing and found a variety of Earth-type cold-weather garb. Boots, hat, gloves, and scarf went over a ridiculous number of layers. I looked like a total dork, but I didn't care.

I hurried down the stairs and to the broad doors that led to the large back lawn. Kehlirik was crouched inside the doors with a book in his hand, and I smiled in relief at seeing him again. My smile spread to a grin when I saw that he was reading *A Game of Thrones.* Oh, I was *so* getting him hooked on television as soon as I got back home.

"It snowed!" I announced, then dashed outside with an unabashed whoop of delight.

Kehlirik set the book down and followed me out as I tromped through what was easily eight inches of snow. He peered at me curiously as I launched into my first-ever attempt to make a snowman.

"Yes, it has snowed," he said. "This brings strong reaction in you?"

"We don't get snow where I live," I told him as I made a sloppy attempt to roll snow into a large ball for the base of my snowman. "I mean, not more than a scuzzy inch or two."

The demon snorted, watching me with open curiosity. "There are other demons who will clear the snow for you."

"I don't want them to clear it for me," I said, slightly breathless. "I want to make snowmen and snow angels and all the stuff I've heard you can do in snow." *I want to have fun*, I added silently as I rolled up a second, smaller ball and placed it atop the first. *I want to forget I'm trapped here and forget how much I miss Jill and Ryan and Tessa and Zack.*

Kehlirik made a huffing sound and poked a claw at my partial snowman. I gave him a sidelong glance as I rolled up the third ball and stuck it on top of the others. "Y'all have fun and play sometimes, right?" I knew the demons seemed to have any number of games, but I had no idea how spontaneous they were, if at all.

"Yes, we play games."

I scanned the area for sticks or rocks or anything to decorate the snowman, but whoever had the job of cleaning up the lawn was apparently pretty damn meticulous. Giving up on the snow sculpture for now, I crouched and packed together a snowball.

"Do y'all ever do snowball fights?" I asked, eyeing him with a sly grin.

He spread his wings and dropped into a menacing crouch, low growl throbbing in his throat. I laughed and let fly with the snowball at him, but he ducked it with ease. In the next instant he took flight, letting out a trumpeting bellow.

"Hey, no fair!" I shouted, laughing as I hurriedly made more snowballs and threw them at the airborne reyza.

I yelped as a snowball smacked me in the back of the head. I whirled to see a faas ducking behind a pillar.

Apparently Kehlirik's bellow had been a "game on!" signal to the rest of the demons. What followed next was the most insanely chaotic and glorious snowball fight in existence. Within less than a minute, the area filled with dozens of demons of damn near every variety. Chinese-dragon-faced kehza took to the air with reyza and zhurn in dog-fights to rival anything out of World War I. On the ground, a cluster of luhrek—demons resembling a cross between a dog and a goat, with the hindquarters of a lion—whipped together a fort constructed of snow and arcane scaffolding, and proceeded to lob volleys at the airborne contingent. Graa darted with lightning speed between air and ground, weaving shields of potency that formed a sting-delivering obstacle course for all players, while young savik methodically dismantled and reformed said shields and slung snowballs at the faas who darted from pillar to pillar.

For my part, I quickly abandoned any attempt at strategy or skill and simply chucked snowballs at any available target.

Another snowball smacked into my head. I spun, expecting to see the devious faas, but to my shock it was a human who ducked behind a pillar.

I stared at the dark-haired man. Tall, a bit stocky, face maddeningly familiar. And then it registered. "Holy shit. Michael?" Michael Moran was the younger brother of Lida Moran, a goth-metal singer who'd ruthlessly used Michael's abilities to create golems—actual creatures of dirt and clay—to get rid of her business rivals. Michael had suffered a head injury when he was young, which had made it far easier for Lida and her boyfriend to cruelly manipulate and use him. After the case had finally been closed—after the deaths of Lida and her boyfriend—Eilahn had suggested I send Michael to the demon realm. I'd agreed. I knew that if Michael stayed on Earth, he'd end up in an institution or even possibly jail for the rest of his life. I figured, if Eilahn said he'd have a chance at a better life, I had to go along with it. I trusted her.

He peered out from behind the pillar, smiling shyly. "Hi, Kara."

I let out a laugh and tromped through the snow to him. "How are you? You look great!" He did, too. His face looked slimmer and far less slack, and his eyes practically sparkled with life.

"You're through playing?" he asked, stepping warily out from behind the pillar in case I was still packing. "The faas are great with snowballs," he added, with another wary look around for any lurking demons. My delight in seeing him grew. It was blindingly obvious that he was more stable and coherent than before.

"Yeah, I'm done," I said, grinning, though I too scanned for faas. "And yeah, those little suckers know how to sling a snowball. They take their games pretty seriously!"

A broad smile lit his face. "And they always travel in pairs! Makes it hard to sneak up on them." His face went abruptly serious, and he looked down and away.

"Michael? What's wrong?"

He wiped at his face with the back of a gloved hand. "I'm really really sorry about all that stuff I did."

"Ah, jeez, Michael, I know you are." I put a hand on his shoulder. "I never blamed you. It's why I had you sent here, so you could have a real chance at a life."

He took a deep breath and let it out quickly. "It's really okay?" he asked, worry darkening his expression as he finally met my gaze. "I mean . . . I've been thinking about it and . . ." He trailed off, swallowing hard.

"It's okay," I reassured him firmly, giving his shoulder a squeeze. "You weren't the bad guy. You were used." I peered at him. "Are you doing okay here? I mean, you're being treated all right?"

He broke into a bright smile again. "Yep, it's the best. They even fixed my head up a bit."

"I can tell," I said, deeply pleased for him. "It's awesome. So, which lord are you with?"

"Seretis and Rayst. I even have my own piano!" He suddenly grimaced and bit his lower lip. "Uh, oh."

"What is it?"

"Lord Amkir and Seretis," he told me. "I hope he doesn't get himself blasted. *Pkkeeeww!*" he added, making a sound like an exploding potency ball.

What the hell? "Wait, who might get blasted?"

"Seretis," he said as if it was *so* obvious. His brow furrowed, and he seemed to be listening to something far away. "Rayst is in with Lord Rhyzkahl in the main hall, so no help there. Lord Vahl is in the far tower library. Lord Kadir is . . ." He grimaced, shook his head. "Elofir is out by the ruins." He paused. "I mean, it's most likely Seretis's fault. He probably made Lord Amkir mad. He's always messing with him.

I just wish he'd do it when Rayst is around." For an instant he sounded like a parent expressing the wish that his child would take his muddy shoes off outside.

I took a few seconds to process this. "Okay, so, you know where all the lords are all the time?"

"Well, *yeah*," he said, then we both flinched as the sound of some sort of arcane discharge came from within the palace—sounding almost exactly like the *pkkeeeww* sound Michael had made.

"Oh, shit," I breathed.

"It's okay," Michael quickly reassured me, head cocked. "I think Seretis stopped it okay." He rolled his eyes. "He won't stop teasing Amkir though."

"Teasing him about what?" I asked, deeply interested in any teasing of Lord Asshole.

"Seretis was teasing him about backing down from Lord Rhyzkahl yesterday."

I tried not to grin too obviously. "I think I'd like Seretis."

"He laughs a lot," Michael said. "Says lots of funny stuff." He winced as the sound of another arcane discharge reached us. "That one stung."

"Michael," I said, "can you see where Mzatal is?"

He nodded. "He's at his palace." His eyes unfocused. "Harder to tell when they're far away. His palace . . . in a dark room. He's drawing all sorts of sigils, I think."

"Is he talking to anyone?"

"Don't think so. Just scowling and drawing." He shrugged. "Hard to see."

I will retrieve you, Mzatal had said. A shiver ran through me that had nothing to do with the snow and cold. Was he working on that even now?

I dragged my thoughts away from that unsettling subject. "Do any of the lords know you can . . . hear them wherever they are?"

A frown puckered his brow. "I can't really hear unless they're pretty close, and then only sometimes," he told me. "Sometimes I can see, and sometimes I just know where they are." His shoulders lifted in a shrug. "Seretis knows, and he said not to tell any of the other lords."

"He's right. Don't tell any lord." I grimaced. "And also be careful which demons you tell." I gave him a worried look. "Michael, this is a *really* useful gift that could be used for the wrong reasons. I don't want to see you taken advantage of again."

Michael's face grew serious. "Okay, I won't. I don't want it to be like before and hurt anyone." He drew in a breath. "Seretis said they can't read it from me since my brain's messed up." A smile lit his face. "Guess that's one good thing about having a scrambled head."

"That's a damn good thing," I said fervently as I gave him a hug. "I'm so glad you're doing well."

"Thanks, Kara," he said, returning the hug. He lifted his head. "I better go. Seretis is calling me." He grinned. "I think he reflected one back at Amkir and stung him good!"

"That's what I like to hear," I said with a laugh. "Take care, Michael."

"Bye, Kara!" He turned and took off at a jog toward the nearest entrance. I watched him go, relieved and pleased that this had worked out so well for him.

A movement in an upstairs window caught my attention as I turned away. I had a feeling it was one of the lords—maybe Jesral? I didn't think it was Rhyzkahl. I tried to picture Rhyzkahl enjoying a snowball fight, but somehow I couldn't see that ever happening. *But I can see Ryan doing it*, I thought with a smile. Ryan would be right in there, slinging snowballs and shouting orders and mock threats.

But would Szerain? My smile faded.

I retreated to a boulder and watched the demons romp in the snow, but it didn't take long for the heat of exertion to wear off and the chill to creep in. Yet I wasn't ready to go back inside, to the place where I had to avoid lords and make myself scarce.

The stone path was already clear of snow, which surprised me until I saw two savik moving along the path, igniting sigils that flared to melt the snow away and keep the paths from refreezing. More snow began to fall, but in a light and powdery dusting that seemed to quiet everything to a respectful hush. I started to walk without any clear destination in mind. I wanted to explore and to stay away from the palace for a while. Glancing up, I saw Kehlirik perched on a buttress. I waved to him and he spread his wings in reply. Pyrenth wheeled overhead in complicated aerial maneuvers as if dodging the scattered snowflakes, but I still had an unerring sense that he watched me as well. I shook my head and laughed softly as I continued to wander the paths. I certainly had no fear that I wasn't well guarded.

Many of the paths ended in little nooks or grottos, each with such a different feel that I suspected they all had unique creators: a small circular pool so clear and deep that it made me dizzy looking down into it; a rock garden of huge hazy crystals which, when touched, resonated with pure tones that went right through me and made me feel cleaner; a garden I visited for no more than a few seconds because the stench from the giant flower-thing at its center was like the worst decomposed corpse I'd ever encountered. Maybe it appealed to demons, but not me.

After exploring a half dozen or so, I came to one that was clearly different from the others. I gained access through a small hedge maze, its center kept clear of snow by softly pulsing wards. A tingle similar to what I felt in Szerain's shrine raised goose bumps head to toe. There was little doubt it was carefully and meticulously maintained; the bushes didn't have even a single leaf out of place, and there wasn't a hint of dirt or debris on the precisely fitted flagstones. In the center stood a waist-high pedestal of black stone with capillaries of gold and silver running through it—an obelisk about a foot across at the base that tapered up to about half that. From the top sprang a flower so lifelike that only the fact that it was the same color as the rest of the stone told me that it wasn't real.

Rhyzkahl holds the flower out to me. "Your favorite, is it not?" I am overcome with joy. He remembered! I take it from his hand. My fingers brush his, and a thrill leaps through me. His eyes are so intent upon me. Will he kiss me? Yes, oh . . . yes, he kisses me, and I am undone. So much more than the kisses of before. I do not want it to ever end, and this time it does not! He gently bears me down to the blanket, brushes my hair from my face then pulls the laces of my dress. My heart leaps. Yes, I am ready! Oh, his touch is all that I dreamed and so much more. I am overcome as he shows me what pleasure awaits. There is only the briefest pain and even that he eases . . .

I lie spent and gasping in his arms as he traces patterns upon my bare flesh. He smiles down at me, and I want to weep again. I am a silly girl—no, not a girl anymore. I am truly a woman now.

I yanked myself out of the memory, for the first time feeling almost like a voyeur. Yet even so, curiosity tugged at me—not about Rhyzkahl popping Elinor's cherry but about Giovanni. Was he in the picture yet? Already out of it? What the hell was the deal with him anyway?

And why can't these damn shadow-memories have time and date stamps on them? I thought sourly. That would certainly make figuring all this shit out a lot easier.

Questions crowded against each other in my head as I regarded the stone flower—the same kind as the one he'd given me. There was no doubt at all that this was a shrine to Elinor. *Yet he keeps her portrait covered.* Maybe this one was all right because it was so far away from the palace? Or maybe because there was no likeness of her here?

I stroked a finger over the stone petals. Szerain carved this. It had his *feel* about it, as if at any moment it could stir in the breeze, turn its face to the winter sun. A pang of longing for Ryan struck me, accompanied by a wave of confusion. Here I was Rhyzkahl's eager bedmate, yet I clearly had strong feelings for Ryan. What the hell was wrong with me?

I needed Jill, needed her keen insight and no-nonsense attitude. I wanted desperately to tell her that, before I was summoned, Ryan told me he loved me. I badly wanted her take on it. I knew she'd frown on my feeling any sort of guilt about casual, consensual sex, but it was hard not to feel a certain amount of angst and doubt given the current situation—in all its many and gloriously fucked-up layers.

The most fucked-up of which was the possibility that Ryan wasn't . . . *real.*

Was I supposed to remain loyal to a personality that might be completely fabricated? My heart clenched at the thought that the Ryan I knew and had come to care for—and yes, even love—could simply be turned off someday. Yet I had to accept that was likely the brutal reality, especially since Turek had told me Szerain's exile couldn't be permanent.

I dropped to sit on the dry stone and tried to imagine what Jill would likely say, ticking points off on her fingers: "You're fucking Rhyzkahl because *A*, he's a hot and sexy stud who gives you lots and lots of orgasms, and *B*, because you're deliberately putting obstacles between you and Ryan to protect yourself in the event things with him don't work out."

Groaning, I dropped my head into my hands. Yep, that pretty much summed it up.

And then there was Rhyzkahl. He might not have loved Elinor, but he'd certainly cared for her. And while I had no illusions that he loved me, it was clear there was some sort of affection in play. I sighed. There was no easy answer to any of this.

Cold and confused, I made my way back to the palace.

Chapter 17

I stood at the broad window in the arboretum, arms clasped loosely around myself as I watched the demons in the yard below. They were already involved in some new game. Not that I had any clue what the rules were. Two faas hunkered on one side of the courtyard, and a zhurn and reyza stood still as statues on the other. At apparently random intervals one from each side would dash to the middle and go through a series of odd sparring type moves. But it wasn't sparring. That would be ludicrous between a faas and a reyza. After a minute, they'd break apart and go back to their side. Then later, another pair would go out and do the same thing. Lather. Rinse. Repeat. I didn't get it, but they sure looked like they were having a good time.

I should teach them football, I thought with amusement. Football with the use of the arcane, and with a variety of creatures, some of whom had the ability to fly. Yeah, that might require a few adjustments to the rules.

I let my gaze drift to the grove. I was banned from going to it, but now I knew that didn't mean it was completely inaccessible. Gently, I pulled a trickle of power, allowed myself to revel in the comfort of it.

I startled as arms encircled me from behind, then relaxed as I recognized the warm power of Rhyzkahl's presence.

"You seem pensive," he murmured. I dropped my head back against him, sighed. He brought his right hand up to lay it against the side of my face. "And you are clouded."

"No, I actually feel fine," I said. "Totally clear."

"Perhaps clear to you," he said. "Not clear to me."

I scowled. The hand on the side of my face wasn't affection. It was him trying to read me, and for whatever reason, he wasn't having much success. I pulled away and turned to face him. "Don't read my damn mind then," I said with a falsely sweet smile. "Problem solved."

Rhyzkahl tilted his head, gave me a disarming yet suggestive smile. "There are times when you most assuredly enjoy it."

Well, he had me there. There was a lot to be said for having a lover who knew exactly what revved your engines. "Okay . . . but those are the only times!" Then I sighed. "Rhyzkahl, this place is great, but I'm so ready to go home."

"It is what I came to tell you," he said. "With Jesral's assistance, the foundation has been laid for the ritual."

"Really?" I smiled broadly. "I'm going home?"

He slid his arms around me. "Tonight, yes. It is a difficult and complex ritual to open a portal without a summoner working the pattern," he cautioned. "But I am confident that I will be able to guide you as needed."

I pressed close to him. "I can follow orders when necessary."

Smiling, he lifted his other hand to stroke my hair back from my face. "We shall soon see." He kissed me, then straightened. "And now I must go make final preparations," he said. The smile remained on his face, yet his eyes seemed deeply veiled. "I will send for you at sunset. Bathe and don what the faas lay out for you."

Excitement and relief twined together within me. "I'll be ready."

He touched my cheek then turned and departed without another word.

I watched him go. Was it at all possible that he was going to miss me? Was that why he was being so strangely tender? I shook my head to dismiss the thought. Right now all I wanted to worry about was getting my ass back home.

I returned to my room, bathed, then stood frowning at the simple, pretty pullover dress laid out on the bed. I'd been thinking jeans, a zrila-shirt, and sneakers would be ideal for going home, but for all I knew, clothes might have significance in demon-side rituals. *Whatever*. All that mattered right now was getting home. After dressing and combing out my hair, I had nothing left to do but wait impatiently and watch the progress of the sun toward the horizon.

Shortly after the sun began to set a faas burst through the door, baring teeth. "Come! Come! Qaztahl waits!"

"Okay, okay!" I said with a smile. The faas hopped out, and I followed it down the corridor. It stopped at the open door to this wing's smaller library and pointed inside.

"Here here heeeeere."

"Rhyzkahl's waiting for me *here*?" I asked, brow furrowed.

The faas peered at me as though I was a silly but very lovable human. "No! Jesral waiting!"

Doubt tightened my stomach. I took a settling breath and wished I was wearing more than the very simple dress with no bra, then entered the small library.

Indeed, Jesral was there, draped casually in a chair, sitting partially sideways with one leg over the other. There was nothing casual, though, behind his eyes or in his aura. Slim, with short brown hair, sharp features, and a keen gaze, he didn't radiate *scary* the way Mzatal did but felt more like a silent, stalking jungle cat—deadly, but able to hide it when he desired. He wore a grey turtleneck beneath a dark blue velvet suit that did absolutely nothing to decrease the subtle aura of danger. He turned his head to look at me as I entered, while the rest of his posture remained in total comfortable casualness.

"Ah, Kara Gillian," he said, flashing me a smile. "I am Lord Jesral. I have heard so much about you. What a delight to finally have the chance to meet you properly."

I inclined my head, wary. "Lord Jesral, I confess I don't know much, if anything, about you." I gave him a small and careful smile.

His eyes widened. "Rhyzkahl has not spoken of me?" He shook his head and made a single *tsk* sound. "He has spoken of you at length. Though there was cause in that, and perhaps not so the other way."

I folded my arms over my chest as I studied him. "And why have I been the subject of so much conversation?"

"Most recently, regarding the ritual," he said, eyes on me, still smiling. "To which I will escort you, that you may return to Earth."

"And why do you care whether I return to Earth?"

He laughed. "What matter would it have to me if you stay or go? I aid because Rhyzkahl asks it."

I lifted an eyebrow. "And do you do everything he asks of you?"

"Clever, clever girl." His face shifted from the smile to a far more penetrating look. "Would you believe any answer I gave you?"

I affected a casual shrug, though inside my pulse raced. I couldn't shake the feeling that this light conversational banter carried higher stakes than I could ever imagine. "Lies and truth are all information of some sort, Lord Jesral."

He dropped his crossed leg to the floor, gaze intense and flat out disturbing in a far different way than any of the others. A strange smile of cold satisfaction crept over his face, as though I'd managed to confirm some suspicion he'd been harboring.

"This is so very true," he said, standing and flicking nonexistent dust from his sleeves. "Though it is helpful to discern a lie from truth in order to glean the most refined information. I can offer one as easily as the other."

I unfolded my arms. "I'm a cop. I'm used to lies. But how about you humor me and tell me the truth." I lowered my head and kept the smile on my face. His too-friendly demeanor disturbed the hell out of me. "Why is it that you so eagerly leap to do Rhyzkahl's bidding? Do you fear him? Love him? Owe him? Or are you merely sucking up in order to keep in his good favor?"

He adjusted his clothing with a few smooth, practiced moves, then gestured toward the door. "We have a mutually beneficial working relationship," he said, "and he would just as readily *leap* at my bidding."

I headed to the door and allowed myself to be escorted. I was more than ready to get the fuck away from the demon realm and all of these lords. "A working relationship?" I gave him an ingenuous smile. "And what sort of work do you and Rhyzkahl do?"

Jesral laughed in a way that wasn't at all comforting. "If Rhyzkahl has chosen not to even *speak* of me to his marked summoner, there must be a reason. It is not for me to step between the two of you and spoil it."

I pressed my lips together and continued on in silence, utterly sick of this place and the bullshit intrigue. Shadow memories flickered as we walked, but I did my best to keep a careful lid on them.

Jesral finally stopped before the double doors to the antechamber. He flicked a hand to open one of them by about a foot. "And so here you are, Kara Gillian. I will see you again soon, I am certain." He took my hand before I could pull it away, lifted it to his mouth without bending, kissed the back, and released it.

I wanted badly to say something cutting and clever, but I couldn't come up with a damn thing. No doubt I would in about five minutes. Instead I simply gave him a nod and a tight smile, then ducked through the door.

Chapter 18

The antechamber swallowed me, overly spacious, overly white, and utterly barren, as though decor had gone missing. The opulence and splashes of color in the rest of the palace warmed and augmented the white, but here, it was unbroken winter. I hurried across the expanse of floor, demon-marble chilling my bare feet.

With a breath of relief, I passed through the open door of the summoning chamber itself, its dark gray walls and floor and pleasing warmth a startling contrast to the room behind me. It seemed the lords had identical summoning chambers, which I guessed had to do with function rather than taste. Hundreds of sigils ringed the chamber, too many to even begin to puzzle out their purpose or meaning. All pulsed faintly, yet to be ignited and activated. *That's what we'll be doing*, I realized, tension and a vague worry twined with a near breathless excitement. I didn't know how this sort of ritual worked, but it still excited me to be intimately involved in such a creation.

Rhyzkahl stood with his back to me, barefoot and wearing almost the same thing he'd worn on my first accidental summoning of him: cream-colored leather breeches that hugged the muscles of his legs, and a white shirt of some sort of silky material. I controlled my impatience and nerves while he completed a sigil. Finally, he turned to me.

"Close the door," he said. "Then ignite the sigil upon it."

I shut the heavy door but paused, frowning as I peered at the sigil. It was a deeply complex thing, with whispers of something intimately familiar. Yet I had no idea how to do what he asked.

"Use your connection with the grove. Ignite it as you would a closure seal for a portal, but draw the grove energy as well," Rhyzkahl said. "It is a source of deep power, and its use to ignite the master seal will offer the greatest anchoring and shielding for the ritual."

I nodded, then drew on the grove and extended to the sigil. An instant later it flared to life, igniting a chain of patterns that ran along the perimeter of the chamber. I exhaled in delight, the weirdness with Jesral forgotten.

"Excellent," Rhyzkahl said. "Without a summoner controlling the portal from the exterior, it is vital that the room be deeply shielded and solidly anchored when the portal opens."

I didn't have to ask him what could go wrong if it wasn't. An unshielded portal could do very bad things. I wanted to get back to Earth in one piece, thank you.

"Are you ready to begin?" he asked.

"I am," I replied, smiling.

He lowered his head slightly, hair falling forward to frame his face and drop it into shadow as he held his hand out to me. My pulse quickened as I crossed through the diagram to take his hand.

With his other hand he sealed the patterns, then pulled me in closer. He looked down on me, eyes veiled and distant. "You have come to me, dear one," he said, a smile with a hint of sadness curving his mouth. "To go home."

After my encounter with Jesral, I didn't know what Rhyzkahl had gone through to make this ritual happen. Something sure seemed to weigh on him, and I didn't want to add to it, just go home. I smiled up at him. "Yeah. And thank you," I said, giving his hand a squeeze.

Slowly, he lifted his head to look beyond me as if thinking of something else. Mentally prepping for the ritual, I figured. Excitement wound through me for multiple reasons, and I had to firmly tamp down the desire to jump up and down or laugh or anything else that would no doubt seriously fuck up Rhyzkahl's focus.

I glanced around at the myriad of sigils, then scanned the arcanely traced glyphs on the floor. There'd only been about a half dozen in Mzatal's purification ritual. Here, they covered a good portion of the summoning chamber floor. My eyes rested on the center—Rhyzkahl's mark. I frowned.

Something about the glyph next to it looked familiar. I was sure I'd seen it before, but damn, I couldn't place it.

I looked up as Rhyzkahl drew a deep breath and dropped his gaze back to me. "I do not always get what I want," he said, which confused me at first until I remembered that I'd asked him that question the other day. But why was he telling me now? Did he want me to stay here in the demon realm?

He released my hand, expression unreadable as he laid a hand against the side of my face. "Soon you will be gone," he murmured.

I raised an eyebrow. "Don't tell me you're going to miss me."

His only response was to look out over my head again, muscle in his jaw twitching. Maybe he really would miss me? He wasn't one for sharing his deeper feelings, but he certainly didn't seem to be eager to send me on my way. A whisper of doubt crept in. As much as I enjoyed my time with the lord, I had no desire to stay here any longer.

I put my arms around him and gave him a light squeeze. "Don't worry," I told him with a smile. "I'll summon you soon enough. We still have another two and half years or so on our current deal."

But to my surprise he put his hands on my shoulders and pushed me back enough to disengage from my embrace. His face hardened briefly before he turned away from me. "There is much more than summoning."

My doubt increased. "I know. I've seen so much." Surely he wasn't reconsidering sending me home? "I'll definitely have new and interesting questions for you next time I summon you." My smile slipped as he remained facing away, hands clenched into fists at his sides, shoulders rising and falling with quickened breaths. "Rhyzkahl?" I set a hand gently on his back. "You okay?"

He went still at my touch, so still I wasn't even certain he breathed. I slid my hand up to his shoulder. "Rhyzkahl, please tell me what's wrong." I gave a somewhat shaky laugh. "You're kinda freaking me out a bit."

He turned and looked down at me, face alive with emotions I'd never seen in him before. Uncertainty. Worry. Something akin to desperation flickered in his eyes as he caught my face in his hands. What the hell was going on with him? More bullshit with other lords? Something with Jesral? That one sure as hell had his own agenda. Definitely time for me to get my ass back home before I got dragged into any of that lord shit.

"It's going to be okay," I said softly. "How about a goodbye kiss?"

Rhyzkahl hesitated only a heartbeat before dropping his mouth to mine in an ardent kiss. I relaxed eagerly into it as I skimmed my hands up his chest and around his neck, slid my fingers through the white-blond silk of his hair. I felt the tension in him ease as he wrapped arms around me, clinging to me. I was going to miss him too, I realized, as odd as our relationship was.

I expected him to break the kiss and begin the ritual, but he continued as if he couldn't get enough of me. He pulled me close to him, one hand sliding down to cup my ass. A shudder ran through me, and I obligingly rocked my hips against the growing evidence that he was possibly wanting more than a simple goodbye kiss. Some hot sex for the road? Yeah, I was okay with that. I quickly worked the buttons of his shirt loose and slipped it from his shoulders. He shook it free of his arms to let it fall to the floor, then brought his hands to my waist, gathering the dress and breaking the kiss to pull it over my head. His eyes flashed with hunger and the hint of desperation again. But it was gone before I could fully register that it was there at all.

He gently lowered me to the floor in the center of the diagram. I flicked a quick glance at the sigils, for a moment paranoid that this "goodbye fuck" was somehow meant to power the diagram, but they remained quiescent. Good. Because that would've been weird.

He slipped his breeches off and returned to cover me, hair falling over me in a curtain of silk as he held my face gently between thumb and fingers of one hand. "In this moment, we are right here, right now," he said, voice resonating with intensity. "Nothing else is of import."

Smiling, I wrapped my arms around him. "We are here," I echoed.

He lowered his head to kiss me again, but this time with a tenderness that damn near brought tears to my eyes. He'd never touched me like this before—sweet and gentle, yet with a passion beneath it that spoke of genuine affection.

His hands moved over me as if memorizing every inch of my skin, and I eagerly responded, more fired and moved by this display of true ardor than by any of his prior attentions.

He made love to me. There was no other word for it. Not possessive or fierce but with a fervor that brought us together into a perfect joining. And my climax was just as perfect, fantastic and overwhelming, spiraling together with his as we clung to each other and trembled with the fierce joy of it.

Sighing in deep, contented pleasure, I relaxed against him. He cradled me close, idly stroking sweat-damp hair back from my face. I gave him a languid smile before casting my gaze around at the pattern of sigils that surrounded us. "It's beautiful," I murmured.

A shudder passed through him. "Yes, it is. Very beautiful," he said, an odd catch in his voice that I'd never heard from him before. He pulled away and stood, back to me, focusing his attention on the slowly pulsing diagram. A lift of his hand sent the entire pattern into a slow spin and then he was still, silhouetted against the softly shifting light.

I pushed up on my elbows. As goodbyes went, that had been a doozy, but now it was time to get down to business. "How do we ignite it? What do we need to do?"

His head dropped. It was several seconds before he spoke. "More. Much more."

The obvious tension in his body and the taut undercurrent in his voice sent a chill racing over my skin. I wondered about the implications of those little words.

"Rhyzkahl. What's wrong? Please tell me."

He crouched and picked up his breeches, tugged them on in silence. "Too much is in motion," he finally said with something akin to regret in his voice. He picked up his shirt, slipped it on and began to button it. "I cannot stop it now. I can only move forward."

I wanted to ask him if he could be any vaguer, but this was freaking me out a little so I opted for a more direct question. "What are you talking about?"

He turned fully to me, beautiful and terrible, like I'd imagine a fallen angel to be if there were such things. The words fell heavily in measured slowness. "Potency. Plans. Agreements. Oaths. Treachery."

The last word issued with a slight hiss and baring of teeth. As it all pretty much summed up what I'd seen of the bullshit that went on between lords in the past few days, I figured one of the rat bastards had fucked him over. "Anything I can do to help?"

In response he stepped forward, extended a hand to me, pulled me up when I took it. He laid his hands against the sides of my face and tenderly traced the line of my cheekbones with his thumbs. His eyes held mine, deep, enigmatic and . . . tormented? I'd never seen that in him before, not like this. He lowered his head to kiss me, body pressing against mine as he tangled his hands in my hair, claiming my mouth as passionately as if he feared he would never kiss me again.

The chill of the moment before slid away as I opened to the kiss, willing it to ease whatever troubled him so. I gave a soft moan when he finally broke it but smiled as I met his eyes again. "Better?"

His hands slid down to my shoulders, and he shook his head, the haunted flicker in his eyes sending a shiver of doubt through me. He bent and picked up my dress, eyes on me as he held it up in his right hand.

"Right. Time to get dressed," I said, relieved. Things were getting weird again. "Would raise some eyebrows if I showed up back home in the buff." Then I chuckled. "Did that once already."

He inhaled deeply as I reached for the dress. Potency flashed from him, incinerating it to ash right before I touched it.

Shock coursed through me. I yelped and took a step back. "Rhyzkahl, what the fuck?" My confusion rose higher as the diagram abruptly flared.

Rhyzkahl lifted his hand, and I felt an oscillating wall of potency behind me as I backed near the inner ring of sigils. "You will not need it," he said with a shake of his head.

Apprehensive, my gaze went from him to the diagram and back. "What's going on?" I asked as the diagram continued to pulse. "Rhyzkahl, why won't I need clothing? Are you sending me home or not?"

"Home," he said, as though tasting the word for the first time. "A new home, yes." His eyes flicked to the sigils as they flared once again, echoing the spike of fear that went through me.

"New home?" I shook my head as my anxiety climbed. "I don't want a new home. I want *my* home. What the hell's going on?"

"That which must be done," he replied, disquiet ghosting across his face. To my horror he flicked a lasso of potency around my right wrist and pulled me toward the center. "You will know it as home and feel no loss."

My fear rose, then climbed higher as the diagram flared. It didn't take a rocket scientist to figure out that this ritual was somehow keyed to strong emotion, and not the good kind either, since it had remained quiet during our love-making.

"Rhyzkahl, I don't want to forget my home," I said, heart pounding. I tried to remain as calm as possible, fought the urge to twist and struggle against the lasso. Whatever was going on, he didn't seem fully committed to it. Maybe there was still a chance to talk my way out of it. "Please." I kept my voice quiet and intense. "Let me go."

Rhyzkahl went demonic-lord still, closing his eyes. He kept the tension on the lasso, but didn't pull me closer with it. The diagram dimmed, and I allowed a whisper of hope to creep in. I'd talked people down from high-stress situations before. I didn't know what the hell was going on with Rhyzkahl, but the best thing I could do right then was to stay calm and talk my ass out of this chamber.

"Too much is in motion," he murmured, eyes still closed.

The diagram dimmed a bit more. My eyes flicked from the sigils and back to him. "It's okay," I said, keeping my voice low and calm. "Everything's okay. Just let me go . . . and we'll start over."

"Start over." He opened his eyes, and to my dismay the ritual brightened again. "Yes, that is what this is. Starting over." He tightened the pull on the lasso and lifted his right hand.

My cop vibe went code red. "No, Rhyzkahl. Wait!" I didn't know what was coming. I only knew it was bad.

The palm of his hand shimmered blue, and the haunted look faded from his eyes. "I have no choice." He drew a deep breath, face sliding into an icy mask. As he opened his hand, a blade began to coalesce within it, bristling with thorny protrusions along its hilt, blue gem in the pommel dark and shadowed. A vile whisper slid through my mind. *You are mine.*

Deep, primal terror flooded me. I struggled to flee, run, anything, but a flick of Rhyzkahl's left hand bound my arms behind me. Another flick pulled them up so that my wrists were at my lower back.

Eyes on the blade, I breathed in gasping pants. "No, Rhyzkahl, please. . . . It's not too late."

The blade glimmered oily blue, fully formed in his hand.

"It is too late . . . *now*," he said, voice laden with deadly promise.

And I knew without doubt it was true. A heartbreaking ache of disappointment flashed through me. I'd wanted so badly to trust him, but it didn't matter. He was going to do something terrible to me.

But right on the heels of that disappointment came an equally profound disappointment and anger at myself. I'd always known he was up to something, and hadn't fully trusted him. The hints and clues had been there all along, but, damn it, I hadn't wanted to look at any of it objectively. My own need and angst kept me nicely wrapped up in ego-stroking denial. He'd attempted to coerce me in our very first encounter, placed his mark on me in a moment of true duress, dribbled information to me on his own terms, used my computer while I slept—and who knew what else. And there'd been numerous moments where he showed flickers of indecision that echoed those he displayed just now, right after our lovemaking. Yeah, great cop sense, Kara. He wasn't simply a charismatic "bad boy." No, Rhyzkahl was far, far worse.

I felt the shift in his aura, heavy and vile. I thrashed in the bindings, sure that if I could break free I could find a way to escape. I had to get away, *had to*. But no. No freedom. The blade whispered. Rhyzkahl lifted it and deep red fire ignited along its length, illuminated sporadically by scintillating arcs.

"Rhyzkahl, don't do this." I felt my lips move, felt the clench in my throat, but heard no sound.

Rhyzkahl heard. "It is already done," he said, voice terrifying in a different way than Mzatal's scary-as-fuck voice—colder and carrying a promise of horror. "Can you not feel it? There is more. Much more." Lifting my wrists a smidge higher, he moved me to the very center of the diagram.

I let out a squeal of discomfort and fear as he pulled my wrists even higher up behind me. Strappado. That's what this torturous position was called. I only knew that because I had a case last year of consensual BDSM that went too far. And now I understood Mzatal's warnings, far too late. Had he known what lay in store for me? And, if so, why hadn't he fucking *told* me? My heart slammed within my chest. I knew I was deeply and seriously fucked. I tried to pull grove power, but it felt as if I ran up against a smooth wall.

"It cannot touch you here," he said. "You yourself sealed the chamber against the grove."

Sick horror filled me. "You *swore* not to do me any harm!"

He didn't even pause before responding. "'During that time in *your world*,'" he said, clearly quoting the words of our agreement back to me, "'I will do nothing with the intent of causing you harm.'"

My world. *Stupid. Stupid!* "Stop! Don't do this!" I didn't even know what "this" was, I only knew it was going to be bad.

Rhyzkahl made certain I was in the very center of the diagram, then lifted my wrists until they were slightly higher than my shoulders, forcing me to lean forward to relieve some of the burn of the uncomfortable position.

"Mzatal," he said, snarling the name. "He thought to keep you from me, use you himself." He gave a cold smile. "He will pay for his audacity." His breath hissed, and I saw that the thorny protrusions on the blade hilt had molded around his fingers. Deep red fire wreathed his hand and crept up his forearm. I had the very bad feeling he couldn't release the blade even if he wanted to, at least not until this ritual was finished.

My gut clenched as I stared at him. "Why are you doing this?" I swallowed hard. "Is this what happened to Elinor? Did you kill her too?"

Pain exploded in my face as he backhanded me hard, knocking me off balance, and I gave a strangled cry as my shoulders wrenched in the bindings. Dizzy from the vicious blow, I struggled to get my feet beneath me again. As soon as I did so, Rhyzkahl gripped my chin hard and turned my face fully toward him. "I did not kill her!" he said, fury replacing the ice in his voice. "Never speak that again." His gaze slid over the puffiness of my eye, but it didn't seem to touch him. "Look. At. Me."

Whimpering softly, I met his eyes. My terror increased at the darkness I saw there.

"Twelve," he said. "We will begin with the number twelve." The grip on my chin tightened. "Look well, Kara Helene Gillian." His eyes penetrated me with dark intensity. "By the time we reach one, you will no longer have the resolve to look into my eyes. And when we are complete, that name will be a forgotten whisper, and you will have a new one."

The truth of it was etched in his perfect features. He wasn't going to kill me. Whatever my fate, it would be much worse. I spit into his face, knowing it would surely be my last act of defiance.

Rhyzkahl didn't show a flicker of reaction. Still gripping my chin, he wiped the spittle away with the back of the hand that held the blade, then shifted to lay his other palm against the side of my face. "Only by breaking you, dear one, can I rebuild you into a greater existence, a new life," he said with a sickening gentleness of tone. "Enthralled, you will be safe, cherished." He smiled at me, caressing my cheek with his thumb. "You will thank me when you fully understand what I have done for you, when you understand that I have saved you."

He lifted me in the arcane bindings until I was on my toes. My breath hissed through my teeth in bursts with the strain in my shoulders. "Bullshit . . . you . . . insane . . . fucker."

All hint of the deranged gentleness evaporated as he leaned close, breath hot on my face. "Through you we gain Szerain's blade. Through you, we open a gateway to a new world. Then you will be with me forever." The bindings grew into a sheath that enveloped me, preventing my body from moving even a millimeter. Only my head was free. I thrashed futilely with a blossoming panic.

He brought the blade close to my face. I let out a breathless scream, sick with horror as I reflexively tried to jerk away.

"You have met Xhan before, under tame circumstances," he said, moving the blade before my eyes, voice cold and penetrating again. "This time, it reveals itself fully to you."

You are mine.

I recoiled from the horrific presence of Rhyzkahl and the blade, unable to jerk anything but my head away, and that only a few inches.

Snarling, he wound fingers in my hair close to my scalp, pulled my head up, and bound it in that position, stripping even that small freedom of movement from me. With a gesture, he lifted me completely off my feet so that my chest was at his eye level, yet he kept me in the sheath so that the strain on my arms and shoulders wasn't as great as it could have been. He placed his left hand in the center of my chest. "We begin with the first sigil here," he said in a cold and unwavering voice that told me that he was not fucking stopping. He dropped his hand and placed the tip of the blade against my skin. I let out another scream at the touch of the blade. I thrashed and struggled to no avail—his power held me immobile, though my muscles fought to respond.

A low hiss that sounded like pleasure came from him as he began to work, knife biting precisely as he carved my flesh. I cried out as pain seared through my chest, every bite of the blade like a window into the depths of hell. My vision began to gray, and I didn't fight it. If I couldn't escape through death, at least perhaps I could find a temporary oblivion.

Rhyzkahl looked up into my face as I began to pass out. "No!" He said, clenching his teeth as he yanked the oblivion away from me. Full awareness returned like a slap, and I let out a low sob.

He continued to work methodically, precisely. Occasionally he would look up into my face after doing a section, as though looking for something. At times it almost seemed as if the blade led him.

I trembled, panting in ragged gasps of breath. Finally, he lifted the blade from my skin and passed his hand over the incisions. I shuddered in relief, whimpering at the pain in my shoulders, wrists, and chest. He stepped back, eyes on the sigil he'd just carved, and spoke a few distinct words in demon. With a flick of his left hand, he removed the encasing sheath, allowing me to fully sag in the bindings with my feet still far from the floor. Another keening scream escaped me as I kicked my legs futilely, struggling for nonexistent purchase as my shoulders shrieked in agony. The diagram flared in eager response.

The red flame coiled around his arm from blade to shoulder, arcs shimmering with a discordant potency that I knew was far different from what I'd always worked with. "It is beautiful." His eyes dropped to the sigil. "And now, together, we bring it to life," he said, voice unspeakably scary in its soft intimacy, as though we were actually working together.

Tears streamed down my face. I shook my head as much as I could. "No, please . . . no . . ."

Rhyzkahl moved close to me again, laid his left hand alongside my face. "In the pain, dear one," he said in the same scary intimate voice, "is the true connection made. Without it, all of this," he gestured vaguely with the knife, "is for naught."

He stepped back two paces, lowered his head. He inhaled as he brought the knife upright before his chest, gripping the hilt in both hands. I shook in the bonds, knowing he didn't mean simply the pain from my shoulders and the carving he'd made in my skin.

"NO!"

He lowered the blade and pointed toward my feet, wrapping each in roiling sheets of viscous black shot through with flickers of brilliant red, burning like fire that did not consume my flesh. I screamed, thrashing, desperately wanting to pass out but utterly unable. His face settled into intense calm as he drew the fire up my legs, and I shrieked in agony.

He brought the dark fire up to the level of the sigil, hissing as ruby lightning leaped from the blade to connect fully with the ignited sigil. I couldn't even scream anymore, could only jerk in the bindings. He held it for ten heartbeats of eternity, then dropped all the arcane pain instantly, leaving only the ghost of its memory. Yet I wasn't burned. It didn't seem possible that such unspeakable agony could leave no physical damage in its wake.

He wrapped me again in the sheath of potency, taking some of the weight off my arms. My breath wheezed, and I twitched. I could barely think, but I knew I needed to be able to think, to remember myself. He'd told me I would forget, forget who I was, forget my name. I wanted desperately to lose myself; it was my only possible escape. But I also knew once I did, I would never come back.

"Kara . . . I'm Kara," I managed to whisper.

He closed the distance between us, stroked the back of his fingers down the line of my jaw in a move that was more possessive than tender. "You will have a new name soon, and a new life."

Licking dry lips, I fought to focus on him, barely able to believe that I'd endured such pain only seconds before. "I'm Kara . . ."

He placed his hand on the right side of my chest, just below the collarbone. "For now, yes." My pain faded more with his touch. "And I will ever remember you as you were."

I wheezed out a breath. "Fuck you . . . hate you."

"That serves well for now." He removed his hand, brought the blade to the base of my throat. "And so we begin anew."

My tears fell as he began to slice. "Kara . . . I'm Kara."

We went through the cycle again. And again. Carve the sigil, fire it with a new form of pain. Begin again.

I lost track of how many times we'd gone through this. Maybe it was only three . . . or seven . . . or thirty. Eventually I began to wonder if there was ever a time when I wasn't here, wasn't a canvas for sigils, wasn't in agony. I tried to remind myself who I was.

I tried to remember who I was.

"You are Rowan," Rhyzkahl said, helping me. He lifted my lolling head, looked into my eyes. "Rowan."

I dragged in a breath, feeling the name. He brought the pain, but then he stopped the pain. Perhaps he was right. I tasted it on my tongue.

He put a hand to the side of my face, cool and smooth, easing the pain. "Yes, say it," he said voice soft and soothing. "Say your name."

Kara . . . Kara . . .

A name. Felt more than heard, as if from an incredible distance. I tasted it, found it more right than the other. "Kara," I managed to rasp.

He took a long deep breath, lifted his hand, allowing the pain to return. "No. Rowan." He moved around to my left side, began another sigil, ignored my keening wail of a scream.

Kara . . .

"You are Rowan," Rhyzkahl said, returning to stand before me. Once again he laid his hand on my cheek, once again gave me numb refuge from the pain.

I heard him. Heard the name. Heard the distant call.

Kara . . .

"I'm . . . K-Kara."

He pulled his hand away, allowing the pain to flood in. I spasmed in the bindings, vision going red as my shoulders dislocated.

"You bring the pain upon yourself," he told me as he brought the blade before me. "Speak your name—Rowan—and end it."

Kara . . . Kara . . .Kara . . .

I moaned, unable to say either name.

Stepping back, he gestured, pulling my arms out to my sides, though keeping them twisted enough to maintain the searing agony in my shoulders. Another gesture pulled my legs apart until I was stretched in a vicious spread-eagle about a foot off the ground.

Once again he bound me in potency to keep me from twitching and marring his work. He set the blade on my upper back, slowly parting my flesh in the complex pattern.

Once again, he brought the pain.

I hung limp in the cruel position, twitching within the imprisoning sheath as he began a new sigil. A thousand times we'd been through this. Surely it had been that many. Yet other than the carving of my flesh and the ruin of my shoulders, I was undamaged. Each bout of agony was only that, yet all of that.

I couldn't pass out. That way was closed off to me. But another way beckoned, shimmered with a promise of ease, of a different sort of oblivion. All I had to do was relax my grip on myself. Let go, and the pain would fade away. I could drift there and be nothing.

Kara . . .KARA!

I moaned. No. I couldn't let go. I'd never find my way back. ". . . here," I whispered.

Rhyzkahl lifted his head. "*Mzatal.*" He bared his teeth and growled a very nonhuman sound. "*Dahn!*" He moved swiftly to grip my hair, hauled my face close to his. "What have you done?" He snarled, face contorted in fury.

". . . here," I gasped, ". . . Kara."

He released my hair with a shove, then backhanded me. "He will not know you. Your name is *ROWAN.*"

I shuddered in pain, uncertain which name was right. He moved to my back, drew a breath, and began a new sigil.

Kara . . . Kara . . . Kara . . .

Twitching, I whimpered, ". . . here."

Rhyzkahl carved the sigil into my lower back, taking far longer with this one than any other. At last he finished, moved back around to look into my face. "After this, you *will* know your name," he said, voice hard again and full of fury. "And he will no longer touch you."

The pain was about to come again. I saw it in his eyes, in his snarl. This one would be worse than all the others.

Rhyzkahl lowered his head, lifted the blade before him. The red fire writhed over his arm and torso as he called down the agony, bringing pain upon pain, making me feel as if my very bones were on fire. Lost in the agony, I couldn't even scream.

The relentless torment abruptly flickered and died, and I dimly heard a cry of pain that wasn't my own. I struggled to focus on Rhyzkahl. His breath hissed through his teeth as he looked down at the knife in his hand. Brilliant blue fire surrounded his fist, and the azure gem in the pommel glowed as though lit by an internal sun. He shook his hand as though to release the blade but the cruel spikes on the hilt still curled around his fingers, locking it in his grip.

I gasped for breath in the brief surcease. He raised the blade before him again, igniting the pattern around us both and in every nerve in my body. "Rowan . . . *Rowan!*" he growled.

There was no way to think beyond the pain. No way to hold onto myself. No oblivion to escape to.

Kara!

The entire diagram stuttered. Rhyzkahl screamed in fury and frustration as the rings of sigils fractured in a cascade of arcane sparks. Within three heartbeats all were dark, leaving only a lone amber sigil above us to cast any light. I hung, twitching, as the name, *my* name, reverberated in my essence. *Kara.*

"... *here*," I breathed.

Rhyzkahl stood with hands clenched as he assessed the ruin of the diagram, clearly seeking what could be salvaged. With a flick of his hand he released the bindings holding me. I crumpled hard to the floor, barely feeling it amidst the other pain. I no longer heard the call, but it didn't matter now. I knew who I was. I didn't know much else, but I knew that.

My breath rasped as Rhyzkahl moved to me. He stood over me, looking down, right hand still locked onto the hilt of the knife. It no longer burned with the red fire. Now it gave off a mist, like dry ice.

Breath hissing through his teeth, he crouched and grabbed my left wrist, hauling my arm forward and sending another electric jolt of pain through the dislocated shoulder.

"... please," I whimpered, "no ... more."

Rhyzkahl's eyes lifted to mine, then lowered to the mark on my forearm. "I salvage that which can be salvaged," he said, setting the hideous blade against my skin above the mark. I tried to jerk away, but his grip was too strong, and I was too weak.

"I take back that which I gave to you," he said through clenched teeth as he sliced the skin of my arm. He began to excise the mark from me, breath coming heavily as the strands shuddered. "And we will begin anew."

Of all the pain he'd dealt me, all the mind-fucking torments—my skin doused with acid, my organs shriveling and squeezing, my bones on fire—none could compare to the pure hell of this right now. The mark was more than an arcane brand or a mere symbol. Its strands hooked deeply into my essence, and as that horrible blade sliced through my flesh, it was as if all of those strands were ripped from me, tearing and stretching at the very core of my being. I screamed through a throat already raw, arching my back, near blind from the torment. A shudder went through Rhyzkahl, and a tiny part of me knew that the pain of the excision wracked him as well.

He dropped my arm and staggered upright, holding the strip of flesh in one hand and the blade in the other. I sucked in shallow gasps of breath as the echoes of the unholy pain continued to reverberate through me.

I jerked at a sudden harsh tug, though no one was touching me.

Kara

"... *here*," I gasped.

Rhyzkahl gave a cry of primal rage. "Dahn. *Dahn!*" He dropped to his knees and dragged me up, holding my chest to his with his left arm as I sagged. "He will not have you!" He let out an animal scream. "You will not have her!" Breathing heavily, he brought the blade to my throat, looked down into my face.

I felt the blade part the first layers of skin. I met his eyes and forced my words through split and swollen lips. "I ... am ... Kara." Even if I died now, at least I remained me.

The tug deepened, and I sucked in a ragged breath. Rhyzkahl continued to hold the blade at my throat, yet didn't press it deeper, didn't draw it across to make the slice that would end me.

His eyes stayed on mine as the pull increased.

"Kara!" My name burst from his lips in a harsh scream, reverberating through me as I dropped away from him and into the void.

Chapter 19

I felt smooth stone beneath me, cooler than the floor of Rhyzkahl's summoning chamber. I lay sprawled on my right side and stomach, my arms twisted at impossible angles. Pain seared through my shoulders and the rest of me, but I could only twitch and whimper. Everything about me felt wrong, unclean, as if I'd been immersed in slime.

Shouted words penetrated the fog of pain, but I couldn't understand them. The wrongness persisted, as did the shouted commands. I tried to see through swollen eyes. I thought I knew the two men in the room. I knew that neither were the Tormentor. I didn't know much else.

"Kara!"

My name. That was my name. I knew that too. The dark-haired one shouted my name. He stood several feet from me, as if reluctant to approach. Barefooted. Never seen him barefooted. Face twisted in concentration, he worked the arcane with blinding speed, tracing sigils and patterns and sending them to do . . . I had no idea what.

"Kara!" He shouted again. "Rhyzkahl seeks to follow. You must cast him back. Push him back through the conduit." He turned to the blond one. "Prepare to seal it as soon as it is clear."

Cast him back? I struggled to comprehend. I was Kara. Everything hurt. The sense of wrongness filled me, and I let out a mewling cry. I felt him, the Tormentor. He still sought to touch me, to pull me back. I dragged in a wretched breath and struggled to push the wrongness away, gathered what shreds of will I still had to drive back the smothering miasma.

"Kara! Again. Cast him from you!"

I moaned and recoiled as the foul touch returned. *You are mine*, it whispered. *No other may touch you thus. You will be eternal.*

I sucked breath through a throat raw from too much screaming. Shaking, I threw my head back, channeled rage and pain and betrayal and hatred, then let it all loose upon the wrongness, upon the Tormentor, shoving him back and away from me with everything I had left.

And then I collapsed, spent. I could see the blond one tracing quickly. I no longer felt the Tormentor, as if the door had been closed upon him. Yet I still felt wrong, deeply soiled, and awash with relentless pain.

The dark-haired one crouched, still several feet away, eyes intent upon me. "Kara." He inched forward, reached out a hand even though he was still far from me, pulled something from the air around me and, with a flick of his fingers, dispersed it. It stung, whatever it was he did, and I flinched and whimpered.

"Kara." *Kara.*

I heard my name, *felt* my name. "*Here*," I whispered, lips barely moving.

He continued to inch forward, continued to pluck *things* from around me. Each time he did so it stung, like the snap of a rubber band against my skin, but with every sting the sense of *yuck* seemed to fade.

"Idris," the dark-haired man said over his shoulder without taking his eyes from me. "Prepare a support diagram with my tertiary parameters."

The blond man nodded, beginning to rapidly trace. He glanced over at me for the first time, and his face paled. He looked quickly away, throat working as if holding back the urge to spew.

I knew this dark-haired one. Not the Tormenter, but one of his ilk.

"Mzatal," I breathed.

"Yes, Kara, Mzatal," he responded, exuding utter calm as he slowly crept forward, pulling, dispersing, steadily clearing the arcane crap that clung to me. Behind him, the blond one—Idris, yes, that was his name—Idris finished tracing a diagram and ignited it. Mzatal instantly breathed deeper, and I could sense the flow of power as he drew potency from the new pattern.

I wanted oblivion. I wanted to pass out, escape the pain, escape everything I'd just been through, but that relief eluded me as though behind a locked door with no key. My gaze drifted to the pattern. I didn't try and focus on it. I didn't want to focus on anything. My mind wanted to drift, and I let it. I didn't want to be aware or awake. I didn't want to be in the here and now.

Kara!

I jerked back to myself, whimpered as the movement sent fresh pain lancing through me. "Mzatal," I moaned. He wasn't going to let me drift. Wasn't going to let me lose myself. *I might never find my way back.* ". . . you . . . called me."

"Yes," he said, still working his way forward. "And I am still calling you."

I fought to work moisture into my mouth. "You . . . have me." He'd sworn to retrieve me. And he had. I was right back in his control, right back to being his prisoner.

"Yes, almost," he replied. "And until I can touch you, I will continue to call you so that you do not slip away."

He did continue to call to me, sometimes sharply, when I began to drift. Every time, his voice and an incorporeal touch—more intimate and penetrating than words—brought me back. After what felt like an eternity, he reached me and placed a hand very lightly on my shoulder. The simple touch dragged me back to myself, as if surfacing from the depths of water. Pain flared, and I sucked in a ragged breath.

Mzatal shifted to sit cross-legged beside me and laid his hand carefully on my cheek, easing the bruising and swelling of my face. His fingers came away bloody, and I realized that Rhyzkahl's ring must have cut me when he'd backhanded me.

"Tired," I mumbled, easier now with my lips and face not so swollen. "Sleep."

"Not yet, Kara," he said. "The sigils are still active." He took a blanket offered by a faas, rolled it and positioned it under my head, then spread a second one over me, giving me at least that bit of coverage and dignity, for which I was deeply grateful. I'd had my fill of humiliation, but if he hadn't provided a blanket, I wouldn't have had the energy to ask for one.

Mzatal placed both hands on my shoulder. Delicious

warmth flowed through to me, and my breathing eased somewhat.

"Foot massage . . . and cabana boys . . . peeled grapes . . ."

A whisper of a smile touched his mouth. "I can have a faas feed you taba fruit."

A shudder went through me as the heat in my shoulder intensified. "No deal," I murmured. "Idris . . . in loincloth. . . ."

"That is a possibility I will take under consideration," he said. Idris blinked and straightened, casting a horrified look at Mzatal's back. I wanted to laugh, but I knew it would hurt far too much. "You will, for the moment, settle for replenishment from tunjen juice, once I have straightened this shoulder," Mzatal continued. He took my arm and straightened it into a more natural position. I tensed, expecting excruciating pain, but he had blocked it such that I felt little more than a dull ache and a *pop* as the shoulder shifted back into its proper configuration. "The binding that held you dislocated both of your shoulders," he told me. "I must make adjustments on them before you can be moved."

I managed to focus on him. "Yeah . . . how'd you know . . . binding?"

"The marks on your wrists," he said after a moment. "And I witnessed it."

My eyes sought his. "How? Why . . . ?"

"Through Rhyzkahl," he replied. "Through the blade. Xhan."

I struggled to process this.

"It is how I knew when to call to you so that you would not lose yourself," he said. "And the physical recall, regrettably, depended on Rhyzkahl's removing your mark."

A shudder went through me, bringing with it new spasms of pain. It was several heartbeats before I could speak. "And that's what . . . you always wanted . . . me, unmarked."

He shifted his hands slightly, seeking the worst of the damage. "Yes, though this was not a means I would have chosen."

Despair rose. Betrayed and tortured by Rhyzkahl, and now right back to being Mzatal's prisoner again. More trapped than ever. I swallowed hard, still not daring to move my arm. I had no doubt there was plenty of muscle damage.

Mzatal moved his hands to my forearm, covering the

wound from the excision of Rhyzkahl's mark. A strangled breath escaped me as memories of the essence-rending pain echoed. He exhaled forcibly and shook his head, as if he could feel it too. When he lifted his hands from me, he looked like he wanted to puke.

I shuddered. "Bad . . . ?"

He answered with a nod and traced a pygah over us. "I am going to turn you to your other side," Mzatal said. "But before that, you will drink juice."

I nodded, then gasped at the pain the movement brought. Gestamar moved forward and helped Mzatal get me into a semi-upright position, supporting my head so that I could drink from the mug Mzatal held for me. I was so weak it was a struggle to drink. Juice dribbled onto my chest, and I let out a low cry of pain as it hit the raw sigils, burning and stinging.

"More," Mzatal urged when I tried to stop. "You must drink it all." Wearily, I complied, though he was more careful not to let any spill. My stomach roiled as he and Gestamar eased me to my other side, and I fought the brief wave of nausea. Mzatal placed his hands on my other shoulder and sent healing warmth through it.

I knew it would take him a while to get me fixed up totally, but then he'd finally have me right where he wanted me: a nice, whole summoner of his very own, one with grove affinity and a tie to the cataclysm. A wave of homesickness swept over me, briefly overshadowing the pain, and I closed my eyes to hold back tears. I wanted to be with the people who *really* cared.

"Kara," he murmured, as he manipulated the shoulder back into its joint. "Kara," he repeated softly, and I knew he was calling to me as before.

I exhaled a shaking breath, tears leaking. "Here." *Forever.*

He popped the shoulder into place, then gently shifted me to my back. "Yes. Here. I will not allow him to have you again."

I stayed silent, aching far beyond the physical. Gestamar moved forward to pick me up but, gesturing him back, Mzatal slid his arms beneath me, lifting as if I weighed no more than a feather. My head lolled against his shoulder, and I tried without success to hold back the whimper.

I knew Mzatal was easing the pain as best he could, but there was only so much he could do in this moment. My shoulders were back in their sockets, but the damage was still there, and the sigils covering my torso were still raw and open.

The disjointed thought of his nice white dress shirt floated in. "Mess up . . . your shirt."

Mzatal looked down at me, and that faint smile touched his lips again. "It is already done, so there is no purpose in dwelling upon it."

I expected him to take me to a sick room or some other area assigned for my use, but instead, he carried me upstairs and down a long corridor. He reached a set of double doors intricately carved with impossible figures like an Escher print, opened them without a touch and strode through. These were his rooms. There was no mistaking that. What the hell was going on? He passed through the outer chamber—simple and spacious, the far wall fully glass with a balcony beyond—and then into a bedroom: two adjacent walls of glass, big bed, three ilius coiled by the pillows, and it *felt* like Mzatal. He gently shooed the ilius off the bed as if they were cats, then waited as a faas spread a heavy quilt over the bed.

"Kara, I am going to place you on your belly for a time," he told me as he gently settled me on the bed and moved me into position. "I will begin with your back."

I held my breath, trembling, as the pain flared. He got me settled and my arms into the most comfortable possible position then adjusted the blanket over my legs and butt. I stared out at the setting sun, the sky alight in orange and purple and pink.

Mzatal splayed both hands over my upper back, then jerked them away as if recoiling from a shock. A heartbeat later I felt his hands on my back again, trembling so slightly I wasn't sure if I imagined it. Gradually the familiar warmth began to flow from his hands. With every heartbeat the pain faded and my breathing grew easier.

I drifted as he worked, but not like before where I thought I might lose myself. This was more the not-quite-sleep I'd go into on those rare occasions when I could afford a full body massage. Not that this was anything like a full body massage, but the sense of deep relief and easing was the same as he seemed to literally pull the pain from me. I wanted to sleep, but that was still impossible.

He lifted his hands from me, and I roused from my light stupor. Fully night beyond the glass now. "Is it working?" I mumbled. "Are you getting them off?" Already it was far easier to speak and breathe, though I was still a long way away from being pain free. But the sense of *yuck* and wrongness had definitely lessened.

Mzatal didn't answer for a moment, and when he did his voice carried none of its usual potency and richness. "Your back is complete," he said, fatigue and faint quaver in his tone. "I will shift you now so that I may work on your front."

He rolled me as gently as possible. It still hurt, but it was so much less than before that I only cried out once. I looked up into his face as he tugged the blanket back up to my waist. His eyes lacked their usual bright intensity, and he held his mouth in a tight line as if holding back the urge to spew.

He took a warm wet cloth from a faas and began carefully wiping the blood away, gaze flicking over the sigils, reading the patterns. The arcane cauterization of the blade left the cuts seeping—nothing like the bloody mess that would have resulted from a normal knife.

An odd tug of worry went through me at his appearance. It didn't make sense that I should be worried about the well-being of my captor, yet even so it was clear that he'd pushed himself to the brink of collapse to get me back. Whatever the hell his motives were, he'd saved me from a deeply horrible fate, and dealing with the sigils clearly sucked ass.

"You okay?" I asked.

Mzatal gave a slight nod as if to say, *yes I'm just dandy*, but then gave a faint grimace and shook his head. "I require a moment," he said, voice sounding as normal as anyone else's, which felt utterly wrong coming from him. "This is difficult."

"It's cool." I paused. "Thanks."

He knelt beside the bed, one hand resting lightly on my upper arm. He closed his eyes, bowed his head. I wondered if he was still drawing from Idris's support diagram. I had the strangest desire to cover his hand with mine, though I was sure I still couldn't move my arm to do so. Probably a lot better that way. I was fucked up in so many ways right now, and I *knew* my judgment was completely bonked. Hell, that's how I'd ended up in this mess.

Mzatal remained still and silent for what had to be at least five minutes. Finally he lifted his head and opened his eyes. They held a bit more of their normal vitality, though still far from their usual keen intensity. "Now I will finish," he said. "And you will be able to sleep."

"Sleep . . . here?" I asked, brow creasing.

"Yes, it is safest." He set one hand on my upper chest and one on my abdomen, took a deep breath as if gathering the resources to begin again. "And under my eye."

"Right." I exhaled a shaking sigh. "Under your eye. Guess I won't be allowed to go on hikes to the grove."

His gaze shifted from my sternum to my face, silent.

"Why didn't you just . . . tell me?" I asked, voice cracking badly. "Why not . . . just say: Hey, Kara, he's going to fuck you up?"

The fatigue on his face seemed to deepen. He looked back to the sigils and began to work. "I intended to tell you as soon as I removed the mark, and you were clear of Rhyzkahl's influence. Even then, you would likely not have believed me. But the information could have served you later, while you were at his palace." He breathed slowly and somewhat unsteadily, and with each breath the pain from the sigils faded more. "He has never done anything this extreme before."

I let out a low sigh. He was right. I wouldn't have believed him, but I sure as hell might have caught on to the undercurrent at Rhyzkahl's if I'd had the warning.

"I'm never going home again, am I?" I asked after a while.

He looked visibly ill, though I was fairly sure it had nothing to do with my question and everything to do with the fucking sigils. "If you mean to Earth, then I cannot say for certain, though it is in the realm of possibility that you will not."

It was the answer I'd expected, but that didn't make it hurt any less. "I'm unmarked now," I said, watching his face carefully. "If I *don't* agree to work for you, then why the hell would you possibly let me continue to live?"

Mzatal shifted his hands to the very first sigil that had

been carved upon me, and now the last one to be healed. What seemed like an eternity ago, he'd asked me my heart's desire. My life had depended on my answer then, and he echoed it back to me now. "Because, Kara Gillian, you have yet to reach your full potential."

I looked away. "You're a slick motherfucker."

He exhaled, and in the next heartbeat searing heat flooded through all the sigils. My hands clenched in the sheet as he kept firm contact on me. A shudder went through him, and his breath hissed through his teeth. Finally the heat faded, and his hands slid from me. Gasping in relief, I took several deep breaths. The sense of *wrong* was gone now. I remained plenty fucked in other ways, but at least I didn't feel as if I'd been dipped in sewage.

Mzatal sank back to his heels, head bowed, trembling slightly as his hands dropped limply into his lap. Shock ran through me at the pained grimace on his face.

Worry for him rose. "Mzatal? . . . Mzatal?"

He remained perfectly still as my inexplicable worry increased. At long last he took a deep breath and lifted his head, though I had the sense it took incredible effort to do even that.

His gaze touched mine. "Here," he replied softly. "Now you sleep."

And I did.

Chapter 20

"Come, Rowan." Jesral tugged on my leash, rousing me from my fitful doze. "You have work to do."

I drew back from him. "No, please."

The slim lord scowled. He gave the leash another sharp tug, then lifted a quirt and smacked it across my bare hip. I yelped and scrambled to my feet.

"Come," he repeated as he turned and began to walk. Heart pounding, I hurried after him. I knew he'd drag me if I didn't.

He pulled me to the center of Rhyzkahl's summoning chamber, then disappeared into darkness, leaving me alone. Cold air sent gooseflesh rippling over my bare skin. Dim red light streamed from a sigil high above, and as I stood shivering, more sigils flared into life to surround me in a slowly spinning circle. Shying away from them, I cast a frantic gaze around. "Mzatal?"

Rhyzkahl caught my chin and tipped my head up. "He is not here, dear one." He gave a soft smile. "It is so much better this way. He would only use you. I told you."

I recoiled. "You. You hurt me!" A lasso of potency wrapped around my wrist, but it didn't come from Rhyzkahl. I looked back in shock to see Mzatal, face angry and hard as he dragged me toward him.

"I *am* here," he snarled. "I will retrieve you, and I will hold you."

I struggled against the lasso. Kadir's cold laugh echoed through the darkness.

"Pain is ephemeral," Rhyzkahl said, before me again as he raised the blood-slick blade. "You are eternal. Mine."

Jesral stepped out of the darkness. "Ours."

Mzatal bared his teeth and dragged me closer to him.

Dull pain flared in my shoulders as I jerked awake. I stared at the ceiling, domed and painted to look like the night sky, replete with softly winking stars. Not Rhyzkahl's summoning chamber. A bedroom. Mzatal's. I squeezed my eyes shut, choking back a sob of both relief and dismay.

Mzatal moved into my view. "Kara. A dream. It was a dream."

No. It wasn't a dream. I let out a shuddering breath and focused on him. He was still wearing the same white dress shirt he'd had on before, now patterned with dried blood that I knew was mine. Dark circles rimmed his eyes, and I had a feeling he'd woken only an instant before I had.

He poured tunjen juice into a glass, then slipped an arm beneath me to help me sit up, releasing me as soon as I was upright. "Drink. You need much fluid."

I took it with both hands and drank, wincing at residual pain in my shoulders. After I finished and held out the empty glass, he simply refilled it and pressed it into my hand again.

I stared down at the pale pink juice, struggling to find a way to get everything to make sense. *I should have seen Rhyzkahl's betrayal coming.* How could I have been so fucking gullible?

"Drink more," Mzatal prompted. Numbly, I lifted the glass and drank. "There is more work to be done on your shoulders," he said as soon as I finished, "then that aspect will be complete." He took the empty glass and set it on the side table, helped me lie back.

I looked away as he began to work, shame continuing to knot my gut. There'd been a million things I could have done differently. Yet I'd stumbled blindly on and right into Rhyzkahl's trap.

Mzatal leaned over me, laying one hand on each shoulder. Warmth flowed into me, chasing the pain away. He remained silent while he worked, either because of his own obvious fatigue, or perhaps because he knew that a bunch of talk wasn't what I needed right now. I turned my head to the right and watched clouds drift in the pale grey of the early morning sky. Fresh air from the open glass doors carried the scent of rain and flowers, and the incessant low roar of the waterfall offered a soothing backdrop of sound.

Eventually, he withdrew his hands. "You have much to consider and process, Kara."

I scowled. "Ya think?"

He remained unruffled by my snark. "Yes, I do. Helori will take you away from here for a time, to regain yourself."

A frown tugged at my mouth. "What do you mean, away? And who's Helori?"

"Helori is a demahnk syraza," he told me. "Away from here. You need time and space to recover."

I looked away from him, watched as an ilius coiled its way across the floor to settle in a corner of the room. "Guess I'm not much good to you all busted up inside and out, huh?"

He didn't argue the point. "Nor are you serving yourself in any way." He reached and ran his hands three times from my neck down over the points of my shoulders, then straightened and clasped his hands behind his back.

I sat up. Nothing hurt anymore, and that felt strange. "Thank you," I said. "Where are you sending me?"

He inclined his head to me. "I trust Helori to take you to places appropriate for you to regain something of yourself."

My eyes drifted to the grove beyond the southern window wall. *Home. I could be myself at home*, I thought, wishing the grove could take me there. *I wish I'd never become a summoner.* I sure as hell didn't want to ever summon again.

"Give it time, Kara," Mzatal said in a curiously gentle voice. "You have much potential and will remember that when you come to yourself again."

I stiffened. "Stop reading my mind," I snarled. "I fucking hate that shit."

"I cannot," he replied, moving out to the doorway of the balcony. "As I have noted before, it is as invisibly natural as the beating of my heart."

"Well, *try*." My hands shook, and I clenched them in the sheet. *Rhyzkahl* read my fears and weaknesses, used them against me ruthlessly. "It's like a mental assault."

He exhaled. "As I said, I cannot. Though I give you my word that I will not use it to your detriment."

His word. Right. I didn't have a whole lot of trust for

lords going on at the moment. Shivering, I pulled the sheet up. My hands brushed my torso, and I froze, felt the blood drain from my face. "There are scars." My voice shook badly. "They scarred." None of my other wounds he'd healed had scarred. Why these?

"I did all that could be done," he said, regret coloring his voice. "The nature of their creation—the taint of *rakkuhr*—prevented more."

I flinched. "I have to live with them forever?" I struggled to process the knowledge that I would have a constant reminder of what happened to me.

"Unless a means beyond my understanding comes forward, yes."

He doesn't care, I thought, mood suddenly bleak. Why should he? He wanted me as his summoner. Didn't matter to him whether I was all scarred up. I pulled the sheet back up, shivers going through me in waves. I couldn't seem to hold a thought in my head for more than a few seconds. I knew I was in deep shock and suffering from all sorts of post-trauma stress, but knowing it and being able to do something about it were two completely different things. I felt utterly fractured, and I didn't have the faintest idea of how to even begin putting myself back together.

Mzatal turned back to me, brow furrowed, looking as though he was about to say something, then he shifted his attention to the door. "Helori is here to take you."

I followed his gaze to see a syraza crouched silently by the door. Larger than Ilana and apparently male, he also had the ridges on head and torso that marked him as an Elder. I hadn't heard him come in. For all I knew he'd been there since before I woke up. How was I supposed to prepare for a trip with him? Was I supposed to pack or something?

Helori rose fluidly and moved to the side of the bed, crouched again. "I am Helori," he said with a teeth-baring smile. "And I would be honored if you would accompany me on a journey."

I dragged up an unsteady smile from somewhere. "Okay." I didn't know what else to say after that.

Apparently it was enough. Helori lifted his eyes to Mzatal. "I have her now."

Mzatal gave the syraza a nod, eyes traveling over me before he turned and departed.

"Do I . . . ?" I frowned, tried again. "Should I pack something?"

"I have done so for you," he told me, "and am happy to add anything, though I will have access to most necessities while we are away."

"I don't think I need anything." My frown deepened. I was pretty sure that was true.

Helori stood, and now I saw he had clothing in his hand. "I have these for you," he said, setting on the foot of the bed the necessary underwear as well as shirt and pants made of a pale blue gauzy material. He placed simple slip-on shoes on the floor nearby. "If they do not suit, I will find others." He tilted his head. "Yes? No?"

"Yeah," I said, glad not to be faced with any weightier decision than that. "That's good."

He moved to the balcony. "I will be here when you are ready."

I waited for him to leave, then reached cautiously for the clothing, anticipating pain and surprised when it didn't come. I dressed slowly, then tugged my hands through my hair, expecting and finding it tangled and greasy. Someone had cleaned the blood off me while I slept, but I still felt yucky. Yet I also didn't want to bathe here. I didn't want to spend any more time here than necessary. And I trusted Helori, an Elder, more than I trusted Mzatal.

I slipped the shoes on and stepped out to the balcony. "I guess I'm ready."

Helori smiled. "Come then. We will go to the grove." He took my hand and led me back through Mzatal's chambers and out. I followed without question or resistance as he led me out of the palace and toward the grove, his hand firm and comfortable on mine, our entire journey remarkably free of demons or humans or lords.

Helori greeted the mehnta as we entered the grove, then pulled me to the center and gave my hand a light squeeze. "Where would you like to go?"

Someplace safe, I thought. *Someplace calm and beautiful and far away from lords. Far far away from lords.* But to Helori I only gave a small shrug.

The syraza squeezed my hand again, nodded to the mehnta, and then we were gone.

Chapter 21

Helori led me up the tree tunnel of the grove at our destination and onto the narrow trail, through oversized plants with leaves twice my height pressing close and arching above. The rushing sound of surging surf came from ahead, punctuated by sharp cries and squawks from a variety of unseen creatures.

"Perhaps here will suit," he said as we stepped out into the open.

I breathed in the warm salt air, felt the brush of the light breeze ruffle my shirt. "It's perfect," I murmured.

White sand met the gentle surf of brilliant sea, waves of turquoise and rich blue catching the afternoon sun. The beach stretched left and right as far as I could see, bounded by rich greens and purples of giant trees and plants.

"You swim," he said as we moved down toward the water. "This is good for swimming. Very good."

The water was beautiful, but I still hesitated. I didn't want to take my shirt off. I didn't want to see or show the sigils. "That's okay," I said. "I... I'll just sit on the beach awhile."

Helori kept the loose hold on my hand as he continued down the beach. "You would not regret it. The seas here can be very soothing."

I didn't want to make a scene, and so I continued on down to the water's edge with him. I simply didn't have it in me to argue. "Sure." I could leave my shirt on. That would work.

Helori knelt and slipped my shoes off, carried them in

one hand and took my hand again with the other as he led me over the fine-grained sand into the fringe of the surf. The water whooshed and swirled around my ankles in random, yet hypnotic movement. I didn't pull away from him. The water seemed to help me forget, at least briefly, how broken I was.

He gradually led me deeper, keeping a comfortable hold on my hand. I didn't fear the water or the depths. I was actually a really good swimmer, and didn't need his hand for physical support, but I knew that wasn't why he maintained the light grip. Looking out to the horizon, I tried to hold onto this sense of peace. I knew too damn well how fragile it was.

"How long do I have here?" I asked. "When did Mzatal say you have to bring me back?"

"He did not specify," Helori replied. "It will fall to us to decide."

My brow furrowed. "Us? What are you talking about?"

The syraza chimed softly. "Us. You and me. We will decide when to return."

Frowning, I struggled to process this, but I couldn't think straight enough for it to make sense. "Why would Mzatal let *me* have any say in when I returned?"

"You have *all* of the say," Helori told me. "With me as guidance for as much as you will accept. You are not his prisoner."

I stared at him, then laughed. "Oh, right. Is that what he told you?"

"Mzatal did not need to tell me," Helori said as he led me a little deeper. "I know this. You are not a prisoner, and I am not your guard. He would have you work with him, but he will not force it."

I stopped and turned to face him. "What if I never wanted to touch the arcane again?" Because there was a part of me that was considering exactly that. I'd had more than my fill of arcane shit.

His amethyst eyes were deep upon me. "It is most certainly a choice you can make, though it is not a choice you must make now in this moment. Should you choose to shun the arcane, you would still not be a prisoner."

The syraza was completely serious, I realized. I shook my

head as I tried to mentally reconfigure *everything*. "Then why . . ." I trailed off, struggled to get my thoughts straight. "But he was going to kill me."

Helori took both my hands in his. "It was a very present possibility on several occasions, yes," he said with full honesty. "In the early instances, for the preservation of the realm. In the instance prior to your surprising departure, to keep you from the hand of Rhyzkahl, though in doing so it protected the realm as well."

"And what if he decides the realm needs protecting again?" I asked quietly.

The syraza seemed to look *into* me. "He would do what he must," he replied, not lying—which, I supposed, was better than a line of bullshit. "He takes his stewardship quite seriously. However, I know him well. With all that has happened, he will do everything in his power to see that it does not come to that."

"But how am I supposed to live knowing that at any moment he *could*?" I asked, deeply shaken. "And would?" Was I safe anywhere?

Helori lowered his head, gaze intensifying. "That is a question only you can answer. You know something of what is possible on a personal level from your time as a guardian of others." I knew he was referring to my career as a police officer. "Answer for yourself what you would want in such a situation. Answer for yourself if you knew many others would die so that you may live. Speak to Mzatal of it. He will not lie to you and will tell you precisely where he stands. And you can tell him precisely where you stand."

Even though I understood Helori, and agreed, I still felt myself trembling at the thought of having such a conversation with Mzatal. "I'm not ready to do that." I'd never be able to hold myself together for a talk like that. Not now, not feeling so fucked up. *Will I ever be not fucked up?* I couldn't even imagine it.

"No, you are not ready," he said. "And you do not need to be yet. We will not return until you feel more yourself. And I will care for you until then. You have my word on that."

Throat tight, I nodded as the truth of it wound around me like a warm blanket. Pulling away from his hand, I turned away. I knew I was about to start crying, and I quickly ducked under the water to get my face wet so it wasn't so obvious. I didn't want to have to deal with any of the shit that went along with crying, like being comforted, or anything like that.

"I want to swim," I told him, and didn't wait for a response before diving into an oncoming swell.

He didn't appear to take any sort of offense. He retreated to the beach with a smile then took to the air in a graceful leap. Probably to better watch over me, I supposed, while I did my swimming and crying thing.

I continued until I was fairly tired out—which didn't take all that long since I was still recovering from a lot of crap. I made my way back up to the beach. Though Helori wasn't in sight, he had spread out a blanket beneath the shade of trees as large as oaks, but with graceful draping limbs like a willow. I still felt empty, but in a slightly better way than before.

A pile of neatly folded dry clothing lay on the blanket. I changed quickly, grateful to Helori for the consideration. A few minutes later, he landed neatly in the sand a few yards away.

"The water is lovely, yes?" he said.

"Yeah," I said with a small smile. "It's pretty awesome."

He crouched near me. "You chose one of my favorite destinations for swimming."

I gave him a puzzled look. "*I* chose?"

"Yes, you chose." His mouth curved into a syraza-smile. "You let the grove know what you wanted, even if you did not realize it."

I processed that for a few seconds. "It's nice and calm here."

"And it is safe." He placed a three-fingered hand on my arm. "Would it trouble you if I changed to human form?"

"No," I replied. "I've seen Eilahn do it. Do you need help?"

"Thank you, Kara. I am able to change independently, as can all of the Elders." He stood. "It is the younger syraza who need assistance."

He stretched his wings out as far as they would go, then pulled them in tightly, at the same time drawing a gauzy cloth from . . . elsewhere. "It is a fascinating process," he said. "You should tell me if Hollywood special effects are better than the real thing," he added with a syraza-laugh.

I made mental note of his casual Earth references and understandings. I'd seen Eilahn shift, but Helori's was a seamless morph that kicked the ass of any CGI. Only a few seconds later he smiled at me from a human face, then drew the gauze cloth around his waist and tucked it in a fluid motion. About the height of Mzatal, lean and lithe, he wouldn't have stood out in a crowd. That kind of surprised me since Eilahn was an absolute knockout in human form, and most of the lords seemed pretty damn good-looking. He did have the same multi-racial quality as Eilahn, but it served to make him blend rather than stand out.

He came over to sit cross-legged on the blanket, then planted his elbows on knees and chin on fists as he peered at me. "Hungry? Thirsty? Sleepy?"

"Not sleepy," I said. "Tired, but not sleepy. I could eat, though."

He seemed to go distant for a moment, then reached and drew cheese, a knife, and a round loaf of bread from . . . elsewhere and set them all before me. That was a pretty cool trick.

"I'll be right back." He winked, leapt up, and disappeared into the trees. I watched him go, then cut some bread and cheese and began to eat. A few minutes later Helori returned and deposited a double handful of cranberry-looking things on the blanket. "That should help tame your appetite," he said with a smile.

Trusting that he wouldn't give me anything nasty, I tried one and found it to be sweet and juicy, with a texture like a cross between an apple and grape. "These are good," I said. "Thanks."

Helori dropped to sit beside me again. "I do realize that what the demon realm calls 'good' may be 'horrendous' on Earth. I will do my best to offer only tasty tidbits, though I encourage you to always test because I might misjudge." He grinned.

"Will do." I held up a berry. "These look a lot like cranberries. My aunt and I string cranberries and popcorn garlands for the Christmas tree every year." Lowering my hand, I let out a soft sigh. "I'm still hoping to make it back home for Christmas this year."

"That is only a couple of weeks away," he replied, obviously familiar with the Earth date. I made a mental note of that. "Perhaps with an escort," he continued, "but not alone, not that soon."

I popped the berry into my mouth and nodded. "Eilahn made me promise not to leave my house or another warded place until I could summon her back."

"She is wise for her youth and quite devoted." He glanced over at me. "She would not be denied in her determination to go to you."

"I thought Rhyzkahl asked her to go," I said, surprised.

"Well, yes he did." Helori's eyes crinkled in a smile. "Though it became his idea to do so through the counsel of Olihr, who conspired with Eilahn."

My surprise deepened. "But why? I mean, how could she possibly know about me, let alone want to be my protector?"

"Your existence became well known among the syraza as soon as you brought Rhyzkahl through the first time," he told me. "She touched in to the impression and resonated instantly."

"That's . . . wow." Amazed and deeply flattered, I had no idea what to say about that. "I do like her very much."

"Good!" he said with a chuckle. "Because I think you're stuck with her. Though Eilahn alone is not adequate protection for you yet."

"I know how to be careful." But a frown tugged at my mouth. Being careful hadn't helped me the past few days, had it? "My house and the police station are warded like crazy." I could take care of myself at home. Yeah, I'd have to become a hermit, but it would be worth it simply to be back.

Helori wasn't smiling anymore. "You know how to be careful in your old paradigm," he said, serious. "It served well enough for a time with Zakaar and Eilahn watching over you, and limited interest in you from other than Rhyzkahl. You are known now, so that interest is no longer limited. Others will seek you, and you are yet unschooled in the arcane beyond basics."

A sick knot began to form in my gut. "What are you saying, Helori? That I can't go home?"

He shook his head. "No, I'm saying that you need to be

far better prepared before going home. Even a brief visit before then would require an escort in addition to Eilahn, and it would still be inadvisable."

"Okay, so I'll summon more demons," I said, desperately clinging to the comforting thought of getting away from this place soon. "I'll owe favors if I have to."

He reached and laid a hand on my arm. "You have had a brief glimpse of the work that Idris does, yet you comprehend only a fraction of it," he said with quiet insistence. "You know now that there is so much more apart from rudimentary Earth-side summoning. You need expanded skills, and you have the resources, now, to acquire them."

My eyes dropped to my hands in my lap. The low breeze stirred my shirt, brushing the fabric against the scars covering my torso. A nameless dread rose within me. "I can't stay here," I said hoarsely. "My aunt and my friends, they don't know what happened to me. They don't know if I'm alive or dead."

"They can be notified through Gestamar, when next he is summoned," Helori said quietly.

I let out a harsh laugh utterly devoid of humor. "Yeah, that'd be some letter home. 'Hey, y'all, weather's great here. Miss you tons. Oh, by the way, I got the shit tortured out of me, and everything's all fucked up. Write soon!' "

"They would know you lived," was his gentle reply. "Your choice to stay here and learn is critical, Kara. To best protect those on Earth, as well as yourself, you need to be as strong and capable as possible. Zakaar will most certainly be watching over your friends and family in your absence, though his primary focus is Ryan."

I heard what he was saying. I would put everyone in danger if I returned home. Not just myself. Heartsick, I let the hope of going home anytime soon crumble to ash.

Helori shifted his hand from my arm to the base of my throat, touching the sigil carved there.

I drew back. "Don't. Don't touch them."

He kept his hand extended toward the sigil. "You must look," he urged. "You must know."

I stiffened. "I've seen them."

"You will not even glance at them now." His eyes darkened with concern. "They are a part of you. You need to *know* them."

"I know them, I promise," I said, voice cracking. "I remember every agonizing instant that went into the making of them. Every day, for the rest of my life, I get to have the reminder of how stupid and gullible I was."

He shifted to crouch beside me, looking every inch the syraza even though he was in human form. "You can use them to remind you of that, or you can use them to remind you, every moment of every day, of how strong you are to have thrived despite the motherfucker's best efforts to destroy you." He cocked his head, dropped his eyes to the scars that showed above the neckline of my shirt. "I look at them and see tenacity and strength. You need to know *what* Rhyzkahl put on you, not just that he put them on."

I scrubbed at my face. "I look back at my time with him and see all the hints and clues that I should've picked up on."

"When you first realized his intentions, what did you feel?" Helori asked quietly.

My lower lip quivered despite all efforts to maintain control. "I was . . . I don't know. I was disappointed." I scowled. "That was my main feeling. So fucking disappointed that he turned out to be such a . . ." Shaking, I took a deep breath and screamed it: *"FUCKING DICK!"*

Searing anger rose, near startling me with how foreign the sensation seemed after being so long immersed in panic and fear. I'd been ready to direct the anger at myself, yet now I knew that wouldn't do me any good. *I* was the goddamn victim.

"Were he standing here right now," Helori said, "what would you do?"

I swiped at my eyes, not surprised to find that I was crying. "I sure as hell wouldn't scream anything. Not even a choice name." I took a deep breath. "I won't scream for him anymore. I've screamed too much for him already." My gaze drifted to a flock of iridescent green sea birds swooping and diving into the water. Last time I'd seen a flock wheeling, I'd been in the gazebo at Rhyzkahl's. "I hate him. He's less than scum." Then I smiled very slightly as I returned my attention to Helori. "But if he was standing right here, I might very well kick him really hard in the goddamn balls."

A whisper of a smile touched his face.

I drew a deep breath and then blew it out. "Mzatal

healed my body," I continued. "Nothing hurts anymore." I toyed with a patch of sand that had made its way onto the blanket, drew random patterns in it while I spoke. "The problem with healing my body of the injuries is that my mind feels like it should be healed as well." I paused. "It's not. It's just as stretched and twisted and shattered as my shoulders were. I can be a real tenacious bitch." I shook my head, gulped. "But this. . . . It's like I'm barely holding onto myself."

"Yes. I know," Helori said. "It is why I proposed this time away for you. It is why we are here—to help you regain that hold."

"*You* proposed it?" I gave him a puzzled look.

"Mzatal was exhausted and truly confounded about how to expediently work with the loss of yourself." He gave me a gentle smile. "I offered this as a possible means."

"Thanks," I said softly. "I didn't even know you before this."

"As I said, once you summoned Rhyzkahl single-handedly, you became known among the syraza," he said, then chuckled low. "And now you are getting to know something of me, though that can be a blessing and a curse."

I laughed weakly. "I'm infamous. Great."

My gaze returned to the gull-things. I could do this now. I *had* to do this now. Hands shaking and heart pounding, I shifted to kneel. I grabbed my shirt before I could panic and change my mind, then practically ripped it and my bra off and threw them aside. Breathing shallowly, I knelt half-nude before him.

Helori traced a sigil in the air above us. I flinched before realizing it was just the damn pygah, then scowled at my reaction.

"Be gentle on yourself," he murmured. "As he was not." He traced three more sigils around the pygah and set it spinning slowly above us.

"I made it this far, didn't I?" I replied, though my voice quavered. The resonance of the pygah combined with the other sigils to form an almost palpable cocoon of calm. Slowly, I unclenched my hands, though I still wasn't ready to look at the pygah or myself yet.

He took gentle hold of my left wrist, straightened my arm, and held it nearly straight out from my shoulder, so that I didn't have to look down to see the scar where the mark used to be. "Look first here," he said. "The first evidence of your betrayal."

Ghostly echoes of the essence agony shimmered through me as I forced my eyes to the long, rippled scar. Sweat stung my armpits. "The fucker," I whispered.

"He knew when he placed the mark that he meant to use you," he told me. "Though the way you were used shifted from the original intent."

My gaze rose to him. "Shifted? What do you mean?"

Helori lowered my arm. "You were initially slated to be used to retrieve Vsuhl, and then to die in a ritual to create a permanent gate to Earth," he said. "Your value changed once Rhyzkahl became aware of your grove affinity." He stroked a thumb lightly over the scar on my forearm, then looked back up to my face. "That affinity made you far more valuable and useful, and thus they chose to make you a thrall, so you could be a long-term tool for their use. You would have been powerful, utterly compliant, and obliviously content."

I'd heard some of this from Rhyzkahl during the ritual, but here, away from the torment, it abruptly clicked into place. "That son of a bitch," I breathed. I'd never been able to understand why Amkir had treated me with such open hostility from the moment I met him, nor why Rhyzkahl had left me and not intervened in the altercation sooner. *It was a test*, I realized. Those assholes had set me up. I'd told Rhyzkahl about using the grove power on Mzatal, and they wanted to see if I could do it again.

My anger rose, and I let it keep going, let it burn away at the panic and fear. I scowled up at the pygah, tempted to bat it away. I didn't want to be calm right now. I dropped my gaze back to Helori. "Tell me about these sigils."

"United, they are a key to the potency of this world," he said while dissipating the pygah. "The ritual was not completed, and so this purpose was thwarted."

I listened carefully, jaw tight. "Why twelve?"

"The twelfth is the unifier, but the ritual failed before it was ignited."

"So, a sigil for each lord?" I asked.

"Yes, one for each, plus the unifier," he said, watching me closely.

"Tell me," I said, holding my anger close to me like armor. "Tell me about each one."

Helori shifted forward, touched the sigil over my sternum and part of my breasts—the first that Rhyzkahl had carved. "This one represents Mzatal, laid as an anchoring presence for the rest."

That surprised me. "Why? Is Mzatal stronger than the others?"

"He is the oldest," Helori stated. "And has proven to be a stabilizer for all of them."

I pointed to the sigil that spread across my upper chest, above Mzatal's. "He made this one next."

"Rhyzkahl," he said and placed a hand over it while I exhaled a shaking breath.

His hands traveled over my body while he traced the sigils and murmured the names. There was nothing sexual about his touch. It held only ease and recognition.

"Jesral," he said, touching the one on my lower abdomen that wound up and over the lowest part of my breasts. My lip curled at the name.

"He knew," I said, hatred flaring. "He walked me to the ritual."

"He would have shared mastery over you upon completion," Helori stated.

"Mastery." I tasted the word. "Fuck him. Fuck them all."

He nodded agreement, shifted his hand to lay it fully over a convoluted and uneven sigil on my right side. "Kadir."

A shiver raced over me. "Bad Monkey."

"Bad Monkey. Yes," Helori agreed. "Very Bad Monkey."

I gave a small smile. He understood perfectly.

He shifted around me, naming more, then touched the one on the lowest part of my back, a sigil that dove to my tailbone. "Amkir."

I snorted. "He's an asshole," I said. "Appropriate that he should be close to mine."

Helori chuckled softly. "Yes, he is. Definitively."

I exhaled as Helori placed his hand on the only one he had yet to name—the sigil that began at the nape of my neck, flowed over much of my upper back, and coalesced in a focal spiral between my shoulder blades. I'd never seen it, but I remembered fully every slice of Rhyzkahl's blade across my skin. "Szerain," I murmured. *One of the few I don't despise*, I thought, but then frowned. I only knew Ryan. I didn't know Szerain. There was every chance I could despise him as well.

"The last, here," he said, touching my lower back. "The sigil was completed, but not ignited. Idris and Mzatal disrupted the ritual to assure it was not."

I turned to look at him. "Could it still be?" I asked, speaking my fear.

He shook his head. "The unifying sigil carries its own potency, as does each of the others. But they are not united and cannot be simply through ignition of this last one, now."

"What does it mean for me, that I bear these?" I asked.

"You are unique," he said. "I do not know the full implications."

I fell silent while I struggled to put everything into some sort of order that made sense. My anger slipped away, and I let it go. I couldn't hold it indefinitely. It felt as if some of the panic went with it, though I knew I still had a lot more to deal with. I reached for my bra and shirt and pulled them back on, then sighed and lay back on the blanket.

Well, I definitely learned one new thing while I was with Rhyzkahl, I thought, as I watched puffy clouds drift across the too-blue sky. *I was totally wrong in thinking that demonic lords don't lie.* What else was I completely wrong about? What other misconceptions would come back to bite me in the ass?

Helori set the pygah to slowly spin above me, then left me alone to brood and ponder.

Chapter 22

Apparently I brooded and pondered so hard I fell asleep. Or perhaps Helori added something to the pygah. Either way, when I woke it was morning, with the sun in glorious display over the water. *I could get used to starting my days like this*, I decided, though preferably without the whole recovering-from-torture bit.

Helori had put a blanket over me and tucked a pillow under my head. When I sat up I saw that he'd also left a mug of juice and an assortment of fruits and nuts on the blanket for me.

He was out in the water, gamboling in the surf with the unabashed enthusiasm of a five-year-old. I ate and drank a bit, then pulled my clothing off, ran down to the water naked, and dove into the waves.

I swam for a while, reveling in the simple feel of the pull of my muscles against the resistance of the water and the rhythm of the waves. After what was probably half an hour, I came out of the water and took refuge in the shade to prevent the appearance of Red Kara. A few minutes later Helori plopped down onto the blanket beside me.

"I met Turek," I said as I tugged my shirt and pants back on. "The savik at Szerain's palace."

He smiled. "Yes, you did."

"He was clearly incredibly intelligent, with a strong ability in the arcane." I frowned. "So, why the hell are savik considered only second-level? And, for that matter, why are syraza only eleventh? Y'all totally kick ass and take names as far as the arcane goes."

Helori grinned. "Because, the summoner Isabel Blackburn made a note to herself as a numbered list in the margin of a text in 1212 Earth time. In 1352, it was discovered and became set in stone. I don't even know what she was referencing with the list."

I blinked, then laughed. "Holy shitballs, that's hysterical," I said. "I'd always been taught that the order of demons *meant* something as far as ability and power." I laughed again. It felt really good.

Helori joined me in the laughter. "I know! That would mean a savik is less powerful than a kehza!"

"I never met a savik as large as Turek," I said, still astonished. "The only ones I'd ever summoned, or heard of, were about a third the size."

Helori reached elsewhere and then set a handful of small cakes before me. "The ones summoned are immature," he explained as I nibbled one of the cakes experimentally. In texture, it reminded me of cornbread stuffed with savory shredded meat, but the crust part tasted more like buttery bacon than corn. *Mmmm, bacon.*

"Once mature," he continued, "they tend to strike their names and claim a new one, which they do not divulge for summoners. They are reclusive and solitary during that stage, and mostly discounted because they do not interact. They are, however, highly skilled with the arcane."

"I am shockingly ignorant of the creatures I summon," I said, grimacing. "Why are you lot called demons anyway?"

"The English designation evolved from various forms of the name for the Elders, demahnk," he explained. "In Latin it was *daemonium*, in Greek *daimónion*, referencing a thing of divine nature." He gave a light shrug. "For some, that twisted into evil nature or evil spirit."

That made sense. I took a deep breath. "So, what's on the agenda for today, Doctor Hel?"

He appeared to consider. "There are many places to visit, each with its own unique gifts." But then he smiled. "However, I know the first place I want to take you." He extended his hand to me, and I took it without hesitation.

A heartbeat later we were in a crystal cave—crystalline walls, huge crystal points, and prismatic light that seemed to originate from inside the crystal rather than reflecting light from outside. At first it was hard to *be* there. As soon as we arrived, every cell of my body vibrated—or at least, that's what it felt like. I wanted to take time to look around, do the whole "gaze in wonder" thing, but Helori tugged me forward, leading me through tunnels and broad passages and over narrow crystalline bridges, before finally stopping before a pool that shimmered with subtle hints of all colors.

"She is in stasis yet," Helori said with a gesture toward the depths of the pool. "But she is aware you are here."

Perplexed, I looked down into the pool. It wasn't filled with water, but instead seemed to be brimming with, well, liquid light was the only description I could come up with, as though all the reflections and colors from the crystals coalesced into a beautiful fluid. And there, a few feet down, was Eilahn, curled into a cute little ball with her knees tucked to her chin, her arms wrapped around her legs and her wings folded like a case around her. In all the time I'd been in the demon realm, I'd never wanted a camera more than at that moment. Because this was some *awesome* blackmail material.

Smiling, I gave Helori's hand a squeeze. "Thanks."

He returned the squeeze. "And now we visit some of my favorite places."

Helori had strange taste in favorite places, I decided. Our first stop was mud. That was it: mud as far as the eye could see. We immediately sank neck-deep in it, achieving some sort of neutral buoyancy, and then remained there for what seemed like hours while I received the best massage of my life from some I-really-really-didn't-want-to-know sort of creatures within the mud.

After that, a waterfall straight out of a shampoo commercial, then to watch a pair of breeding luhnk—which was strange and bizarre only because the female resembled a six-legged mammoth in size and shape, and the male was closer to the size of a German Shepherd. After that, we visited the lower branches of a massive tree with a trunk at least thirty feet in diameter.

Helori draped himself over a branch as thick as his waist, and I did likewise a couple of feet away. He pointed toward the ground, and I looked to see a teeming mass of carnivorous ants as big as terriers tearing into a cow-like thing twice the size of an elephant.

As I watched the industry of the giant ants, I found myself grinning; somehow I didn't think Mzatal would approve of me being in such a potentially perilous position after he'd spent so much energy and effort to retrieve me. My gaze slid to Helori. He wouldn't let me be in any true danger. I knew that, deep in my essence.

"What's going to happen to me after we return to Mzatal's palace?" I asked.

"Mzatal will train you," he replied, "though I do not know what terms of agreement he would set."

I mentally recoiled. "I don't want to be marked," I said firmly. "I can't—won't—do that again."

"He would not propose marking you now," Helori reassured me. "It is a lengthy process, and in any case, Katashi currently bears his mark, and having a second is inadvisable. He will, without doubt, require an agreement."

My brow furrowed. "Idris said something about that. What's the difference?"

"An agreement is a short term arrangement—perhaps a few months to a few years—with specific terms negotiated," Helori said. "Marking is long-term, usually lifelong."

I gave a slow nod. "Okay. I'll think about that." I had yet to fully wrap my head around the notion that Mzatal wasn't my enemy—at least, not at the moment. The idea of willingly working with him still seemed incredibly foreign. I peered at Helori. "Do you trust Mzatal?"

"Do I trust him to always make choices I agree with? No." Helori said. "Do I trust him to speak the truth to me and follow through on what he says to the best of his ability? Yes."

I took it all in, considered. Mzatal had certainly followed through on his promise to retrieve me. "I guess I can handle that."

Helori's golden-brown eyes met mine. "I have not known him to willfully break an agreement with a summoner," he told me. "Dealings with other lords, however, have their own rules."

"Some of those lords are batshit fucked-up." I snorted. "I mean, did their mamas not hug them or something?"

Helori's eternal smile faded a little, and he closed his eyes, as if in pain.

I grimaced. "Shit. Sorry. I was trying to make a joke. I

guess a bad one." But my brow furrowed. What nerve had I struck?

He let out his breath in a soft exhalation and looked back over at me. "In jest, you hit very near the mark."

My confusion increased. "Why are there no female lords? Do they not *have* mothers?"

"Genetics and arcane levels determined gender," he said. "Though it was possible for there to be a female of their kind, it did not occur."

Questions crowded together in my head, but before I could ask any of them he reached and took my hand.

"My beautiful Kara," he said, clear and ancient eyes on mine, "they do not know their origin. And I ask you to trust me that, for now, it is for the best."

My cop instincts poked at me to find out more, to continue to question, but I regretfully slapped said instincts down. For now. "All right." Damn it.

"It cannot remain thus for much longer," he said, expression briefly shadowed. "There is so much in flux now." He stood and nimbly leaped over to my branch, then pulled me to my feet. "And, speaking of flux, I am taking you now to the Zadek Kah—a polar atmospheric anomaly that acts as a kaleidoscope-type prism. The play of colored light over the landscape of ice is indescribable." He grinned. "It is *awesome*."

And before I could blink, we were off again.

Since we seemed to flit all over the planet, I lost track of time. Yet it was clear that Helori wasn't trying to distract me from either the horror I'd endured or my post-traumatic stress. Each place seemed to be a new opportunity for contemplation or conversation or simple self-discovery—like therapy at super-speed.

That second night, we slept curled up in a den of skarl—hyena-like creatures as friendly as house cats. I was dubious at first, especially since the den reeked of skarl-musk, but it turned out that the skarl gave off a comforting vibe that allowed me the best damn sleep I'd ever had in my life. As soon as I woke, though, Helori traveled us to hot springs surrounded by ice and snow to bathe the thick skarl odor away.

After bathing, I lounged on a smooth rock, neck deep in

the water. "If you can teleport pretty much anywhere," I asked, "why did we take the grove to the beach that first day?" That first day—only two days ago, yet it felt like a century.

"It was so it could truly be your choice," he told me. "You were not ready to tell me what you wanted, but you could tell the grove."

That made sense. "The climate and terrain here is a lot like Earth," I said. "The fact that humans can live here so easily, on a completely different world, is kind of mind-boggling." I gave Helori a questioning look.

He ducked under the water to slick his hair back, then nimbly climbed out of the pool and crouched beside it, apparently impervious or oblivious to the subfreezing temperatures. "Earth and this realm are closely tied in many ways, like sister worlds," he told me. "A very close family resemblance."

My lips pursed as I considered that. "Is the geography the same?" I asked. "I mean, is there a North America and Africa and all that? But, you know, with different names."

"No," he said with a shake of his head, eyes crinkling with humor. "Same family, not identical twins."

I chuckled. "I can handle that."

He laughed. "I am delighted, as I do not think it will change."

Snorting, I rolled my eyes. "Okay, my mad syraza, what do you have planned for me today?"

Taking my hand, he hauled me out of the pool, ignoring my protest, though I was surprised to find that the warmth of the hot spring seemed to insulate me from the frigid air. A heartbeat later, I thought we were standing at the mouth of a cave very high above the ground. Then I realized there was far too much wind, and that the cave itself sure seemed to be moving around a lot. Plus the floor was weirdly squishy.

I groaned. I'd seen Star Wars. I looked askance at Helori. "Are we in some sort of giant flying demon worm thing?"

He laughed. "Not a worm. A nehkil. Reminiscent of the Earth basking shark, except more reptilian, and it flies. But don't worry," he said as my expression no doubt betrayed my apprehension. "We are far too large to make it down his gullet. Ethereal spores prevalent along the coastline are his primary sustenance. You could say that he soars for spores," he said, laughing.

I gave him a pained grimace.

"You may note them passing in as flickers of light," he said, then gestured beyond the open mouth of the nehkil. "Is it not a glorious view?"

I had to agree with him there. It was pretty damn awesome. I'd only flown in airplanes a few times in my life, but I figured we were probably a couple thousand feet up. Sea spread off to the horizon on the right, in varying shades of blue and green from near black to luminescent turquoise. Shifting white marked the places it crashed into land or partially submerged rocks. Verdant forested mountains veined with waterfalls and rivers rose to the left.

Helori pulled a blanket from elsewhere and spread it out on the beastie's, er, tongue, I assumed. I found myself inordinately glad for the blanket, since I was still buck-naked from the hot springs. But, since Helori was nude as well, I didn't see a point in making a fuss about clothing, and after only a few minutes I forgot about it completely.

We stayed there for what was probably most of the day. The nehkil's mouth and tongue were nowhere near as moist as I'd expected, and Helori explained that its salivary glands shut down during this open-mouthed basking in order to prevent it from dehydrating. I alternated between enjoying the view, napping, and general navel-gazing while the nehkil flew along the coastline.

The sun was beginning to dip toward the west when I saw a huge arch of stone stretching from a mountain into the sea. Though I was pretty sure that part was natural, there was something about the shapes around and on top of it that were not. As we got closer, I could make out windows, balconies, and arched doorways, all blending beautifully into the stone and greenery of the arch.

"What's that?" I asked Helori.

Helori lounged on his side, propped on one elbow. "That's the home of Rayst and Seretis."

"Both of them?" I asked. "They live there together?"

He nodded. "They each have their own sections, but most is common use."

"I met Rayst during the conclave," I said, "He seemed very nice." I paused. "I don't despise him."

"On the scale of lordly ratings, 'nice' serves," Helori said with a smile. "He involves himself with the power games as little as possible, but will not hesitate to step in if he sees the need."

As my gaze traveled over the palace, I caught a glimpse of iridescent wings atop the stone arch.

"Rayst and Seretis had a lot of syraza with them at the conclave," I said. "Do the syraza like them more or something?"

"It is a preference," he replied. "The potency environment is not only stronger there with two lords together, but also more comfortable due to the nature of those two. And thus many of the younger syraza live near and associate closely with Rayst and Seretis." Helori smiled. "It took much for the other lords to agree to the shift—for both to be in the same geographic location—because the entire structure of the potency flows had to be reconstructed. But it was long enough ago that all came to agree on it."

I pursed my lips in a frown. "Ilana is Mzatal's syraza-counselor, his ptarl, and Zack . . . Zakaar is Rhyzkahl's. Where is Szerain's?"

"Xharbek." Helori exhaled. "Xharbek is in hiding."

My brow furrowed. "Because Szerain is in exile? Or because of *why* he's in exile?"

"Both." He fell silent for several heartbeats before speaking again. "Xharbek is thought dead by, well, most."

I regarded him, considered his words. "But you don't think he is."

His eyes met mine. "No. I do not."

Interesting. Yet another addition to the mental clue board. At this rate I was going to need a mental clue wall.

I lifted my chin toward the structure as we came closer. "It's not as Palace-y as the others I've seen."

"Each lord builds according to taste and purpose," Helori said. "Simply viewing and feeling the residences gives much information."

That seemed quite true from what I'd seen so far. I glanced back at Helori. "Rayst and Seretis. Are they *together* together?"

He raised an eyebrow. "Yes. And have been for a very long time."

I chuckled. "Well, no wonder they're happier than all the other lords. Or at least they seem that way."

"More at peace," he said with a nod. "Though that too is a relative term."

The nehkil veered slowly away from the dwelling. The faint flicker at the edge of my sight told me that there were probably aversions or some other sort of protective wards in place to keep wildlife away. I stayed silent long after the home of Rayst and Seretis disappeared from view, pondering everything that had happened since my arrival in the demon realm.

When the sun touched the horizon I turned back to Helori.

"I think it's time for me to go back now."

Chapter 23

I exited the tree tunnel in Mzatal's realm with Helori by my side. My steps slowed as I looked out at the greens and dark greys of the mountains, the glinting glass of Mzatal's palace, and the dark finger of the column. I wasn't healed, not by a long stretch, but now I felt as if the fracture had at least been set. And I was ready to face Mzatal.

Helori, still in human form, slid a look at me as we made our way down the stone path and stairs. "Idris is working in the entry hall."

Shame tightened my gut. I'd had the fucking gall to think that *he* was the naïve one. Wasn't that a laugh.

"He was instrumental in your recall," he continued. "Mzatal could not have accomplished it on his own. Both worked continuously from the time of your departure until the time of your recall."

I stayed silent for several heartbeats. "I understand now why he stays with Mzatal."

"It is as perfect a pairing of student and teacher as I have ever seen," Helori replied.

The simple cave-like entryway beyond the stone and glass doors struck me as refreshingly unpretentious after the opulent grandeur of Rhyzkahl's palace. Idris stood near the wall to the right, crafting a ward with an ease and elegance that I could only dream of someday having. He glanced my way as we entered, and his eyes lit up with surprise and delight. "Kara!" He turned to me and nearly fumbled the ward, then grinned in relief as Helori lifted a hand and kept it from completely unwinding.

Helori moved off, leaving me alone with Idris. "Yeah, it's me," I said, instantly realizing how dumb that sounded.

But his grin only widened. "God, Kara, you look so much better than—" He flushed. "I mean . . . shit. Sorry. You look great."

I held back a low laugh. "Thanks. I feel a lot better, too," I said with a sigh. "I'm sorry you had to go through so much to get me back. Running away to Rhyzkahl was about the stupidest thing I've ever done."

"Yeah, but you didn't *know* it was stupid at the time," he said with a scowl. "It was *Rhyzkahl* you were dealing with. How would you know?" He shook his head. "I mean, back on Earth, that is. When you got here, Lord Mzatal should have . . ." He trailed off, then straightened his shoulders. "He should have told you more," he said definitively.

Damn. Idris grew a spine while I was gone.

"Anyway, I'm glad you're back," he continued. "I, um, we were really worried about you."

"Well, thanks for everything," I said with a small smile. "I owe you, big-time."

He flushed and smiled sheepishly. "Nah. It was no biggie. You're kinda special, y'know?"

Special? Was he crushing on me? Weird. "No, I just managed to attract the attention of some powerful people. A perfect storm of Shit Happens." Sighing again, I leaned my back against the wall. "The first time I summoned Rhyzkahl was an *accident*. I was trying to summon Rhyzel, a luhrek, at the same time that Peter Cerise—the Symbol Man killer—was trying to summon Rhyzkahl. The lord simply hijacked my summoning to escape Cerise's binding."

Idris began tracing a new ward. "Yeah, whatever. I couldn't do it."

I frowned and tilted my head. "Have you ever tried? I mean, summoning a lord?"

His gaze snapped to mine. "You gotta be kidding! No way!"

"Then how do you know you can't do it?" I asked, raising an eyebrow. "Maybe when you get back to Earth you can try summoning Mzatal."

He stared at me as if I'd tried to tell him that two plus two equaled three. "You're serious."

"Well, yeah," I said. "I mean, as long as Mzatal's willing.

That's what matters most. And I could show you the storage diagram I used so that I had enough power. What do you have to lose?"

"My measly life?" he said, then grinned and shook his head. "I dunno. Katashi is using four summoners to summon Lord Mzatal. And Lord Mzatal has always been willing."

That didn't make sense to me. "I always thought it was easier to summon Rhyzkahl because he was willing." I shrugged and made a mental note to find out more later. "Well, if you do give it a try, don't summon any of the other lords." I wasn't smiling anymore. "Especially not Amkir, Kadir, Jesral . . . or Rhyzkahl."

"I wouldn't dream of it," he assured me. "Even talking about summoning Mzatal is a stretch for me."

"Yeah, well, don't even be alone with any of them." A shiver ran down my spine. "Especially Kadir. He's twisted."

He nodded slowly. "Yeah, his portrait freaked me out enough. Don't need to see the real thing. Since I've been here, Lords Vahl, Elofir, and Seretis have been here a few times, but none of the others."

"Portrait?"

"In Szerain's gallery," Idris said. "On the third level of his palace. There's portraits of demons, humans, all the lords, all sorts of stuff." He whistled low and shook his head. "And you know how Szerain's paintings and sculptures are. Well, that portrait of Kadir felt like he was about an inch away, breathing on me. Scared the shit out of me!" He made a face at the memory.

"I didn't know about any gallery. I saw lots of his stuff in the rest of the palace," I said, then scowled blackly as a shadow memory flickered. Why the hell couldn't I have had a fucking Elinor memory about the gallery when I was actually *there* at Szerain's palace?

Idris shrugged. "Yeah, but no lords outside the gallery. At least none that I've ever seen."

Helori returned and touched my arm. "Mzatal will meet you in the plexus."

I nodded, then looked back to Idris. "I'll see you later. Thank you for everything." I gave him a quick hug, then turned and walked quickly away before either of us could get too embarrassed or maudlin.

Helori led the way, which was damn good since I didn't know where anything was. When Mzatal had first brought me here, he'd taken me straight to the summoning chamber, after which we went right back to the grove, and of course, then I escaped.

My loss, though, because Mzatal's palace was damn impressive, in a much different way than Rhyzkahl's. Where Rhyzkahl's palace rose to lofty white heights with a myriad of towers, balconies, and the feel of opulent indulgence, Mzatal's curved with the flow of the cliff, dark stone accented with bursts of color from tapestries and intricate wall hangings. Glass comprised most every outside wall, floor-to-ceiling, wall-to-wall, like in modern high-rise buildings giving the place an open feel and loads of natural light. Helori led me to the spacious atrium with its rising mezzanines, then up stairs and more stairs, down a corridor, and then yet more stairs.

At the top, we entered a broad, high-ceilinged corridor carpeted in luxurious deep blue. "And now we enter Mzatal's private area," Helori said, indicating the narrow line of beautiful flickering wards inlaid in the paneling.

We passed several doorless arches leading to glass-walled rooms, including a library, a sitting area, a large barren room, and a solarium. I glanced at the double doors of Mzatal's chambers—which I recognized only because of the Escher-like carving—odd because of the rarity of doors in the palace. Both Szerain and Rhyzkahl had plenty of doors, so Mzatal's lack didn't seem to be characteristic of the demon realm. At the very end of the corridor, we stopped before the only other door. Carvings of interwoven sigils covered it, and their intricacy and grace reminded me of Szerain's work.

"He is engaged," Helori told me, "but he is aware you are here." He pushed the door open enough for me to pass. "Go. Await him." Smiling, he bent and touched his forehead to mine.

I threw my arms around him in a hug. "Thank you."

With a low chuckle, he wrapped his arms around me and hugged me close. Grinning, I blinked back the silly tears that sprang up, then quickly released him and entered the room before I could totally start bawling.

Windowless and close, the room crackled with potency.

Mzatal stood on the other side of a stone pedestal topped with a basin, much like the one I saw in Szerain's shrine. Intense focus etched his face while sigils and strands of potency danced from his fingers above the surface of the water. Fascinated, I watched the interplay of light and color. I had zero clue what he was doing, but it was still amazing and beautiful.

I closed the door quietly behind me and waited for him to finish. I didn't have any sense he was making me wait on purpose, which made it much easier for me to be patient. It was like watching the coolest laser show ever, except without lasers. Instead, glowing streamers were caught and woven back into place, and wobbly things were set to spin smoothly. Mzatal moved around the table in a graceful flow, wasting no motion and doing things almost before I realized there was anything to engage.

Finally he lowered his hands and sent the remaining "stuff" down into the basin, then set a single orb about a foot in diameter spinning above it. He lowered his head, assessing its movement and moving fingers slightly until it spun smoothly.

Stepping back, he gave a little nod of completion, not unlike the one he'd given after that weird as hell kiss. What the hell had that kiss been all about, anyway?

He watched the orb for another few heartbeats, then turned to face me, eyes full of a deep resonant potency.

"Kara," he said, speaking my name like an extension of that power.

"Mzatal," I replied with a slight nod.

He moved toward me, and for the barest instant I had the bizarre impression that he was going to hug me, but then he clasped his hands behind his back in standard Mzatal-pose. "You seem more yourself."

"I'm . . . better." I still didn't feel totally like me, but at least I knew who *me* was. "So what now?"

Mzatal opened the door without touching it. Convenient trick, I figured, since he had his hands behind his back so much. "Come. The plexus is stable." He glanced back at the spinning orb, then headed out. "We can talk of what is to come next in more comfort."

I cast one last glance at the orb thingy, then followed him.

Chapter 24

We went back down the corridor and entered the archway of the solarium. The high ceiling as well as the wall opposite the archway were constructed of glass. It reminded me of Rhyzkahl's arboretum without the trees. The glass doors stood open to the balcony and the expanse of sea beyond, and fresh air touched with salt flowed over me. The side walls alternated wide vertical bands of the natural dark stone and softly gleaming gold, embossed with scenes of demons and humans. Near the balcony waited two low, comfortable-looking chairs with a table between. It felt as though they'd been arranged for this moment.

Mzatal gestured to one of the chairs. I sat, nerves beginning to set in as he took the other. Shit was about to get real.

"How was your journey?"

"It was very interesting," I said, smile twitching briefly. Somehow I doubted that Mzatal would have approved of the more dangerous parts. "And I don't feel like I'm about to break into a million pieces anymore."

Mzatal smiled—the most genuine smile I'd ever seen on him. "I can feel it. You will be able to move forward now, no longer mired."

I sighed. "Helori explained why it isn't in my best interests to return to Earth right now, and how I need to be better prepared, better able to protect myself and others, before I can go home." I still hated it, but I understood it. "He also says that you can be trusted to abide by your word."

He gave a quick nod. "I do not break my agreements with summoners."

I spread my hands on the cool wood of the table. "Then

why don't you start with the terms you desire, and then we can go from there."

"A simple framework," Mzatal began. "A five year agreement to provide summoning services from this realm and from Earth, as required and specified in the agreement. One full year of training here before assessing the possibility of return to Earth. You will take no action that is against my best interests—which, by the end of a year, you will know how to discern. I will provide full training—all that you are able to absorb."

My eyebrows lifted. "Five years?" I asked, incredulous. "No way. Nothing more than three years, and we will decide *together* the possibility of my return to Earth after six months. And in the event of an impasse, Helori will make the final decision."

A frown touched his mouth at my counter-offer, but I had a feeling he'd deliberately asked for a larger amount of time, knowing I'd bargain it down. "Consideration at six months or beyond *only* on the condition that you have passed the shikvihr initiation."

Shikvihr. I frowned. Where had I heard that before?

From Rayst, I suddenly remembered. *"How far along is she in the shikvihr?"* he'd asked Rhyzkahl. That ritual foundation thing.

"I can't agree to that when I have no idea how long that typically takes to master." I leaned back and folded my arms. "For all I know you could be placing this condition on a skill that takes decades to learn." Helori said I could trust him at his word. He hadn't said a damn thing about the part that came before actually swearing the oath.

"Calvus Atilia passed the shikvihr initiation in seven months. The longest any has taken to pass it is eighteen months."

Well, eighteen months sucked. *So I'll study my ass off*, I told myself. "Very well. I also want to be able to send and receive messages from home, via whatever agents you might have in place on Earth or by my own means."

"It can be arranged," he said, eyes on mine. "Through me."

I pursed my lips. "Will you respect my privacy?"

Mzatal inclined his head. "As you will be in agreement to act only in my best interests, yes."

I steeled myself for the next point I wanted to raise. Rhyzkahl had sworn not to harm me—on Earth, which hadn't done me a fat lot of good. "I—" My voice cracked. I took a deep breath and tried again. "I want to discuss what would happen in the event that I were to fall into the hands of another lord." I met his eyes. "I don't want to become anyone's thrall."

He leaned forward. "First, I will do all within my ability to keep that circumstance from arising," he said. "There are possibilities of implants for recall and such, though there is always the chance of those being detected." He paused. "There are other, more drastic options."

I spoke as quietly and calmly as possible, though my voice still had a slight quaver. "I expect you to do all in your ability to keep such a situation from arising and to extricate me should precautions and safeguards fail. I expect you to do me no harm at any time during our agreement, regardless of location, realm, dimension, or other locale, with the sole exception of a scenario where, in your best and most honorable discretion, you believe that I would prefer death, or a scenario in which the lives or fates of innocents would be spared by harming or killing me."

Mzatal listened carefully. "Define harm."

"Shit that hurts that I don't want done to me!" I snapped, then winced at my outburst. "Sorry. I . . . I mean physical injury or maiming as well as any sort of arcane torture. And no mental harm either. Or memory stripping." Damn it, I knew I was missing stuff. What good would this agreement do me if I fucked it up? I dropped my hands into my lap and clutched the fabric of my shirt beneath the table.

"There must be conditions," Mzatal replied calmly, "otherwise training will be impossible. One would be to do you no *willful or nonconsensual* harm. Accidents can occur in training, as well as times when harm may be a part of the process." His expression was reassuring. "In other ways, I will not seek to harm you."

"R-right. Yeah. No willful or nonconsensual harm."

There was more after that, though nothing anywhere near as unnerving or fraught; details and fine tuning concerning training and protocols, that sort of thing. Nothing leaped out at me as being onerous or untenable, and after what was probably a couple of hours, the sun set and papers were drawn up in English and demon, with Ilana and Helori verifying that the translation was precise. We signed in ordinary ink and then swore to it, with about as much drama as the times I'd been sworn in to testify in court. Yet I had no doubt that the oath was just as binding as if we'd chanted naked and signed in blood. Probably far more so, actually.

With the agreement signed and sworn on, I felt oddly at loose ends, though relieved to have the details out of the way. I pushed down the niggling fear that I'd missed some loophole that Mzatal could use to take advantage of me, and held onto Helori's assurance that Mzatal was true to his word.

"So what now?" I asked.

"First, the balcony." Mzatal stood and picked up a wine bottle and glasses from the side table. I followed him out into the pleasantly cool night. He exhaled softly, appearing to relax as soon as he was in the open air. It didn't seem as if he disliked the indoors, but more as if he craved something that could only be found in wide open spaces. Even sitting behind the glass of the solarium seemed to confine him. Or maybe I was reading far too much into it.

He poured a glass and passed it to me. I took a long drink and looked up at the stars. A sliver of moon shone high overhead with a cluster of stars twinkling near it, looking as if they'd been poured out of the crescent. A thin cloud drifted before the moon, set briefly aglow before it passed on.

Mzatal took a sip, then set his glass aside and stood, hands behind back, as he took a deep breath and released it slowly. "They are so beautiful," he murmured, looking out at the stars. He wouldn't get any argument from me. With practically no ambient light to impede viewing, the sky seemed utterly packed with stars. The only time I'd ever seen the sky like that was the day after Hurricane Katrina blew through, and most of south Louisiana had been without power. I'd seen the Milky Way for the first time. *And the last time?* I wondered. No. I'd get back home. I'd work and study my ass off and do whatever I had to do.

Still, I couldn't hold back the wistful sigh. "I don't recognize any of the constellations."

"Nothing of Earth here," he said. He looked at me then back at the sky. "I never tire of them." He gave a small shake of his head. "At times it feels as though I could simply move through them if I chose to." He pointed to a cluster of stars a handspan above the horizon. "There, the bellowing reyza." He traced it in a pale light for me to see, then extinguished it.

I smiled a bit. "What others?"

"Many constellations named by the demons seem to have no relevance to their names." A whisper of amusement touched his eyes. "I will show you some that do. There—the summoner, and the portal, and kzak's bane," he said, pointing and lighting each one in turn for me to see.

"I had an encounter with a kzak once," I remarked, looking up at the constellation. "Still don't know if it was sent after me or Ryan."

He looked over at me. "When? What were the circumstances?"

"Not long before I was sworn to—" I grimaced. "Before I was marked. Ryan and I were eating lunch at a kinda shitty restaurant, and a kzak came in and attacked us. We managed to wound it, and then Zack finished it off."

Mzatal turned to face me. "You. It would have been sent after you. None who could send a kzak would send it after . . . the other one. It would be futile."

Sighing, I set my glass down and leaned my forearms on the balcony railing. I looked out toward the grove and let the calm peace of it touch me for a few minutes before I spoke again.

"You should have told me about Rhyzkahl," I said quietly, controlling the emotion as much as I could. When Mzatal healed me, he'd said he planned to tell me after he removed the mark. Too little, too late. "Even if I hadn't believed you—which, I admit, I probably wouldn't have—there was stuff that happened there that I might have questioned, that might have made me suspect."

He turned to look back out at the stars and remained silent.

Exhaling, I ran my hands through my hair. "Look, if we're going to work together, I need to know that you'll share information with me whether you think I'll believe it or not, whether you think I'll like it or not, or whether you think it'll hurt my feelings or not." I straightened and regarded his profile. "I'm used to building cases based on separate pieces of evidence," I said, narrowing my eyes. "I might not believe you about something, but if I'm faced with a similar bit of evidence elsewhere, then yeah, I'm more likely to take a harder look."

Mzatal lowered his head. "It was a tragic error on my

part," he said, surprising me with the admission. "Once he made the demand for your return, telling you would have better served both of us."

"Promise me that you won't do that again," I said. "Please."

He lifted his head. I watched as his gaze focused on the stars. "That which relates to you, I will tell."

I nodded, throat tight. "Thank you for getting me back. And for not keeping me prisoner."

He turned to me again and placed his hands on my shoulders. "Kara, I could no more keep you prisoner now than cage the lightning or bottle the surging sea. It is not my desire."

I blinked, nonplussed. I had a brief impulse to say something snarky or silly to break the sudden, strange mood, but at the same time I didn't want to do that to this moment. Yet I had no idea what to say.

Fortunately he spoke first. "I am truly pleased that you are here," he said. He dropped his hands from my shoulders and clasped them behind his back again. "And that the formalities of the agreement are behind us."

I frowned up at him. "You've confused the shit out of me, you know. You summoned, imprisoned, terrified, and threatened me." My eyes narrowed. "Now you're pleased that I'm here. Don't get me wrong. I'm grateful as hell to be here rather with Rhyzkahl, but what's the fucking deal?"

"When you were first summoned," he said without hesitation, "many—most—of my actions and your circumstances served as carefully calculated assessment tools. I had but a short time in which to weigh grave risk against enormous benefit."

That required a moment of mulling. "The risk that I could fuck up your world versus the chance I could be of use to you later," I said. "It was all a bunch of mind games and extreme bullshit so you could determine whether to kill me or keep me." It'd been pretty clear at times, but this admission gave me a broader perspective.

"That is a simplistic, though adequately accurate statement." He paused. "By the time I sought to remove the mark, I knew I wanted to work with you, and that it would be mutually beneficial. And then," he said with a shake of his head, "you were gone."

A flush of anger washed through me. "I can't even begin to tell you how fucked up all of that is. I mean . . ." I trailed off. Yeah it was a total ethical catastrophe, but I couldn't get past the fact that, despite his willful domination and abuse of power, he'd pulled my ass away from Rhyzkahl and been more than accommodating since then.

I took a settling breath and shifted to a more in-the-moment question. "You played at everything from being a totally scary motherfucker to halfway decent to get what you wanted from me," I said, narrowing my eyes at him. "Is 'Mr. Nice Lord' another carefully calculated tool to get what you want now?"

He stood silent for a moment, and I had the feeling the question disturbed him. "I cannot deny that everything I do is to get what I want," he said quietly. "What I want from you is your dedication to becoming the best summoner you can be. That serves your best interests and mine, and will serve to thwart Rhyzkahl and others."

It didn't exactly answer my question, but was probably the best I'd get from him. *Rhyzkahl.* I gave Mzatal a sharp look. "Are you sure—absolutely *sure*—that Rhyzkahl doesn't have any way to recall me? No more implants or anything like that?"

"I checked you thoroughly before, during, and after the healing," he said. "There is a streak of arrogance in Rhyzkahl. Once he had you, he did not think he could lose you."

Goosebumps skimmed over me that had nothing to do with the temperature of the air. "I'd rather not depend on his arrogance," I said, rubbing my arms. "*You* were able to hide a recall from him."

"We did a full purification ritual on you while you slept," he said. "and found nothing noteworthy."

A frown tugged at my mouth. "Rhyzkahl found an implant of yours and removed it," I said. "He told me you'd triggered it to kill me."

"He lied," Mzatal said without hesitation. "When you were with Pyrenth at Rhyzkahl's grove, I sought to activate my primary recall implant, here." Mzatal lightly touched the center of my chest. "Unfortunately, it failed and unraveled. There was nothing in it to kill you."

I nodded slowly as I processed his answer. "So you had

two implants on me. How—" I couldn't control the slight shiver that ran through me. "How did you put them in me?"

He exhaled. "The first—the one that failed—I implanted during the purification ritual upon your arrival."

"And the second?"

"The second was conditional, a failsafe for the first," he explained. "When you disrupted the removal of the mark, the mark was damaged. We were in a critical window of time with a high chance that Rhyzkahl would recover you before I could remove it completely." Mzatal's mouth tightened. "If he did, I knew he would have to remove the mark eventually and replace it. I set the implant to trigger upon its removal, which it did." He paused before continuing. "I implanted it in the antechamber before we went to the grove, before your escape."

I blinked in realization. "That weird-as-hell kiss."

"Only a heartbeat before, it had not been my intention to implant it in that manner," he said slowly, "but, yes."

I processed *that* and decided another change of subject was in order. "What about these?" I asked, touching one of the sigils on my chest. "Could he use these against me somehow? Does he have any connection to them?"

"There are no direct connections," he told me, "but as was in your mark, there are residuals of both the blade and the *rakkuhr* that taints it." A shudder passed through him. "Had any of those sigils been cut with the purpose of recall, there would be no doubt. But they were not." He exhaled. "As it is, Kara, I cannot be absolutely certain about the potential those sigils hold. Szerain knows more. He was the one who first worked with *rakkuhr* and determined it was incompatible with us, with this realm. And Rhyzkahl and Jesral, based on what I witnessed of the ritual, have harnessed it in new ways."

"What *is* it?" I asked. Memory of its touch brushed me, the foul miasma . . . Clawing panic rose, and I had to take several deep breaths to fight it down.

"I do not know its full nature as it is a potency alien to this world," Mzatal replied, eyes darkening. "It subtly alters arcane harmonics, and its use has the potential to cause much disruption." He grimaced. "It affects me deeply. It affects Idris as well, but not nearly as much." His eyes went to mine. "Kara, I will do all in my power to keep you from falling into their hands again." He said it quietly but backed with deep intensity. "Idris has great skill and determination. He will work on this as well."

Some of the tension in my gut uncoiled with the understanding of his solid support. "When do we start?"

"You should rest tonight, and we will begin your training tomorrow."

I scrubbed at my face. "I have so much to learn. I mean, I don't know shit. I don't know most of the sigils, or the shikvihr, or . . ."

"These I can teach you," he reassured me. "I have taught many. And you have a quick mind and innate talent."

"No pressure," I said with a weak laugh. "I guess I'd better go get some sleep." I met his eyes. "Thanks again."

"You are most welcome, Kara Gillian. Come, this way." He gestured for me to go with him, and together we walked down the length of the balcony to the corner, the sea to our right and the grove ahead. He passed through the open doors in the glass wall and called up a soft light within. I entered, then stopped, confused.

"These are your rooms."

"Yes. I would prefer you stay here."

A protest formed on my lips, but it died unvoiced at one look at his face. He had no intention of taking advantage of me. He wanted me to stay here because that way he could keep a closer watch over me. Guardian, not guard. And, as much I hated the weakness of it, I knew I'd feel safer here as well.

"Um, sure. Okay," I said instead.

"If, after this night, you truly prefer different quarters," he said gently, "I will make the arrangements."

"Yeah, that's cool," I replied, shifting uncertainly. "I don't have any clothes or, uh, night things."

"The zrila have made a small supply for you," he told me. "You will find those items in the rose chest in the dressing room off the bath chamber."

I smiled with only a bit of tension. "I guess I'll be occupying your bedroom then."

He leaned down and kissed my forehead. "Sleep well, Kara," he said, then departed.

Surprisingly, I did.

Chapter 25

Rhyzkahl stood before me, glorious and beautiful. "You left too soon, dear one." Dark fire flickered over his blade as he stepped closer, and a terrible smile curved his mouth. "We were not finished . . . Rowan."

I tried to back away, but ropes of potency held me immobile. The bindings cut into my wrists, and pain seared my shoulders. A strangled cry of horror slipped from my lips as he brought the blade close to me.

He stroked the back of his hand over my cheek, tilted his head as his eyes met mine. "Ah, Rowan, you are meant to be thus." I tried to protest, to say my name, but I couldn't make my mouth form the word. His smile widened as he lifted the blade and touched it to my flesh.

I screamed as the pain tore through me, and I writhed in the bindings.

Kara!

A hand on my shoulder. My name. I held fast to it. Reached for them both.

"Kara!"

Rhyzkahl fractured and dissipated as strong arms pulled me from him.

"You are dreaming, Kara," the voice said, gathering me close. "I am here."

I clung to him, to Mzatal, I realized as the nightmare shattered and dispersed. He sat on the edge of the bed, holding me securely, but gently. To my horror I burst into tears, but he simply shifted to cradle my head to his chest. He murmured something as I felt the unmistakable touch of the pygah, but he did nothing more. Didn't tell me to breathe or chill or anything like that. Simply held me, radiating a solid security while I wept.

Gradually, I calmed down, but I continued to hold on to him even after I got control of the stupid sobbing. I hated feeling like this, despised this weakness in me. And right now I desperately needed this feeling of safety.

"I'm sorry," I whispered.

He shifted so that he sat up against the headboard, keeping an arm around me so that my head was cradled on his shoulder. "There is no need to apologize. I know something of nightmares."

I let out a ragged breath and felt as if I should pull away from him now, but I couldn't bring myself to do it just yet. "Guess you're regretting letting me stay in your rooms now," I said, trying for humor but not quite reaching it.

He gave me a light squeeze. "No, Kara," he said, voice calm and melodious. "I have no regrets in that."

I sighed against him. "Good thing, 'cause I think you're stuck with me."

He was fully clothed, in dark grey pants and a white caftan-style shirt covered with intricate silver embroidery. A comfortable chair and ottoman had been pulled near the bed, and a small side table held some papers and a half-full wine glass.

He'd been sitting there only moments before, I realized. Watching me sleep. But somehow the thought didn't creep me out at all. Instead I found myself deeply appreciating the care, especially now, after the nightmare.

I was definitely calmer now, but I still wasn't quite ready to shift away from him. "How much did you know about me before you had me summoned?"

Mzatal drew a deep breath and released it slowly. "I knew you were Rhyzkahl's marked summoner," he said. "I knew what Katashi had told me of you. I knew from reports of demons that you function as a Guardian—police person—to maintain order in segments of the human populace. I had more details from closer surveillance in the weeks leading up to your summoning."

I still had my head against his upper chest, calmed by the steady beat of his heart. "I kind of wondered, especially when I saw that the, uh, feminine supplies that you had here were the same brand I usually use." I smiled, finding that stupidly amusing, and I had to bite back a giggle as I had a sudden image of a reyza poking through the cabinet beneath my sink and holding up a tampon in confusion.

Mzatal gave my shoulders a squeeze. "It was my desire to be prepared for your arrival. I did not know—" He paused, and I felt him give a low sigh. "I did not know when I summoned you if you would be with me indefinitely or for a very short time."

My amusement faded as I remembered how close he came to killing me in those first few hours after I was summoned. Though I appreciated his candor, the topic unsettled me. I shifted to sit more upright, wrapped my arms around my legs, and rested my chin on my knees.

"Rhyzkahl wanted to use me to get Szerain's blade." A shiver passed over me at the memory. "Why? I mean, why me? And why does he—and you for that matter—want it so goddamn badly?"

"The most likely reason he chose you as a ritual surrogate is your demonstrated ability to summon a qaztahl single-handedly using only chalk and blood. That, coupled with the similarities to Elinor's energy signature, were compelling reasons." Mzatal drew a deep breath and released it in a slow sigh. "Control of a single blade offers a substantial increase in potency and focus. With control of two," he said, shaking his head, "there is an exponential increase in power."

My eyes narrowed. "You sound like you're speaking from experience."

Mzatal met my gaze steadily. "Yes. Szerain, Rhyzkahl, and I stood long unchallenged and unchallengeable."

Holy crap. I'd known they had the blades, but hadn't put it together that they had their own little power bloc. That called for more investigation later, both on its nature and its dissolution. Those three sure as hell didn't stand together now.

"Rhyzkahl wants it for someone else, doesn't he?" I asked. "Jesral or Amkir, to set up a new regime." Kadir had a hand in there too, but my gut told me he wasn't a candidate.

Mzatal nodded. "With Rhyzkahl bearing Xhan, and Vsuhl likely destined for Jesral, they would hold much influence and be in a position to advance other plans, including designs on Earth."

"But they can't get Szerain's blade without me, can they?" I asked. "Otherwise, wouldn't they already have done it?"

Mzatal remained silent a moment, his mouth drawn in a tight line. "With you, the task would be far easier. What I do not know is if Rhyzkahl gained enough from you in the ritual to make an attempt by another means."

"Well that sucks," I said, hugging my knees a bit tighter as I considered everything. "Back in that fucked-up time when you tried to remove the mark," I continued after a moment, "you told me you wanted to get the blade. Is it possible for me—us—to get it first? I mean, without it being really painful or horrible or anything like that?"

Mzatal laced his fingers over his solar plexus. "When I first said that, all I knew, based upon what I sensed from the mark, was that Rhyzkahl sought the blade. His methods proved to be brutal, though ultimately would have been effective. He sought to forge you into a tool for greater purpose, and may yet seek to finish that task. One of the uses of that tool would have been to retrieve Vsuhl." He gave me a gentle smile. "However, based on my observation of his ritual, I do not believe he ever sensed your subtle affinity to the iliur, the essence energy that ignites the blades. I sensed it clearly in the close contact of the healing."

I frowned in thought, considering this new tidbit. "What does that mean? That makes it easier?"

"I believe that it does. I have deep connection with all three blades. Working with that, in tandem with your unique gifts, we have an excellent chance of securing Vsuhl with minimal complications."

I shifted to sit cross-legged and absently rubbed the scar on my left forearm with the palm of my other hand. "Okay. Well, that sounds promising," I said. "Turek showed me the image of Szerain's blade. Why are his and your blades so beautiful and Rhyzkahl's so—" I grimaced. "—hideous?"

A shadow of what seemed to be grief passed over his face. "It did not always appear thus." He lifted a hand and traced a sigil. A heartbeat later a slightly translucent image appeared of Rhyzkahl's knife, but without the thorns on the hilt. A softly glowing blue gem adorned the pommel, and the oily blue sheen I'd seen on the blade shone here as a clear, shimmering layer of potency. "Rhyzkahl dabbled secretly with the *rakkuhr* for many years, bringing the taint upon himself. The corruption of Xhan is recent." He dispelled the image with a sharp flick of his fingers, as if it pained him to see what the blade had once looked like.

"This *rakkuhr*," I said. "Is it like a 'dark side of the Force' sort of thing?"

A flicker of question lit his eyes, but then it cleared as he no doubt read the meaning of the reference from me. He shook his head. "No. It is not 'evil' any more than the potency you and I use is. But, while powerful, it is insidiously disruptive." He paused. "You have felt it. It is anathema. I do not fully understand it. Szerain knows more, and now Rhyzkahl," he said with regret.

I let out a long, slow breath, seeing flashes of red and shadow, feeling an echo of the Wrongness. "I think I understand far more than I want to," I murmured. With a shudder I willfully changed the subject. "How is this all going to work? Getting Szerain's blade, I mean."

Mzatal narrowed his eyes. "The specifics are not finalized as there is much to be determined through our work." He regarded me as though weighing what to tell me. "However, the plan is to utilize my nexus as the seat of a beacon ritual to locate and transfix Vsuhl. When that ritual is set, it will require tending until it culminates—a matter of hours to weeks. Once it is complete, we will perform the actual retrieval of the blade at Szerain's nexus since that has the strongest connection for Vsuhl."

"Okay. What's a nexus?" The rest kinda made sense—at least enough for now.

"A focal point. A link to the source potency," he said. "Szerain's is the columned platform in his courtyard. Mine is here, at the base of the cliff."

"All right," I said. "So when do we start work?" It felt good to finally have a goal and direction.

"It will coincide with your training," he said. "It is near dawn now. Meet me in the workroom at midmorning." He stood from the bed, clasped his hands behind his back. Chatty-time was over, and a sliver of relief went through me. I felt comfortable around this lord, and that in itself made me uncomfortable and wary. I sure as hell wasn't ready to blindly trust any of these qaztahl. I *was* ready to focus on something—anything—to move this along.

"Sounds like a plan," I said as I climbed off the bed. "I'm

going to hit the bath first and spare you my dreaded Stinky Summoner power." Mzatal gave me a slight smile and nod, then left for his table in the outer room.

I headed to the bath chamber, then peeled off my nightshirt and undies and dropped them on the marble bench by the wall. I almost never took baths at home anymore, but if I had a bath like this, I sure as hell would. It wasn't a bathtub, but a pool cut into the natural basalt of the cliff that backed the palace. Steam rose and the surface stirred gently as though the water circulated. Steps led down into it, and a shallow shelf with a headrest for lounging beckoned invitingly.

I crouched and dabbled my fingers in the water. Perfect temp. Damn near perfect everything. Okay, great, I was trapped away from home, but I could sure as hell enjoy the luxuries.

I stood and moved to retrieve a towel from the shelves. A wave of dizziness flowed through me and was gone, but as it retreated color leached from everything as an all-encompassing grey fog rose. Heart pounding, I went still as I struggled to make sense of the sudden, surreal shift.

Rhyzkahl appeared in the fog about ten feet from me, beautiful and terrible, wearing the same white and cream he'd worn during the ritual. I sucked in a shocked breath. Adrenaline dumped into my system, sending my heart pounding. *He's not really here*, I realized, though that didn't calm my racing pulse. It was a dream-sending. I knew from experience how real and potentially dangerous they were—an actual contact with the lord, not a product of my subconscious. This one had greater presence than any of the previous ones, like the difference between a black and white photo and one in color.

"Get the hell away from me!" I said, voice shaking.

He took a step forward. "Kara."

"No. No!" I gasped, taking a reflexive step backward. "Get away from me!"

Rhyzkahl raised his hand, and I stepped back against an unyielding barrier of potency. "Kara, come," he said softly. "It will be different."

Sweat trickled down my sides as I fought back panic. "No you'll *make* me different!" I pressed back against the barrier. "Fuck off! I'm staying me!"

Rhyzkahl took another step forward. "Yes. That is what I am here to tell you. I will reverse all." His eyes traveled over my scars. "*All.*" His breath came heavily as though it challenged him to say this. "Come."

His gaze felt like a foul touch. "I trusted you once," I shot back with a curl of my lip. "Never again. You fucking *tortured* me."

He stepped within a pace of me, aura surrounding me, suffocating me. "It can be undone," he said with a shake of his head. "Dear one, it is not too late."

"Yes it *is!* You can't undo the fact that it happened, not without destroying me in the process." My breath came in shallow gasps. He wasn't even projecting terror at me in that way, but his presence alone brought it forth. "You're the one who said it was too late, and now you sound like a psycho stalker." I pressed back against the potency barrier. "I'm not going with you. I'll *never* go with you. You can't undo this."

Another aura. Mzatal. I vaguely felt his arm across my chest, but it was as if he was the dream and Rhyzkahl the reality. Rhyzkahl sensed it too. He looked beyond me then snapped his focus back to my eyes and spoke with measured intensity, breath hissing. "You do not understand." He caught my face between his hands. "Kara, all will be well. I will take you away. Away from here. Away from the realm. And you will be you and whole."

Mzatal was there, somewhere—an invisible support. "No," I said, baring teeth. "I do understand." Though my heart still slammed, I gathered myself, gripped Rhyzkahl's wrists and tugged, seeking to get his vile touch off my face. "I *understand* that you would give me over to Jesral and those other fuckers. I understand you lied to me and betrayed me. I will never *ever* go with you. Get that through your blond head right now."

A whisper passed through my mind, and I knew Rhyzkahl read the truth of my words. Good.

His breath quickened. He released my face and took a step back, hands lifted as though he still held me. A stricken look swept over his features, and he shook his head, looking strangely lost.

I felt Mzatal's physical hold on me more clearly as well as his nonphysical touch. "Rhyzkahl. Leave me *now*," I said as I took a step toward him, *willing* him away.

He retreated another step.

A flush of determined anger seared through me. "Go! Leave me alone."

Potency surged over me as he tensed and dropped his hands to his sides. "Ungrateful chikdah." He spat the words and took another step back, visibly shaking in what could only be anger.

I blinked in true surprise at the slur. "Wow. Yeah, dude. A couple of pointers here if you want keep a girl. First, don't torture her. Second, calling her ugly names is also a no-no." I held steady to my core and the supporting presence of Mzatal. "Get away from me. I don't ever want to see you again."

"You think your savior's hands are clean?" he asked with a short, cold laugh. "You will see me again. Soon."

Mzatal's encouragement to continue to resist and push came through clearly, and I did so with ferocity. I shook, there was no doubt about that. But I also had no doubt that I could and would push this fucker away. My fingernails bit into my palms as I rejected his presence with every fiber of my being.

Rhyzkahl took a forced step back and growled an angry curse. He turned his back on me, lifted his open right hand. "You had all within your grasp and cast it aside. You *will* be mine." He made a fist and ripped it forward, wrenching the dream-sending away.

I gasped and my knees buckled. Mzatal held me securely from behind, his left arm over my shoulder and across my chest until I could get my legs to support me again. I managed to do so, then pressed the heels of my hands into my eyes. "Shit."

Mzatal muttered something in demon as he half-carried me back into the bedchamber and settled me in his chair. He dragged the sheet from the bed and draped it over me, then crouched and peered up into my face.

"What was that?" he asked, naked concern etched in his features. "I could only peripherally sense it."

I grimaced as my head throbbed. "Dream. A dream-sending from Rhyzkahl."

"That was no dream. This has happened before?"

"Yeah, shit. A bunch of times on Earth," I replied, rubbing my temples. "This time it was way stronger than before though. When I died, the link was broken, but he hooked it right back up next time I summoned him. The bastard."

Mzatal laid his hands over mine at my temples and eased the headache, then drew my hands down into my lap and held them there. Without taking his eyes from mine he called out to Gestamar. "Have Idris prepare a purification *now*, with the last quadrant open. I will need to specialize it."

I heard Gestamar's acknowledging grunt from the other room. Mzatal squeezed my hands. "It would have been useful to know of this sooner."

I gave the lord a sour look. "Well, he hasn't done it in a long time, and I figured you'd tromped through my head enough to know every fucking thing about me. I mean you know what goddamn brand of *tampons* I use."

Mzatal closed his eyes and shook his head. "And understandable to draw that conclusion. But this is something I could not detect, and even when active, I could not follow it."

That didn't sound good. "Can you get rid of it?"

"I gathered enough during the contact to localize it," he said, opening his eyes again and looking into mine. "I *will* deactivate it."

So far he'd followed through on what he said he'd do. No reason not to trust him in this as well. I managed a weak smile. "I guess training will come later?"

"Priorities. This first. Definitely this first." He gave my hands a final squeeze then released them. "Tell me what happened," he said, and moved to sit on the edge of the bed.

And I did. By the time I finished, a slight frown curved his mouth, and he seemed deep in thought.

"What is it?" I asked.

Mzatal shook his head. "He is dangerous in a new way. He has shown signs of true jealousy. I witnessed it clearly during the ritual, and it colored much of your interaction in the dream-sending."

"He's possessive," I agreed "What's so bad about that? I mean apart from it being totally psycho that it's directed at me."

"I have known Rhyzkahl for millennia, and he has *never* shown jealousy," Mzatal said with a slow shake of his head. "Possessive power displays between qaztahl, yes. That is normal for all of us. Personal jealousy such as he has shown is alien. It is not our nature."

I took that in, though it was hard to get my head around the idea of the lords not being jealous. "Well it sure as hell looks like his nature now," I said, scowling. "He seemed to lose it when I told him I would never go with him." I put the puzzle pieces together. "You're saying he's an unknown because you don't have a precedent for it, and therefore he's dangerous. More dangerous."

Mzatal nodded. "Yes, and we will need to take that into account."

"What did he mean when he said, 'You think your saviour's hands are clean?'" I asked, watching him carefully.

Mzatal exhaled. "I have lived millennia, Kara, and done much that would revolt you. My hands are not clean."

I realized I didn't really want to know the details right then, not with everything else I already had to deal with. The fact that he hadn't tried to dance around the question was sufficient—for the moment. I didn't hold any illusions that he was a saint; he was a demonic lord, and I'd had a glimpse of his darker side.

I nodded in acknowledgement. "Fair enough, for now."

He stood. "Go bathe, then come to the summoning chamber, and we will disengage this link. Gestamar will stay with you."

I looked up at him and nodded, tension leaching out of me. He gave me a quick smile and departed, hands clasped behind his back. I watched him go, grateful to him on innumerable levels. Though I was the one who'd pushed Rhyzkahl away, I wasn't sure if I could have done it without Mzatal's support—at least not yet. I owed him big time. Again.

Was he keeping score? And if so, what would the payoff be?

Chapter 26

I tried to avoid thinking about the coming ritual as I made my way to the summoning chamber. *It's a purification*, I told myself sharply. *Not even as dangerous as a summoning, and I've done a kajillion of those.* Didn't help. The curl of tension still sat like a rock in my chest.

I stopped before the double doors, heart suddenly pounding a mile a minute. I didn't reach for the handle to pull the doors open. I didn't want to go in there. Bad things happened in summoning chambers.

He held his hand out, and I stepped forward and took it. He smiled down at me. Pain. Blood.

I startled as Mzatal placed his hands on my shoulders from behind, and I realized I'd been standing in one place, staring at the doors for what had to have been at least ten minutes, so absorbed I hadn't even felt his approach. Yet he didn't say anything, simply held my shoulders and let me know he was there.

"I'm sick of trying to be strong," I whispered hoarsely. "I'm not. I'm not strong at all. I fake it and pretend to be tough, but I can't do this." I shook my head in a sharp motion, eyes on the doors. "I . . . I can't go in there."

"In there or out here," Mzatal said in quiet, resonant tones, "it is the same. It is a horrific ghost that haunts you, wherever you are. What you carry, what you fear, is as potent on this side of the door as it is within the chamber, though its manifestation is clearer there." His gave my shoulders a light squeeze. "Your victory is in facing the ghost where it manifests strongest. Turn from it now, and Rhyzkahl triumphs, and you, and those you care for, no longer face a ghost but a certainty. Face it now with me beside you, and you are a step closer to banishing the ghost forever."

I breathed out a curse. "Oprah needs to have you on her show," I said sourly, feeling the truth of his words. I hated it, yet I also knew I had to accept it.

Steeling myself, I grabbed the handles and yanked. They opened far more easily than I expected, and only Mzatal's hands on my shoulders saved me from toppling back on my ass. I grimaced. Yeah, this was a great way to start things off.

I headed through the antechamber and into the chamber itself. Idris was already there, standing by a much simpler and smaller diagram than the one that had been used on me previously. Mzatal moved past me to inspect the diagram, but I stayed where I was, near the door. Sigils twisted and glimmered a foot off the floor in ordered rings, mesmerizing even unignited. I tried to breathe normally and not like a hyperventilating chihuahua, but I could feel sweat pricking the small of my back.

"Do I need to do anything?" I asked Mzatal when he looked my way.

He shook his head. "There are no special preparations needed."

I raised and eyebrow. "Really? No being led around hooded, and scary thrumming, and all of that? Really?"

"There will be thrumming during the process itself, but not before," he said. "There is no purpose for that now, nor for a hood."

Slick motherfucker. Now I understood. He pushed buttons as part of the damned assessment. Yeah, he'd needed to purify me when I first arrived, but the rest of it was all to see how I'd react. I leveled a scowl at him. "Is there anything in our agreement that says I can't call you names?"

He crouched and added a few touches to the diagram. A very faint smile curved his mouth. "No."

My own mouth twitched. "So, *hypothetically*, if I were to call you an asshole, there'd be no reprisals?" I asked with an innocent look. "Hypothetically, of course."

Idris glanced up sharply, then hissed and drew back his hand as the sigil he was working on stung him.

"Nothing of that sort is covered by the agreement," was Mzatal's mild reply.

I chuckled under my breath. “I think I’ll just call you Boss.”

He glanced over at me with a raised eyebrow. I smiled sweetly in response. Mzatal straightened, turned fully to me, hands behind back and head lowered slightly, and still with the faint hint of a smile. “There could be consequences.”

I shrugged, still smiling. “What fun would it be if there weren’t?”

Mzatal lifted his head. “None whatsoever,” he said, his face betraying a hint of amusement as he moved to the center of the diagram.

My smile faded as he turned to face me. Somehow I’d forgotten the pesky detail where I had to go *into* the diagram.

He held out his hand to me. My mouth went dry. Rhyzkahl had done this same thing—stood in the center of the diagram, invited me to cross over, to walk gullibly to my own doom.

My gaze snapped to the door of the chamber as I looked for the sigil that would seal it. *No, it’s Mzatal’s chamber, not Rhyzkahl’s.* Almost identical. I squeezed my eyes shut and took a deep breath. *Stop being such a fucking pussy!* I railed at myself.

Opening my eyes, I looked to him. He waited patiently, exuding calm and stability. I moved jerkily forward, like an automaton that hadn’t been oiled, but I made it to the diagram and passed through the sigils. I took his hand, all too aware that my own was probably gross and sweaty and clammy right now.

He gave my gross, sweaty hand a squeeze and ignited the diagram with a flick of his fingers.

“Thanks, Boss,” I whispered.

His eyes met mine, deep, ancient, and intense. “You are most welcome, Kara Gillian.”

He helped me down to lie on my back, then retreated from the circle. I closed my eyes and waited for the shit to start.

The next thing I knew, someone called my name and a hand squeezed my shoulder.

“Mzatal?” I blinked awake to see the lord crouched beside me, his forehead covered in a sheen of sweat. "It's done?"

"Yes. The link has been cleared."

I squinted at him as I sat up, my eyes feeling oversensitive to the light. "You okay? I can't believe I fell asleep."

He gave a quick nod. "With a triple pygah set above you, you would have found it challenging to stay awake, and I needed the stillness of your mind."

"Well, it worked," I said as I watched Idris clear the last of a support diagram that hadn't been there when the ritual started. "It was hard?"

His mouth curved in a faint smile. "Rhyzkahl does not relinquish his treasures easily."

"I bet he doesn't." I met his eyes. "Thanks."

"You are welcome." He stood and held his hand out to me. "I searched for anything else that had been integrated using *rakkuhr* and found nothing."

I pushed aside the thought of Mzatal digging through my head before it could weird me out. It had to be done. As I straightened my clothes, I found myself looking down at the deactivated glyph in the center of the floor. I frowned. There'd been a pair in the center of Rhyzkahl's ritual. One had been Rhyzkahl's mark, and the other one naggingly familiar though I couldn't place it.

I nodded toward the glyph. "Is that your mark?"

He crouched and passed his hand over the glyph, igniting it to a soft blue glow. "Yes, with a few variations for this specific ritual." He traced around a section with his finger. "Here is the core of it."

"So any ritual you do has your mark in it?"

He looked up at me and nodded. "Yes, the qaztahl's mark is the hub of any ritual in the demon realm."

"In . . . in *his* ritual, his mark was there along with another. I didn't realize it then, but it had to have been a qaztahl's mark as well. Probably Jesral's, right?"

"Yes, Jesral's mark was there," he said. He stood slowly, eyes on mine. "What troubles you?"

"It looked so familiar." I pinched the bridge of my nose, trying to place it. "I didn't have time to think about it then though, y'know? But I've seen it before. On Earth." I struggled to remember. "Shit."

"Pygah," Mzatal said, reminding me to use my resources. "That you've seen Jesral's mark on Earth is significant."

I called the pygah and breathed, but the connection still eluded me. "Damn it," I said, knowing I *needed* to remember. "Can you, um, help?"

He smiled a bit, probably amused that I asked him to do something I'd so strenuously resisted before. "Yes. A simple prompt, nothing more."

A second later, I knew. I could hear the water drip in the shower, smell the soap, feel the humidity of steam. "Tattoo," I said. "On one of Katashi's senior students. Tsuneo." A smooth-faced Japanese man a few years younger than me who'd been studying with Katashi for five or six years. I didn't know much more about him. Katashi didn't have more than a few students with him at any time, and his more senior students tended to live and practice elsewhere, only coming to Katashi's mansion for summonings. "It was down by his hip where no one would normally see it," I continued, "but I walked in on him in the bathroom. It was small, but I *know* it was the same."

Mzatal went still, only the muscle in his jaw shifting as he ground his teeth.

"Why would one of Katashi's students have a tat of Jesral's mark?" I asked, not liking any of the answers I came up with.

Mzatal remained silent for another moment, and when he spoke, power boiled behind the words. "Only if Jesral has influence in Katashi's enclave."

Everything about that was disturbing. Jesral with a foothold in Mzatal's Earth presence held implications beyond my puny knowledge, but I knew enough to label it a Really Bad Thing. "I guess it's too much to hope that Tsuneo simply found it in a book and thought it would make a cool tat?"

Mzatal took my hand in a firm grip and strode toward the doors. We passed through the antechamber, crossed the corridor and exited onto the balcony.

He breathed deeply and closed his eyes as he released my hand, undoubtedly calling up the pygah. "A chance that he came upon it by accident? Yes," he said, then he shook his head. "Likely? No."

I leaned on the rail and rubbed at my temples. "Shit gets more and more fun," I said with a sigh. "So when do you start training me? I think I'm going to need it, and soon."

He stood beside me, looking out to the sea and sky. "You need everything I can teach you, all that you can absorb," he said, voice still brimming with power. "Meet me at the column at midday wearing clothing suitable for working out."

I straightened and regarded his profile. The set of his jaw betrayed his deep turmoil. "You got it, Boss," I said, laying my hand briefly on his shoulder before I turned and departed.

Chapter 27

Workout clothing? An ilius—Tata, I think—coiled out of my way as I passed through the main room and into the bedroom. To my utter shock, I found a tank top, something that looked very much like a sports bra, socks and shorts. Apparently the zrila had been busy sewing like, well, demons. I quickly threw the clothing on, then spent several frustrating minutes looking for my sneakers, finally finding them in the insane location known as the-bottom-of-the-wardrobe-where-they-belong. Crazy faas!

I raked my hair back into a ponytail as I headed out and reached the column just as the midday tone resonated through me. I looked up. It rose three stories or so, about ten feet in diameter at the base, narrowing gradually to a flat top that was half that. Though of the same ubiquitous basalt of the area, its polished surface glimmered in other-sight as though coated with a thin layer of potency. As good a place to meet as any I supposed. What the heck did the lord have planned for me that required workout clothing? Exercise? The Arcane? I sucked equally at both.

A few minutes later Mzatal approached down the long path from the palace. I allowed myself an appreciative smile at his appearance. Barefooted and bare-chested, he wore loose pants of deep blue low on his hips, and a sleeveless and flowing knee-length open tunic in a fabric that shimmered impossibly between gold, maroon, and dark green. His braid hung over his right shoulder, though calling it simply a braid did little justice to the intricate weave. It had to be at least a dozen strands, wound through with cords of silver, gold, and bronze. He looked damn good.

As he neared I gave him a grin. "Nice duds, Boss. Looking sharp."

With a glance and faint smile, he continued past me and to the column. Placing his right hand on the surface, he murmured something too low for me to hear, then clasped both hands behind his back and turned to regard me, smiling enigmatically.

I gave him a wary look. "What's the plan for today?"

"This is where it begins," he said, voice rich and intense, "and this is where it ends. The Primary Initiation."

"Okaaay," I said, totally baffled. "And what does that mean?"

"This segment of training begins now and ends when you survive the execution of a perfect shikvihr atop the column."

Survive?? I tipped my head back to look at the column. How the hell was I supposed to climb that thing?

I dragged my eyes from the column and back to Mzatal. "You're fucking kidding me."

His smile didn't waver. "No, I am not. It is an arduous undertaking, and one that will serve you well."

I frowned. Clearly I was missing something incredibly obvious. I hated weird challenges like this, because I always seemed to miss the really obvious thing. "Okay, lemme make sure I have this straight," I said. "I have to climb this smooth, really high column and then do a shikvihr? I don't even know what that is yet."

"The shikvihr is a full pattern lay, consisting of eleven rings with eleven sigils per ring," he explained patiently. "It is a ritual foundation that greatly enhances ability to control and focus potency. When done properly, it flows like a harmonious dance. The column will adapt to the level of your preparedness. Step back ten paces, and I will demonstrate an initiate level shikvihr."

Yeah, I was off to a great damn start. I backed up the requisite distance.

Mzatal turned to the column and placed both palms on it, murmuring low again. As I watched, the surface of the column began to flow and change. Ridges and footholds appeared and disappeared in an undulating rhythm. He ascended with a grace to make Nureyev weep, shifting effortlessly from each protrusion to the next as they ebbed and flowed around him. Some of the ridges couldn't have been more than an inch or two deep, yet Mzatal seemed to glide up the column like a rock climber in zero gravity.

I craned my neck back as he reached the top and began what looked like a dance, or kata. He flowed around the perimeter of the top, a hair's-breadth from the edge at times, laying sigils in a flowing chain, with movements so beautiful it made my heart ache. With a final sweep of his hand he ignited the sigils, sending a resonant tone through the column that vibrated my teeth in an impossibly good way.

Another wave of his hand dissipated the sigils. He descended as beautifully as he'd ascended, then placed a hand on the column again. It shimmered and became dormant. He turned and beckoned for me to approach.

"This was without the distractions that accompany the final trial," he said with a slight smile.

I suddenly felt like a fifth grader who'd been handed a calculus test. Only a few weeks ago I'd been so damn confident in my summoning abilities, yet now there was no denying there were *major* gaps in my knowledge base.

Throat tight, I gestured to the column. "I don't even know how to begin, to get to . . ." I shook my head. "I don't know *any* of this."

"It is why we are here," he said, exuding calm. "It is why we are training. You *will* know it. You *will* understand it intimately. You *will* be able to dance the shikvihr even though the world breaks apart beneath your feet. It is your foundation. It is your salvation."

Clearly, he'd never seen me dance. "Okay, fine. What do I do first?"

"You climb," he said, placing his hand on the column again. It shimmered and then a narrow stair spiraled around it to the top.

Nice that the column has a "kindergarten" level, I thought. "Just climb?" I asked him.

"To the top. Go."

I gave him one last doubtful look, then started up the stairs. I fully expected them to start shifting beneath my feet, but they remained stable, though they seemed to narrow considerably the higher I climbed. I kept my back pressed against the column and took my time, and finally eased up over the edge.

A swell of potency engulfed me like an emptiness needing to be filled. I dropped to my knees, fighting the surge of panic as I realized the top of the column wasn't solid. I knelt on a perimeter about a foot and a half wide, but in the middle was a two foot diameter . . . hole? I didn't know what it was. Deep blackness radiated potency like a ravenous maw, and whatever it was, I knew I didn't want to step on it. Or touch it. Or be anywhere near it.

Panic continued to claw at me. I squeezed my eyes shut, called up a stupid pygah, and focused on my breathing. I didn't have to see the hole to feel it, and even shifting out of othersight didn't do much. It still lurked there, dark and unknown, sucking at me, tugging with questing fingers.

I had no idea how long I was up there doing my impression of a treed cat, but at long last I cracked my eyes open and peered down at Mzatal.

"Can I come down now?" I called, damn near pleading.

Eyes on me, he nodded. Getting back onto the narrow stairs was the hardest part of the climb, but I managed to crab my way down. By the time I reached the ground I was drenched with sweat.

Scrubbing at my face, I trudged back to Mzatal. *Look at me, I couldn't even stand on the top.* Trust me to flunk kindergarten.

Yet when I looked into his face, he was smiling. "Many do not make the climb," he told me. "Some who make the climb cannot step onto the top. It is a start. Your body rebels more than your mind."

My spirits lifted a fraction of a smidge. "You mean I didn't fail?" I had a hard time believing that I managed to get through something others couldn't, especially as fucked up as I currently was.

He shook his head. "You did not fail, and it was indeed a trial, its outcome determining the course of your training."

I snorted. "You needed *this* to find out I don't know shit?"

His mouth twitched. "That I already knew. I needed to know something more of your heart and your mettle." He looked up toward the column. "The void can consume the resolve of even the most stalwart." He returned his attention to me. "And now we train your body."

He stepped into a wide stance—one arm stiff to the side, wrist flexed, and the other straight out in front, palm forward—and beckoned for me to copy it. I did so, though a thousand times klutzier. From there he led me through a kung-fu-tai-chi-yoga type of routine that left me sweating and shaking. At first everything in me screamed that it sucked—it was exercise, after all—but it was so freeing that by the time we were done, I was almost sorry it was over. Almost.

I felt the grove activate as we finished. "Someone's coming."

Mzatal went still. "It will be Seretis. He is early." He straightened, adjusted his tunic. He wasn't sweating or even breathing hard, the bastard. Luckily, I was doing enough for both of us.

Though I'd never actually met Seretis, I remembered the lord's quick smile as he'd passed me on the way to deal with the anomaly at Rhyzkahl's palace; seen a glimpse of his character as manifest in the residence he shared with Rayst. And Michael Moran had certainly spoken highly of him after our snowball fight. "Why is he here?"

"He asked to meet with me concerning a matter raised at the conclave." He looked past me, down the steep, rocky slope that dropped from the far side of the column. "Do you see the pile of bricks at the bottom of the hill?"

I peered that way and saw a stack of dark basalt bricks about twenty-five yards away. "Yeah."

"While I am gone you will move ten of those bricks from the pile to the base of the column."

I blinked in astonishment and *almost* asked him if he was fucking kidding, but managed to hold it back. He wasn't. Not one little bit.

"Sure thing, Boss." I scowled and picked my way down the hill while he turned toward the grove. Yeah, and I intended to sing "It's a Small World" in my head the next time his mind-reading-ass was trying to concentrate.

The bricks weighed probably about ten pounds each, which wouldn't have been too bad to carry over flat terrain. But the hill had a slope of about forty-five degrees, and ranged from rubble to thigh high "steps," which meant that this particular exercise *suuuuuucked*.

Gestamar landed by the column as I reached the top of the hill. "Heya, Gestamar," I said breathlessly.

He rumbled in what I suspected was amusement. "Greetings, Kara Gillian."

As much as I liked Gestamar, I didn't want to waste

breath with casual conversation. He simply continued to watch while I lugged brick after brick. The uneven footing and the climb over the big shelves made the whole thing one big pain in the ass. By the ninth brick my muscles were pure jelly. I was *so* going to hurt tomorrow.

"A long bath in the hot pool will serve you well tonight," Gestamar said, rumbling louder, and this time I knew damn well he was laughing.

"Yeah, thanks, darlin'," I panted as I headed back down the damn hill.

I stepped down from a boulder onto gravel, lost my footing and landed on my ass, though I caught myself before sliding. That would have left some ugly road rash. *Still gonna have a bruise,* I grumbled silently as my posterior protested. I grabbed the last brick and slogged my way back up the damn hill, but when I reached the top, Seretis leaned casually against the column where Gestamar had been. Yep, still totally looked like he belonged on a Spanish-language soap opera. He watched me, smiling, as I staggered past him. Lord or not, I wasn't about to stop when I was so close to being done.

I stacked the brick with the others, then sat heavily and lay back in the grass, breathing hard. I turned my head to peer at him. "Hi, I'm Kara Gillian. Figure you already know that though, right?"

He smiled broadly. "I know it of certainty now. I am Seretis," he said, voice light and damn near cheery. "It is a true pleasure to meet you, Kara Gillian, as delightfully sweaty as you are in this moment."

I pushed up onto my elbows, liking him already. "Michael speaks highly of you."

"And well he should," Seretis said with a laugh. "I pay him enough to do so!"

"So, you and Mzatal meet up for weekly poker games or something?" Though even as I said it, I damn near busted out laughing at the thought of a bunch of lords getting together for poker night.

Smiling, he bent and picked up one of the big bricks, shook his head. "Nothing so amusing as that this time," he said, giving me a wink. "Some qaztahl matters. And questions about you."

I rolled my eyes and sat up. "I'm so popular!" Then I sobered. "Mzatal told you what happened to me?"

"He did, though I also knew some from them." Seretis gestured to the three syraza sunning themselves on the roof of the palace. "There are those who think you dangerous, Kara Gillian."

"Are you one of them?" I had to remind myself that simply because he seemed nice and had a sense of humor didn't mean he wouldn't prefer to see me dead.

His face still held a smile, though his eyes were serious now. "I could have been," he said, turning the brick over in his hands, "had Mzatal's answers been different, and had you assessed differently than you do."

The sweat froze on my skin. I knew it would take only a flick of his hand for him to smash my skull with the brick. I swallowed to work moisture back into my mouth. "And you believe him? Trust his judgment?"

Seretis tilted his head and nodded slowly, regarding me with keen, hazel eyes. "If he says it, I know it to be truth to the best of his knowledge. It is in what he does not say," he offered with a shake of his head, "that his shrewd genius abides."

I nodded slowly, some of the tension slipping away. "I have no intention of destroying the world," I said, "for whatever that's worth,"

"I know this," he said with quiet power. "I truly do. You carry a 'danger' that some would like to harness, and no," he said with a smile, answering the question before I asked it, "I am not one of them."

"I said once before that dangerous things are used, destroyed, or contained," I told him. "Are you content with how Mzatal intends to contain and use me?"

His gaze went to the pile of bricks at the bottom of the hill. "I would rather hold—as Mzatal does—that you have the will, courage, and heart to contain yourself and to make use of your potential. Should that prove not to be the case, then I would need to reassess."

I let out a low sigh. "I guess we'll find out."

Seretis looked back to me, held the brick out. "You disliked carrying these up the hill."

I took it, weirdly relieved to have it out of his hand, even though I knew damn well there were a hundred other ways for him to kill me before I could even blink. But by passing it to me it seemed as if he relinquished my fate back over to my control. "Exercise and I don't always get along." I told him. "We agree to disagree."

He crouched. "Amkir. Jesral. Rhyzkahl. Kadir."

My gut clenched, and I made a sour face. "You mean the Four Dickwads?"

Seretis let out a soft snort of amusement. "The Four *Mraztur*."

"Sounds like a nasty word."

"There is no direct translation," he said, "but, in your vernacular, perhaps 'motherfucking asshole dickwad defilers' will serve." His gaze penetrated me, and when he spoke again, the air seemed to tremble around him. "Every brick you carry, every time you climb the column, you strengthen yourself against them. They do not rest in their purposes. Dance the full shikvihr and you become a true thorn in their side," he said, eying me appraisingly. "Mzatal believes you have the passion, resolve, and skill to do it."

My eyes went to the top of the column. Memory of the terror of that yawning void whispered through me, and I shuddered. "I have a long way to go," I murmured, then looked back to him. "But I've been described as a tenacious bitch more than once."

He chuckled, then his smile softened. "You would not have survived Rhyzkahl's venom or Mzatal's assessments were you not, Kara," he said gently. "The Four seek you, and they seek Earth. They believe you carried power in the form of Elinor's essence and they seek to use you to advance their plans." He shook his head. "You were more than they had bargained for and less of what they thought they had."

I turned his words over in my head. "What do they want of Earth?" I asked, though I had a feeling I already knew the answer.

"What most all of us lordlings want," he said, tilting his head. "Connection. Access. Since the cataclysm, we know it is critical for stability and control of the arcane, as well as the vitality of the qaztahl." His smile faded. "The Four Mraztur want more though. Benevolent alliance is not what they seek."

I scowled. "I'm not going to let them fuck up my world," I said, though I was fully aware those were big words for someone who could barely carry ten bricks up a hill.

"Perhaps that purpose and determination will make this—" He tapped the brick in my hand. "—lighter."

"Nothing will make the burden lighter," I replied. "But it sure as shit makes me more willing to bear it."

"It is much to bear." His eyes dropped to the sigils that were visible above the neckline of my tank top. For the first time his smile faded completely, as if a light had gone out. He lifted a hand toward me then paused. His face was unreadable, yet I could see in his eyes his need to touch the sigils and his loathing to do so.

I went very still, sensing the silent, motionless battle within him. My pulse thudded as I waited, and I realized I wanted him to touch the sigils, wanted him to *really* know what I went through.

He shifted his attention up to the trio of syraza on the tower, though his hand didn't waver. His gaze stayed on them for half a dozen heartbeats, and I had a feeling there was a silent discussion going on between them.

Seretis looked back to me, eyes haunted. "May I?" he asked softly. Beneath the words I felt his hope that I'd say no.

I worked moisture into my mouth. "Yes."

He shifted closer, pausing with his fingers barely an inch above the sigil on my sternum. Unbidden, the memory of the torture that fired this sigil flared. *It is as though I am immersed in acid and my skin boils away as I scream and thrash.* Clenching my hands into fists, I tried in vain to control the shudder.

Grief shadowed across his face as he absorbed the memory. He visibly shook, then sucked in a sharp breath, eyes widening in brief horror as if the power that had formed the sigils reached for him. He recoiled hard enough that he lost his balance and landed awkwardly on his backside, breathing heavily, eyes never leaving the sigil.

I realized I was staring at him in shock, and I quickly controlled my expression as best I could. "Yeah, that's usually the reaction guys have when they look at my boobs," I said lightly, trying to break the bizarre tension and give him a chance to recover.

Seretis closed his eyes and drew three controlled breaths, clearly drawing on the pygah and possibly others. After a moment he exhaled and opened his eyes. The horror had faded, yet the revulsion and grief still remained. He shifted to a half cross-legged position with one knee up, similar to the kneel/sit that the syraza so often used, then raised his eyes to mine.

"I am so very sorry," he said, voice barely above a whisper but with no less strength.

"It is what it is," I replied quietly.

A soft smile returned to his face. He reached and brushed my cheek lightly with the tips of his fingers. "And you are here, forged in fiery torment," he pulled his hand back, rested his forearm on his knee, "prepared to kick the ass, as Michael would say, of the Four Dickwads."

A shiver of lingering terror raced over me, but I gave him the low chuckle he no doubt expected. I didn't feel anywhere near strong enough to even look any of them in the eye, much less kick any asses.

He laughed, a beautiful sound that helped disperse my residual fears—and his as well, perhaps. "Trust me, you don't want to look them in the eye. Ugly, the lot of them." He stood smoothly and held a hand out for me.

I allowed him to pull me to my feet and gave him a more genuine smile. I didn't even mind that he'd clearly read my thoughts. He kept hold of my hand, laughing eyes on mine as he bowed toward me and brushed his lips across my knuckles—sharp contrast to Jesral who hadn't bowed at all, though I doubted Seretis was aware of it.

"And now, my sweaty, fiery summoner," he said, releasing my hand. "I must take my leave of you as Mzatal awaits me again."

"It was my pleasure to meet you, Lord Seretis," I said, actually meaning it.

Seretis beamed. "And a delight to meet you, Kara Gillian." He turned and began to walk away, then stopped and looked back. "You could surprise Mzatal and carry all the bricks down again." He took two steps, then stopped again. "On reconsideration, surprising Mzatal is not always the wisest course of action." He laughed and continued toward the palace, whistling.

Grinning, I watched him go, then looked over at the bricks.

Nope.

Instead I lay down in the soft grass in the shadow of the column, and took a nap.

Chapter 28

I felt as if an entire new universe was opening up for me. Mzatal introduced me to the concepts of constructing floaters, starting me out with floor glyphs: chalk first, then transitioning to pure arcane energy. That alone took several days, which gave me plenty of time to get frustrated at my lack of success and apparent inadequacy. Mzatal, however, was the model of patience, though he sure as hell wasn't always Mr. Nice Guy, and it was clear he had no intention of coddling me or easing me into training. As Idris had warned me oh-so long ago in our first conversation back on Szerain's tower, Mzatal had no problem letting me know when I'd screwed up. Yet, he also was quick to offer deserved praise and stuck with me until I finally had my lightbulb-over-the-head moment of understanding.

The next couple of days flew by unnoticed as he led me through grueling preparatory practices of how to manage and channel the potency flows. Some of it was familiar—refinements on known techniques—and some completely new. But by the end of the week we were both satisfied that I was ready for the next step.

Mzatal had told me that the shikvihr could only be taught by a lord, and the same held true for floaters. I thought that simply meant it wasn't *allowed* to be taught by others. I was wrong. A summoner *required* direct initiation from a lord to shape floaters. I could see, but not influence the needed potency strands. He explained that first, a summoner had to have an innate capacity to control potency combined with acquired skill. If those prerequisites were met, then it was simply a matter of fine-tuning what was already there, which was successful about half the time. I'd already been assessed through the first part, so all that remained was the second, which he accomplished in about ten minutes of holding my hands clasped between his. I didn't feel any different, but I could sure as hell touch the strands afterwards.

He asked if I wanted to wait until the next day for the actual floaters since it was so late, but I knew the sooner I could get this shit down, the better, so I opted to forge ahead. Besides, I was pretty damned excited to try it. A couple of hours later, I had the kick-all-the-ass, mind-blowing "aha!" breakthrough on the floaters, and by dawn could lay consistent anchors and had a grasp on tracing multi-sigil series.

"And now it is time for you to sleep," Mzatal told me, giving me one of his this-is-not-up-for-discussion looks when I began to protest that I was fine and could keep working. I closed my mouth, gave him a sheepish grin, and nodded assent instead.

"Come to the workroom at the mid-afternoon tone," he said. "We will go to my nexus point and begin work directly related to recovering Szerain's blade."

I blinked in surprise. "I'm ready for that?"

"This is not the actual recovery, nor is it even part of the seeking," he explained. "However, what we do will determine how we will construct those rituals in order to best utilize your unique energy signature."

I wanted to quiz him more, but he turned me bodily and pushed me toward the bedroom. "Get in bed and sleep," he ordered.

"Pushy fucker," I muttered, but did as he commanded and was asleep within seconds of hitting the pillow.

After sound sleep, a bath, and plenty of food, I headed down to the workroom a little earlier than the appointed time so that I could practice all of the new stuff on my own. After about half an hour, Ilana came in and peered expectantly at me.

"You are ready?" she asked, her lovely chiming as soothing as ever.

I gave her a puzzled look. "Yeah, I guess. You're working with us today?"

"Only to transport you to the beach," she said with a delicate flutter of wings. "Mzatal is still in the plexus and will be here momentarily,"

I nodded and finished the sigil I was practicing, then shifted my attention to her. "Ilana, what's the deal with Zack AKA Zakaar? Is he as off-the-charts insane as Rhyzkahl?" He'd never shown any signs of treachery but then neither had Rhyzkahl before I'd arrived in his realm. The thought of Jill, Ryan, and Tessa at the mercy of a Rhyzkahl devotee gnawed at me.

Ilana shook her head. "Zakaar is demahnk—an Elder like Helori, like me. He is separated from Rhyzkahl for two reasons, one being that he stood resolutely against Rhyzkahl's choices several decades ago."

"And the other?" I asked. "Or is that something you're not allowed to talk about?"

"He chose a guardianship, also because of Rhyzkahl's actions."

I tugged a hand through my hair, grimacing. "Zack is close to a friend of mine. Is she safe with him?" That he was one of the elder syraza eased much of my concern, but I really *needed* to hear it straight from Ilana.

She moved in close and laid her hand on my arm. "If this is one he has chosen to protect, she could not be safer. Zakaar is the most resolute of us all."

I released a breath I hadn't realized I was holding. "Thanks." I still had plenty to worry about around my friends and family, but at least I could put Zakaar's being a diabolical fiend on the back burner.

Mzatal entered, one hand behind his back and a document in the other. He wore all black today, a mid-thigh tunic-coat, pants, and boots. Strands of metallic gold woven through his complex braid were his only ornamentation.

"Afternoon, Boss," I said, giving him a quick smile.

"Good afternoon, Kara," he said, his eyes traveling over me in a quick assessment of who-knew-what as he moved close to Ilana. He held up the glyph-covered paper. "Today we will attempt the first ring of the beacon ritual at the nexus."

"Cool." I stepped in close. I'd done enough travel with Helori to know the drill. I felt no small relief that we were going to the beach this way, since I'd learned from Jekki and

Faruk that the standard way down was by about a billion stairs along the cliff face.

A heartbeat later we arrived on a high beach of tumbled rock and black sand nestled in a curve of the cliffs just south of Mzatal's palace. Ahead, more stairs led down to a lower sandy beach where I saw Idris kneeling in the light surf, splashing water over his head. I assumed he'd come down the cliff stairs, but *why*? About fifty yards to the right, the waterfall cascaded with a roar into a deep sea-pool. Off to the left stood a circular platform of basalt surrounded by eleven dark columns. Apart from color, it was a near match to the pavilion in Szerain's courtyard. This was Mzatal's nexus. He strode immediately toward it, glancing back at me with a jerk of his head to indicate I should follow. I did so. I didn't have the faintest idea what I would need to do, but I was more than ready to do it.

I stepped up onto the stone next to Mzatal, then threw out my hands as a wave of vertigo struck. *Whoa.* It was like stepping into a slowly spinning vortex. Szerain's nexus had felt like it was sleeping, but this baby was definitely awake.

Mzatal caught my arm and held it for the moment it took me to accustom myself to the energies. "This afternoon is about experimentation, determining the ideal configuration for the base ring of the beacon diagram," he said, a bare hint of eagerness in his voice as though the task itself or the method excited him. "Come."

I followed him to the center, mild uneasiness coiling through me, though I couldn't put my finger on why.

He turned to face me. "I spent time in the plexus seeking any sign that Rhyzkahl has activated a ritual recently, but found none," he said with a last glance at the paper he held before tucking it away in a pocket.

"That's a good thing, right?"

"Yes. Very good. And as we progress, it will be our goal to minimize disruptions in the potency flow so that we do not alert him to our work until absolutely necessary. For now, Idris and I will monitor that aspect until you are ready."

"Sounds good to me," I said with a nod. I had no idea how to keep flows low-profile, but I was confident he'd teach me what I needed to know. *Yeah, like I was confident Rhyzkahl would send me home?* I shoved the thought aside. This was nothing like that. Right?

"As soon as possible, we will create the beacon here to locate Vsuhl," he said. He turned a slow circle, his eyes traveling over the platform and the columns. "Now we must determine how best to integrate your unique energy signature into the calling. I have laid out the initial parameters." He patted the pocket that held the paper.

I peered up at him. "And since that's theory only, you want to know how it works in a live setting." That made sense, though the part about integrating my signature spiked my uneasiness. *Am I being as naïve about Mzatal as I was about Rhyzkahl?* An insistent thread of doubt twisted through me.

"Yes," he said with a nod and a quick smile. I had the feeling we were in his element, something he actually enjoyed. "We seek the bridge between theory and practical application." He rapidly traced a line of eleven floaters in front of us. "What do you see as the commonality between these three sections?" he asked, indicating the sections, then glancing at me.

Damn. A test. I examined the series and, to my relief, found a small link. "Well, the lateral vectors correlate."

His mouth drew into a tight line, and his brow furrowed. Crap. That obviously wasn't the answer he was looking for. I had a feeling my answer was about as dumb as saying that the commonality between a group of typed words was that the ink was black. With a pass of his hand along the line, he ignited the sigils, then moved behind me. "This may help you to see more clearly. Pygah with your eyes closed and *feel* the series. Then open your eyes and see what correlations you find."

I felt as if I'd been handed an exam I hadn't studied for, and it must have shown.

Mzatal laid his hand briefly on my shoulder. "This is not a test, Kara. I know that I am missing an aspect, and I want to determine what you can see in order to fill that gap."

Well, that was a new one. With a slight frown, I moved to the exact center of the line of sigils and followed Mzatal's instructions, very aware of his presence behind me. I extended my senses and *felt* into the series, then opened my eyes, finding it more vibrantly clear now. I smiled, feeling not only the common harmony between the sections, but the delicate relationships between individual sigils. "It's not really about the sections. Each sigil is connected to every other sigil, some doubly so."

Mzatal stepped up beside me, clasped his hands behind his back, and squinted at the line. "Show me."

I saw Idris watching a couple of feet from the edge of the platform, frowning slightly, hair dripping seawater.

Was this part of some strange game Mzatal was playing? Except it sure felt sincere. I traced several of the sigil strands with my index finger. "See? These are the doubles. And here are the singles," I said, as I pointed them out. "They have a different resonance that feels . . . off."

Mzatal narrowed his eyes, leaned in, and examined the series for at least a full minute, deeply absorbed. With a sudden intake of breath, he straightened, nodding. "Yes. Excellent." He made some adjustments to the line. "And now?"

I'd followed the feel of what he did and was already trying to figure out how to say in words what I sensed. I gestured to the sigil on the end. "That one," I said, shaking my head, "is the wrong, um, hue?" Damn it. That wasn't right.

The lord peered at the sigil, then shook his head definitively. "I do not see it," he said. "It would clarify for me if I read it directly through you."

I tensed involuntarily, though I knew it was the best way for him to see what I couldn't explain. And at least he asked. "Uh, yeah. Sure."

He laid his hand on my shoulder, nothing more. "Now show me."

I examined the sigil carefully, *feeling* into the slight discordance of the hue. My nails bit into the palms of my clenched hands, though I couldn't even feel a whisper of his presence. Apparently looking *through* me wasn't the same as reading me.

Mzatal remained still for a bit, then muttered something in demon. A moment later he lifted his hand from my shoulder. "I have it," he said. He made a quick adjustment, then spun the line into a ring around us. "You completed the series," he said, turning fully to me with a smile.

I exhaled in relief that he was out of my head, and echoed his smile with a slight one of my own. But the mild discomfort twitched up another notch. I'd given him something he couldn't get without me. He'd said he would use me. Was I falling into his trap? "Guess I'm not totally hopeless," I said lightly.

"Kara Gillian, you are far from hopeless," he said with a shake of his head. "Now you have but to ignite it."

Right. Ignite it. I rubbed sweaty palms on my pants. This wasn't Rhyzkahl. Mzatal and I had an agreement. *Get over it*, I told myself. So far there was nothing to indicate that Mzatal intended to screw me over. I took a deep breath, lifted my hand, and sent a focused burst of potency to the ring. Its resonance struck me in a dissonant wave as it ignited, off just enough to be uncomfortable.

Mzatal turned in a circle, examining the ring. "Perfect. This is our foundation," he said, nodding approval. "Now, bring it into alignment and see if you can attain full resonance."

I made adjustments and brought the alignment as far as I could. The resonance improved, but remained unsettling and definitely not right.

Mzatal had his shoulders drawn up; obviously, he enjoyed the discordance as much as I did. "More, Kara. Slide the anchoring until the harmonics align, then you will have it."

I gritted my teeth and tried to make the adjustments, took it a little farther, but no. Grimacing, I withdrew from the series. "It's not . . ." I shook my head. "No. It's not right. It's not working."

Mzatal exhaled, and though I wasn't looking at him, I felt his eyes on me. "Take it down," he said.

Annoyance and frustration seared through me, and a zillion thoughts consumed my mind, even though I knew most were irrational. Why the hell couldn't I do this one stupid little thing? And who the hell gave these lords the right to fuck with my life? *My* life. Everything had been fine until the asshole lords got involved.

I grounded the ring, then dispelled it with several arm sweeps that felt more like attacks than artistry. At least I could do that much right. Without looking at Mzatal, I turned and stalked to the edge of the platform, then stepped down onto the sand.

Idris hurried over. "It's okay," he said. "You almost had it." He gave me a you'll-get-it-next-time smile that made me want to slug him, but I knew none of it was his fault. Except that I was here at all. Yeah, that.

I gave him a tight smile and moved off a bit. All I wanted was to be by myself. Hugging my arms around me, I stared out at the ocean, unsettled, annoyed, and *angry*.

"Idris," Mzatal said from somewhere behind me. "Proceed with the stabilization of the nexus in preparation for the full foundation. I do not know when we will be ready, though, ideally, by the next full moon on Earth."

Didn't know when we would be ready because I couldn't do my part. *Fuck.*

"Kara, we will return home and continue our work tomorrow," he said with irritating calm. "Take the stairs. Stop at each switchback and count to one hundred twenty-one, then continue."

Blinking in disbelief, I turned fully on him. He stood with his hands locked behind his back and face set in impassive judgment. "Not *my* home," I retorted, damn near snarling it. "And count? Like, count out loud to one twenty-one?" I looked over at the stairs that zigzagged up the five-hundred foot cliff. Punishment for messing up the ritual thing. *I hate this shit.*

"It is not necessary to speak," he said. "It *is* necessary to acknowledge each number."

"Sure," I said tightly. "No problem." Yeah, this was turning into a lovely shittastic day.

"End the count with a pygah," he added, then turned and strode toward Ilana. I stared at his back and bit back a choice reply. Idris walked the perimeter of the nexus over and over, oblivious to the bullshit taking place in my world.

I pivoted and stalked to the stairs, looked up and shook my head. "You've got to be kidding me," I muttered. They rose steeply, cut from the basalt itself or built out where needed. Narrow. No rail. Great.

I started up, thighs complaining even before I reached the first switchback. Back home, stair climbing was pretty much limited to my basement and porch steps, with all others avoided unless absolutely necessary. Upon reaching the turn, I stopped and did the stupid count and pygah, then peered over the edge. It was already a *looong* way down. Idris, shirtless now, traced in the center of the nexus, surrounded by a growing ring of sigils. Damn, but he made it look so easy.

Up. And more up. On the fourth switchback, I stopped to catch my breath, hands on my hips, thighs burning like crazy. I looked up and immediately realized that ignorance was indeed bliss. Still a helluva long way to the top. *Shit!* I tried to nurse the anger, but it slid away to a simmer, my body demanding the lion's share of my attention. A glimpse of blue caught my attention from a couple of switchbacks up. Possibly a faas heading down, I figured.

I leaned back against the cliff, both to rest a bit and to keep well away from the edge since, at this point, it was like being on a ledge of a twenty-story building. I had a healthy respect for though not a particular fear of heights, but this was definitely pushing the envelope.

I took a deep breath, did the count and the pygah. When I opened my eyes, Faruk hopped down the last few steps to my switchback and stood vibrating before me, a plastic sports bottle—very obviously from Earth—clutched between its hands.

"Tunjen for youuuuuuu, Kara Gillian," the faas said, holding the bottle out to me.

"Thanks," I said with an unsteady smile, realizing how much I really needed this right now. Faruk hopped up and down, teeth bared, then ran up the stairs on all six legs as though running on flat ground. For a second, I considered sitting, then decided against it. The way this day was going, it'd be against the rules, and I'd have to do the whole thing over or something stupid like that. Sighing, I lifted the bottle to drink and saw it had my name painted on it in delicate gold letters. I couldn't help but smile a bit at that.

Reluctantly, I shoved off the wall and tackled the stairs again, thighs seriously shrieking. Walking tomorrow was going to be fun. *I hate this shit.*

On the last switchback, I sat heavily on a step, panting. My legs were shredded, so sitting and counting *really* slowly felt like the best plan. Screw the consequences. To my great annoyance, as I finished my count and pygah, Idris bounded up from below, grinning and sweating.

"Best view ever!" he said as he dropped into a squat beside me and began a quiet and methodical count.

"Yeah. Great view," I muttered, giving him a doubtful look. With a groan I couldn't suppress, I heaved myself to my feet and continued up the last section. I kept close to the wall, thankful that there was only a light breeze and no gusts. Holy shit, but this was seriously high.

"Kara! Hug the wall," Idris called out from below. "I'll be passing on the left."

"Yeah. No problem there, dude." I pressed my back against the wall to make absolutely sure I was out of the way, not at all liking the thought of getting knocked off these stairs.

Idris, the bastard, dashed up the steps, sometimes two at a time, obviously familiar with their varying heights. He passed me with a stopwatch in his hand and his face set with fierce determination and focus.

Frowning, I watched until he reached the top, my emotions churning between admiration and feeling even more inadequate. My throat went horribly tight. I sank to sit on a step and looked out over the ocean. I tried to hold it back, tried not to be a baby, but I couldn't. There was too much. I gave in and let it flow in a full blown sob-fest. Lonely. Homesick. Missing everyone. Totally stressed out. Betrayed. Recovering from torture. Stuck here. Unsure of where I stood. All of it came up.

After several minutes I finally got my shit somewhat together and wiped my eyes. Letting out a long sigh, I dragged myself up and somehow managed to finish the climb, subdued and with *everything* hurting. To my dismay, as I reached the top, I saw Idris hurrying toward me. My eyes burned and felt swollen. *Damn it.* I sighed and plastered on a smile. Maybe it would pass for just being flushed from exercise.

But no. He moved in close, brow deeply creased with worry. "Um, Kara, you okay?"

"I'm good," I said, plodding up the trail toward the palace without stopping. "Tired. That's all. Lots of stairs, and I'm an out of shape clod."

"Yeah. It's a lot of stairs. You did *great* making it to the top!" He hovered beside me, a spring in his step as if he hadn't recently bounded up, what, fifty plus stories?

I knew he didn't mean it to be as patronizing as it sounded, but damn. "Yeah, yeah. Thanks," I managed. "So, uh, Mzatal does this kind of thing a lot? Assigning exercise?"

"Yeah, he did at first for me," Idris replied with a shrug. "I pretty much do it on my own now, though he'll still come up with stuff sometimes."

"You look like you're in pretty good shape." My legs didn't want to move, but I trudged on. I didn't want to lose what little momentum I had.

"I wasn't when I got here," he said. "I mean, I wasn't a slug or anything since Katashi kept me moving, but it really took off once I came to the demon realm." He peered anxiously at me. "You wanna sit down for a bit? There's a bench up ahead, and the sunset's gonna be awesome."

Even as wiped out as I was, I still had enough perception to know that sitting down with Idris and watching the sunset would probably send the wrong message. "No. Thanks. If I stop, I'll never get moving again. I just want to get back and collapse."

"Um, yeah. Sure," he said, visibly losing a little of his spring and looking crestfallen. "It's not much farther."

"Thanks," I said. I really wished he would go on without me, but I couldn't come up with a damned thing to say that wouldn't hurt his feelings.

Idris continued at my side, almost saying something several times, then, thankfully, not. Once we reached the atrium, he finally showed signs of going his own way. "I, uh, guess I'll see you in the morning," he said.

"Yeah. Thanks for walking with me." I gave him a tired smile. "See ya, Idris," I said as I turned for the stairs. More goddamn stairs. Yay.

"Bye, Kara," he called out, and I could feel his eyes still on me.

I gave a final unenthusiastic wave without looking back and sighed in relief as I got out of his sight. And, even better, in another minute I'd be able to Stop Walking.

Mzatal sat at the table in the main chamber of his rooms, leafing through a journal. He'd changed from the black into a roomy blue brocade coat, and looked totally refreshed, his braid hanging over his shoulder now wound with silver instead of gold. The fucker.

He set the journal aside as I closed the door and gave me a gentle smile. "A long soak will feel good. Food will be waiting when you are finished."

Something about the cover of the journal gave me a déjà

vu memory moment, but I couldn't place it and was too damn tired to try to figure it out right then. I gave Mzatal a faint nod and headed straight to the bath chamber, shedding my clothes along the way. I sank to my neck in the deliciously warm water of the pool, then pulled myself onto the shelf that served for lounging and rested my head in the smooth dip made for that purpose. I didn't want to fall asleep, I told myself as I closed my eyes, just rest a bit.

I jerked awake to my name being called and a hand on my shoulder. Mzatal. "Shit."

Mzatal crouched at the edge of the pool, holding a towel spread before him, ready for me.

"Shit," I said again as I willed my jellified muscles to drag me out of the bath. Mzatal wrapped the towel around me as soon as I stepped out, then picked up another.

"Thanks," I said. "Sorry." I gave him a rueful smile as he dried my shoulders and arms then scrunched the towel through my hair. "I didn't mean to fall asleep. That was stupid."

"You are tired and have had a challenging day," he said gently, not seeming in any way annoyed. "Come." He put his arm behind me and very lightly urged me toward the bedchamber.

I didn't resist. "Challenging." I snorted. "Yeah, that's a word for it." I clutched the towel around me as he guided me to the bed and pulled the covers down. I frowned, wearily casting my gaze around the room. "I don't know where my night things are."

"They are in the dresser," he said. "Though you may be more comfortable sleeping as you would at home. I will bring something for you to eat." He turned and exited to the main room.

I blinked at his back, wondering how the hell he knew how I slept at home. Then again, probably not much of a stretch considering he knew plenty of other intimate details about me. I set the towel on the end of the bed. Screw it. He'd seen me naked plenty of times already, and I slept much better in the nude. I groaned as I crawled into the bed and pulled the covers up. Tomorrow would be a day of hurrrrrrt.

Mzatal returned a moment later carrying a plate of the yummy cat-turd-looking things and some sliced fruit, and a glass of tunjen juice. I sat up and tucked the sheet around me as he held the glass out for me. "Drink at least half now," he said as he set the plate on my thighs and smiled. "You will sleep deeply tonight."

I obediently took a long drink of the juice. "I'm sorry I messed up the ritual."

Mzatal shook his head and sank to sit on the edge of the bed. "You completed the first series, saw that which I could not, and you ignited the ring. The rest will come."

I peered at him. "Oh. I thought you were . . ." I trailed off, trying to find the right word. "Mad" wasn't right, but I was too tired to figure it out.

He met my eyes evenly, and I wondered if it had really been judgment I saw earlier in his face or simply my distorted perception. "I was—*am*—deeply pleased that you were able to work so intuitively with the sigils," he said. "That ability is a vital element of this." He laid a hand on my right ankle over the covers. I sighed in relief as the healing warmth spread up my leg. Though of course it did him no good for me to be crippled for a couple of days, so it made sense for him to make sure I could walk tomorrow.

"If we ever do get this blade, what happens then?" I asked. "I mean, to me."

He tilted his head slightly and lifted a finger toward the glass of forgotten juice in my hand. "We *will* retrieve Vsuhl. After that, you continue to train. We have an agreement."

I drained the glass and set it on the side table. "But what about the blade? You'll have two of them."

"It is my intention to hold it for Szerain," he said, then moved his hand to my other ankle.

"Oh. Right. Makes sense." I nibbled some of the food. I didn't have much of an appetite, but I knew I needed to eat something. "By the way, where do you sleep? I haven't noticed you crawling into bed here," I said.

"Qaztahl require far less sleep than humans," he explained. "Usually only a night every ten days or so. Great potency drain or disruption also requires sleep for quickest restoration." He glanced to the big comfy chair near the bed. "I slept there the night after your healing, and I've not required more."

I gave a slow nod. When he woke me from the nightmare the other day, he'd been working in that chair, watching over me. "I feel guilty for putting you out of your bed," I told him.

He gave my ankle a light squeeze and lifted his hand. "Such guilt is wasted," he said as he stood. "Do try to eat more. You need it." He poured more tunjen juice into my glass, then touched my shoulder briefly. "Sleep well, Kara." With that he turned and departed.

I watched him go. He seemed to give an actual crap about me. But then again, so had Rhyzkahl. I sighed and ate a couple of pieces of fruit, then snuggled down under the covers. Mzatal needed me and wished to use me; he was quite clear on that point. It was his ultimate motives that I wasn't too sure about.

I tried to push my doubts away, but even as tired as I was, it was a long time before I could sleep.

Chapter 29

I dreamed of coffee. A steaming cup of my favorite Café du Monde coffee with chicory, plenty of cream and sugar. There may have been donuts in the dream as well, but it was the rich scent of coffee that invaded my sleep and teased me with the promise of alertness and calories.

The dream evaporated as a mental touch from Mzatal nudged me from sleep. I groaned and pulled the pillow over my head, desperately trying to recapture the scent, the flavor of coffee—even if it was only dream coffee.

A heartbeat later I lifted my head. I still smelled the coffee. How the hell could I still be smelling coffee? I turned over and saw Mzatal sitting in his chair perusing a stack of papers. I held the sheet around me and sat up, blinking in disbelief at the steaming mug, cream and sugar on the side table. "Is that . . . coffee?"

Mzatal smiled. "Yes, real coffee."

I stared at him. "You got me coffee?"

"Yes," he said as he set his papers aside. "You have been craving it since the morning after I first summoned you."

"Thanks! Wow." I shifted so I could reach it and quickly loaded it up with cream and sugar. I held it close, took a sip, and damn near let out a moan of ecstasy. Okay, maybe I did make a bit of an O-face. "Holy shit, that's good," I breathed.

Mzatal's smile widened, watching me. "Excellent."

I settled back against the pillows, making sure the sheet was securely tucked around me. I cradled the coffee like the precious thing it was and sipped. "No, really. Holy shit, I've missed this."

"Yes, I know," he said, eyes crinkling in amusement. "It is why I acquired it."

In that moment, my heart melted just a teensy bit. I also realized with relief that I was only a little sore from yesterday's exertions. "Keep this up and I may start to like you."

Mzatal shook his head. "Perhaps suspend your opinion until after today's training."

I actually chuckled. "More stairs? Or do you have something worse in mind?"

He regarded me for a moment. "We will be summoning Katashi this evening."

Well, that would no doubt be interesting, especially considering the whole question of whether Jesral had been in contact with Katashi. " 'We.' Does that mean you want me there with you?"

Mzatal raised an eyebrow. "Absolutely. And you will assist Idris in preparation, which will introduce you to the nuances of summonings from here."

I nodded and sipped delicious coffee. "Speaking of Idris. Um, has he ever had a girlfriend?"

Mzatal's brows drew together, and he pursed his lips in thought. "There has not been opportunity since he has been here. On Earth, I do not know."

I frowned and shook my head. "Doubtful on Earth either, if he was with Katashi." I gave Mzatal a penetrating glare. "Idris needs a girlfriend or at least needs to get laid. And neither one of them needs to be me."

His eyes snapped to mine. "I'm in total agreement that it should not be you," he replied firmly. "He has been distracted by you to the point of having atypical errors in his work." He tapped the pile of papers on the table. "As in this from last night. Such distraction can be devastating to a summoner, particularly here in the realm."

"He's a nice guy. But." I sighed and shook my head. "Not only is he way too young for me, it . . ." I trailed off and shrugged. "I don't feel anything beyond friendship."

Mzatal gave a decisive nod. "I will manage this. It cannot continue to interfere with his work. Too much is at stake."

I raised an eyebrow. "How do you intend to manage it?"

"I will tell him the truth and outline the consequences."

I was surprised Mzatal didn't shrivel away from the look

I gave him. "Dude. Seriously? You expect him to stop crushing on me because you *forbid* it?"

Mzatal frowned, contemplative. "Perhaps not ideal given the entanglement of human emotions, though there is no time for it to drag on," he said, as if he actually knew what he was talking about. "If he knows you have no interest and sees how his distractions have affected his work, he will subside enough for now."

My withering look became glacial. "Boss, you're completely awesome in many ways, but you are *so* off-base with this it's not even funny." I rolled my eyes. "I've already ramped 'No Interest' up to eleven on the dial and, at this point, he doesn't *care* if his work suffers." I took a big gulp of coffee, then ran my fingers through my tangled hair. "Let me deal with it. Normally I'm not into direct confrontation with this sort of shit, but there's isn't enough time for it to fizzle out on its own."

Mzatal regarded me with that damned unreadable mask which he'd slipped on as I was talking. Great. Lords weren't much on being told they were wrong, but it had to be said.

After a long moment he gave a nod. "You are correct. It will serve better—for all of us—if you are the one to do this."

"Damn," I said, taken aback. I gave him a wry smile. "I was hoping you'd tell me I was wrong, and that I should simply slap him or something." I chuckled, then sighed and shook my head. "Does he have some sort of favorite food or escape or activity?"

Mzatal appeared to consider for a moment. "His focal activities in the last months have been physical challenges: the cliff stairs, free climbing, running, swimming. He loses himself and finds himself there. He does have a particular liking for fruit ices." He cocked an eyebrow at me. "Helpful?"

I nodded and drained the coffee mug. "Have some of those fruit ice things ready," I told him. I threw the covers off and headed to the bath chamber, only realizing when I was neck deep in the water that I'd been nude. Oh well. Making Mzatal see my flabby butt was more than sufficient payback for having to confront Idris.

After the awesome bath, I headed to the workroom with my notes. I totally was *not* looking forward to seeing Idris, but it needed to be done, and especially before Mzatal attempted to do it his way. I snorted in amusement at Mzatal's surprising naiveté. Forbid the crush. Right. Had the dude never read *Romeo and Juliet*?

The workroom was empty, and so I got busy. Mzatal had taught me each of the sigils for the foundation ring of the beacon, and even if I couldn't align the thing yet, I could practice setting it up. It was new and pretty damn exciting. Except for the last part. Every time I tried to progress from the tenth to the eleventh, the whole series destabilized and collapsed. Every single time, and I had no idea why.

On the fifth try, I thought I had it. The tenth ring held stable. I paused, took a deep breath, and began to trace the eleventh, and before I could even blink the whole thing unwound and dissipated. "Fucking shitholes!"

Someone cleared their throat behind me. I cast a glowering glance back to see Idris. "I can't get the stupid thing to set," I said and brusquely started tracing anew.

"You're starting out wrong, and by the time you get to the end, it's propagated the error ten times," he told me. "But you're only missing one connection," he said, as he moved in closer. "I'll, um, show you if you want."

"Sure, I'd appreciate that." No denying he knew what the hell he was doing. And then we'd have The Talk. Yeah, that was going to be fun. *Sigh.*

Idris moved up close behind and to my right. He looked down at Mzatal's notes on the table. "Think of each sigil as a section of code in a computer program," he said. "If you don't tell it how to move on to the next part, it won't work."

I scrubbed a hand over my face. "Idris. I can barely turn my computer on. A different analogy please?"

He smiled and traced the first two sigils. "See? Just tie the final loop of the first into the initial one of the second, and you'll be stable the rest of the way. Like, um, Christmas tree lights. Go ahead. Try it."

I peered at his loops, then smiled as I damn near *felt* understanding click in. "Now that makes sense!" I finished the series and stood gazing at my accomplishment with pride. I glanced over to Idris to find him watching me, not the series, with a dreamy not-all-there look in his eyes.

Shit. *I hate this*, I thought as I took a half step away from him.

He blinked and looked from me to the series, then back to me. "Oh, yeah. You did it. Just needed that one tweak," he said, then fidgeted. "Kara, have you ever been out to the little waterfall? Um, I wouldn't mind showing it to you sometime. Maybe tomorrow. You'll like it." He stepped closer.

I took a deep breath and released it, steeling myself for what I had to do. "Idris," I said, consciously keeping my voice very calm. "I'm about to say five words that no man ever wants to hear."

Idris blinked at me.

"'You're a great guy, but—'" I shook my head. "Idris, this 'you and me' can't happen for way too many reasons to count."

He stared, mouth open for a moment. "But . . . but you're not even giving it a chance! What about the hug the other day and the talks we've had. You can't say all that didn't happen!"

I pursed my lips. "I consider you a friend. And I'm from the South. We're some seriously huggy folk down there." I let out a sigh. "Idris, you didn't even see that I'd finished the series. You're totally distracted. I can't afford any distractions, and neither can you." My gaze narrowed, and I pulled the neckline of my shirt down enough to really show the sigils on my chest. "*This* is how high the stakes are now. If you hadn't been as focused as you were to retrieve me, Rhyzkahl and Jesral would've succeeded. I'd be their thrall, their weapon, and they'd probably have Szerain's blade by now. Where do you think that would leave you and Mzatal?"

He looked shell-shocked, so I continued as I pulled my shirt back up. "They're not giving up," I told him. "I have to stay on my toes, and I need you to be at my back, as a friend and ally."

The poor guy took a step back, looking as if he'd had a bucket of ice water thrown on him. He shook his head, face flushing, then turned and hurried out without another word.

"Fuuuuuuck," I groaned. I hoped to hell that Mzatal had been monitoring and had the damn fruit ices ready.

Fretting about Idris, I settled into practicing the series. To my relief, I had no trouble getting it to remain stable. Even his computer program analogy began to make sense, now that I understood that the sigils and series were simply chunks of instructions, ways to shape potency for each step of the process.

I continued to practice and trace, losing myself in the focus and pausing only to grab a quick lunch that Faruk brought.

Shortly after the midday tone, Idris returned. I looked over at him, my brow furrowed, totally unsure what to say, if anything. He looked calm. Really calm. A curl of dread formed in my chest. Shit. Had he simply buried it all?

Idris smiled and headed my way. I returned the smile cautiously. He stopped a couple of feet away and leaned against the edge of the table.

"Thanks, Kara," he said, his voice sounding as calm as he looked. "I needed that."

"You're okay?" I asked uncertainly. "Dude, I wasn't trying to hurt your feelings or anything. I swear."

Idris ran his hand over his hair. "Yeah, I'm good. For real. I let everything get all blown out of proportion," he said, opening his hands and shrugging. "I went and ran the stairs. Talked to Jekki and the reyza Juntihr. Everything's straight now." He gave me a sincere smile. "You don't have to worry about me stalking you anymore."

"It wasn't that," I said with a grimace. "I mean, not all that." I paused. "Okay, that was a lot of it." I gave him a wry smile. "But it was also that I don't think I'm the one who can make you happy. I think I'd be a better wingman for you than a girlfriend." I gave a snort. "Because, *dude,* have you not figured out that I have some major issues?"

Idris laughed. "Yeah, you do," he said. "Anyway, I realized that I don't need *any* girlfriend right now. Not until some of the shit settles." He drew a breath and released it slowly. "And yeah, I care about you. A lot. And that's one of the reasons it's important for me to focus on what we're doing here, with the ritual and everything else. Any one of us loses focus—you, Mzatal, me—the whole thing caves."

Some of my tension slid away, and I breathed a sigh of relief. "Thanks," I said. "Time to get back to work then." He grinned in response and within a minute had surrounded himself with a ring of floaters.

Smiling, I watched him for a moment while I wondered what the hell he did to chill out so quickly. We both worked in focused silence for a while, me on my basics, and he on diagram diagnostics.

After about a half hour, Idris stood in the center of a complete diagram, looking it over and making minor tweaks. "This is one thing I love about working in the demon realm," he said, "being able to use the floaters instead of chalk. I mean, apart from it being way more efficient, it's so much easier to make adjustments." He shook his head, let out a low whistle. "I still can't believe you summoned Lord Rhyzkahl. On your own. With *chalk*."

I lifted my shoulders in a self-conscious shrug. "I didn't think it was that big a deal."

The exasperated look he gave me told me exactly how naïve I sounded.

I cast my gaze over the shimmering ring around him, then looked back at him, frowning. "Wait. If I didn't use chalk, then how the hell else would I do it on Earth?"

"Well, with floaters," he said with a *duh!* tone. "But of course you haven't finished the shikvihr, so that's not possible for you yet."

My bafflement increased. "You can use floaters on Earth? And what does the shikvihr have to do with it?"

He looked up at me, blinked. "Everything!" Idris took a big breath. "Okay, so you've seen the shikvihr, right?" He didn't even wait for me to nod, simply hurried on, clearly excited by the topic. "See, there's eleven rings to it. Each ring learned here causes a permanent enhancement to potency-holding and general skills usage. In the demon realm, you can dance the rings you know and use the specific attributes of those rings. With me so far?"

"Sure," I said. "It's like a magic kata-thing that trains mind and body and all that."

A pained expression flickered over his face, but apparently I wasn't wrong enough for him to correct the finer details of my analogy. "There's an exponential increase between the rings, so it's a *huge* advantage to learn as much as possible," he continued. "And even though you can't dance the shikvihr on Earth unless you know the whole thing, the passive enhancement *does* carry over, so it boosts summoning and warding and stuff."

"So a summoner on Earth could have it, but it wouldn't be anything obvious."

"Yeah, but it's not common anymore since it can only be learned in the demon realm from a lord. Plus, it's a super big challenge to learn."

Considering I'd never even heard of it before, I had to agree with him about its not being common. "But what does that have to do with using floaters on Earth?" I asked again.

He grinned. "Sorry. If you complete the full shikvihr here, then you can actually dance the shikvihr, floaters and all, on Earth. Once you've laid the shikvihr, you can use other floaters. No need for chalk and blood!"

Well, that sounded cool as shit. Looked like the damn thing was worth learning after all and not simply as a stepping stone for returning home.

Mzatal entered, glanced at me, then approached the diagram Idris had created, eyes traveling over it in assessment.

Idris made one final adjustment. "I've reset the parameters you wanted, my lord. How does it look?"

"Stable," Mzatal said, nodding approval. "It will serve. Go lay it in the chamber now."

Idris grinned and dissipated the diagram with several broad sweeps of his arms, then headed out.

Mzatal's gaze followed him as he exited.

"Well, that whole confrontation went better than expected," I said.

"Idris is an exceptional young man," Mzatal said, his eyes still on the empty doorway.

"He's amazing," I said. "Crazy talented and, holy shit, really has his head on straight."

Mzatal's mouth tightened. "Unusual focus and talent."

There was something he wasn't saying. "What's wrong?"

He finally pulled his gaze back to me, expression oddly troubled, which made no sense considering that Idris had done nothing but be generally Awesome.

"Katashi reported that Idris's biological mother had only a smattering of arcane ability," Mzatal said. "It does not fit."

"Well maybe his dad kicked ass?" I offered. "Or maybe he's a genetic mutant. I mean, is arcane ability always genetic?"

"No, not always," he said. "Though many attempts to manipulate potential proved ill-advised. Perhaps a high-potency father, but one completely unknown to Katashi." He shook his head slowly. "I cannot pinpoint the issue, but it gnaws at me. Especially after witnessing Idris's process today."

"Process?" I asked. "You mean, how he dealt with me telling him to back off?"

Mzatal nodded. "It was swift and definitive," he said. "He considered, analyzed, and accepted. Another noteworthy aspect."

I blew out my breath. "Yeah, I've never met a nineteen-year-old who could react that maturely." I snorted. "Hell, for that matter I'm not sure I've ever met a *thirty*-nine-year-old with that much maturity."

"Agreed," he said. He dropped his arm over my shoulders, surprising me with the gesture, though only for an instant. It felt curiously natural and utterly platonic, and I found myself not minding it one little bit.

"In light of other suspicions," Mzatal continued, "I believe Katashi knows more than he has told." A hint of suppressed anger colored his tone.

"You train pretty much all summoners who come to the demon realm, right?" I asked with a slight frown.

"Most, yes," he said. "The other qaztahl—in the past—have sent promising summoners to me, those whom they wished to excel. Some were not sent to me, though, if they were only to receive basic training."

"How many summoners are there?" I asked with a tilt of my head. "I mean, I used to think there were hundreds, but that was before I knew about the cataclysm."

Mzatal drew a deep breath. "There have never been hundreds of summoners. Hundreds, even thousands, with the potential, yes. However only a small percentage of those have adequate innate talent along with the ability and desire to channel the energies. Often the propensity found other outlets. Currently, there are fewer than a hundred with potential identified, and barely thirty who have performed a summoning." His arm tensed over my shoulders. "If Katashi is to be believed."

My own tension wound higher. "And you lords, you really need summoners, don't you."

"Yes, we do," he said, looking over at me. "What troubles you?"

I pulled away from him and looked into his face. "How do y'all *find* summoners?"

His eyes met mine steadily. "Since the ways reopened, most work is done through Katashi and his agents. Demons—kehza and nyssor—assist as well with assessments." His brow creased. "Kara, what is it that disturbs you?"

My pulse pounded unevenly as my tension wound into a tight knot inside my chest. "How . . . how do you make sure those with ability become summoners?"

"It is not a matter of making sure they become summoners," he replied, eyes on mine and a hint of concern showing through. "For the generations during and after the cataclysm, those hundreds of years while the ways to Earth were closed, skills faded. As the skills were not used, the genetics shifted as well, as a continuous flow of potency is critical." Mzatal spread his hands. "There simply are not as many potential summoners as there once were. Those that are located are assessed, and if they show promise, then training evaluations can be made. Thus, we are slowly rebuilding the population."

I took a step back, shaking my head, wishing I could dislodge the sense that something was seriously fucked up. "I mean, if you knew of someone with the ability, you'd make sure he or she ended up in training, right?"

"That opportunity is provided, yes," he said. "Through Katashi and his agents." The concern in his eyes deepened. "Kara?"

"Before Tracy Gordon died," I said, very aware of the unsteadiness of my voice, "he said, 'they make sure we become summoners.' Tracy's grandparents were summoners, and his parents died under strange circumstances. If my dad hadn't died, I'd never have been raised by my aunt—my *summoner* aunt." My hands tightened into fists, nails biting into my palms. "How far do you go to make sure summoners become summoners?"

Mzatal's face abruptly slid into the unreadable mask. Without a word, he pivoted and exited to the balcony, hands clenched into fists behind his back.

I stared after him, going cold. "Mzatal?" I hesitated, then followed him out. "Mzatal, what the fuck?" I asked, my gut clenching even tighter as I stood behind him. My dad had been killed by a drunk driver, or so I'd believed until recently.

Have you ever looked at the accident report? Tracy had said. *I have. He shouldn't have died in that wreck.*

My breath clogged in my throat. "Did . . . did you have my dad killed?"

Mzatal dropped his head and gripped the rail, not answering.

A red haze filled my vision. "Did you kill my dad?" I hauled off and punched him hard in the back by the right kidney. He tensed, but I didn't give a shit about reprisals or consequences. "*Did you?* Answer me, motherfucker!"

"Not directly. No," he said, head still lowered and his voice strained though filled with intensity.

"Turn around, goddammit!" I demanded, my voice shaking and my hands clenched into hard fists. "What do you mean, 'not directly'? Did you order it?"

Mzatal turned to face me, his eyes deeply haunted. "I mean that if—*if*—this was a deliberate act at the hands of Katashi or his agents, then I am responsible," he said, shaking his head. "I did not order it."

"Swear it," I gasped, chest clenched so tight I could barely breathe. "Swear to me that you know nothing of any plan or plot to kill the parents of potential summoners."

Mzatal went demon-lord still, tension palpable. "I give you my oath, Kara Gillian. I do not condone such."

Relief flooded me along with a pang of grief, and I threw my arms around him as a low sob caught in my throat. He returned the embrace and lowered his head over mine, his breathing unsteady. I trembled, absolutely knowing—*knowing*—my dad was murdered, yet trusting Mzatal fully in his oath.

After a long moment, he spoke, the words issuing as though they came at great personal cost. "Jesral would condone such."

It took a moment for me to gather why saying as much would have such an effect on Mzatal; he had already suspected Jesral's involvement. Then I realized, *My Dad's death was nineteen years ago.* Whether Jesral had been involved with Katashi that long or had an independent Earth presence, I didn't know, but both possibilities held their own brand of ugliness. Of course, there was always the chance that Jesral wasn't involved at all, but given the clues and his behavior to me, his innocence seemed unlikely.

"I will have answers from Katashi tonight," Mzatal stated, voice tight.

I drew a ragged breath, nodded, then released him to step away. He seemed reluctant to let me go, and I wondered if maybe he wanted comfort and reassurance as much as I did. Not that a demonic lord would ever admit something like that.

"Isn't Katashi your sworn summoner?" I asked. "Wouldn't you know if he was doing shit behind your back?"

"Yes," he said through gritted teeth. "He is. And I *should* know." He clasped his hands behind his back and turned to look out into the open space. "However with another qaztahl involved, and the possible use of *rakkuhr*, there are many possibilities for blurring and interference."

"What will you do with—" I started to ask, then shook my head and turned away. "Nevermind." I realized I didn't want to know what he would do with a traitor of that depth.

He inhaled, expression hardening. "I have been blind."

I shoved a hand through my hair, exhaling. "Yeah, well, I know how it feels."

"Yes, you do." He turned to face me and laid his hands on my shoulders, squeezing them lightly.

I looked up at him, my throat tight. "Betrayal sucks. I'm sorry you have to go through it."

A muscle in his jaw leaped. "I have been many things, but rarely a fool."

I narrowed my eyes. "Hang on now. You didn't let me wallow in self blame, so you're deluded if you think I'll let you."

He lowered his head slightly, and a smile ghosted over his lips. "You speak truth, Kara Gillian. I will cease to wallow."

"That's more like it," I said, managing a smile. "How long before this damn summoning? Is there time for ice cream or junk food or anything good like that?"

"Idris should be ready very soon," he said. "The ice cream will need to wait until after, unless you choose it over the summoning."

I made a big show of hesitating and considering, then finally heaved a dramatic sigh. "Fine. I'll do your damn summoning." Especially since it looked like it was going to be a doozy of a confrontation with Katashi. The cop in me wouldn't miss that for a million bucks. "But I do need to go change."

Mzatal dropped his hands from my shoulders and raised an eyebrow. "What you wear is inadequate?"

"As if!" I rolled my eyes.

Mzatal smiled just a bit more. "Go then."

I turned and headed out, but once outside the workroom, my smile quickly faded. The cop in me was ready for a confrontation with Katashi, but I couldn't shake the feeling that some bad shit was coming our way.

Chapter 30

After grabbing a quick bite, I bathed and dressed in flowing crimson pants and a black wrap-type shirt that belted at the waist with a broad white sash. Apparently the zrila really liked the challenge of making clothing for someone new, and I wasn't about to complain. I'd never been any sort of clotheshorse before—preferring the easy comfort of jeans and t-shirts—but I'd also never had a team of designers making custom clothing for me either. I could totally get used to this, and was already plotting ways to bring my new wardrobe back to Earth.

If I ever get back to Earth, I thought with a sudden burst of homesickness. I did my best to push it aside while I allowed Faruk to coil my hair up into something cool and intricate. By the time I finished preparing and stepped out into the main room, Mzatal had returned and was patiently waiting for me.

"I'm ready," I said, doing my best to keep at bay the insistent trepidation of being in the chamber with a ritual, any ritual. Fucking Rhyzkahl.

His eyes traveled over me, assessing. "You are indeed." He took my hand. "Come."

Mzatal's hand felt good in mine. Strong, comforting, and simply present. And, as much as I hated to admit it, I was grateful for the contact. Some of the tension within me eased as we exited and headed to the summoning chamber. I didn't have to participate, simply observe. That was safe enough.

Idris crouched in the center of an impressive pattern. He

looked up as we entered and gave me a quick smile before returning his focus to the diagrams.

Mzatal gently disengaged from my hand to go examine a nearby section of the pattern. I crouched and peered at the tracings, fascinated by their beauty and complexity. I understood some of the sigils now, saw how they linked together. No way could I lay a pattern like this yet, but it was wonderful to start seeing that there really *was* a pattern.

"Dude. This is amazing."

Idris's gaze jumped to me and then back to the diagram as a proud smile spread across his face. "Thanks." He made a final tweak to a section, then stood. "My lord, it is ready."

Mzatal rose fluidly to his feet. "And well done," he replied with an approving nod. He began to add an overlay of tracings with impressive speed and elegance. I retreated to the wall to watch and stay out of the way, while I struggled, with a modicum of success, to follow what he was doing.

Mzatal glanced over to me. "To summon from here requires the addition of patterns not accessible to summoners."

"So a demon-side summoning is, by its nature, a partnership?"

"It is most definitely a partnership," he said, continuing an outer perimeter of tracings. "You will feel the shift in the energy as I lay the over-pattern. It becomes more central and focused." With that he touched it, igniting the entirety of the already glowing pattern into a glittering, flickering, utterly beautiful construct.

It also reminded me way too much of Rhyzkahl's initial diagram, even though the patterns were different. Palms sweating, I quickly looked away, found a spot on the opposite wall to focus on while I breathed deeply in an effort to slow my racing pulse.

"Idris," Mzatal said, "go prepare. We will summon upon your return."

Idris nodded and departed. As soon as he was gone, I dropped to a crouch and pressed my forehead to my knees, holding my fisted hands on top of my head. I shook and cursed under my breath, trying to focus on how much I hated Rhyzkahl instead of how much the patterns freaked me out. *I'm a summoner, damn it*, I railed at myself. *I can't do that, can't protect myself if I can't stand to be near a ritual.*

I felt Mzatal's presence, but he didn't move to rescue me, for which I was strangely grateful. Simply knowing he was there and aware of me was enough for the moment. After a few minutes I lifted my head and forced myself to stare at the pattern, to look at the actual sigils and identify their purposes. Hey, look, I was getting better at this whole not-panicking thing.

Idris returned, dressed in black jeans, boots, and a black silk shirt. Confidence seemed to shimmer off him. This was *his* turf. There was no doubt he felt most comfortable working a ritual diagram. Gestamar entered behind him and crouched silently near the doors.

"We will bring Katashi in," Mzatal said, "and I will assess him." His voice remained intense, verging on scary. "Once the perimeter is down, Gestamar will escort him to secure chambers" He held his hand out for me, and I took it, grateful. After drawing me to his side, he headed around the diagram, pausing to lay a hand on Idris's shoulder for a heartbeat before continuing to the opposite side of the pattern from him.

As soon as we were in place, Idris began. Mzatal spoke to me in a low voice as Idris initiated the call and proceeded through the ritual, explaining precisely what Idris was doing and why, and detailing the aspects that were different from Earth-side summonings. I listened intently, not only for the knowledge but also because the running commentary helped remind me that this ritual was nothing like the one I'd endured.

Idris anchored the portal with a smooth precision that impressed me deeply. Mzatal lifted a hand, focusing the diagram, continuing to explain what he was doing and why. Idris glanced up at Mzatal, saw that he was set, then made the call for Katashi.

My hand tightened convulsively on Mzatal's as the diagram flared. I quickly relaxed my grip, embarrassed at my reaction, but Mzatal simply kept his hand firm on mine.

A heartbeat later Katashi sprawled in the center of the diagram. The glowing pattern faded, leaving the room in comparative darkness.

Mzatal set a sigil alight in the ceiling, casting the room in a pale yellow glow. In the circle, Katashi struggled to his hands and knees, breath rasping. Despite everything, a whisper of sympathy stole through me. I knew how much summonings hurt.

Jekki bounded into the room as if on cue, slipped through the floor tracings to hold a basin and towel out for Katashi. He took it with shaking hands, murmuring thanks.

I shot a glance at Mzatal to see his eyes narrowed to slits. On the other side of the diagram Idris smoothly gathered the flows and sealed the conduit, a look of pleased satisfaction on his face. Mzatal released my hand to stand with his hands clasped behind his back, and I moved a few feet away to let him do the full Lord thing.

Katashi finished wiping his face and stood with the help of the faas. He turned to Mzatal and gave a formal bow. "My Lord Mzatal," he said, voice shaking slightly, which surprised me. I'd never known the old man to show even the slightest bit of worry or strain. Across the diagram I could see Idris frowning, so apparently it surprised him as well. *Well, what have you been up to, old man?*

Mzatal lowered his head. "Katashi." His voice was potent and terrifying, much like when he'd first summoned me.

Katashi flinched under the Scary Voice. "What is your will, my lord?" he asked, voice shaking even more. Crap. Was he about to have a heart attack? If so, I sure as hell wasn't going to do CPR on him. But right now he looked guilty as hell about *something*.

Mzatal snapped his gaze to Idris. "Drop the perimeter."

Idris quickly complied. Eyes still narrowed, Mzatal lifted his right hand and beckoned Katashi forward with a twitch of his index and middle finger.

The old man straightened as calm seemed to settle over him. His gaze flicked briefly to me, lit with a strangely desperate intensity. My cop-sense woke up. *He's about to do something.*

Unfortunately, my brain was too slow to listen to my cop-sense. In the blink of an eye, Katashi lunged and clamped his hand on my left wrist in an iron grip. I let out a startled yelp and backpedaled, but an instant later recovered and slammed a fist into the old man's face. Eilahn would be so damn proud. But Katashi was a lot tougher than he looked, and even though my punch caused him to stagger back half a step, it didn't budge his grip. He bared his teeth and tightened his hold.

I hauled off to slug him again, but faltered as a too-familiar tugging sensation shot through me from his hand on my arm. *A recall!* Panic flared. I opened my mouth to cry out for Mzatal to help me, but he clearly sensed it as well. With a sharp flick of his hand, he whipped out a tether of potency to loop around Katashi's forearm. He dropped back into a wide stance and yanked viciously on the strand, severing the wrist with a hissing sizzle. Katashi opened his mouth to scream as I staggered back, but in the next instant he was gone.

Katashi's severed hand dropped to the floor, its end smoking faintly. Mzatal released the strand and turned to me. I suddenly realized I'd backed to the wall, and I had no doubt I looked like a panicked mess. But that shit had been way too close. *Another second*, I thought, still taking ragged breaths. Another second, and I'd have been gone.

"My lord! My lord!" Idris shouted. I dragged my gaze to him. He gripped a thin strand of potency in his left hand that led to the middle of the diagram and seemed to terminate in mid-air.

"Speak, Idris," Mzatal said without taking his eyes from me. He reached out and grasped my hand.

"I'm tracking him!" Idris exclaimed, voice betraying excitement and terror as he gripped the thin strand. "My lord! I'm tracking him. I put a tracker on him right before he went!"

Mzatal pulled me over by Idris. I followed numbly while I tried not to think about how close I'd come to being taken again. Yeah, like not thinking about the pink giraffe.

"Excellent work, Idris," Mzatal said. I was pretty damn impressed myself. I'd barely had the presence of mind to punch the asshole. "What do you sense?"

Idris's eyes unfocused. "Rhyzkahl. He's at Rhyzkahl's palace and—" Power shot up the strand in a blinding flash. Idris let out a sharp cry of pain and released the strand. He turned his hand over to peer at his palm, then paled. "Oh, fuck," he breathed.

I tried not to show any reaction to the sight of the vicious burn, but I could see the white of the bone even from where

I was. I moved to push Mzatal toward Idris, but I needn't have bothered. He'd already moved with demonic-lord speed to clasp the injured hand between his own.

"That was very well done, Idris," he said, voice carrying his sincerity clearly. Idris gave a very shaky smile, then hissed as Mzatal began the healing.

"I'm sorry I couldn't hold it," Idris said, clearly trying hard to be stoic. "But he went to Rhyzkahl. I saw that."

"Idris, sit," Mzatal commanded. The young summoner did so, collapsing into a cross-legged position. Mzatal crouched, maintaining his hold on the injured hand.

"My lord," Idris said, "Jesral was there too."

"All pre-planned," Mzatal replied, exuding calm. "Though I do not know if Katashi knew Kara was here, or if he made the decision to take her when he saw her. Either way, it is clear he knew her worth to those two."

I rubbed at my temples, still trying to rid myself of the vestiges of reaction. "If Katashi had a recall implant," I said, grimacing, "it means Rhyzkahl probably set it during one of the times I summoned him."

Mzatal nodded, shifting his gaze to me. "Yes, and he likely has much more in place as well." His expression darkened. "With such unprecedented access to Earth, he would not have wasted even a tenth of a heartbeat of that time."

I scowled at how thoroughly I'd been duped. Mzatal looked back to Idris.

"Pygah and breathe," he said as the young man paled. Idris gulped, eyes unfocusing slightly as he deepened his breathing. After a few moments Mzatal released his hand to turn it palm up. "The strike was tainted with *rakkuhr*," he said. "It will be scarred."

Idris's eyes dropped to the ropy scar that ran across his palm. I watched as he attempted to close his hand into a fist and wiggle his fingers, and my heart clenched at the deep dismay on his face as he clearly had difficulty doing either.

Fear flickered behind his eyes as he looked up into Mzatal's face. "How can I do tracings?" he asked, voice trembling.

"You can trace with it now," Mzatal assured him, "though not with the fluidity of before. With work you will increase the movement and adapt so that it is again natural to you." Confidence and calm flowed from him as he placed a hand on Idris's shoulder. "Of this I have no doubt."

"Physical therapy, dude," I told him with as encouraging a smile as I could manage. "You'll be knitting sweaters out of potency in no time."

Idris gave me a shaky smile of his own as he flexed his hand a few times. "Yeah. Knitting." He drew a breath, then released it in a rush. "I gotta lot of work to do."

My smile faded as I looked at the scar on his palm. Anger seared through me, burning away the last of the fear and panic.

"We all do."

Chapter 31

I sat on the chaise on the solarium balcony, elbows on knees, with a glass of chilled wine held to my forehead. Mzatal stood a few feet away, hands clenched at his sides as he looked out into the darkness. He was pissed, and I didn't need to be able to read his mind to know it.

I straightened and took a long drink, worry curling through me for Idris and for myself. "I'm really glad you chopped that asshole's arm off."

"I was blind and I was a fool." He spat the words out, fists tightening. "And I am unaccustomed to being either." He exhaled forcefully. "He was within a heartbeat of taking you."

"Yeah, that part kinda sucked," I said, trying to make light of it and failing. Sighing, I set my glass down, then moved to Mzatal and wrapped my arms around him from behind. "He didn't take me. You stopped him. I'm still here to annoy the crap out of you."

Some of the tension left his body as he folded his arms over mine. He drew a deep breath and released it slowly. "Annoy. Is that what you do to me?"

I let out a soft laugh. "That's what I keep *trying* to do," I said. "Not sure if I'm succeeding."

He turned and wrapped his arms around me, a whisper of a smile on his face as he cradled my head to his chest. "You are failing utterly in the moment."

Exhaling, I relaxed against him. "That's cool. Failure builds character."

He held me close for a moment, then released me gently and draped an arm over my shoulders. Heavy clouds shielded stars and moon, and only the surging crash of waves far below reminded me that I gazed into physical darkness and not the void. He tucked me in close, and moved his other hand behind his back. "In your perception," he began, "what has shifted on Earth in the time since Rhyzkahl first came through?"

I considered for a moment. "Well, I suppose it starts, at least for me, with finding out last spring that Peter Cerise was the Symbol Man: a serial killer who was trying to summon and bind Rhyzkahl."

"Yes. Cerise lost his balance and all reason decades ago when—" Mzatal stopped, and I could see him mentally rephrasing it, "when his foundation was stripped from him. He was a chosen of Szerain and quite brilliant. He disappeared, and Katashi claimed no knowledge of his whereabouts."

That he was a chosen of Szerain's made sense to me and helped explain why Cerise had attempted to summon that lord to aid his ailing wife. "Okay, well . . ." I hesitated, unsure how to go into the subject of Ryan. Then I snorted. Mzatal *knew* I knew, so dancing around the subject seemed ridiculous at this point. Mzatal was oathbound about pretty much anything to do with Ryan/Szerain, but I wasn't constrained by any pesky oaths. "It was during that time that I met Ryan and Zack."

"That would not be a coincidence," Mzatal said with a nod.

"Yeah, I'm starting to realize that." *But engineered by whom?* "Ryan and I have become close," I said. "Friends and, well, more than friends, too." I shook my head. "Anyway, it wasn't long after Eilahn came to protect me that we had a case go to shit, and we ended up in a weird fight with a bunch of golems. Things went downhill, and at one point I got knocked down. I was about to get totally squished by a golem, and Ryan . . ." I took a deep breath. "Ryan's face went to ice. He pulled potency and blasted the fuck out of the golem, saving me." A shudder raced down my spine. "And then he collapsed. Zack ran to him—snarled at us and told us he'd take care of Ryan." I paused, gathering my thoughts. "I didn't see Ryan for a week, and by then he was back to—" I winced. "—normal."

"You spoke to Turek at Szerain's shrine," Mzatal said

after a moment. "And so you know something more than you did when you arrived." A whisper of frustration touched his eyes. I had a pretty strong feeling that he wanted to ask questions, but was constrained by the damn oath that prohibited talk of Szerain's exile.

"I know Ryan is Szerain," I said. "And I know Zack is Zakaar. But Ryan doesn't know. And Turek says it's dangerous for him to know himself."

"Because Rhyzkahl will take more definitive measures to—" Mzatal paused. "He would take more definitive measures."

"Is he . . ." I trailed off. I desperately wanted to know if Szerain and Ryan were at all alike, but I knew that Mzatal wouldn't be able to answer me directly. "If, um, a lord were to be exiled," I tried instead, "would their exiled persona be very different from their true personality?"

Mzatal's whole body tensed as a deep anger seemed to flow from him, though I was fairly certain it wasn't directed at me. "I *cannot* speak of this, of him," he said through clenched teeth. "But I will speak of something else," he continued, lifting the arm from my shoulders. "A mere story about possibilities with me and with you."

The intensity in his voice sent a frisson of cold fear through me, but I had a feeling that if I didn't find out all I could now, I might never know. *And I need to know.*

"Were I to diminish you," he said in a low, dark voice, "to strip you of the ability to use your skills or to even maintain memory of yourself, there are many ways I could accomplish this. Some would leave you with nothing of yourself and some would leave you with more." He lowered his head.

A chill crawled through me. "Go on," I managed.

"One very particular way would leave you with all memory of yourself, but only the ability to express that which fits a certain predetermined model." The tension returned to his body, and he breathed a word that was most definitely a demon curse.

The cold in my gut deepened. "S-so, I would be completely aware but trapped behind a wall?"

"No," he replied, voice going even more intense. "That is far too mild of a description for how I would submerge you."

My hands tightened into fists. "How would you do it?"

Mzatal turned to me, potency flaring. "How deeply do you wish to understand, Kara Gillian?"

I hesitated, then straightened, lifting my chin, though my heart pounded. "I *need* to know. Show me what was done to Szerain."

He shook his head, eyes never leaving mine. "I cannot speak of that, nor do that." He paused, and the air around us seemed to grow heavy and charged. "I *can* show you precisely how I would submerge you were I to do so to bring about the greatest torment."

My mouth went dry as my resolve wavered. *It's only a demonstration*, I told myself. *I can trust him.* I dragged in a careful breath. I'd survived Rhyzkahl's torture. I could endure this submersion for a few minutes. And I *needed* to know, for Ryan, and for myself.

"Yes," I heard myself saying. "Show me that."

A faint smile touched his mouth but didn't reach his eyes. *I trust him*, I told myself again. *Right?*

Mzatal drew a deep breath and closed his eyes. I braced myself and tried to prepare for . . . I had no idea what.

When he opened his eyes, it was like looking through a window into a nightmare. Moving with demonic lord speed he seized my head between his hands, face abruptly and coldly vindictive and purposeful. The nightmare behind his eyes flooded out to inundate me, and I sucked in a breath, recoiling.

"No, wait!" I struggled against his hold, then cried out in shock as Gestamar moved swiftly in from the main chamber and wrapped an arm around my waist from behind. "No. Stop!"

Mzatal didn't move, but I felt the stab of potency slide through me in a surgical strike, and in the next instant I went limp in Gestamar's hold as Mzatal stripped my physical control.

But only the physical. I still had full awareness, still felt Mzatal's hands on my head. I could still silently yell at myself for being the biggest goddamn moron who'd ever walked the Earth. I fought to move, to twitch, *anything*.

"Fool," Mzatal snarled in a voice that was his, yet not his. "It could have been so easy for you."

My body couldn't move, but my Self jerked in shock as

what felt like a viscous goo began to rise around me. It wasn't physical—there was nothing I could see or taste or smell, but it was cold. So incredibly cold. The arcane constriction continued to rise around my essence, everything that was me. I panicked as fully as if it was a corporeal substance threatening to drown me. My Self thrashed and flailed, but the advance was inexorable, and I couldn't find any purchase.

Mzatal's lip curled. "All in our grasp. All." His teeth clenched harder. "And you choose—*choose*—to withhold it from me." He pushed me lower while I thrashed and fought the submersion.

I felt the reyza's strong grip, his hot breath on my neck. I hung limp as Mzatal held my head, while within I fought the unrelenting push.

He forced me down. The only way to describe it was as if I was in a narrow pipe, with barely any room to twitch or move, and that pipe was filled with icy goo, and then a grate placed over the top and sealed down. I had less than an inch of "space" between the grate and the goo, forcing me to constantly scrabble for purchase, to press my face against that grate simply to exist.

Mzatal drove the "grate" fully down upon me until it felt as if I was a hair's breadth away from being lost completely, then blatantly and clearly sealed the prison. "How long can you bear this?" he hissed. "How long until even *you* break?"

Panicked, I pressed my Self against the barricade. I wanted to sob, scream, anything, but all I had was the total quiescence of my body in Gestamar's arms.

Mzatal held my head for another ten heartbeats, then released me and straightened, face returning to its normal Mzatal-ness.

"Kara, I have some matters to attend," he said. "Wait for me inside." He turned and headed off down the balcony.

Gestamar released me, and I straightened. I glanced up at the demon, then moved inside to Mzatal's chambers. Pursing my lips, I looked around, then began opening cabinets, methodically searching. I knew it had to be here somewhere.

This is me, I realize. I scrabble and press against the barrier. The confinement is horrific, but the rest isn't so bad, is it? He called me Kara. At least I'm still me. But what the hell am I looking for? I extend, desperately trying to understand, and as I do, it's like sticking my finger into an electrical outlet as the jolt of connection slams home. I am fully myself, know myself, am myself, and I'm also this walking, breathing, thinking Pretender that seeks a confiscated bag of weed. I feel myself animating her through a slender tendril of essence that winds through the grate. Her thoughts, chaotic and irrational, tumble beside Mine in a confusing torrent, and I experience a new sort of drowning as they invade Me. Panic. I know her. Panic. I am her. Panic. I am myself. Panic. Who am I?

She found it in the bottom drawer and grinned. Not warded or protected in any way. She took the baggie to the table in the bedroom, sat, and began to expertly roll a joint.

Who am I? The Observer. Boundaries. Must set boundaries. I am myself. I am—she is—the Pretender. Thoughts are intimately entwined. I cling to mine and willfully keep hers at bay, still glaringly present, but separate. I witness the Pretender using my body. It's been over fifteen years since I've done any sort of drugs. I know I can't experiment or have one joint just for fun. She knows this as well, but denies it. Wake up! Don't do this!

She moved to the balcony and leaned against the rail. She lit the joint easily with a quick sigil.

No. Damn it. I can't smoke pot. I'm not going to go back to any of that shit. I know myself too well. I struggle against the grate, struggle to extend control through the connecting strand. It's still my body! Surely I can stop me, her, us from doing this. But it's like steering a car with my pinky while tied in the backseat.

She lifted the joint and took a long pull, then sighed out the smoke with a relaxed smile.

That's what I needed. *Her thought rolls over me. Damn it! I witness the Pretender abuse my body. I want to smack her.*

She jerked in surprise as Mzatal reached and plucked the joint from her fingers.

"You have dishonored my hospitality, taken that which is not yours, and do not have the control to use such without succumbing to it." He glowered down at Us as he incinerated the joint with a flick of his fingers.

"Are you fucking kidding me?" She scowled up at the lord. "It was my damn weed in the first place. I was merely recovering my own property that you 'confiscated.'" She made obnoxious quote marks with Our fingers.

Holy shit. I know this Pretender. I had that attitude when I was about nineteen or so. I was off the drugs by then, but She is the Me of then, still on drugs. I can't live like this! I reach through the strand and it's like fighting through a vat of tar, sticky, searing heat against the ice of my Self. Agonizing. Exhausting.

"And what the hell does it matter anyway if I smoke a joint?" she continued, rolling Our eyes. "This summoning shit is a pain in the ass and the pot chills me out."

"I do not jest," he replied in a hard voice. "For some it would not matter. For you it does. You lose yourself."

He's so right. Why won't she listen? No, this isn't me. This . . . this is a very small part of who I might have been. This isn't me! I can't do this.

"I don't lose myself," she said with a snort. "Oh my god, it's just pot. And what the fuck do you care? You wanted a summoner. Well, here I am." She gave a showy curtsey.

"Smoking breaks your agreement with me. This is of much relevance." Mzatal looked to Gestamar. "Destroy the remainder of the herb."

She gave a snotty laugh. "Oh no, I did something against the magic contract. Does that mean I get a spanking?"

You stupid little bitch, stop talking before you get into real trouble! I continue to struggle to reach through the strand.

Mzatal's eyes were hard upon Us. "Gestamar, Kara will be leaving us. Tell Idris to prepare a diagram. We will proceed within the hour."

Yeah. Trouble like that.

I press against the barrier. I can't relax, can't rest. All I can do is gasp in what existence I can through the seal. I can't take much more of this.

She stared in shock. "You're going to send me back for one fucking joint? You f-fu—"

I slam on the brakes! I force myself through the strand and manage to make her stop before she can call him a fucking asshole. The thought is there, the words formed, ready to spill. Stop it. I want to weep, but she has my body. Exhausted. This tiny influence exhausts me. I can't do this. Please, you have to stop this. Mzatal, please! I'm trying not to panic, but there's so little room. Please. Please.

Mzatal moved to me and took my head in his hands, unsealed the barrier. I sagged and clutched at him as he released it, eyes wide as the goo slowly retreated. He pulled me to him, kept one arm wrapped around me and the other cradling my head to his chest. I could feel him continuing to dismantle the suppression. With every heartbeat it loosened more, until finally it was completely gone. I was me again. Fully me.

But shudders spasmed through me, and I had to clamp down hard on the urge to cry. "That was me." I whispered.

He continued to hold me close, even though the cruel submersion was over and dismantled. "Was," he replied. "It was an aspect of you. You would not be who you are today without that aspect. It is a gift."

A shiver raced through me. "You know all about that time in my life."

"Yes," he replied quietly.

Of course he did, I realized. He probably knew me better than I knew myself. He'd gone trouncing through my memories and life when he was deciding whether or not to snap my neck.

"Fuck," I breathed. Shame coiled through me, but I pushed it down. I wasn't that person anymore. And I could be damn glad that I didn't have to live my existence watching me be that person, be something I despised. "This submersion," I said, then paused, considering my words. He couldn't answer a direct question, but he could, perhaps comment. "I don't know how anyone could bear it for more than a few minutes, much less many years."

Mzatal went very still. "I do not know how it could be endured for so long."

Again, I chose my words carefully. "I wonder if anyone else could be as . . . reviled and shamed by the actions of their outer personality as I was." Did Szerain detest how Ryan conducted himself?

"Yes," he said, exhaling. "Perhaps not as instantaneously, since your overlay was drawn from a painful era of your past. But without the control, without the influence, any actions could emerge. Surely you have watched another and judged their actions. It is similar with a foreign overlay."

I struggled to process it all. Now I knew—or at least had a taste of—what Szerain endured. But Szerain had been submerged under the overlay of someone else's life. It was bad enough under a shadow of myself. What would it be like to have the superficial memories of Jane Doe overlaid and my features shaped into hers? And Szerain chose this. Surely, he didn't know how bad it would be. Turek's words came back to me. *He despised being submerged. He will not willingly submit to it again.*

"There were a couple of minutes there where I thought you'd really done it. I thought you'd really submerged me." I looked up at him. "I'm sorry I doubted."

He met my eyes steadily. "You wanted to know what it was like. That aspect was crucial to your understanding. I reinforced it with specific intention." He shook his head. "There is no need for apology."

Reinforced with specific intention. The words he spoke when he submerged me. They'd made little sense at the time, and now I thought maybe I knew why. Were those Rhyzkahl's words when he submerged Szerain? Was this the only way Mzatal could tell me?

I tensed as the grove flared. "Someone's coming." I paused, feeling the resonance. "It's Lord Vahl. Were you expecting him?"

"No," he said through clenched teeth. I winced in sympathy. Mzatal was having a Bad Day. I knew those far too well.

"Do you need me to leave?"

"Only if you choose to do so," he replied. "Otherwise, I would have you abide." Left unspoken was the implication that, while he wanted me with him, he would not mandate it.

"I'll stay then," I said, pleased and oddly flattered. I gave his hand a squeeze. "I'm kind of a nosy bitch."

A smile ghosted across his face. He leaned down and kissed my forehead, then released my hand. "I need a moment to prepare."

"Of course," I said. He'd want to be in top form to face another one of the lords with their perpetual head games and intrigue. "Would you like me to get wine?"

"Wine would be excellent." He faced the balcony railing and closed his eyes, breathing deeply.

I headed inside to the demon realm version of a wet bar and grabbed wine and three glasses. I also wolfed down a couple of pieces of cheese and a slice of fruit since I was starving. Clutching the glasses and wine carefully, I returned to the balcony and set them out quietly so as not to disturb him.

A moment later he opened his eyes and regarded me. "Fog yourself, Kara."

"Huh?"

"When you hold grove power it is far more difficult to read you," he said.

I blinked. "Oh, right." Rhyzkahl had said something about my being fogged right before the big bad ritual. Reaching for the grove, I pulled a trickle of power, then looked to Mzatal.

He shook his head. "Draw more," he instructed. "I can still read with a very slight probing. Learn how much you need and pull only that."

Complying, I pulled slightly more, then brought up an image of me doing an obnoxious booty-shake.

Mzatal gave a nod. "Perfect."

I hoped he meant the fogging and not the booty-shake itself. "Where do you want me?" I asked. "Standing? Sitting?" I grinned. "Sprawled suggestively?"

"You already stand with me," he said quietly. "But for this, sit." He gestured to a chair.

My smile widened. I poured a glass of wine for myself and settled into one of the big comfortable chairs.

"He comes," Mzatal said, face shifting with unnerving speed into a cold, hard mask. Radiating a feral potency, he turned to look out over the rail, hands clasped behind his back. I composed my own face and held my glass of wine.

I felt Vahl's approach before I saw him. He stopped in the balcony doorway, dark eyes on Mzatal's back. He still had that "dangerously appealing" feel about him, which was certainly helped by the snug black shirt and pants he wore. Due to the angle, he didn't appear to see me, and since I'd fogged myself, he couldn't pick me up through reading.

He spoke in demon to Mzatal, and with the grove power I got the gist of "meetings are complete" or something to that effect. I remained quiet and still, only moving to take a sip of wine.

Mzatal answered in English. "And what have you come to tell me?"

Vahl blinked, clearly wondering why the hell Mzatal spoke in English. He glanced around and a quick flash of surprise lit his eyes as he saw me. He'd surely been expecting me to be here in Mzatal's realm, but probably not here by his side sipping wine.

Vahl barely missed a beat, though he was obviously taken aback. He looked from me to Mzatal and continued in English. "The rotations were agreed upon, with yours remaining allocated to the threes and elevens with general oversight in the eleventh month. Much time was spent in negotiations brought forward by Rayst and Seretis concerning— " Vahl stopped abruptly as Mzatal dropped his hands to his sides.

I took a very casual sip, watching Vahl. The lord obviously took that simple movement of Mzatal's hands as a potential threat. He barely breathed, eyes intent on Mzatal's back.

"You are in Rhyzkahl's debt," Mzatal said, slowly opening his right hand. "What is your true purpose for being here?"

Vahl took a half step back, apprehension flickering in his eyes. "Mzatal . . ."

"I will speak for you since you cannot find the fortitude to do it yourself," Mzatal said in the silky and oh-so-scary tone I knew far too well and which seemed to have an effect even on Vahl. "You have come to see what you can determine on the status of Kara Gillian so that you can report to the one who holds your tether."

I suppressed a shiver with effort and made certain to maintain contact with the grove.

Vahl shrank back just a hair, eyes on Mzatal's right hand as if he watched a revolver cocked, loaded, and aimed at his head. But then he pulled himself up to full height and drew a breath, clearly determined not to go down cringing. "Yes." He glanced to me and back to the hand. I had a feeling Mzatal could call and cast power before Vahl could even blink. "He wants to know," Vahl added.

"What did he tell you of how she came to be with me?" Mzatal asked, still with the silky deathly voice. My grip tightened on my glass as I willed my hand not to shake. This would *not* be a good time for me to go into any sort of meltdown.

Vahl's brow furrowed at the question. "He said he was in the midst of working with her in a ritual, and that you activated a recall you had implanted." A brief flicker of admiration touched his face, likely for the skill required to accomplish such a difficult feat. Tension knotted my back at the "with her" bit, and I had to fight the urge to bare my teeth.

Mzatal pivoted to face Vahl. Without taking his eyes from the other lord, Mzatal held a hand out to me, extending with his presence as well. "Kara."

I set my glass down, then stood and took his hand, calming at the comfort of both the physical and mental touch. "Lord Mzatal," I murmured.

Vahl's eyes flicked over me, no doubt noting everything from my collarless state, to my unreadability, to my comfort with Mzatal. Mzatal drew me to him and looked down at me with a very obvious gentling of his features and a smile that I knew was for Vahl's benefit as much as mine. He was sending a clear message to Rhyzkahl via Vahl: *Kara is here with me.* He pulled me to stand in front of him with my back against his chest, then slid a hand down my left arm and lifted it, showing Vahl the long scar.

"Did he tell you he excised his mark with Xhan?" Mzatal asked, eyes on Vahl.

Vahl's eyes dropped to my arm. I watched as his lips parted in reaction. Surely he knew what arcane agony the act had held. Vahl tore his gaze away and looked directly at Mzatal, an odd combination of repulsion, horror, and fascination on his face. "Why torture himself—and the girl—thus, severing a mark physically?" he asked, voice incredulous.

Oh, Rhyzkahl suffered? Poor fucking baby. I glanced back at Mzatal with an "it's okay" look, then locked my gaze with Vahl's. I tugged my blouse open at the top so that he could clearly see the intricate tracing of scars on my upper chest. "No, Lord Vahl, *this* is torture. These were carved with that same blade."

He took another half-step back, clearly shocked. His eyes rested on the sigils, revulsion whispering across his face as if they spoke to him in crazed murmurs.

I closed my blouse, readjusted my clothing. "There was more," I told him. "Much more." A tremble went through me as I echoed Rhyzkahl's words. Mzatal set a hand very gently on my shoulder, calming me, letting me know he was there for me.

"Vahl," Mzatal said, "tell me what you know of this ritual."

The other lord visibly suppressed a shudder, eyes remaining on me. "On the morning of the ritual, Jesral and Rhyzkahl cloistered themselves in a room near the summoning chamber for hours." He shook his head. "I do not know with certainty, but I believe it was related. There were also ties to Amkir and Kadir."

Mzatal leaned forward ever so slightly, increasing the contact with me. I kept my expression as controlled as possible, feeling him at my back in more ways than one and grateful for the support.

Vahl ran a hand over his head. "Something went horribly wrong with the ritual and—"

"No! It didn't go wrong!" I cut him off, voice cracking. "It went exactly as intended. As Rhyzkahl intended." I swallowed hard. "He bound me in potency, carved my flesh, and *tortured* me to charge the sigils and diagram. It was only when he sliced the mark from my arm that Mzatal was able to retrieve me." Potency flared from Mzatal, backing my words.

Vahl didn't argue, obviously disturbed. "When Kara was recalled, the patterns imploded." His mouth drew into a flat line. "Everybody was aware that something had happened. The entire palace shook." He lifted his gaze to Mzatal. "Rhyzkahl went down, but no one knew for sure at first because he had sealed the doors such that no one could open them. And none of the syraza would touch it."

I had to smile. I was the one who'd sealed the damn chamber with the grove power. "He tried to follow me through the conduit," I told Vahl, sneering. "I threw him back."

He looked at me, eyes haunted. "He emerged later and went straight to his chambers for a full day and night and half of the next day." He exhaled. "I know nothing more of it."

Anger shuddered through me. I would have to bear these scars for the rest of my life, while Rhyzkahl simply had to take a long fucking nap.

Mzatal dropped his arm over my left shoulder and across

my chest, pulling me close and supporting me on many levels. I lightly crossed my arms over his and leaned back against him, let my anger trickle away.

"When next you see Rhyzkahl," Mzatal said, "tell him Kara Gillian is under agreement with me and has my *full* protection." He paused. "Tell him also that I know what he has done to Xhan."

Vahl grimaced, nodded. I didn't have to read him to know that he wasn't keen on making that report.

"And, Vahl," Mzatal continued, but in a much less scary tone, "that report need not be in his presence. It was an arduous conclave. Perhaps a few days rest here." The potency eased in Mzatal. "There is the potential for discussions of mutual interest."

Relief coupled with uncertainty crossed Vahl's face. "I will send him a sigil," he finally replied. "And I am honored to accept your invitation."

Well, the next few days will certainly be interesting, I thought to myself.

Mzatal and Vahl exchanged slight nods, then Vahl turned and left. I let out a breath and turned in Mzatal's arms, sliding arms around him and leaning my head against his chest. "Thank you."

Mzatal put his other arm around me and released the power he'd been holding. "There is no need for thanks," he replied softly. "It is what had to be done."

I tilted my head to look into his face. "No. I mean it. Thank you for being so *here* for me. I don't think I could get through this without your help."

A smile touched the corners of his mouth. "I will ever be here for you, Kara Gillian."

The truth of his statement made me feel warm all over. I gave him a light squeeze. "I'm starving. Are you starving? I think we should eat food that's terribly bad for us."

One silky eyebrow lifted. "I promised you ice cream."

I grinned. "So you did."

He slipped an arm around my waist and led me inside. "Come then. The faas will prepare a feast of that which is bad for us."

Chapter 32

The next week was a flurry of training with little time to do anything extra but eat and grab what sleep we could. However, I managed to get halfway through the first ring of the shikvihr without blasting the crap out of myself, and only had one teeny little incident where I accidentally set all of my notes and papers on fire. Fortunately I was on the balcony at the time, and the faas were quick with water to douse the small blaze.

And that, boys and girls, is why you should never sigil in bed, I thought with a low laugh as I cleaned up the mess.

Mzatal attended to my training as much as possible; there were many hours, however, during which he remained in closed-door meetings with Vahl. Fortunately, I was at a point where the best thing I could do was practice practice practice what I'd already learned. Idris would have helped, but the boy wonder was tied up with some sort of from-scratch development of a new interlinking diagram method that he and Mzatal had brainstormed. Thankfully, Gestamar stayed close by to help me in case I had questions. Or maybe he stuck close by in case I tried to set the place on fire again. Either was possible.

"Tomorrow is the full moon on Earth," Gestamar abruptly said, startling me enough that I lost control of the sigil I was crafting. He quickly flicked a claw and dispelled it before it could do more than deliver a light sting.

I gave him a somewhat sour look. "Okay. But we don't have to worry about phases of the moon here, do we? I mean, there's shitloads of available potency."

The tip of his tail twitched. "Dahn, but demons will be

summoned to earth from here, and I am often among those summoned."

"Because you're so awesome?" I grinned.

"Kri," he replied with a proud lift of his chin. "But this is not why I tell you of the full moon." His eyes met mine as he folded his wings in close. "Jekki and the zhurn Bezik are also oft-summoned, and we have agreed to carry letters for you and do what we can to have them safely delivered to your loved ones."

For the longest moment I could only stare at him while I processed this. "Thank you," I finally managed. He was offering me a chance to personally let Tessa and the others know I was safe and sound. Mzatal's communication with Earth was shot to hell with Katashi's defection, and he wouldn't have a solid back-up system in effect for at least a couple of months. He did have some sort of verbal arrangement in place to get word to my people in case any of his demons were summoned, but, by his own admission, it was unreliable at best, especially since the communication skills of many of the demons weren't the greatest. A physical letter made it all feel real, as if I could touch the folks back home.

"I . . . wow." I swiped at my eyes, which had somehow become a bit moist. "Thank you," I repeated.

Gestamar gave a gentle rumble. "Go and write three copies of a letter." He paused. "And best not to set them on fire."

"Will I ever live that down?" I asked with a laugh.

The reyza snorted. "Dahn. Demons have long memories and are easily amused."

It took me most of the rest of the day to write a letter to Tessa, primarily because I had no idea how to explain everything. I finally gave up and kept it short and simple, telling her I was all right and would be home as soon as possible. I didn't want to go into any of the other stuff in a letter, and the most important thing was to let her know I was alive and reasonably safe.

There was no sign of Mzatal that night or the next morning, but around mid-afternoon Jekki handed me a trifold parchment with Mzatal's seal in wax on it. The elegant, handwritten note simply said to please go to the atrium for the evening tone. *Please.*

An actual written invitation? Weird.

I turned to ask Jekki what it was all about, but forgot my question entirely at the sight of the faas laying clothing out upon the bed.

"This wear!" the faas burbled, pointing to what looked like flowing pants and shirt in a rich maroon. "Tonight. Bathe now and hair Faruk do."

My eyebrows lifted as my bafflement increased, but I knew better than to defy Jekki's directive. I cleaned up, allowed Faruk to do my hair in a complex braid complete with gold and silver strands woven through, donned the new clothing and elegant jeweled sandals, and then headed to the atrium.

Idris stood watching the beginning of the sunset when I stepped off the stairs. He was dressed to the nines as well, in black jeans, a crisp white tailored shirt, and a grey silk and wool blend jacket. It was a good look for him. Even his hair had been tamed. A bit.

"Hey, Idris," I said, "do you know what this is about?"

"No clue," he replied with a smile. "It's a first for me."

"Maybe we're being fired," I said, "for being simply awful."

Idris laughed along with me. "Somehow I don't think that would come with a fancy invite. Did the faas dress you too?"

Grinning, I looked down and ran my hands over my outfit. "Yep. Good thing or I'd have shown up in workout clothing."

A soft scrape of sound alerted us, and we turned to see Mzatal step into the atrium, wearing the dark Armani suit, white shirt, and a deep red tie. His braid hung over his shoulder wound with extra strands of silver cord, and he looked sharp as all hell.

"This way," he said with an enigmatic smile. He turned and headed down stairs I'd yet to explore. With a glance at Idris, I followed, curious and puzzled. After a couple of turns of the spiral stair, we stepped out into a room dancing with light and color. As everywhere else, a wall of glass faced the sea and sunset, but here, the waterfall cascaded before it, spectacular rays of the setting sun streaming through.

Then came the bewildering part.

Mzatal strode to the head of a dining table elaborately laid with crystal, silver, and fine china. He glanced at us and gestured to the chairs on each side of the table. Gestamar came in behind us and moved to crouch near Mzatal.

Idris slid a look at me, and I gave him a what-the-fucking-fuck look right back. I moved to a chair, pulled it out, and sank into it, utterly mystified. Idris sat across from me with a look on his face that mirrored how I felt. I got that we'd apparently been invited to a meal, but that in itself was weird. I'd eaten plenty of times around Mzatal, but apart from wine and tunjen, I rarely saw him eat, and had certainly never shared a meal with him

Mzatal stood behind his chair, a faint smile curving his lips. "You have both worked very hard," he said, "and are away from your homes." He waited while the faas poured wine in our three glasses, then drew a breath as though delaying a moment more to choose his words. "With the fullness of your schedules, you have lost track of your Earth time," he continued. "This is a day that each of you typically celebrate with your family and with your friends. I cannot offer those, but I can offer the recognition and something of the celebration. Happy Christmas, Idris Palatino and Kara Gillian."

A weird jolt went through me, a strange combination of dismay and pleased surprise. Idris simply stared, brow slightly furrowed.

I'm going to miss Christmas with Tessa. My throat tightened in preparation for a lovely bout of feeling sorry for myself. *But Idris is away from his family, too*, I reminded myself. And he had to lie to them; through Katashi, they'd been told he was in Japan. Now that Katashi proved himself untrustworthy, who knew what, if anything, Idris's family was being told. Ruthlessly I shoved the self-pity down.

Mzatal lifted his glass, smile fading a bit, obviously sensing the muddled emotions. "Here. Drink."

I forced a smile as I picked up my glass and took a sip of the really good dark wine. "Merry Christmas, Boss. Thanks for remembering."

Idris cleared his throat, seeming to have recovered a bit from his initial shock. "Yeah, um. Thanks. Really," he said and lifted his glass.

The doubt seemed to linger in Mzatal's eyes, and I realized it had to run fairly deep if it was actually showing. Damn it, he'd made an all out effort to do something for us, even if it did sting. Sure, I could get into a big pity party about having to miss Christmas with the folks back home, but that would pretty much guarantee that my Christmas here would suck shit. Truth was, I couldn't find it in me anymore to resent Mzatal for summoning me. If he and Idris hadn't brought me here, then Rhyzkahl certainly would've carried out his plans, and there wouldn't have been anyone to rescue me.

Time to lighten the mood in this room. "Wait," I said with a laugh. "This isn't at all like the Christmases I'm used to. There's no smell of burnt turkey." I grinned. "Tessa can't cook for shit, and neither can I."

Some of the uncertainty faded from Mzatal's expression. He downed half a glass of wine, his other hand resting on the back of the chair. "The faas have prepared a meal that they assure me contains your favorites from here and even some from Earth," he said, inclining his head slightly. "It is unlikely anything will be burnt unless I specifically asked for it, and then it would be under protest."

"No, that's quite all right." I shook my head emphatically. "Not-burned sounds good to me." I looked up and gave him a teasing smile. "Mzatal, sit the hell down so we can all relax, okay?"

He gave a slight nod and pulled the chair out. *Finally*.

With that the mood eased enough for us to engage in some light conversation while we waited for the food. I told the others how Tessa and I always went to Lake o' Butter pancake house the morning after Christmas, before hitting the stores for the day-after-Christmas sales. Idris told us about how his family had a tradition of getting together on Christmas eve, making cocoa, and taking turns at verses of Christmas carols with on-the-spot, fabricated lyrics. He grinned so much in telling the story—and during his rendition of a snortingly funny verse of *Silent Night*—that I knew he really considered them family, though they'd adopted him as a teen.

Mzatal finished his wine and set the glass aside to be speedily refilled by Faruk. He reached into his pockets and pulled out two little boxes of delicately carved wood, then placed one before each of us. "I do greatly appreciate your work and your efforts."

I set my glass down, hesitated, then reached for the box and opened it. Inside was a ring. *Uh oh.* I slid a glance to Idris. With relief, I saw he had a ring, too, and with that the weirdness factor evaporated.

Intrigued, I lifted the ring out of the box. Silver and gold interwove to form an intricate yet solid band, and a rich blue stone sparkled in the setting. I exhaled and lifted my gaze to Mzatal. "It's beautiful," I said, smiling. "Thank you."

"You are welcome, Kara," he said. "It suits you well."

Idris sat, stunned to silence, staring at his ring. His was silver and a dark grey metal, with a deep red stone. He looked up at Mzatal and back at the ring. "Holy shit," he breathed, then looked up again, a smile lighting his face like a kid at, well, Christmas. "My lord, wow. Thank you," he said and carefully removed it from the box.

I wasn't one to wear jewelry much, but I knew I'd wear this. I slid it onto the middle finger of my right hand, instantly loving the look and feel of it. It wasn't girly or prissy at all. It was almost like a man's ring but for a woman—solid and strong, yet still utterly lovely. "Mzatal," I said, guilt tugging at me, "I didn't get you anything."

He shook his head, face betraying nothing of expectation or disappointment. "You did not know. Enjoy."

Idris, in his own world, slipped his ring on. "Holy fuck," he said in an extended exhale. I grinned. Apparently he liked his ring.

Jekki, Faruk, and two other faas brought the first wave of food. They burbled and fussed so much over everything, I had no doubt that they got a kick out of the whole concept.

We settled into some serious eating. Mzatal sat and watched us with a small, steady smile on his face. He drank wine and picked at a plate of fruit, cheeses, and some sort of custard drizzled with what looked like honey, while Idris and I stuffed ourselves and swapped more silly Christmas stories. Gestamar listened and rumbled in reyza-laughter periodically.

I'd had a little wine, and Mzatal was way too quiet. "Y'all ever have parties or celebrations here?" I asked him. "I mean back before the cataclysm, when there were more humans."

Mzatal twirled the stem of his glass between his fingers. "Yes," he said with a slow contemplative nod. "In the atrium and the rooms that open from it."

I tilted my head and peered at him. "And what were those like? Did those seventeenth-century folks know how to get down?" I asked, grinning.

Mzatal lifted an eyebrow and hesitated a second, likely reading the meaning of "get down" from me, then smiled. "They were lively indeed. I tended to observe from the mezzanine," he said, his smile widening. "Unless, of course, a reveler caught my eye."

Okay. Now that was interesting. "Oh? Do go on," I urged.

He took a drink before continuing. "It was usually a smooth process. I would catch the glances thrown my way and note which appealed most in the moment," he said with a slight shrug. "Later I would descend to the atrium and rescue the chosen one from the throngs." Amusement lit his face. "They did so love to be rescued."

"I'm sure they did," I said, laughing.

Gestamar snorted, and I slid a glance to him. "I bet you saw some interesting shit," I said.

"Much," the reyza said, rumbling. "Bedding a qaztahl ranked highly for many, and wine loosened inhibitions and dampened fear." He bared his teeth and looked at Mzatal. "I know a story they will enjoy. Tell them of Marguerite Deshayes."

Go, Gestamar. I leaned forward. "Yes, tell us about Marguerite."

Idris sipped wine and waited, a look on his face as if he couldn't believe we might get a *story* from the lord.

Mzatal gave Gestamar a *look* then stared down into his glass. I kept my eyes on him, knowing how to play the waiting game. He shook his head and lifted his eyes to me. "It is a truly silly tale," he said, a smile playing on his lips.

"The best kind," I said, grinning. "Spill it!"

Gestamar rumbled, and Mzatal settled back in his chair. "It was your year, sixteen thirty-two," Mzatal said. "When I arrived in the atrium, Marguerite, a busty and hitherto unobtrusive woman in her late thirties, approached and sought to press her advantage, obviously quite inebriated."

Gestamar elaborated. "She threw her arms around his neck and pressed everything against him. Including her advantage."

Mzatal gave a grudging nod. "I simply put her aside and

thought the matter done," he said. "However, when I ascended to my chambers later, I found her naked at the top of the stairs unable to get past the warding to my bedchamber, which had likely been her goal. And I never *bed* in my bed." He shook his head and smiled. "She was spread, and ready, and reaching for me."

I laughed, though I almost felt sorry for the woman. "And what did you do?"

"She was far too much in the wine," Mzatal said, "and would not have approached me without. I moved to step past her so Gestamar could carry her down, and . . ." He paused, drained his glass.

The reyza tapped the table with a claw, rumbling. "If you do not finish it, I will."

I looked to Gestamar. "I think you'd better. I have a feeling he's going to leave out all the juicy bits."

Gestamar snorted. "She grabbed his cock through his breeches and held on like a graa on a tagan fruit." I gathered from the way the reyza clenched his hand that he meant to convey with *great* ferocity.

Mzatal cursed softly in demon. "To this day I do not know how she managed it."

Gestamar continued. "She yelled out all of the things she could do for him, and he was . . . in shock."

I didn't think I'd ever before heard a reyza rumble that heavily with laughter.

Mzatal leveled a frown at Gestamar. "It was unexpected and hurt *quite* a lot." He looked back to Idris and me. "As Gestamar said, I was indeed stunned. Though I had no physical shielding active, the assault was still startling," he said, then hesitated. "I first tried to simply wrest her hand away."

"That was unwise," Gestamar commented.

Idris cringed noticeably. I burst out laughing. "Oh no."

Mzatal cleared his throat. "When I recovered from my *error*, I breathed a pygah and used potency to prize her fingers off. And still the woman screamed what she could do for me," he said with a shake of his head and an amused smile. "I stayed well away from her reach."

I wiped tears away from laughing so hard. "Did she ever leave? Or did you have her carted off?"

"Mzatal set a triple pygah," Gestamar told us, "which, along with the wine she had consumed, eased her greatly."

Mzatal nodded. "The faas reclothed her, and Gestamar carried her back to her quarters. And I continued to mine."

"He continued slowly and *carefully* to his chambers," Gestamar clarified.

I tried hard not to snort my wine. "Did she remember any of it the next day?"

"Only vague remnants," Mzatal said, "though I remembered all."

"And the parties were never the same after that, I bet."

"I maintained light physical shielding among the humans," he said with a smile. "But Marguerite . . ." He paused and his eyes went distant as though remembering, a slow smile growing. "All of the delicious acts she screamed out? She could perform every one and more." His eyes flashed with good humor. "This I determined in the next week when I encountered her by the little waterfall."

That got even more laughter. "And I bet she was much more fun when she wasn't blitzed," I said.

Mzatal raised an eyebrow. "Indeed. I prefer coherent, cognizant, and inclined," he said. "While inebriated, she was most inclined, but neither coherent nor cognizant."

I leaned back and sipped my wine. It was clear that the lord was far from chaste, but I had to appreciate his desire for a willing partner in full control of her faculties. Hell, better than a lot of guys back home who'd have taken advantage of a situation like that in a heartbeat.

Mzatal opened his mouth to speak again, then turned and looked at Faruk. He stood abruptly, strode to the faas and crouched while Gestamar hissed softly.

I set my glass down. "What's going on?"

Mzatal laid his hand on Faruk's back and spoke softly in demon. The faas seemed to huddle in on itself, tip of its tail trembling like a rattlesnake's.

Idris glanced over at me. "Faruk is being summoned to Earth." His brow furrowed. "It doesn't happen often for her."

"Her?" I blurted, then grimaced at how stupid that sounded. But none of the faas had any sort of visual or behavioral features to indicate gender. I usually winged it and guessed, but I had a feeling Idris actually knew.

His eyes crinkled. "Yes, and Jekki is male. They're a mated pair." His gaze went back to Faruk, and I stood, deeply curious about what a summoning looked like from this side.

Faruk detached her pouch of kek tokens from her belt and tossed it to Gestamar, then laid her hand on Mzatal's knee. Wind swirled around them, and the whine of a portal overrode the incessant rush of the waterfall. Mzatal stood and stepped backward to the table, eyes on Faruk.

The portal opened with a rush of wind and the stench of sulphur, and a heartbeat later, tendrils of luminescent mist-like potency wreathed the faas, and she disappeared. Jekki chittered, his tail twisting and writhing in what I'd come to recognize as faas agitation.

I remembered to breathe again as the arcane wind died away to nothing. "Do you know who summoned her?"

Mzatal nodded slowly, eyes narrowed. "Rasha Hassan Jalal al-Khouri. I had thought her dead, she has been so long without summoning."

The name didn't ring any bells, and I filed it away. I glanced at Gestamar as he moved to clear the residuals from the summoning. A pang of selfish longing tugged, as I wished it had been Gestamar, along with my letters, rather than Faruk. I pushed down my impatience. There were two days yet during this Earth full moon for Gestamar or the other designated letter-carriers, Jekki and Bezik, to be summoned.

Mzatal turned back to Idris and me. "It is late, and we meet early tomorrow," he said, edge in his voice and the set of his face indicating that the party was over for him. Jekki pressed close to his thigh, and the lord laid a hand on the faas's head.

I got it. One of his demons was out, and he was back into serious lord mode. I acknowledged with a nod, hesitated, then moved to give him a quick kiss on the cheek. "You're okay, Boss," I said smiling up at him. "Thanks for the Christmas."

He stood unmoving for a heartbeat, then lifted his hands to the sides of my head, leaned in and kissed my forehead. He tucked his hands behind his back again, inclined his head a smidge. "Rest well, Kara Gillian."

"You too, Mzatal," I said, then gave Idris a hug before heading out. I looked down at the ring on my right hand and smiled. All in all, it had actually been a pretty decent Christmas.

Chapter 33

Thirty. My hand touched the stone at the end of the pool. I tucked my legs as I glided to a stop, pushed off the end, and began another lap. Fifty laps. That was my goal.

Mzatal's palace was full of things that were just plain Awesome. The library with three full floors of books and spiral staircases, the greenhouse on the north end of the roof with its collection of weirdest-plants-of-the-demon-realm, the waterfall walkway that spanned the river where it plunged from the cliff in its rainbow cascade to the sea far below.

But hands down, my favorite was the pool that I'd dubbed The Very Awesome Pool of Awesomeness. This wasn't just some run-of-the-mill indoor pool. Hell, it wasn't even a really fantastic luxury pool that you might find in a mansion or high-end hotel. No, this thing was glorious. Fed by the river, it was like an indoor grotto, with a large inner pool about twenty-five yards long that was perfect for swimming laps; a far deeper section for safe diving—complete with rocky ledges from which to dive; and numerous pools to the side that were either fed by hot springs or warded to be warm. The main pool, however, stayed cool enough for comfortable swimming. The roof above it was thick resin-glass. Rocks and waterfalls surrounded everything, along with lush tropical plant life. The only thing missing was the sounds of birds and monkeys.

Swimming had become a surprise therapy for me in the past several days. Athletics and I had never gotten along, but strangely enough, I'd actually developed a semi-fondness for swimming laps. I was a more-than-decent swimmer, yet also ridiculously self-conscious; I detested swimming laps at the gym or any other public pool. Here, I had the pool to myself more often than not, and there was usually no one but demons to see me. I could have swum naked if I'd so desired, but in the interest of not traumatizing Idris, I had the zrila make up a bathing suit for me. Actually, I asked for one simple bathing suit, but by the next day I had close to a dozen varying styles in my wardrobe. Apparently the zrila really enjoyed a crafting challenge.

I'd started swimming laps as a spur of the moment, Gee-let's-see-if-I-can-actually-still-swim-a-few-laps sort of thing, but I soon discovered that when I swam I could forget. I could lose myself in the rhythm of the strokes and the feel of the water, and for that time I wasn't Kara the demon summoner, or Kara the traumatized survivor of torture. I was simply *Kara*.

But today, I actually thought about summoning while I swam. None of the three demons bearing my letters had been summoned during this full moon, and I forced myself to control the selfish ache. Faruk had seemed nervous, perhaps even frightened before her summoning, but that could easily have been because she was so seldom summoned. Or was there more to it? It had hurt to be summoned when Idris brought me through, like being dragged through broken glass. And from what I'd seen, it had hurt Katashi as well. Yet I had a feeling it wasn't anything that Idris was specifically doing or not doing. Even the times I'd summoned Rhyzkahl it had seemed to take him a few seconds to gather himself, to recover.

I finished my laps and propped myself up along the edge of the pool. I cast my gaze up at the rocks to see if any demons were around. There were usually a few here and there, but this time the only one I saw was Gestamar, perched on the diving ledge. As I looked up at him he made a graceful bound down to a rock closer to me, as if sensing I had a question for him.

"Does it hurt for y'all to be summoned?" I asked him.

He snorted. "Always. Sometimes more than others, depending on the skill of the summoner and the degree of conjunction."

"Then why do it?" I asked, brow creased. "Why put up

with it? I mean surely it's not simply for coffee and popcorn and books?"

"We like coffee and popcorn and books," Gestamar replied.

I laughed. "Okay, I suppose *I* could see doing it for coffee." I tilted my head and peered at him. "Is there some other reason you tolerate it?"

The reyza spread his wings wide. "Kri," he said, then settled his wings in close and bared his teeth.

I waited, then rolled my eyes. "Well, will you tell me?"

Gestamar bared his teeth wider. "Dahn."

Laughing, I splashed at him. He leaped into the air, nimbly avoiding most of the water, then cannonballed into the pool, thoroughly swamping me. Before I knew it the pool area was filled with demons, and an enormous water fight commenced that rivaled the Epic Snowball Fight at Rhyzkahl's palace.

I grinned and escaped the pool, then grabbed my robe and retreated down the corridor. Demons certainly knew how to have fun. That was something I never *ever* would have guessed in a million years.

"They miss having humans around."

I yelped and turned at the resonant voice. Vahl leaned against the wall of the corridor, arms folded, eyes on me. His skin glistened dark and with vibrant health as though salt scrubs, mud baths, and Mega Vitamins for Skin and Hair were the norm. His casual pose reminded me of a mountain lion, sleek and powerful, beautiful and dangerous.

"Lord Vahl," I said, and tried not to think about the fact that I was wearing a tank-style bathing suit and nothing else. "You've been, ah, watching?"

He gave a nod, smiling a little. "They love to play," he said with a glance toward the demons. "And they love the different rules needed to play with humans."

"I've noticed that they do love games." I paused, regarded him. "Michelle says you treat her very well."

He shrugged. "I value her. We all miss humans, though some will not admit it, and the reasons vary."

I narrowed my eyes at him. "She had a really shit life on Earth. Don't fuck her up."

He uncrossed his arms and pushed off the wall. "I've no reason to do so."

"Please keep it that way," I said, well aware that I had zero authority to back up my little mandate.

Vahl snorted softly. "And what of you and Mzatal?" His eyes dropped to the partial sigils visible on my upper chest, then returned to my face.

"What of us?" I responded, shrugging. "I'm in an agreement with him."

Vahl tilted his head and smiled. "There are agreements and *agreements*."

I chuckled low in my throat. "And why do you care?"

"Simple curiosity." His smile widened.

I snorted. What a line of shit. But Vahl wasn't being pushy or obnoxious in any way. He was simply testing the waters. "We don't fuck," I told him. "Is that what you wanted to know?"

He dipped his head in a small nod. "It will serve."

"Okaaaay," I drawled. I glanced back to see how the water war was progressing, surprised to see that it seemed to be finished. Not a demon in sight anywhere. Where the hell had they all disappeared to so quickly?

"They have a tendency to do that," Vahl said. I looked back at him to see his gaze on the pool area as well. "They are here and then not."

It took me a second to realize he'd read my mental wondering about the demons. "Shit," I breathed, annoyed at myself. I quickly drew on the grove to fog my thoughts.

One eyebrow lifted as Vahl noted the fogging. "That makes everything more interesting," he murmured, stepping closer, exuding natural sexiness. "Though reading can make everything very . . . *very* satisfying."

I retreated half a step to find the corridor wall at my back. The man was pretty damn hot, and Michelle definitely had a good thing going on in that regard. I also knew that Mzatal wouldn't blink twice about me sleeping with Vahl as long it was my own choice to do so. "I like keeping my thoughts to myself," I muttered.

Vahl smiled and closed the distance between us. He lifted a hand and pushed a wet tendril of hair from my face. "As I said . . . interesting." My pulse sped as he traced his fingers lightly along my jaw. His eyes stayed on mine while

I gulped softly and wondered whether he was really about to kiss me, wondered if I wanted it, if it was a good idea, and if he was a good kisser.

He leaned down and lightly brushed my lips with his, then kissed me for real, a curl-my-toes kiss, and I lost myself for several heartbeats before remembering both myself and the devious nature of the lords. Yeah, this would probably be good—*great*—sex, but I'd had that with Rhyzkahl and look where that got me. And not that there was a damn thing wrong with casual sex, but right now, I wanted sex to mean something.

I placed my hand in the center of his chest and lightly pushed, breaking the kiss. "That was most enjoyable, Lord Vahl," I said, breath coming a teensy bit raggedly. "But I think that will have to do."

He stepped back without protest, inclined his head in acknowledgment with perhaps just a bit of it's-your-loss thrown in. "Perhaps another time will be more opportune."

I gave him a smile and a nod, but inside I was thinking, *Don't hold your breath.* I turned away, exited the corridor, then headed back through the atrium. Mzatal was on the mezzanine, and when I lifted my eyes to his he gave me a warm smile that touched me down to my toes. He'd been monitoring, I realized, and would have interceded in a heartbeat if Vahl had chosen to press his advance past where I wanted.

Feeling damn good about myself and my situation, I headed back to my room to get out of my wet things..

Chapter 34

The next few days were comfortable routine. Up at daybreak, quick breakfast and a cup of precious coffee, then off to the workroom for several hours of review, drills, new stuff, practice, lather, rinse, repeat. Then a break for lunch and personal time and any "homework" that had been assigned, and back to the workroom in mid-afternoon for yet more reviews, drill, etc. Finally, a break for supper, sleep, and other silly-but-necessary stuff.

To my surprise, I found myself slotting in exercise as silly-but-necessary—and completely by my own choice, at that. Swimming, the damn stairs, and now even running.

Look at me being all athletic and shit, I thought with a snort as I tugged on a sports bra and shorts and laced up my sneakers for a run after supper. Jill wouldn't have any idea who the hell I was by the time I made it home. Hell, I actually had—*gasp*—muscle tone in my legs!

Safar and Gestamar flew sparring patterns above, watching over me as I headed out. The sun drifted low over the sea surrounded by banks of white clouds that promised a glorious sunset, but I estimated I had at least an hour and a half of daylight left. It had been well over a month since I'd last gone jogging with Jill, so I started out at a sedate shuffle. I was a crap judge of distance, but Gestamar had advised me that the path that looped around the lake was approximately two miles.

I had to do the stop-and-walk a few times, but nowhere near as much as I expected. By the time I made it around the lake and headed back toward the palace, I barely even felt sore anymore, though I knew that tomorrow would probably be a much different story.

The path curved up toward the main entrance, but when I neared my favorite pile of bricks at the base of the hill, I left the path and jogged across the grass toward the rocky slope and the column atop it. I could finish up with a speed climb up the hill and then feel super virtuous before collapsing in an exhausted heap. Hey, it was all about making me stronger, right?

My sprint-climb up the hill ended up being more of a gasping, flailing slog, but I eventually made it to the top. To my surprise, a shirtless Idris was there, about fifteen yards from me, doing pushups in the grass beside the column. As I watched, he cranked out another dozen or so perfect pushups, then leaped up and began tracing a series of complex sigils, face a mask of concentration as he worked his scarred hand. As soon as it was done, he waved a hand to dispel the series, then dropped to do more pushups.

I slowly lowered myself to sit cross-legged on the grass, not wanting to interrupt. Idris smoothly pressed out twenty pushups, then rose and began tracing the same series again with a grace that was utterly at odds with his somewhat awkward social skills. For that matter, everything about him right now was so far from the uncertain youth that it was nearly impossible to believe they were the same. Not only the surety of movement and the confidence with which he traced the sigils, but—holy shit, dude was built like a gymnast. He'd been shirtless when he summoned me, but I'd been a bit too preoccupied to notice anything but the fact that, yeah, he wasn't scrawny.

A breeze cooled the sweat on my body as Idris dispelled the sigils and dropped to do yet another twenty pushups. I watched the muscles flow in his shoulders and back. Why the hell had he been wasting his time pining over me? Girls would be falling all over him given the chance.

He rose again, but this time he began to move in what I quickly realized was the beginning of the shikvihr. I remained utterly quiet, watching in fascinated awe as he traced sigils in a fluid dance of movement. He set the first four rings as easily as breathing, slowing only slightly on the fifth, and having only the barest uncertainty as he finished the sixth. He began the seventh ring, made it halfway through, then paused as if he'd run into a wall of molasses. I held my breath as he oh-so-carefully unwound the last sigil without disturbing the rest of the pattern. He went utterly still, and I could practically feel his complete focus.

After nearly half a minute he began to move again, with only a minor adjustment in his stance and in the position of the next sigil, but apparently that was enough. He finished the series and ignited the partial pattern, then gave a whoop of triumph.

I got to my feet, applauding as I headed his way. "Dude, that was amazing!"

Grinning, he met my eyes. He'd been aware of my presence the whole time, I realized. He turned a slow circle, admiring the creation, then made a sweeping motion, dispersing the pattern with a whisper of wind and soft chiming sound. "Yeah!" He lifted his hand for a high five, and I was more than happy to provide one for him.

"How long have you been working on learning this?" I asked.

Idris picked up a towel and water bottle from beside the column, wiped his face, still smiling broadly. "Since about two weeks after I got here. So, four months-ish."

Blinking, I did my best to hide my dismay. "Damn. If it took *you* four months to get to the seventh ring, I'm going to be here for years before I finish it."

He took a slug from the water bottle and shrugged. "Most summoners never finish it. You get whatever you can out of it, and that's what you end up using." The grin spread across his face again. "I'm *psyched* I got through the seventh ring!"

My mouth tightened in annoyance. "Mzatal said I couldn't go home until I learned it."

"Damn," he said. "The whole thing?"

I thought back to the wording of the agreement. "Yep. He definitely said that I had to pass the shikvihr initiation. The whole motherfucking thing." I cursed under my breath, then straightened and shook my head. No, I wasn't going to wallow in homesickness or angst or any of that shit. "So I guess I need to get my ass in gear."

Idris's face was a mask of consternation. "Wait. He said you had to pass the *initiation*?"

"Well, yeah." I frowned. "Why? Is there some difference between learning and passing?"

"Uh-huh," he said. "It's the difference between this," he pointed at the ground, "and that." He hooked his thumb over his shoulder at the column. "Most never complete a full shikvihr on the ground. I think there've only been a handful of summoners in all history who've passed it on the column."

Numb horror flowed through me, and for several seconds I could only stare at Idris. "A handful?" I finally managed. "In what, a few thousand years?" I thought quickly back to Mzatal's words. *That rat fucker.* He hadn't lied. He'd told me how long it had taken people to pass the shikvihr initiation. He'd simply cleverly omitted the detail about it being such a miniscule number. Fury and hurt rose within me.

I turned toward the palace. *"MZATAL! YOU'RE A FILTHY DEVIOUS MOTHERFUCKER!"*

Idris winced and ducked his shoulders as if expecting a lightning strike. "Shit, Kara!"

I clenched and unclenched my hands. "That devious, conniving son of a bitch. He found a way to make *sure* I stay here."

Idris gave me a worried look. "The agreement to go back is based totally on that?"

"Yes!" Anger coiled with the deep sense of betrayal in my gut. I'd trusted him, had actually felt a real connection to him, as though we were far more than summoner and lord, or student and teacher. I'd *liked* the feeling that we were friends, and most of all, I truly needed to be able to trust him. "I can't go back for six months," I told Idris. "I wasn't happy about it, but I could deal with it, y'know? And then he said that after the six months I could go home as soon as I passed the goddamn shikvihr initiation. So I *asked* him how long it took to pass, and he said—" I gritted my teeth. "—he said that some dude passed it in seven months, and the longest anyone's ever taken to pass is eighteen." I shoved a hand through my hair. "He didn't care to mention the odds of never passing at all." *And I was too stupid to ask.*

And the shitty part was that I knew why he did it. I knew perfectly well it wasn't some nefarious scheme with darker purpose. He'd carefully employed that demonic lord deceit in order to keep me here—to protect me and make absolutely sure that I could never go back to Earth anything less than a goddamn superhero.

Didn't matter the purpose. It still cut deeply. How could I trust him if I never knew when he might pull another stunt like that, whether to protect me or not? His words came back to me: *Kara, I could no more keep you prisoner now than cage the lightning or bottle the surging sea.* I snorted. Wasn't that a lovely pile of bullshit?

I summoned the damn pygah and did some damn breathing to calm myself the hell down. Once I stopped feeling murderous, I gave Idris as nice a smile as I could muster. "Congrats on getting the seventh ring, Idris," I said. "I have some things I need to do." I didn't really know what just yet, but I knew I needed to do something.

Heading back up to the palace, I pulled a trickle of grove power, not only to help me calm down but also to make it more difficult to read me. I had no doubt that Mzatal was aware of my pissed-offed-ness, but I didn't want him hearing my thought processes while I tried to work this out. Better for the both of us that way.

Mzatal wasn't in his rooms, for which I was beyond grateful. I took a quick bath and changed clothes, then carefully packed up as much of my stuff as I could carry. And how the hell had I acquired so many clothes? The zrila had gone nuts.

It took a few minutes, but I finally managed to convince a faas that I needed to relocate to different rooms—any that were prepared and ready, though preferably something as far away from Mzatal's chambers as possible. That turned out to be on the north end of the palace in the eerily vacant section where humans once lived. Unfortunately, to be far away from Mzatal meant I was also far away from a view of the grove, though at least I could still feel it clearly. The room itself was comfortable enough with a spacious combined bedroom and living area. No door though. An open archway led straight to the corridor, but at least there was a curtain that could be drawn to screen the bed. By the time the evening bell rang, all of my things were in a pile beside the bed in my new room.

I curled up on the couch with my papers and books, tried

to work through the concepts of the first three rings of the shikvihr. But my focus was crap, and calling up the pygah did nothing to ease the ache within. Eventually I gave up studying and tried to write a letter to Tessa, but after four tries I was ready to give up on that as well.

An ilius coiled by the open archway, and I remembered Idris's comment about the demons being early warning systems for a pending Mzatal arrival. I quickly made certain that I was still holding enough grove power to keep him from reading me, and a few seconds later the sound of footsteps in the hall confirmed Mzatal's approach.

He stopped just beyond the arch, but to my surprise didn't enter. I didn't look directly at him, but my peripheral vision worked overtime.

"Kara."

I took a deep breath. "Lord Mzatal."

He closed his eyes. A wave of reaction passed over his face before he could stop it, and I winced inwardly, realizing that by using his title, other than in show for others, I hurt him. That hadn't been my intention, but the formality defined my boundaries and our roles, so I steeled myself to accept the consequences.

He remained silent longer than necessary to process a response, but finally opened his eyes. "Kara. Come. Walk with me."

I really wasn't ready to talk or hug it out or any shit like that. My own thoughts needed to be a lot clearer first. "Is that a command or request, my lord?"

He drew a deep breath and released it slowly before responding. "A request only."

"Then I will respectfully decline, my lord," I said, keeping my voice as even as I could. "I wouldn't be good company."

Tension tightened his shoulders. For an instant I thought he would enter, but he simply kept his hands clasped behind his back, though I had a feeling they were in fists. "Kara, reconsider your quarters," he said. "It is too soon for you to be away."

"Yes, you've made your stance on that quite clear," I shot back, voice laden with bitterness.

"I speak of the immediate concerns," he replied. "Though the other is what I came to discuss."

I took a steadying breath. "I can't talk to you now," I said. "It would not end well."

He remained silent for a moment, then gave a short nod. "Accepted." He paused again before speaking. "Kara, reconsider your quarters," he repeated, "if only for a few nights."

"If I go back to your rooms now, my lord," I said, calmly and quietly, "you might as well put the collar back on me."

An expression of dismay flashed across his face, then melded into a neutral mask. "That is . . ." He trailed off, shook his head. "So be it. Rest well, Kara Gillian."

My hand tightened on my pen as I gave him a nod. He remained just beyond the archway for a few seconds more before turning and heading back down the hall.

There was no point in trying to study or write letters, not with my focus this screwed up, and so much uncertainty and hurt churning through me. Eventually I gave up and went to bed, but it was a long time before I could fall asleep.

I jolted upright, anguished scream choking off before it could fully form. The nightmare coiled around me, refusing to fully disperse even though I was awake and aware.

"You are mine," Rhyzkahl says with a snarl. "None other may touch you thus." A drop of crimson slides down the keen edge of his blade. My blood. My pain. "You are mine."

Throwing off the covers, I stumbled out of bed and then to the balcony. The cool night air washed over me as I stepped out, but my shivering had little to do with that. *If Mzatal was here . . .* I squeezed my eyes shut. No. Mzatal wasn't here to ease the nightmare. And now I understood his words, his desire for me to "reconsider my quarters." He'd kept the dreams at bay while I stayed with him, let me sleep in peace.

But I need to be able to stand on my own at some point, don't I? I couldn't expect him to be there every second of the day to ease my boo-boos or hug away my fears. And I had no desire to live my life so thoroughly protected. Rhyzkahl had made sweeping decisions about my "safety" as well, such as when he'd denied me the grove. This situation was nothing like that, I knew, for Rhyzkahl's intentions had little to do with my personal safety and everything to do with his own goals. Yet, in a way, knowing Mzatal had the best of intentions—while deceiving me into an agreement that could trap me here forever—was the hardest part. At least I *thought* he had the best of intentions. But how could I really be sure?

I returned inside and went to the bath chamber. My thoughts tumbled over each other as I took a long soak. Dawn came, but when the faas arrived with food, I could barely choke down a few swallows of chak. I tried again to study, but at the morning bell gave up, gathered up all my papers, and headed to the workroom.

Sitting at a table against the back wall, I spread out my notes and sought calm, which proved tough to do when I felt haggard on innumerable levels. I gently pulled power from the grove, as much to mask my thoughts as to seek an elusive peace.

Mzatal entered, and I stood. I didn't do the "Lord Mzatal" thing. He got that message clearly last night.

"Greetings, Kara Gillian," he said, eyes on me and holding himself with a too-smooth façade that spoke volumes more than any expression of hurt or anger could have.

Taking a deep breath, I gave him a nod of acknowledgment. "We could engage in some bullshit about getting down to work, or we could talk about the other shit. Which would you prefer?"

He stepped forward. "The work has no value or substance while the other hangs between us."

"Agreed," I said, a bit surprised at how calm I sounded. I sure as hell didn't feel it. "A question for you then. Assuming we had no agreement stating otherwise, if I were to ask you to have Idris send me home, would you?"

Mzatal shook his head slowly. "No."

I gave a snort of humorless laughter. At least he wasn't lying to me. Though it felt like too little too late, at this point. "Then why did you even bother with that bullshit in the agreement?" I asked. "To lull me into some sort of false ease?"

His eyes narrowed. "You asked what I would do if there was no agreement," he replied, voice oddly tight. "Were there no agreement, there would be many other factors considered as well. There *is* an agreement and it is not . . . bullshit."

"And where in all of those *factors* is a trust in my own

judgment?" I demanded, feeling the hurt of it all keenly. "Am I a toddler who needs her hand held to keep her from running out into traffic? Or am I a grownup who can be told, 'Hey, there are cars out there that'll flatten you. You need to look both ways.'" I shook my head, eyes on him. "After Helori took me away, I came back here, back to you, for two reasons. First, was that I'd come to understand the danger to myself and to my loved ones if I went back to Earth, and I knew I needed further training." I paused, took a deep breath. "But second was because you told me I wasn't a prisoner."

His head lowered, eyes remaining on mine. "Under the agreement, you are not a prisoner."

My mouth twisted. "And you made damn sure I'd agree to it, too. You used that well-honed qaztahl deceit to fudge your answer to my question so that I'd buy it. You knew damn well what I wanted to know." I met his gaze steadily. "You've said yourself—repeatedly—that you can't help reading me. But you *chose* to give me the answer that would ensure I became your prisoner by my own goddamn agreement." I spread my hands. "By all means, let me lock myself in this gilded cage you've created for me."

A whisper of anger or frustration passed over his face. "And what has changed in the time frame given? *Nothing*. I fully intend for you to complete that term and pass the shikvihr initiation. You are creating your own cage by doubting your ability to do so."

Anger churned in my gut. "My doubt or lack of doubt has nothing to do with this," I retorted. "What's changed is that I see the fucking bars now. And you *still* refuse to admit that you employed deceit, because you don't fucking trust me to judge for myself what my best course of action is!"

A shimmer of silver-blue potency flashed in his eyes. "Kara Gillian, you have four qaztahl holding you at the top of their target list," he said, near spitting the words. "I had no time to toy with the devastating introduction of doubt into your process of learning the shikvihr. You do not consider doubt a factor. I *do*. I have watched it eat away at the potential of so very many. You see bars because you choose to see them rather than the door that is open for you."

"Yeah," I said, giving a slight nod. "Well, at least you admit it. And yeah, you did all this for my own safety and for the best reasons, blah, blah." I shrugged. "Only problem with all that is, now I know I can't trust you. From here on out I'll always be wondering what the catch is, where the hidden trap is. Wondering what else you do because you know what's *best* for me." I slowly released my hold on the trickle of grove power. I didn't want to shield my hurt from him any longer. "You said you want to work with me. That can't happen. Not like this. I'll work *for* you." I lifted my chin, mouth tight. "I'll abide by the terms of the agreement. From here on out we are student and Lord."

He didn't move or speak for several heartbeats, then abruptly turned and exited to the balcony, hands in fists at his sides as he went to the far end rather than his usual place right outside the door.

My anger didn't abate with his departure. In a swift, decisive move, I yanked the ring off my right hand and hurled it against the wall as hard as I could. Breathing raggedly, I seized my papers and got the fuck out of the workroom and away.

Chapter 35

I returned to my room and dumped my papers on the bed, tried to pace away my fury and angst, but it was like attempting to put out a house fire with a garden hose. I finally gave up and changed into the first bathing suit I could find, dragged on my robe, and stalked to the pool, all the while praying I wouldn't run into anyone—human, lord, or demon. It wasn't simply that I didn't want to talk to anyone; in my current mood, there was too much chance I'd do or say something I'd no doubt regret later.

Kinda like what I'd already done. My right thumb kept creeping over to where my middle finger met my palm, feeling the absence of the ring as if I'd lost a part of me.

I guess I'd had a hidden fantasy that once we talked openly, everything would sort itself out and *somehow* be okay again. Yeah. That happened. *Why did he have to screw everything up by tricking me?*

I stripped off my robe, threw it onto a chaise, and dove into the pool. I didn't count laps, simply focused on my strokes and the rhythm of the turn at each end, yet still my mind whirled. With Mzatal's bullshit dumped on top of Rhyzkahl's treachery, and the Four Mraztur targeting me, I now had five lords on my shit list and could say with conviction, *lords suck*.

Even as I thought it, I knew lumping Mzatal with the others wasn't fair. But damn it, he'd consciously duped me. I told myself it wasn't the end of the world that we weren't BFFs anymore, but it just felt *wrong*, like a series of sigils with the harmonics off. And I was at an impasse, unable to do anything about it.

I pushed hard off the wall, stroked savagely for the other end. I'd survived a lot of shit before. I could get through this. All of it: recovering from the torture, learning the shikvihr, getting Szerain's blade, being the target of the Four Mraztur, Mzatal's distance. I could do it. Yeah, it would've been better in all sorts of ways with Mzatal's close support, but oh-fucking-well.

The anger wasn't helping and neither was thinking. I kept swimming until I didn't have to think anymore.

By the time I stopped, my muscles burned and trembled, but the fury was gone and my thoughts were clearer. I rested my forehead on the stone at the end and closed my eyes. Yep. My plate was piled high with shit, no doubt about that, but I had a choice. I could easily slide into the torture-fractured, barely-glued-together woman that haunted me—and, thanks to Rhyzkahl, days like this made it hard not to cave in to her. Or I could get my act together, play at being whole, and focus on clearing my plate, with or without Mzatal. *Time to get your head back in the game.*

I pushed away from the wall, stroked over to the rock steps and relocated to a side pool fed by a hot spring. A sigh escaped me as I eased into the water. I draped my arms on the edge and tipped my head back to look up at the mid-morning sky through the thick glass of the ceiling. The shikvihr stood between me and home, and was a tool to use against the Mraztur. No point in wasting time. I began a methodical mental review of the first ring.

A shift of movement caught my attention. I lifted my head to see Vahl gracefully climbing down from the rocks, eyes on me. I quickly got out of the pool, realizing too late that he was between me and my robe. I silently cursed, then sighed, wishing I'd grabbed a tank suit rather than a two piece. Though surely Vahl wouldn't do anything untoward under Mzatal's roof. Besides, I reminded myself, he'd been damn near a gentleman when I'd stopped his kiss the other day.

I straightened and lifted my chin as he approached. A light smile played across his lips, but when his gaze dropped to my torso the smile faded to nothing. He could see the sigils more clearly now. All of them, except for the parts that were covered by the bikini.

"How long have you been here watching me?" I asked, watching him with narrowed eyes.

His eyes traveled over my body, down, then up, then down again, as if reading and memorizing every aspect of each sigil. "I was here when you arrived," he said, not looking at my face.

"Like them?" I asked bitterly. "Rhyzkahl has a future in body art."

He stepped closer, eyes still traveling over the sigils. "Turn around." It wasn't a request.

I hesitated, then complied. Even in Mzatal's realm, he was still a demonic lord, and I'd learned my lesson about needlessly antagonizing any of them.

He pulled the ties at my neck and back before I could even twitch. The top fell to the stone as I swallowed hard and clenched my hands. He wouldn't be foolish enough to assault me here, right? At least I hoped not.

Vahl walked around me, stopping in front, eyes on my breasts but with no lust reflected in them. He set the heel of his hand near my nipple with his fingers pointed toward my throat, and closed his eyes. I sucked in my breath, and a shiver raced over my skin, but he didn't seem to notice. After a moment, he lifted his hand, then set two fingers on the sigil that started below my throat. Rhyzkahl's. A shudder ran through him as he lightly traced it, yet he didn't stop until he completed the symbol.

"What are you doing?" I asked, voice unsteady.

He finally looked up into my face, fingers still on the sigil. "Do you feel them?"

My eyes narrowed in a frown. "No. They're scars. That's all they are to me."

He shifted to trace a sigil that twined around my nipple, eyes on my face. Revulsion and fascination coiled together in his expression. "*Rhyzkahl* did this," he said, as though really taking it in for the first time.

Goosebumps rose on my skin. "Yes. Carved them with an essence blade, then tortured me to fire each one," I said, amazed that I could speak without my voice shaking. Eyes still on his, I lowered my head and called up the memory of the torture. He wanted to know? I was more than happy to give him the gory details.

He dropped his hand and stepped back, shaking his head.

"Yes," I said quietly. "He did this."

Indecision clouded his expression, though I couldn't imagine why. He drew a deep breath, shook his head again, then looked to me with an uncompromising gaze. "Go find Mzatal."

"Huh? Why?"

His eyes unfocused briefly as if he was listening to something, then snapped back to mine. "Run, Kara. Find Mzatal. *Now!*"

I took a step back from him, then turned and snatched up my bikini top and robe. I was two steps from the entryway when I felt the grove activate. I sucked a breath in and whirled to look at Vahl.

"Rhyzkahl," I breathed. Vahl's expression didn't change. He sure as shit didn't look surprised.

I quickly yanked on my robe and fled to find Mzatal.

Chapter 36

Mzatal was descending the stairs as I rushed into the atrium, his shirt and face spattered with blood from a nosebleed.

"Rhyzkahl arrived in the grove," he said with dark intensity as he approached. "I have cast him back and bound the blades so that he cannot use his, but this also means I cannot use mine. And he will return."

Belting my robe more securely around me, I stopped at the base of the stairs and looked up at him. "What do you need me to do?"

"Seek Idris in the summoning chamber. He lays support," he said as he passed. "Shield yourself. Draw all that you are able from the grove."

I started up the steps, then paused. No. That wasn't right. I knew it in my essence. I couldn't simply cower and hide and shield myself. I pivoted back to Mzatal. "I'm going with you."

He stopped and turned to me, mouth drawn to a tight line. "It is *Rhyzkahl*," he said. "And I do not wish to risk you while there is a safer alternative."

"Yeah. And I don't want to hide in a corner and hope for a good outcome," I said, eyes narrowed. "I can shield near the grove as well as in here. Maybe better. So I don't think it's safer."

"Kara," he said with urgent intensity, as he backed down the corridor. "I will be in open conflict and unable to adequately protect you." He shook his head. "Rhyzkahl's initial attack and my counter drained most of my reserves, and he is near untouched."

"All the more reason for me to go with you," I said as I

strode toward him, my eyes locked on his. "If he gets past you, nothing's going to stop him getting me, whether I'm out there or in the summoning chamber. And it *feels* like I need to be out there, where he is. Where *you* are. Trust me, okay?"

Still he hesitated, but finally gave a tight nod. "So be it," he said, turning to move with me. "Stay close." We continued down the corridor to the main entryway and out, heading toward the grove at a brisk pace.

"Vahl knew," I said with a quick glance to him. "He was with me at the pool, and he told me to run and find you, right before I felt the grove activate."

Mzatal's jaw somehow tightened more than it already was. "Vahl has cast aside much." He bit the words out.

I frowned. "What do you mean? Was he here as a mole for Rhyzkahl? If so, he seems to have changed his mind."

"I suspect Rhyzkahl increased pressure on him," Mzatal said, "and recently."

But he warned me. A shiver raced over me. *If he hadn't, if he'd held me or taken me while Rhyzkahl kept Mzatal occupied....* I shook my head, refusing to speculate on what might have happened.

"Aren't you worried that Vahl will join up with Rhyzkahl and help him fight us?"

Mzatal gave a sharp shake of his head. "Such is not our way," he said. "We do not war as on Earth. Engagements are qaztahl to qaztahl. Vahl may go to Rhyzkahl but will not engage, and we need only counter Rhyzkahl." But the tight set of his mouth told me it would be ugly no matter what.

"What about me? Does that mean I can't help?" Though that didn't make sense if Idris was laying a support diagram.

"No," he said. "Summoners are an accepted resource in engagements."

Resource. Hmmf. My palms were sweating, and I wiped them on my stupid flimsy robe. This was not at all how I envisioned eventually facing Rhyzkahl again—barefoot and dressed in a goddamn bikini.

Mzatal stopped about ten yards away from the entrance of the tree tunnel. He called the pygah and began laying the sigils of the first ring of the shikvihr.

I stood out of the way then did my own stupid pygah and

extended to the grove, drawing energy to shield and trying to get a sense of what I could do to help.

Mzatal moved fluidly within the circles. "Once I have the shikvihr set, stay behind me. It will give you additional protection."

My stomach tightened as I nodded. "Mzatal, if this goes bad, don't let him take me."

He paused in his movement, looked over to me. "I will not." He shook his head. "Kara, *I will not.*"

"You do what you have to do," I said with no compromise in my tone despite the knot of cold in my gut. "If it looks like he'll win, you fucking kill me. I mean it."

"I will do what I must," he replied quietly, then resumed his flowing dance of the rings. "He will not have you."

Exhaling, I returned my focus to the grove and delved into the power, expanding my awareness and exploring the energies as I got a feel for its properties. I cursed under my breath as I felt the grove activate. There was no mistaking who was coming through.

"He's coming!" I said. "But I think I can seal the tunnel to stall him."

"If the grove will respond to you thus, do it," he said, words clipped by his intense focus on the dance. "With my reserves tapped and my blade inaccessible, I *need* the augmentation of the shikvihr, and any time you gain for me will be invaluable."

I concentrated on the grove, asked it to guide me even as I guided it to shape its power into a means to slow or stop Rhyzkahl. I felt the grove's assent, its desire to assist, yet even with its touch my efforts felt clumsy and fumbling, like playing on a cathedral organ after barely learning "Chopsticks" on a piano.

Movement near the grove caught my attention. Vahl edged his way to the treeline then crouched, facing us, about ten paces from the tunnel. *Crap*. I sure as hell hoped Mzatal was right about him not interfering.

Through the grove sense, I felt Rhyzkahl's full arrival. My heart gave a sick double-beat. Not just Rhyzkahl. "Mzatal!" I called out. "Amkir's here too!"

Without pausing in his tracings, Mzatal gave me a nod as he began the tenth of the eleven rings. "He will not engage," he said with a surety I didn't feel.

Shit. We sure as hell needed every bit of time I could buy. With a blend of intuition and the arcane principles I'd learned so far, I awkwardly shaped an energy barricade over the exit of the tree tunnel. It sparkled there, a convex film of transparent purple and green iridescence reminiscent of a soap bubble but far more capable of stopping Rhyzkahl. At least I sure as hell hoped so.

Rhyzkahl stalked down the tunnel, a glowing mass of azure potency already prepared in his right hand. He stopped a pace beyond my barrier, his eyes first on Mzatal, then on me.

Shit shit shit. My heart pounded as I saw him, *felt* him again. Terrible memory whispered to me, the icy mask of his expression as he touched the blade to my flesh. I forced the images down, gritted my teeth, and called upon the grove for more energy to reinforce the seal.

Amkir stopped a few feet behind Rhyzkahl and folded his arms across his chest, looking as hard and angry as ever. *Just stay there, asshole.*

Rhyzkahl lifted his left hand to the barrier and began to work at unweaving it. For all its flimsy appearance, I knew the damn thing held a lot of power, and, to my relief, he wasn't able to push straight through it. Yet I also knew it wouldn't stop him for long. Sweat dripped down my sides with the struggle to maintain hold as he picked away at it. I continued to assess and reinforce my construct, but I realized my inexperience left inherent weaknesses in the shield, like a steel door hinged with duct tape.

Rhyzkahl lowered his head, gaze penetrating me. "You are *mine*," he said, his voice clear and resonant.

"The fuck I am!" I called out as I braced myself to hold the seal. "I belong to myself, asshole."

"This is a new trick for a summoner," he said, working his hand into the barrier, his aura radiating angry, focused confidence. "Mzatal has trained you well for me." His eyes narrowed as he sneered. "Do you spread your legs as readily for him as you did for me, chikdah?"

"Name-calling and slut-shaming?" I asked. "Is that the best you can do?" I struggled to keep the power flowing despite the growing fatigue from the effort. "Would it bother you if I'd slept with him?" I knew that it would, and right then anything that might distract him from unweaving my barrier seemed like a good idea. "Would it piss you off if I told you he sucked on my tits then bent me over the table in his chamber and fucked me?"

Rhyzkahl's aura flared, striking me like wind off the desert. *Oh, shit.* Baiting him had refocused rather than distracted him. *Bad move.*

"Kara!" Mzatal called out in a warning, but it was too late for me to take the words back. Rhyzkahl bared his teeth, gave a sharp cry of anger, and tore at the barrier.

I backed hurriedly. Damn it. "Boss!" I called out. "No time left!"

"Ten heartbeats," he said through clenched teeth.

"Don't have it!" I swallowed heavily and took another step back.

"Channel everything you can into the barrier," Mzatal said. "Then move behind me." In a furious swirl of his hands, he slurred the last three sigils together and called for the union of the rings.

"It's going. Shit!" I felt as well as saw my barrier disintegrate as Rhyzkahl ripped through it. I scrambled to move fully behind Mzatal.

Rhyzkahl lifted his hand the instant the barrier cleared and made a vicious cast at the shikvihr. Mzatal swept his arm to ignite the pattern even as the attack struck it.

The shikvihr flared blindingly, then collapsed on itself with an earsplitting *crack* and a concussive jolt that threw me to my hands and knees. I gasped in pain and shock, watched a drop of blood from my nose splat on the stone beneath me as if in slow motion. Mzatal staggered back in the aftershocks, clearly off balance and at a disadvantage. I lifted my head and saw Rhyzkahl look from Mzatal to me, then . . . hesitate. My gut told me he didn't want to hurt me. Not that I had any illusions about it being because he gave a shit about me personally, but because he didn't want to damage his "tool." Cop-mode set in, looking for the advantage and finding it. *Maybe.*

I scrambled to my feet and staggered to Mzatal. Rhyzkahl stepped forward as he called potency to his hand again, beautiful features hardened to ugliness by what could only be hatred.

"Kara," Mzatal said, his breath coming heavily, but his voice strong. "Get behind me."

"The hell I will," I said. "I don't stand a chance without you, and he needs me alive." I only shook a little as I pulled Mzatal's left arm over my shoulder and across my chest in the same way he'd held me when I faced Vahl. Except that now I was a human shield. And though I sure as hell wasn't ready to die, it also positioned me such that Mzatal could easily kill me if things got even worse. Going to Rhyzkahl was *not* an option.

Dissonance abruptly flooded me, as though every cell in my body suddenly awoke and vibrated at an uncomfortable frequency. I nearly gave in to the impulse to pull away from Mzatal, then stopped as a strange familiarity wound through the discomfort. "What the hell?" I said through gritted teeth, eyes locked on Rhyzkahl as he stood statue-still. Hopefully the human shield bit was causing him to reconsider his strike tactics. "Mzatal?" My hands gripped his arm. "Why does this feel so weird?"

Mzatal tightened his arm across me. "I do not know," he said, his breath hissing as though in pain. "But I . . . feel the grove."

Even as he said it I could almost, *almost*, see the interplay of my grove energy and Mzatal's aura, like trying to see something through a fogged window. Rhyzkahl lowered his head and pulled more potency to him. He'd obviously figured out some way to get around my oh-so-noble defense and didn't plan on giving us leisure time to figure out this dissonance.

The familiarity abruptly clicked into place. The sigil series on the beach, the discordance I'd experienced there. "Boss," I gasped. "It's like a series out of alignment."

He inhaled sharply, and in the next instant I *felt* him mentally shift, even as I reached through the fog to him, as if tuning a ring of sigils and clasping Mzatal's mental hand all at once. The dissonance faded, and though I felt that more harmony waited just beyond my perception, I couldn't reach for it right then. Adjustment to the overlap of my grove-fueled power with Mzatal's potency required all my focus. "We can do this together," I told Mzatal with newfound confidence as I leveled my gaze at Rhyzkahl.

Mzatal pulled me tightly to him. "Kara," he said, the richness of that single word conveying his understanding of what I'd done—what *we* had done—on all levels.

Rhyzkahl cast a strike at us, and Mzatal deflected it as if it had been no more than a wiffleball. I drew more power from the grove, intaking breath at the ease with which it flowed into me, into us. I shared that power with Mzatal, offering him a deep reservoir to use as needed. I felt as much as saw the shimmering potency coalesce in Mzatal's right hand.

He extended his hand before us, opening his fingers wide as he channeled power into a wall of interwoven green, gold, and purple strands of light, erected between us and Rhyzkahl. Breathing deeply, Mzatal exerted arcane pressure on the wall, pushing.

I smiled as Mzatal forced Rhyzkahl back a step, and I opened myself more to the grove, feeling the murmurs of its semi-sentience. Rhyzkahl's gaze slid over me, and a ripple of sensation set my skin itching faintly, as though the sigil scars had goose bumps. The memory of the torture rose again, and I dove into the connection with the grove, immersing fully. Power flickered in sparkling green iridescence over my skin and through my being as I focused, added a layer to the arcane wall, and *pushed* with Mzatal.

Rhyzkahl fought to move against the dual force, face hard and determined, neck muscles and braced stance revealing the extreme physical effort that accompanied his resistance. Half-step by grueling half-step, he retreated into the tree tunnel, unable to stand fast in the face of our united effort.

"I will have you," Rhyzkahl growled, the words carrying to us and the mountains beyond.

The threat speared me, igniting pure hatred like a fountain of flame from my gut to my head. "Never!" I shouted. The grove power scorched through me, welcome and unhindered. Mzatal channeled it into a devastating strike that lanced forth in a scintillating burst of green and gold. Rhyzkahl took the blast fully in the chest, and his strangled cry twisted with the sharp *crack* as it took him down.

I bared my teeth, feeling power like a vast, still sea respond to my deep need as he sprawled to his back. Now I had him at *my* control. I wasn't the one writhing in pain this time. Power suffused me. I bore down on him with the grove energy, willing him to suffer. Willing him to *die*.

I leaned back against Mzatal, smiling as I watched Rhyzkahl struggle to shift from the supine position. Amkir stepped toward him, and I raised a barrier of shimmering grove potency between the two lords. Rhyzkahl was *mine.* I opened the floodgates to the sea of power and, through the grove awareness, I knew what Rhyzkahl felt: invisible pressure closing in on him, crushing, taking his breath. I tasted his first flickers of fear, and my smile widened. I dimly felt Mzatal telling me I had to release Rhyzkahl, but the song of the grove washed it aside, raw and wild and torrential. My breath came in shuddering gasps as power seared its way through me. Vahl sought to enter the tree tunnel, to reach the Tormenter, but I held the grove inviolate, allowing none to enter. No one would touch him but me.

I heard Mzatal shouting my name, but the words burned away as soon as they reached me. He shouted to Vahl, to Ilana, to Amkir, but my focus was on the vile sack of shit who even now could barely draw a breath.

A sudden resistance slid between the Tormenter and my power, blocking my vengeance. My eyes narrowed and I pushed harder.

Kara! Kara, you must let go!

Awareness hit me like a slap. The resistance was Mzatal as he fought to keep me from killing Rhyzkahl. *No. He deserves to die!*

Kara!

Mzatal called to me on all levels as he maintained the shield on Rhyzkahl. The loss of even one lord would throw all of the arcane perilously out of balance. Turek had shown me, and Mzatal sought to remind me now. *Mzatal.* I realized with horror that I was about to hurt him as well. Aghast, I hurriedly sought to disengage, but the power rushed through me in torrents, responding only sluggishly to my efforts. Mzatal swayed behind me, his arm locked across my chest. Rhyzkahl went still. Amkir stood in the tunnel beyond the fallen lord and my barrier, face flushed and anger palpable.

Vahl strode toward me, but I had no time to spare for him in my desperate bid to curtail the flow. His eyes narrowed, then he drew back his arm and slugged me hard.

White pain exploded in my face. The power dropped away from me like water from a burst balloon, and I sagged heavily in Mzatal's grasp. As the world spun around me, I thought I heard Mzatal yell to Vahl to get Rhyzkahl out of our grove.

Our grove.

Mzatal went to his knees, breathing heavily and still holding me. "Kara?"

I groaned. Pain throbbed in my jaw, and everything dipped and tilted around me. "Here. Ugh."

His hand came up to cradle my face, easing the worst of the throbbing and the spinning-world effect. "Rhyzkahl is gone."

Somehow I managed a woozy smile. "And you're here," I slurred.

He looked down at me. "*We* are here."

I gave him a radiant smile.

And then I passed the fuck out.

Chapter 37

I woke about a thousand years later, certain that someone had driven a truck through the bed and over me a few dozen times during the night.

Ilana chimed and stroked hair back from my face. I gave her a faintly puzzled smile, while I tried to remember why I ached from head to toe and why Ilana would be so close and attentive. "What happened?"

"Rhyzkahl sought you yesterday," she said as she brushed her hand over my forehead.

Rhyzkahl. All of it flooded back to me. "We won," I said.

She inclined her head. "Yes, you did. Rhyzkahl was denied."

I exhaled. I knew I should be elated at the victory, but tension coiled in the pit of my stomach with the memory of exultation in sharing with Mzatal and then my subsequent loss of control of the grove energy. "And Mzatal? Is he all right?"

She smiled. "Until only a moment past, Mzatal has not left your side, and then only to attend a matter that could not be left longer."

"But he's all right?" I asked again.

She smiled. "He is depleted, though otherwise well."

A feeling of ease and comfort stole through me. "Now I feel bad for waking up after he left," I confessed.

The syraza chimed in laughter. "You woke *because* he left, precious one."

"Hunh?"

"There was a peace upon you while he was here," she told me, "and you slept deeply and well. When he left, you reached for that peace like a blanket that had slipped from you, found it missing and so, awoke."

The truth of it wound through me, and I smiled wryly. "He's still going to be annoyed that he wasn't here."

"Yes, he will be," she replied, violet eyes alight with amusement. "Take the opportunity to bathe, and you will feel more refreshed when he returns." Her head tilted, and her eyes unfocused briefly. "He is still with Idris."

I considered everything that had happened in the past few days, and my smile slipped a bit. "It scared me that I liked him so much." I grimaced. "When we argued, it was like I lost something I couldn't replace. I wondered if maybe it was just Stockholm Syndrome, where a prisoner begins to have, um, positive feelings for their captor, but now . . ." I shook my head.

The syraza leaned forward. "What you name 'Stockholm Syndrome' originates here." She touched my forehead with a long finger. "Determine if the origin of your 'like' of him is here," she tapped my forehead again, "or here," she tapped my chest above my heart, "or somewhere beyond both."

"Before yesterday, I was too confused to know." I sat up and dragged my hand through my hair. "Something happened when we faced Rhyzkahl." I paused, considered. "I'm not confused anymore. It's not about weighing pros and cons in my head, and it's not a weird falling-in-love thing. It's . . ." I trailed off as I realized I didn't have words for it.

"Beyond both," Ilana said quietly. "Find the balance between the head, the heart, and that which lies beyond."

"Easy for you to say," I said with a smile. "But right now I'm going to take a nice long bath. Deep thinking will be a lot easier once I start feeling human again."

I headed to the bath and lounged for awhile as I processed the events of yesterday. We'd beaten Rhyzkahl. *Holy shit. We beat him.* My argument with Mzatal seemed so trivial now, though I knew the core of it still mattered tremendously. I remained a prisoner because of the agreement, yet it was hard to even bring up the same feelings about it. A different light had been shed on the trust between us. I couldn't explain it, but right now I knew I trusted him as much as I could trust anyone. More really.

My hands were nicely pruney by the time I dragged myself out of the bath-pool. I toweled off, slipped on a robe, and headed out, then paused at the sight of Mzatal standing in his usual spot on the balcony, looking out, hands behind his back.

I took a deep breath, padded out in my bare feet. I stood beside him, not saying anything.

"I brought you to these rooms so that I could watch over you," Mzatal said quietly. He exhaled a low breath. "And, I wanted you close."

It took me a few seconds to figure out what he was talking about. Then I realized. *Oh, right. I moved out.* Technically, this wasn't my bedroom anymore.

He shifted and splayed his hands on the rail. "It cannot be like it was."

"Well, I fucking hope not," I replied, with perhaps a hint of acid in my voice. But then I sighed and shook my head. "I hope it can be better."

"It already is," he said. "So much has clarified."

I looked over at Mzatal. I knew much had clarified for me, especially with regard to how much I trusted him. But how much had clarified for him? And, if so, in what way?

His left hand dipped into a pocket then placed a ring on the rail. My ring. The one I'd thrown against the wall. The lovely blue stone had a long crack in it.

I felt a flush rise and opened my mouth to apologize for treating his gift so poorly, but he spoke first.

"While I was on the balcony after leaving you in the workroom yesterday," he said, voice low and resonant, "I had begun considerations for the restructuring of our agreement."

I picked up the ring, ran my thumb over the fracture in the stone. "What sort of restructuring?" I asked, stomach suddenly knotted with tension.

He turned fully to me. "I would ask you to trust me as I trust you, and terminate the agreement altogether. It is a limiting factor."

The tension dropped away so completely that for an instant I felt weightless. "I'd like that," I managed to say through the near-dizzying relief. Mzatal enfolded me in his arms and bent his head over mine as he let out a long breath, murmuring something in demon.

"Thank you," I said.

"Words of gratitude are not needed," he replied. "I cannot give you what is already yours. But I accept them and offer mine to you. *Dak lahn*." He pulled away only far enough to take the ring from my hand. "I will have the stone replaced."

I shook my head. "No. Leave it. I want the reminder, corny symbolism and all." I smiled and held my right hand up, palm down for him. A smile touched his mouth as he slid the ring onto the middle finger.

I tilted my head back to look up at him. "We kicked Rhyzkahl's ass, didn't we?"

His eyes crinkled as his smile widened. "Yes. And well." But his smile faded a heartbeat later. "Kara," he said.

Exhaling, I grimaced. "I know. It got out of control," I said quietly. "I couldn't stop it. I almost—"

"Yes, but you did not," he interrupted. "It is not typical for a summoner to channel such energies and was too much without experience or training."

I thought about that for a moment. "I had something similar on Earth, I mean as far as the big wild energy." My gaze went to the distant sea. "My car went into a river, and I couldn't get out. Thought I was going to drown. Then I felt the river and *somehow* used it to bust my way out of the car. That big power saved my ass there, too, but I never actually had control over it to lose."

A thoughtful look came into his eyes for an instant, but then he gave me a reassuring smile. "I will help you learn to accommodate the grove flows," he said. "It will be a powerful tool in our arsenal against Rhyzkahl and those who stand with him."

"He's not going to give up," I said. "We need to get the damn beacon set for Szerain's blade." I thought back again to that last time on the beach. The discordance. I hadn't trusted myself or Mzatal enough to push through and set the resonance properly. "I know I can do it now."

"Yes, of this I have no doubt," he replied, expression showing nothing but utter faith in me. He paused with an air about him as though deciding whether or not to continue, then drew a deep breath. "When I had you stand before the statue of Elinor," Mzatal said quietly, "when you sank so deeply into her memories, you know that I came within a heartbeat of killing you." He paused while my breath caught at the reminder of those moments of terror. "What would I have wrought had I slain you?" His expression briefly shadowed. "And what would have happened later had my focus not shifted to exploring your potential?"

"A world without me would suck, that's for damn sure, and I'd be here haunting your ass," I said with a touch of heat, but then shook my head. "Everything we do has consequences. Everything." I looked up and met his gaze. "You had no right to do all the shit you did to me, but after going through what I've been through, and how we are now, I'm ready to live for this moment and the future."

Mzatal exhaled, and his shoulders dropped a smidge as if a measure of tension unwound. "Everything has consequences," he echoed, and I had the feeling the words touched far beyond the current topic. He shook his head as though to rid himself of whatever it was and gave me a smile.

"What made your focus shift?" I asked, watching his face for signs of anything he wasn't speaking.

"With the Elinor memories, it was that you had the presence and will to extract yourself from them. Beyond that, I cannot tell you the precise instant, nor the trigger," Mzatal said, closing his eyes and tipping his head back as though trying to recapture a distant moment. When he looked back to me, his expression held a measure of respect. "In a very short time, I came to know that you held a great love of life and possessed admirable tenacity. Both of these I acknowledged as highly desirable for a summoner, as well as useful for the retrieval of Vsuhl. But there was something . . . more." He went quiet with brow furrowed, seeking words for the rest.

"I get it," I said with a straight face. "You needed someone with devastating skills and mastery of the arcane in order to challenge Idris to move beyond the paltry efforts he's shown thus far."

Mzatal smiled. "This is a measure of your magic," he said, eyes crinkling, "your ability to truly lift my spirits. It is a precious gift. And there was—is—a sense of potential beyond my known parameters. I did not, and do not, choose to lose it. Or you."

I met his eyes with a serious gaze. "Mzatal, I promise you now that I will always be the person you can count on to bug the crap out of you and call you on your bullshit."

"And I will hold you to that promise, Kara Gillian," he said. Then, to my surprise, he let out a low laugh. "In reconsideration, perhaps I *do* know of two moments when I truly began to reassess everything about you."

I cocked an eyebrow at him in question.

Smiling, he lifted his hand to his throat, middle finger extended. "When we were last at Szerain's palace, after your injury, you touched the collar thus and said that you knew your place. I had no choice but to leave the room or laugh outright, completely dissolving my carefully maintained demeanor."

I grinned. "And the other?"

"After I told you of Elinor's energy signature. When you referred to it as," his smile spread a bit wider, " 'Elinor's magic kidney,' again it was all I could do not to laugh."

And here I'd thought he was a humorless fuck. "What can I say? I have a unique outlook."

"One I would not trade for anything."

I turned and leaned on the railing to look out at the sea. Distant clouds shrouded the horizon, and flying creatures swooped along the cliff edge. A breeze brought the taste of salt and warmth. Mzatal moved to stand next to me, hip grazing mine.

I flicked a glance his way. "So, when do we go back to finding this stupid knife?"

A hint of amusement curved his mouth. "Vsuhl is far more than a stupid knife."

"I'm not going to call a knife by a name. Especially one as silly as 'Vsuhl,' " I teased with a roll of my eyes, then raised an eyebrow at him. "Is there anything else you name?"

The amusement increased, and he raised an eyebrow right back at me. "I have names for many things. But to answer your question, we begin as soon as Idris prepares." He shifted to drape an arm over my shoulders. "But for now, I wish to enjoy the view. And the company."

Smiling, I slipped an arm around his waist and leaned in to him. "They're both pretty damn nice."

Chapter 38

My favorite faas in the whole world crouched by the side of the bed with a mug of coffee cradled in his hands. I grinned and threw off the covers. "Oh, Jekki, if you weren't already taken . . ."

Jekki tilted his head and gave me a confused burble. "Don't mind me," I said with a laugh as I pulled on a robe. "I'm punchy because I actually got a full night's sleep. And here you are with coffee, ready and waiting!" The last couple of weeks had been psycho busy with training and ritual preparation, but thanks to a progress-halting snag yesterday, I had the luxury of much needed sleep. Okay, it kinda sucked that we'd run into a snag, but, damn, I actually felt halfway rested.

I glanced through the doorway to see Mzatal still sitting at the table in the outer chamber tracing sigils and making notes—exactly where he'd been when I went to bed. I snorted. "Let me guess. He's been there all night and hasn't eaten since, what, yesterday morning? The day before?"

"Ate bits, some, morning two days," Jekki said, holding the coffee out to me.

I took the mug and sipped, then exhaled in pleasure. Jekki knew how to stay on my good side. "Right. Could you please bring a plate of fruit, some cheese, and a fresh jug of tunjen for him?" I asked. As Jekki turned to go, I added, "And a bowl of that honey custard stuff he likes." If nothing else, maybe he'd eat that.

I followed the faas out into the main chamber. Mzatal glanced toward me with a faint smile as I set my coffee on the table and moved behind him, but then immediately returned his focus to the sigil before him.

I placed my hands on his shoulders and began to massage the tight muscles. "Take a break, Boss."

Mzatal set the sigil spinning, then let out an exasperated sigh. "I still cannot determine the sequitur of this final series for the beacon, and we *cannot* proceed without it. All else is complete." He scrubbed his hand over his face in a very rare gesture of frustration.

"Yeah, well, take a break and maybe it'll come to you," I said, continuing with the massage. "You sure as hell won't figure it out when you're tense and hungry and cranky."

He exhaled a that-hurts-but-don't-stop breath and dropped his head back to look up at me. "Tense, admittedly. Hungry, undeniably." His expression turned doubtful with a hint of a smile. "Perhaps methodical, calculating, and focused. But cranky?"

I laughed. "Well, I rescind the cranky label for now, but only if you rest and eat," I said. "I know you're a big bad lord, but you still need food every once in a while." I dug my thumbs into knotted muscles. "Cripes. How long have you been sitting here?"

"Since we concluded last night," Mzatal said. He looked back to the floating sigil, dissipated it with a violent sweep of his arm, then sighed. "I should send for food."

"Way ahead of you." I smiled as Jekki and Faruk hopped in with a tray and jug. I gave his shoulders a final squeeze, then helped the two faas get the food onto the table. "Eat."

Mzatal gestured toward my mug as he poured tunjen for himself. "And what of you? You have only had coffee again," he noted.

"Coffee is the food of the gods," I retorted as I snagged some cheese and a couple of grape-things.

"You do much enjoy it," he said, selecting slices of fruit for his plate. "It is ubiquitous to Earth, yes?"

Taking a sip, I nodded. "It's a huge industry, and there are shops devoted to little more than the sale of coffee in a variety of forms." I let out a dreamy sigh. "Heaven."

"It was relatively new to your world at the time of the cataclysm," he said, "with only a century or so of any significant distribution. Once the ways opened again, I had not considered it until I noted your obsession, then discovered its use to be widespread."

"It's not an obsession," I said, grinning. "It's an addiction. Get it right."

Mzatal smiled. "Obsession with an addiction." He reached over the cheese for the custard. "My favorite," he said, raising the bowl slightly to me. "Dak lahn."

I returned the smile, glad to see him eating. "I know."

He lifted his eyes to mine, held the gaze for a moment. A sense of true appreciation came through to me before he started on the custard. "Idris has completed his work and now awaits me." He shook his head. "I am no nearer a solution than I was last night."

"Still on the final series for the beacon?"

He nodded. "The last three sigils are inharmonious, and I have yet to determine the cause."

"Can't you take a day and do something else, give your mind a break?" I asked. "You could come out and harass me by the column. I'm *soooo* close to finishing the damned first ring of the shikvihr."

"It is likely you would were we to devote the day to it," he said with an approving nod, then grimaced. "But time is short. If the beacon is not set within the next two days, we will be delayed another month, and that is unacceptable. All else is ready except this last series."

I frowned. "Another month? Why?"

"The Earth full moon is four days hence," he said. "The greatest chance of locating and binding Vsuhl is on that day, and the beacon must be completed and tended for at least two days prior in order to be optimally effective."

I gave him my best utterly-baffled look. The high level of potency in the demon realm meant that rituals weren't dependent on the moon cycle, and certainly not on the *Earth* moon cycle. "That makes no sense," I said, perplexed. "What am I missing?"

He finished the custard and set the bowl aside. "Szerain is unrivaled in arcane innovation," he said, tone shifting to one of casual conversation, as if he'd decided to discuss the weather. "Should he choose to hide something, it would not only be very cleverly hidden, but also linked to him. It would . . . resonate with him." He reached for his mug of tunjen, took a long drink.

"Ohhh," I said as comprehension dawned. Vsuhl was Szerain's blade. "So to track Vsuhl we're purposefully coinciding with Earth's highest potency time because Szerain is there." Because of the stupid oath, Mzatal couldn't come right out and say *Szerain is on Earth*, but I could. "Got it."

"To correlate with the lunar full, I *must* complete this series today," he said, a hint of the earlier frustration coloring his tone.

"That's one hell of a time crunch," I said with a grimace. "I wish I could help more."

"You spent half the day yesterday working on it with me. This time it is *my* aspect that is not aligning," he said with another deep sigh. But then he gave me a smile. "And today, you have fed me and eased the significant tension in my shoulders. That is much help, Kara."

"Well I'm going to help even more by grabbing a bath now," I said. "If Idris is free, I'll make him run me through the first ring of the shikvihr until I get it. I'm ready to nail that thing."

"Complete it," he said with a warm smile, "and I will leave this accursed series to culminate the ring for you."

I grinned. "Deal, Boss. That's one way to get you to take a break."

"Until then, though," he said with a shake of his head, "I must refocus on *this*." He traced a sigil and began adjusting strands on it. I didn't remember it being in the series we'd worked on yesterday, but it wouldn't be the first time I had less than a Full Clue.

I stood, picked up my cooling coffee, and took a long sip as I headed off toward the bedchamber. Something about the sigil nagged at me, but I couldn't put my finger on it. Yet I could feel, with increasing unease, every modification Mzatal made to it. Heart pounding unevenly, I turned and walked back to the table, set my mug down. Each adjustment of the sigil brought it closer and closer to—

I didn't ask permission, simply reached out with a shaking hand to shift the axis of rotation of the sigil, then detached an outer strand and set the whole thing into a wobbling spin.

The sigil brightened and issued a low, throbbing tone that sent an itch through my bones. The air crackled palpably and audibly as though with static. *Wrenching shoulder pain. The bite of the blade. The cold mask of his face.*

Mzatal sucked in a sharp breath, stood and backed away so abruptly that he overturned his chair. I cried out as pain like fiery needles flared across my abdomen.

He swept the sigil away with a pass of his hand. The pain vanished but I still clutched at my belly, my breath coming in ragged bursts.

"It burned," I managed to get out.

Mzatal moved swiftly behind me, dropped his arm over my shoulder and pulled me back against him. His other hand slid beneath mine to press against my abdomen where the scars of Jesral's glyph still tingled.

I dropped my head back against his shoulder. "I saw that sigil, in Rhyzkahl's ritual," I said, my voice shaking. "It was directly in front of me, in the inner ring."

"And it affected you now," he said, pressing slightly with his hand. "Jesral's glyph only?"

I closed my eyes and assessed myself just to be sure. "Yeah, that's the only one that flared," I said, slowly easing. "And it's okay now, like it never happened."

Mzatal remained silent and still, likely making his own assessment.

I swallowed. "I guess they aren't just scars after all." Helori had said as much, but denial had been a lot more comfortable.

"They are not what they were created to be," he said quietly, "but they are not quiescent, and I do not know what they *are*."

"Well ain't that goddamn peachy," I said, new apprehension settling in atop the old. I turned around so I could look up into his face, not wanting to dwell on any thoughts of the fucking scars. "I'm sorry I messed with the sigil."

"Admittedly, such could be dangerous and ill-advised," he said. "However, in this case, quite useful. The adjustments you made were an adaptation for *rakkuhr* that I did not know, but that resonates with what has been out of sync in the final ring." He gave me a slight smile. "As impulsively reckless as your action was, I now have enough insight to complete the series."

I snorted. "Go me!"

Mzatal laughed, placed his hands on my shoulders, then

leaned in and kissed me on the forehead. "Go you, indeed. Now bathe and prepare. We will begin the beacon midday at the nexus."

Smiling despite myself at the unexpected sound of his laughter, I headed off to bathe and prepare. But my smile faded as I reached the bath chamber. The scars were clearly more than scars, yet no one seemed to know what the hell they were.

I scowled as I slipped into the tub. It'd been a big deal just to get my ears pierced, and now I had arcane scarification. *Fuck you, Rhyzkahl. Fuck. You.*

Chapter 39

The sun hung low over the sea in an increasingly glorious display of fiery orange and purple, casting the black sand of the beach in shifting hues that reminded me of the album cover for Pink Floyd's *Dark Side of the Moon* album. The mild sea breeze wound around me, cooling the sweat that plastered my shirt to my body as I lay sprawled on my side on the large flat boulder. I smiled wearily. That album would be a pretty nifty soundtrack for this particular scene.

Rippling waves of power pulsed from the active ritual diagram that was set within Mzatal's nexus point. The low crash of surf against rock mingled with the sub-audible hum of the ritual in a strangely rhythmic discordance, both lulling me into a stupor and keeping me from actually drifting off.

Events moved swiftly once Mzatal knew how to tune the series of sigils. That afternoon, he'd brought us back out here to create the ritual to seek out the blade. This was like a message signal, a "Hey, wake up!" to the blade, combined with a way to lock onto it once it was found. And then, assuming that was successful, we would relocate to Szerain's palace and create a new ritual—the final one, where, if all went well, I would actually call it into my hand.

For three days we worked on this diagram, first in the creation and then taking turns tending and maintaining it. In between periods of work on the beacon, we trained and studied and prepared for the next ritual. And, occasionally, Idris and I grabbed naps on blankets spread on the sand. Needless to say, I was damn tired and more than ready to sleep in a real bed. I'd had my fill of camping out during my time with Helori. An outdoorsy chick I was not.

Adding to my fatigue was the fact that the creation of this beacon required a fair amount of bloodletting on my part, since I was the one who would make the final call to the blade. I had no problem with the actual shedding of blood; I'd been taught to summon with a diagram formed of chalk and blood, and I wasn't squeamish about making the cut. However the amount needed in a summoning was never more than a few tablespoons. I figured I'd dumped about a pint for this one so far.

The diagram thrummed and flared on the pavilion, and I smiled in weary satisfaction. In some ways it was similar to the beacon I'd used to call Tessa's essence back to her body, though on a vastly larger scale. *Rhyzkahl gave me that beacon.* I mused on that. I'd developed my storage diagram from it, which made it possible for me to summon whenever I wanted instead of being limited by the phase of the moon. No doubt there was some significance to the fact that Rhyzkahl had given me the parameters to a beacon similar to this one, but I was far too tired to explore it now. Didn't matter. I wasn't retrieving the blade for his punk ass anyway.

Idris staggered over to the big rock, stripped off his sweaty shirt and dropped it beside him. "Shit," he breathed as he watched Mzatal continue to prowl the perimeter of the diagram. The lord wore only flowing silk pants of deep maroon. No shirt or shoes, though his hair remained braided perfectly, as always. I watched with tired detachment as Mzatal tweaked a sigil, tested strands, and added additional potency to the call. Back on Earth the moon was near full, ideal for a beacon to call Szerain's blade while Szerain was on Earth. If this part failed or was performed improperly we would have to wait another month to try again.

My gaze went to where Gestamar crouched, halfway between my boulder and the nexus. Once again he had my letter to Tessa tucked into his pouch in case he was summoned tonight and had the opportunity to arrange for its delivery.

"Idris," I said. "Do you know why the demons put up with it?"

He tugged his boots off and set them on the rock. "Put up with what?"

"Put up with being summoned," I said, watching Gestamar. He had his wings pulled in close as he crouched, making himself as small as he could be, which was a lot smaller than I'd expected a reyza of his size to be capable of. "It hurts," I continued. "A lot. Gestamar told me that it hurts demons, too. But he also implied there was a reason they tolerated it, and not simply for the offerings they received." I flicked a quick glance at him. "Have you ever been summoned?"

He squinched his toes in the sand and shook his head. "No, I came through with Mzatal."

"Yeah, well, trust me, it sucks." I grimaced, remembering. "It's like being stretched and dragged over sharp rocks, and, well, it sucks." My mouth pursed. "But Gestamar told me he gets summoned a *lot*." I really hoped that Gestamar would be summoned tonight, and that shamed me a bit since I knew how much it hurt. It helped that the reyza had freely offered to carry the letter for me.

Idris nodded. "Since I've been here, if Katashi didn't summon him on a full moon, then someone else did. That Gestamar wasn't summoned last month was an oddity, but maybe that was because Katashi is—" He scowled. "—here. And a couple of times he's been summoned on consecutive nights. That's hard on him." His gaze went back to Mzatal, and he sighed. "Crap. He's not stopping."

I shifted my attention to see the lord continuing to tweak and refine. As I watched, he pulled his ritual knife, made a small slice in his left forearm and bled into the quadrant. I winced as the sigils flared blindingly.

"I thought he was done," Idris said. He scrubbed at his eyes, grimaced. He looked damn near as tired as I felt. "I should go lay support."

"I'll be your moral support," I said with a weary grin as I lifted one arm. "Go, Idris, go!"

He snorted, smiled. "Maybe I'll tell Mzatal to chill. That'd totally work."

I chuckled. "Yeah, I'll watch how that goes from waaaaaay over here." I let my arm flop back to the stone, winced as the cut broke open again. "Crapsticks," I muttered. Mzatal hadn't healed it yet, not only because it was hardly life-threatening, but also because there was every chance I would need to bleed again.

"Hopefully, I'll be back soon," Idris said. "Maybe I can get away with only laying it and not working it." He shrugged. "Normally, he'd have already told me to do it. I think he thought he was done, too." He shrugged again, then headed toward the pavilion, leaving shirt and boots on the rock.

I took a few minutes to appreciate the view of the two shirtless men. Sure, Mzatal was my teacher and Idris was, well, not someone I wanted to get involved with, but that didn't mean I couldn't appreciate the fact that both were fine specimens of the male physique.

Laughing at myself, I pressed up to sit, then took several deep breaths as my head briefly swam. Idris completed and ignited his support structure, and immediately it dimmed as Mzatal began to draw from it. Poor Idris.

Gestamar suddenly twitched. I snapped my gaze back to him. Mzatal rose from his crouch and turned to face the reyza fully.

In the blink of an eye Gestamar became a whirlwind of movement, snarling as he laid a series of wards around himself so quickly he'd obviously prepared them earlier and had been holding them ready. I watched, frowning. What the hell was he doing? Faruk hadn't done anything like this. Maybe it was different for reyza?

I flicked a glance at Idris. He stared as well, brow creased in similar bafflement. *But he's seen reyza summoned before*, I reminded myself. If this looked weird to him, then that probably meant it was.

Mzatal called something out in demon, and Gestamar answered, still snarling and laying wards. The lord watched, not moving except to clench his hands at his sides.

Mzatal gestured to Idris, eyes never leaving Gestamar. Idris hurried over, and the two exchanged quick words.

"Kara! C'mon!" Idris called as he turned and ran back to the support diagram.

Grimacing, I pushed off the rock, staggering a few steps before I got my equilibrium back. Idris had barely shed a few tablespoons of blood, the perky fucker.

"What's going on?" I asked as soon as I reached him.

Idris swept an assessing gaze over the diagram, then began to rebuild part of it in swift, precise tracings. "Hostile summoning," he told me, quickly reworking sigils, in full-blown focused summoner mode. "Gestamar resists. Can't assist directly since it's locked straight onto his signature. We're prepping in case his resistance fails." He flicked a quick glance at me. "Lay a full perimeter around this diagram. Use the ascended model, quickly."

Ascended model. I blinked. *Hey, I know that one!* I quickly moved into position and began.

Wind whirled around Gestamar, lifting sand as though he stood in the midst of a mini-tornado. He unhooked and dropped his belt with the pouches, then snorted heavily as blood burst from his nose in a spray. He bellowed and went completely still, features locked in intense focus. My pulse slammed as I finished the perimeter and ignited it with grove power. I'd never seen a demon arrive with any sort of nosebleed or demon equivalent. Then again, I'd never performed any sort of hostile summoning. I couldn't even imagine how much effort it had to take to summon a demon so unwilling. Surely whoever it was had to be using multiple summoners, not only for the power, but also to be able to counteract the resistance quickly and effectively.

Mzatal lifted both hands to trace, wind whipping his silk pants around his legs. Gestamar gave a bellow full of pain and released the hold on his wards, as if unable to maintain anymore. The portal formed as soon as he did so, and I watched in numb horror as the arcane tendrils whipped out and around the demon. Gestamar bellowed again, looked to Mzatal and said three words, then let out a horrible reyza scream as the portal enveloped him.

And then he was gone.

The wind died to nothing, and silence fell, broken only by the whisper of falling sand and the sounds of our harsh breathing.

Idris spat a curse and turned back to his diagram, swiftly reworking sigils to ground the power that rebounded through it. Mzatal moved to where Gestamar had been and began laying sigils.

I turned on Idris. "What the hell is a hostile summoning?" I demanded. "What's going to happen to him?"

"Depends on whether they manage to bind him or not. Fucking insane. Dunno what'll happen." He completed the grounding but then moved on to do something else I didn't recognize at all. "Key now is to lock down any traces here so they don't get a toehold. Can't do shit with the summoning itself, but we can make sure the door is closed and locked."

"Toehold? For what?"

He continued to trace rapidly. The scar on his hand sure as hell didn't slow him down much. "Sucking info from here while Gestamar is there," he said. "I know as much about it as you do. Speed lesson from Mzatal in about four sentences." He jerked his chin toward the lord. "Go over and find anything open and close it down. I'll finish here."

I jogged to Mzatal and began closing everything I could. This was shit I knew how to do. My gut clenched at the sight of the belt and pouches—with my letter—on the sand. Gestamar had dropped them when he realized it was a hostile summoning. Jaw tight, I continued to work.

As I completed the final closing, Mzatal sank to one knee, breathing heavily. I staggered a step back, then sat in the sand.

"What's going to happen to him?" I asked Mzatal, worried. "Who summoned him?"

A muscle worked in Mzatal's jaw, and his voice had a slight waver and hesitancy to it. "Tsuneo, Slavin, and Anton. All Katashi's."

Those were the three words Gestamar had said before succumbing. He'd told Mzatal who was summoning him. And Tsuneo was the one with the Jesral-mark tattoo.

"With good fortune, Gestamar will shred them," Mzatal said. "Without it . . ." He shook his head, hissed softly.

"Without it, what?" I asked, anxious. "What could happen to him?"

"It has been centuries since there has been a hostile summoning. There are many possibilities." Anger and what sure as hell appeared to be distress flared in Mzatal's eyes. "Most likely Tsuneo will bind him as long as possible."

Dismay curled through me. Under normal circumstances, a summoner would dismiss a demon after a few hours, but if a demon was needed for longer, the summoner could adjust the bindings so that the demon could remain a while longer without discomfort. That's what I'd done for Kehlirik when I summoned him to remove the warding on my aunt's house. It had taken him over a day to complete it, and even with the readjustment, he'd still seemed debilitated when I finally dismissed him. If there was no summoner to dismiss a demon, they'd return on their own within about a day, but it was highly uncomfortable for the demon, as they "snapped back" to their own world. At least that's what a nyssor had once patiently explained to me when I was still a fledgling summoner-in-training. Considering how miserable a normal summoning was, the "snap back" had to be truly excruciating.

But to bind an unwilling demon until he could be held no longer? Gooseflesh rippled over me. Not only agonizing for the demon to be held for so long, but the return would be devastating and no doubt put Gestamar out of commission for quite some time.

And that's what Tsuneo wants. Anger flared at the realization.

Mzatal sank fully to sit, fatigue and stress deeply etched into his features. Faruk approached and handed him a mug of juice which he immediately passed to me, his hand visibly shaking. "Drink," he murmured.

I took it and drank, but kept my eyes on him. I couldn't think of any other time that I'd seen him so affected, even when exhausted after retrieving me from Rhyzkahl. "You okay, Boss?" I asked after I downed half the mug.

"My connection to Gestamar is in flux." He passed a hand over his face. "We are essence-bound, and this is disruptive."

Turek had told me that he was essence-bound to Szerain. "Is that like the ptarl? The Elder syraza?" I asked.

He frowned slightly, took another mug from Faruk and drank as he considered. "Similar perhaps, though the ptarl have . . . have always been. An essence bond is a choice."

My worry deepened. These assholes had to have known how much this would fuck with Mzatal. I had no idea if the Earth faction knew about our plans to retrieve Szerain's blade, or if the Four Mraztur and Katashi had managed to get word back to Tsuneo and company about all that was going on, but surely this was done with a mind toward putting Mzatal at a disadvantage.

An idea took hold, and I staggered back to my feet. "We'll summon him back!"

For a variety of reasons, that rescue option hadn't been

a possibility for me when I arrived here, but we had no such limitations on this end. "I may not know much else, but I know how to summon a demon."

When I moved, Mzatal actually startled with a very un-Mzatal-like reaction, which only deepened my conviction that we had to do *something*.

"Idris . . ." He glanced back at the blond young man. "Idris yet holds the strand." Mzatal gave a nod as if adjusting to the idea of a rescue, yet there remained a bleak cast to him, as if he didn't dare pin hopes on it. "Yes. Work with Idris."

"Yeah, Boss. I'll let you know when we're set up and ready for you." I gave Mzatal one last worried look before hurrying over to Idris. Demon realm summonings required partnership between the lord and the summoner, so Mzatal would have to get his act together for that. The world swam briefly, and I scowled, wishing I hadn't given that pint to the other ritual.

"Idris," I began, then grinned. He'd heard me and was already rapidly tracing sigils, his mouth set in a hard line. I moved to the other side of the new diagram, then hesitated. I knew damn well how to create the pattern for a summoning—in two-dimensional chalk sigils. And I knew how to create floaters, but not the specific ones for a summoning diagram. Even if we hadn't been on sand—rendering my usual chalk-and-blood method utterly impossible—the past several weeks of training had shown me with stunning clarity how superior the arcane-only method was. And I had no doubt that we were going to need every possible edge if we were to have any hope of snatching Gestamar back.

Only problem was that converting a two-dimensional chalk sigil to a three-dimensional floater was a brain-melting exercise.

No, don't try and convert, I decided. *Think of what each sigil is supposed to do and then craft the damn thing.* Beginning slowly, I went back to the purest basics of how to structure a summoning circle and began tracing. Idris worked rapidly on the other side, but I did my best to ignore him and not let his speed and skill affect my own efforts. I knew what I was doing. I simply had to adjust to expressing it in a different format. Like sculpting instead of drawing.

By the fifth sigil I had a better feel for how each tracing had to be formed. On the tenth the proverbial light bulb went on, and I *saw* how to do the conversion from two to three dimensions. Breathing a sigh of relief, I picked up speed and managed to finish the perimeter as Idris started in on the conduit parameters.

"Idris," I said, starting the outer veils. "Do a linear pull in that section and link it to the main conduit vertices. Easier flow that way." I'd figured that trick out almost by accident, during the summoning of a zrila, when the polarity shifted and threatened to turn me into a bloody lump. "Trust me," I added, with a glance at Idris. He was a fucking genius when it came to this stuff, but at the same time, I'd been doing Earth-side summonings for over a decade. Sometimes real world experience made all the difference.

To my relief he simply nodded and complied, raising my estimation of him another zillion degrees. Not a cocky bone in his body. After all this shit was over, I was damn well going to find him a girlfriend, because he sure as shit deserved, and needed, one.

I flicked a quick glance at Mzatal. He still sat in the sand near where Gestamar had disappeared. Worry deepening, I returned my attention to the diagram and put the finishing touches on the foundation. All told it had probably taken Idris and me about fifteen minutes to trace it out and set it up. I could *so* get used to doing all my Earth work in the arcane tracings. *Watch out, shikvihr, I'm coming for your ass as soon as I get that stupid knife.*

"Okay, Idris," I said after a quick assessment of the diagram. "You ready?" This would work. It had to work. Surely those fucktards hadn't even remotely suspected that two summoners and a lord were right beside Gestamar when he was summoned, ready to snatch him back.

His eyes swept over the diagram in a similar assessment. Straightening his shoulders, he nodded, his mega-focus settling over him like a cloak as he positioned himself opposite me. Now we needed Mzatal.

I headed over to where the lord sat on the sand, back to us, staring out at the sunset. "Boss? We're ready," I said, touching his shoulder.

Mzatal flinched and staggered to his feet. *Damn.* Though deeply concerned, I took hold of his hand and gave him a reassuring smile. His face was ashen and hand loose in mine. Definitely not the Mzatal I knew. "It's all ready for you," I said. "We'll get him back. Don't worry."

A glance at Idris told me he didn't like the looks of this any more than I did. Something had to shift and now. I hesitated. I had a clever plan in mind to jar him out of his funk. Only tiny drawback was that it could easily end with me squished. Then again, if Mzatal couldn't snap out of this, I might as well be squished.

I drew a deep breath, hoping it wasn't my last, turned fully to Mzatal and slapped him hard across the face.

The lord took a stagger-step back and lifted his right hand. *Shit!* I thought with a cringe, then exhaled in relief as he traced a pygah and inhaled in one fluid motion. He looked at me, still shocky-looking but more focused.

"I am here," he said, voice quiet and raspy.

I took his hand again, squeezed. "Good. Let's get Gestamar."

Mzatal assessed the pattern and added his sigils, with less fluidity than usual, but solid and potent. He ignited the diagram and gave me a grim nod.

Idris and I worked quickly through the forms and readied the conduit. With caution, I extended, focused, and made the contact touch.

I maintained my focus, yet didn't open the portal. I sensed the reyza, but I didn't make the pull, simply maintained the touch for now. If there were other summoners present on the other end I didn't want to alert them. A tug of war with Gestamar in the middle would end badly for all involved.

"Idris," I murmured. "Can you tell if and how he's bound?"

"Gimme a sec," he muttered, and I realized he was already focusing down the channel. I held it as motionless as possible. The ideal scenario would be that Gestamar wasn't bound or warded in any way, but I knew damn well the chances of that were between zilch and none, especially considering the circumstances.

I watched as Idris skillfully maneuvered the summoning strands and twitched the gossamer thread he'd linked in as Gestamar was taken. *Clever*. I realized that he'd likely gotten a lot of practice at doing this sort of thing, not only during his many attempts to summon me from Earth, but also when he and Mzatal sought me at Rhyzkahl's. I smiled despite the gravity of the situation.

Mzatal shifted then went still, eyes faraway in what I knew was an extension to Gestamar.

"Mzatal?" I asked quietly, maintaining a steady hold on the ritual. "What do you feel?"

He squeezed his eyes shut, focusing. "Pain . . . arcane bindings." His eyes flew open, and he bared his teeth in the most overt display of anger I'd ever seen on him. "Kara, Idris, we must reach him. *Must.*"

"That's what we're doing," I said, automatically slipping into my calm cop-handling-a-crisis mode. "Can you do something with the bindings?"

Calming somewhat, Mzatal went to one knee and laid a hand on the perimeter of the pattern. Its resonance deepened as he carefully strengthened and fed it. Idris continued to follow the strands to their terminus, abruptly going still as a statue, barely even breathing.

"One of them is with him now," Idris said in such a soft exhalation I would never have heard him had we not all been connected in the ritual.

"Tsuneo," Mzatal said at a similarly low volume.

I nodded. "Okay. Idris, you maintain the watch, and you let me know the *instant* they leave him alone. Mzatal, you get ready to slip bindings. We're going to play a waiting game and we're going to win it."

Idris breathed a low curse. "I don't think we can wait. There's movement." A frown tugged at his mouth.

"Another ritual," Mzatal said, eyes unfocused. "Idris, can you discern its purpose?"

"No," he replied. "Gestamar is in Katashi's summoning chamber, but the other ritual is in the adjoining room." He paused. "Tsuneo is still with Gestamar."

Crap. So much for waiting for the most opportune moment. "Mzatal, how's Gestamar doing? He needs to be calm and quiet, maybe even feign weakness."

Pain flickered over the lord's face. "Thrashing. I cannot quiet him. The bindings are draining him, and he is in agony."

"If we wait any longer, it's going to get ugly," Idris said, worried expression deepening. Neither one pulled attention from their surveillance, but I could sense as clearly as if both stared at me, that they waited for my instructions. Considering the disruption in the essence bond, Mzatal was doing everything he could to stay focused. I had the most experience as a summoner. I was lead on this, and it was up to me to call the shots. It made sense, but it still felt weird as all hell.

"Fuckballs," I muttered. "Okay. Plan B, folks, since we may not be able to wait for them to leave him alone. Any shift of focus off of him will do. Idris, you give the word and hold the conduit, Mzatal, you slip bindings, and we'll yank his big ass out. With any luck at all we should be able to make it one perfectly coordinated movement, because we are awesome like that."

Idris suddenly grimaced. "Shit, all three in the room now."

Damn it! "Fine. Plan C it is. Fuck stealth. Mzatal, can you send any sort of strike through the conduit?"

A smile ghosted across his lips. "I can."

"Good. On three then. Idris hold the damn conduit wide, and I'll focus on the call. Mzatal, you zap and unbind, then we'll pull. One, two, *three!*"

The word was barely out of my mouth when Mzatal unleashed power through the conduit. I damn near lost hold as part of it reflected back on me, but Idris managed to steady the strands.

"Now!" Mzatal shouted, and we *puuuulled.* The diagram shuddered, and then with a *crack* that shook the beach, Gestamar appeared sprawled and bleeding.

"Idris, seal it!" I shouted as I quickly anchored and watched for any attempt to follow the reyza. Together, Idris and I shut down the flows and dropped protections, allowing Mzatal to go to the stricken demon. Gestamar was alive, I could see that much. He was a mess, but he was back and in what appeared to be one piece.

"Mzatal?" I asked. "Is he okay?"

The lord dropped to one knee beside Gestamar, then looked back to me, relief swimming in his eyes. "Nothing permanent." He looked up as Helori and Ilana joined him to crouch by the reyza. I blinked. Where the hell had they come from? Had they been here this whole time?

Idris and I finished shutting everything down and

cleaned up residuals. After a few minutes the two syraza disappeared with Gestamar. I grinned over at Idris. "Dude, we kicked ass."

He gave a whoop of delight in response.

"Recalling the blade will be a walk in the park after this." I laughed as I said it, yet at the same time, I meant it. We'd worked superbly as a team. Even if Rhyzkahl showed up, we could handle him.

Still grinning, Idris loped over to the big rock to retrieve his shirt and boots. Mzatal sat cross-legged where Gestamar had lain, head lowered. I crouched beside him and slipped an arm around his shoulders.

"Hey, you okay?"

"I am tired," he said without lifting his head, and for an instant I had the impression that he spoke of a fatigue that went far beyond the physical, a weight comprised of millennia of schemes and plans and plots. I had to resist a sudden weird urge to stroke his hair back from his face, which made no sense since it was still perfectly braided as always.

"C'mon, Boss," I said, taking his hand. "Everything's going to be fine."

Mzatal remained utterly still for another moment, then squeezed my hand and stood. "Were it all in your control, Kara Gillian, I would know that to be the truth."

"I'm a tenacious bitch, remember?"

He began to smile, then abruptly straightened and turned fully to the beacon diagram, grip tightening on my hand.

My fatigue dropped away as excitement flared. "Did it find it? Is it working?"

He didn't answer, barely even breathing as he kept his full focus on the beacon. A few seconds later the ritual flared, the sigils carved on the columns flickered to life with a faint blue glow, and a single clear tone sounded.

I sucked in a sharp breath as the tone seared through me, seeming to set every cell in my body alight. The sensation faded after a few seconds, though I still felt a bit strange, as if someone was watching me from the inside.

Idris came up beside me, face alight with wonder though he didn't seem as flattened by the tone as I was. Then again, I was the focus, the one who'd be calling the blade. Made sense that it would hit me the hardest.

Mzatal released my hand and draped his arm over my shoulder. "Rhyzkahl knows now."

I nodded. Mzatal had warned us earlier that the beacon would be impossible to hide. "When do we go?"

"Tomorrow. We will arrive at Szerain's palace at dawn."

I smiled. "Does this mean I can take a bath tonight and sleep in a real bed?"

He dropped his gaze to me, gave me a smile haunted by concern for Gestamar and possibly more. "Yes. We both need—" He took a deep breath. "Yes. Bath and rest for you."

"You need to sleep too," I said with a glare, though I had to admit, he already looked way better than while Gestamar was gone. "Make tonight your weekly nap." I swept my gaze around, taking in the beacon ritual and the disturbed sand that was all that remained of the battle for Gestamar. "This is going to work. We're a damn good team. I mean, look at what we just did. We kicked those asstards in the goddamn balls."

A measure of the morose pall seemed to lift from him. "Yes, it was truly harmonious."

"Harmonious asskicking," I said. "It doesn't get any better than that."

Chapter 40

I came fully and suddenly awake, as if a switch had been thrown, then lay perfectly still, listening and cautiously sensing with othersight as I tried to figure out what had roused me so thoroughly. A light breeze drifted through the open balcony doors, bringing with it the scent of the sea and of the demon-realm equivalent of pines. Far in the distance some sort of night creature called and received an answering cry. It was still full night, but the moon was higher in the sky than when I drifted off. I'd been asleep for a few hours at least.

But nothing seemed amiss. None of the wards had been tripped. No intruder or danger, as far as I could tell. Mzatal wasn't in the bedroom or bath chamber, and I didn't sense his presence in the main room. I looked to the balcony, but I didn't see him in his usual spot by the railing either. Most likely he was with Gestamar, or in the summoning chamber, in final preparations for the morning.

The grove shimmered in the distance, casting a scintillating aura of green, purple and gold unlike anything I'd ever seen from it before. I pulled the sheet from the bed and wrapped it around me as I moved out to the balcony. When I reached the rail, I tucked the sheet a little more securely, then spread my hands on the cool stone. The starry sky glittered in a cloudless expanse above, and the moon drifted high, half full. I gazed across at the curiously activated grove and carefully extended, touching the semi-sentience, gently exploring its ancient power and beauty. It responded in kind, extending questing tendrils. Still and silent on the balcony, I communed with the grove, pulled power and let it flicker over my skin in green and gold iridescence.

My understanding of it grew, as did my grasp of how to best use its potency, and, most importantly, how to control it. It wasn't "mother nature" or "Earth power" or anything like that, but more like a strange, alien power source that had been nurtured and shaped by beings long gone from this world.

And how long will I be gone from my own world? I allowed the feelings to rise of how homesick I was, how desperately I missed my aunt and all my friends. I swallowed against the lump in my throat and felt the grove respond like a song in my essence. "I miss them," I whispered. Its potency swirled around me whispering back. Though I couldn't translate what it said, I knew what it meant for me to do. Inhaling deeply, I gathered more power, enough to coalesce into a radiant orb before me.

I want them to know I'm safe.

Lifting my arms, I pulled the power into a tight coil, breathed my wish into it, then released it and watched it disperse across the balcony and to the grove and beyond in a transparent shimmering wave. Slowly the grove subsided to its usual softly glowing quiescence, though I still vibrated with the energy.

After several minutes the power settled to a gentle and peaceful resonance, and I shivered in the faint chill of the night breeze, unnoticed while I'd communed with the grove. Smiling, I turned and headed back inside.

Three steps in I stopped dead in my tracks.

Mzatal stood at the end of the bed, radiating potency, and without a trace of the earlier weariness. He wore only his robe: sumptuous deep red silk with sleeves and hem adorned in intricate silver stitching. His thick braid hung over his right shoulder, and, as I stared, he deftly unwound the silver cord that bound it. His eyes stayed on me as he dropped the cord and ran his fingers though the bottom half of the complex braid, separating the shining black strands.

My pulse made a weird double-beat. I'd never *ever* seen his hair unbraided.

"You are exquisite," he murmured, gaze devouring me as he slid his fingers through the twists of hair, freeing more of the thick fall until it hung loose below his shoulder. I took a slow step toward him, heart pounding at the effect those three words had on me.

Mzatal lowered his head, eyes intense as he lifted his arms and reached back to unweave the last of the braid. His robe parted as he did so, and . . . yeah. He ran his fingers through his hair, then shook it out over his shoulders, gaze never leaving me.

"Exquisite," he murmured again, and I damn near forgot to breathe. Unbound, his hair hung past his ass in a perfect, rippling fall straight out of a shampoo commercial. Holy shit, but he was gorgeous. Not beautiful like Rhyzkahl, but hot and male and . . . wow.

I let the sheet fall to the floor. It was a totally cliché move, but, yep, had to be done.

Mzatal smoothly shrugged off the robe and dropped it onto the chair beside him. The air between us crackled with the potency he held and the grove power that still hummed within me. His eyes traveled over my body as I slowly moved toward him, every inch of my skin tingling in acknowledgement of his gaze.

He closed the distance between us, cradled my face in his hands the same way he had when he'd kissed me to place the recall implant. The tip of his erection brushed my belly as he murmured something in demon.

"Goddamnit," I said in a rough voice. "Kiss me already."

Smiling, he did so, gently at first, then with more intensity. There was nothing pure or weird about this kiss, and that was damn fine with me. His hair fell over us as he held my head with one hand and slid the other to the small of my back. He pulled me close against him, erection hard between us as he near growled into the kiss. I knew I didn't need to ask him not to get me pregnant. Not only did I know in my essence that he would not without my permission, but I had my own means now, my own power to make certain of such things.

Groaning low, I skimmed my hands over his hips and back to cup his ass. His glutes tightened deliciously in my grasp as he rocked against me. His hand tangled in my hair, holding my mouth to his in an uncompromising assault on my senses. I welcomed it eagerly, moaning with pleasure.

His other hand moved to cup my breast, caught my nipple between thumb and forefinger and lightly squeezed. My breath quickened, and a low whimper escaped my throat. My hands stroked up his back, heat rising in my belly at the play of muscle beneath his skin. I reached higher and fisted my hands in that glorious mane.

Mzatal broke the kiss, breath shuddering as he throbbed between us. I smiled and raised an eyebrow. The big bad scary mofo demonic lord liked having his hair pulled? I tightened my grip and he groaned in response. I chuckled low in my throat, ridiculously pleased that I'd discovered something that could fire him. Despite all the time I'd spent with Rhyzkahl, I couldn't name a single thing that I knew turned him on or fired a deeper reaction. He'd always been in perfect control, never revealing himself. That Mzatal would open himself to me like this touched me deeply. Desire lit his eyes as they met mine, and he smiled, acknowledging.

In the next heartbeat he lifted me as if I'd never eaten a donut in my life, near shoving me onto the dresser, then dropped his head to my right breast. Heat flared through me as his teeth found my nipple, and I gasped in a breath. I'd found one of his buttons, but he sure as hell knew what mine were, too.

"Mzatal," I groaned and wrapped my legs around him. He was thick and hard and more than ready, and holy shit I wanted him inside me. He continued to suck and bite my breasts, wringing a variety of incoherent noises from me. I clutched at his hair, grinding against him, my breath coming in ragged gasps. "Come on, damn it."

He lifted from my breasts, gaze smoldering as he positioned against me. Passion, dangerous and heady, seethed behind his eyes. Both hands slid down to grip my ass, yet maddeningly he still didn't pull me onto him. Instead, he bent his forehead to mine, went perfectly still for what felt like forever though it was probably only a second or two. The physical retreated, and we entwined in utterly silent dreamlike spaciousness, the whole universe too small to contain us. Timeless. Transparent. He lifted his head from me, and the glorious sensations rushed in again, intensity and awareness impossibly heightened.

In a swift motion, he pressed in hard to full depth and held me there while I whimpered, nearly overwhelmed by the sensations and need.

A smile curved his mouth, and his hands tightened on my ass as he began to thrust, pulling me onto him with each deep stroke. I locked my legs around him, urging him on. His potency resonated deep within me, echoing with elusive familiarity. Instinctively, I touched the grove, pulled that power to meld with his, then sucked in a sharp breath as everything about him leaped in response. Our potencies merged in exquisite perfection, like the tone that sounded when a ritual came into alignment, but more. Every sensation, every movement, every mental touch snapped into breathtaking clarity.

Mzatal tangled a hand in my hair, pulled my head back to nuzzle my neck as he murmured something in demon. The meaning of it wound through me as he began to thrust with greater urgency. *I have missed you. And I did not know anything was missing.*

Yeah, I had what he was missing. And he sure as hell had what I wanted. Yet even as I thought it, I knew there was so much more to it than this moment of physical pleasure, and that knowledge spiked it all even higher. I made a low guttural noise as I wrapped my hands hard in his hair. His breath hissed as I pulled, and he thrust harder, which was pretty much the reaction I was hoping for. "Yes," I gasped. "More."

He was happy to oblige, grip uncompromising as he drove into me, deep cries accompanying each thrust. The scent and sound of him wound through my senses, and the feel of his skin was like a thousand points of familiar pressure. A coil of heat writhed in my belly, fired by the combined potency and his ardent attention.

He spoke in demon again as he shuddered against me, driving deep. *Come home to me, beloved. Come home.*

"Fuck . . . oh, hell yeah," I gasped. Not as poetic, but it got the point across. It only took another few seconds before I tightened my legs spasmodically, crying out as I clenched around him. Waves of shuddering pleasure expanded into limitless space, rebounding and shaking me again and again. A deep cry ripped from his throat as I climaxed, and in three more thrusts he released as well, throbbing deep within me as we mingled, merged and complete.

My breath came in uneven gasps as he slowed. My hands clenched and unclenched in his hair. I pulled him close, then nuzzled the crook of his neck as our combined potency thrummed between and through us.

Still within me, he shifted his grasp, slid his hands up my back to hold me close.

"*Zharkat*," he murmured as he nuzzled my neck. A nameless thrill went through me. Beloved.

Straightening, Mzatal lifted me from the edge of the dresser, then held me firm in his arms, keeping me deliciously impaled upon him as he moved to the bed. I kept my legs tight around him as he lowered me to the soft quilt. He looked down at me with a smile that lit his entire face and kissed my forehead, eyes and cheeks, before lowering his head to nuzzle my neck. Already he was hard within me again, and I made a pleased sound in the back of my throat as I arched into him. There was a lot to like about the stamina and quick recovery time of demonic lords, and Mzatal had no problem demonstrating exactly how easily he could bring me right back up to the peak. His hands and mouth and cock worked me into a gasping frenzy that had me begging for yet another release. With merged potencies and deep passion, we carried each other to new realms. In the end, we collapsed together in a glorious tangle of limbs and hair, spent and shuddering and smiling.

At long last I caught my breath and regained the ability to speak. I grinned over at him where he lay propped up on one elbow beside me. "Thanks, Boss."

Mzatal laughed, stroked fingers down my cheek. "I am forever dubbed thus."

"Yep, you're stuck with it!" I said, then gave a languid sigh as my body hummed delightfully with pleasure and potency.

He shifted and swept all his hair over his shoulder. I eagerly reached out to slide my fingers through the silky mass. "There is time yet for sleep," he murmured with a smile, skimming a hand over my breasts and down my belly.

My loins tightened at his touch. I could get used to this merged-potency-multiple-orgasm-thing. "I'm not sleepy at all," I said with a sly grin.

He raised an eyebrow, then his face mirrored mine in a smile. "Wrap your hands in my hair again, and I will do . . . bad things . . . to you."

I gathered a handful of hair, tugged. "How bad are we talking?" I asked. I tugged again, harder.

He closed his eyes briefly, muttered a sentence in demon that meant something along the lines of *holy fucking shit it feels good when you do that*. His reaction sent my pulse racing and heat rushing to my naughty bits.

"Bad," Mzatal murmured. "Very *very* bad." He shifted between my legs and pushed my thighs apart, lowered his head to me. I groaned and wound my hands in his hair, kept my grip firm as he did bad things that made me cry out and scream and clench in very good ways. Once I recovered, I proceeded to do bad things to him, which he seemed to find just as good.

Eventually we lay limp against each other, spent and sated. He wrapped his arms around me, held me close until our breathing slowed, then turned me to my right side and shifted to lie behind me. He dropped his left arm over me, reminiscent of how he held me during the confrontation with Rhyzkahl, pulled me back against him and snuggled his head over mine. "*Zharkat*," he murmured.

I smiled, content. "*Boss*."

He laughed—a free, beautiful sound—and held me close as we both slipped into sleep.

Chapter 41

I opened my eyes to sunlight and the distant song of unknown creatures greeting the morning. Above me the stars of the domed ceiling still twinkled. Languor and deep peace drifted through me, and I smiled as I felt an arm draped across my hips and a black curtain of hair spread over my breasts.

He stayed, I thought in delighted wonder. *He stayed and slept with me.* I shifted very carefully to face him. Mzatal had dozed in the chair less than a week ago, so I knew he'd *chosen* to sleep with me. Rhyzkahl had never made that choice, even when I asked him to. As I looked upon the sleeping lord, I realized I'd never doubted that he would.

And he was, indeed, asleep. I reached and stroked his hair back from his face, wanting to see how he looked in repose.

Beautiful. He breathed deeply and evenly, face relaxed and carrying none of the controlled mask that he usually wore, whether smiling-controlled, or scary-mofo-controlled. For the first time I felt as if I had a glimpse of the true Mzatal, and I reveled in it.

I coiled a lock of hair around my finger while I reflected on, well, everything. I cared for Mzatal quite deeply, yet I knew this wasn't any sort of "romantic" love. It was far more than that. I didn't have words to explain it, and didn't feel any need to do so. It just *was*. Even if we never slept together again, we'd always have this amazing shared closeness.

A smile twitched across my mouth. Though it wouldn't

be at all bad to do it again. Maybe some post-ritual celebration?

Mzatal drew a deep breath and stirred, a smile playing on his lips as he muttered something. I stroked his hair, and a moment later he stirred again, opened his eyes and looked into mine. He lifted his hand and set it against my cheek.

"Zharkat."

I smiled. "Hi."

His hand slipped to the back of my neck, and he brought me close for a kiss that did a lovely job of waking me up fully. He pulled back, smiling a smile that reached all the way to his eyes and shone out. "There are no words adequate," he murmured.

I let a lock of his hair slide through my fingers. "I'm not even going to try," I said with a chuckle. "And today we retrieve the blade."

Mzatal slid his hand over my shoulder and down to my hip. "Yes, we do," he said, still smiling. "And with Vsuhl, forestall much."

"We will kick all the ass," I said, deeply enjoying how at ease I felt with him.

Laughing, he wrapped me in his arms and rolled, pulling me atop him. "Is that what we will do, zharkat?" he asked. "Kick all the ass?"

I grinned, utterly delighted at the sound of his laugh. "Damn straight. We are badass, and all should fear us." I lowered my head and nestled it into the crook of his neck. Despite my brave words there was a hell of a lot to be nervous about. And I was. I exhaled softly. "I could stay like this all day."

Mzatal wrapped his arms around me. "And I as well," he said. "Were it any other day, I would not leave these chambers."

I shifted to nuzzle his neck. "After this is done, we must research how to conduct rituals from bed."

He laughed. "What do you think I have been contemplating this morning?"

"You do know I sometimes set things on fire?"

"I have faith that your skills have improved since that incident," he replied, giving me a squeeze.

Grinning, I sat up, still straddling him as I sketched a

quick series of sigils, surprising myself with how easily and fluidly I could do so. "This could totally work!" I laughed and wiggled upon him, then dispelled the series.

I felt him harden—more of that demonic lord quick recovery and response at work. His hands went to my hips, and then he lifted me with ridiculous ease and slid within me. I let out a low groan and began to move against him.

"Trace again," he said, smiling in enigmatic innocence.

I chuckled low in my throat, then did so while he did his utmost to break my concentration. After that he found new and interesting ways to distract me as I traced the next series, and the next. At long last I found myself—somehow—upon the table in the main room, the final series of the upcoming ritual drifting in luminescent perfection above me, and my body humming with languid pleasure.

"I think I know the series pretty well now," I said, grinning up at him.

Mzatal leaned down and kissed me. "You have mastered it, indeed."

"Please tell me you don't train Idris like this?" I asked, cocking an eyebrow at him.

He laughed, shook his head. "No, you have a unique advantage." He pushed off me, then picked me up and carried me toward the bath chamber. "And now it is time to prepare, that you may kick all the ass in the coming ritual."

After a bath that we somehow managed to finish without any more distractions, it was time to dress and get ready for departure.

My usual style of clothing for ritual fell into the comfortable, casual, easy-to-move-in category. Today's wasn't going to be much different, though I stayed away from anything silky and flowy. I wanted to be able to run and move and all that good stuff, but I also wanted to wear something durable enough that it wouldn't get ripped right off me in a fight. That would probably be a *little* distracting.

But since I had the style sense of a near-sighted hamster, I'd decided to throw caution to the wind and leave my wardrobe up to the zrila.

And wow, did they ever rise to the challenge: comfortable knee-high boots, black pants made out of durable denim-like material but a lot softer and a lot more flexible, and a really cool sleeveless wrap shirt with a black sash to belt it all in at the waist.

I preened in front of the mirror. "I look like a badass," I announced.

Mzatal had the grace not to laugh at my posturing. "You are indeed glorious."

I flashed him a grin. "A glorious badass." Turning away from the mirror, I took a settling breath. "I guess I'm ready to go," I said.

He took my hand. "The others await."

My nerves rose again. I had the brief impulse to pounce on Mzatal and enjoy some stress relief, but I knew that was simply a delaying tactic. Okay, it would definitely relieve some stress, but I'd still have to go and do this thing no matter what.

He slid me a look as we walked, a hint of a smile twitching his mouth. "It would be a shame to dishevel the braiding Faruk made in your hair," he murmured, telling me clearly that he'd read my impulse. His own hair was once again perfectly contained in a complex braid, its utter blackness beautiful against the grey and silver brocade of his tunic coat.

"I bet you could find a way to do it without messing up my hair," I said slyly.

His hand briefly tightened on mine. "If I were to take you now," he said, "your hair and clothing *would* be quite disheveled."

I laughed. "Tease." But even the simple banter was enough to quell my nerves. Well, somewhat. This was still a huge thing we were about to do. And neither of us had any doubt that Rhyzkahl would make an appearance.

Our footsteps on the stone path seemed loud in the still morning air as we headed to the grove's tree tunnel. The others were there waiting—Idris, Safar, Ilana, a big reyza I didn't know, as well as two zhurn and two kehza I also didn't know. Gestamar was still recovering, his absence palpable. Everyone was so damn quiet that I had the brief urge to shout, "Let's do this thing!" but I decided it wasn't the right moment. Still, I smiled at the thought.

Mzatal paced beside me, contemplative. "If you remain open to me during the ritual, it will be helpful," he said. "After last night, I am certain there is much we can accomplish together that we cannot alone."

I smiled. "I know we can."

Idris glanced up from his papers as we approached. His eyes flicked to our joined hands and then back up to my face. He gave me a nervous smile, one that I knew would vanish as soon as he was involved in the patterning.

"Hey, Kara," he said. "Big day."

I exhaled. "Yeah, not sure I'll ever be able to top this."

Puzzled, he furrowed his brow as he looked from me to Mzatal, then back to me, expression deepening into a frown.

"Yes, you will need to make adjustments," Mzatal told Idris. "The shift is likely permanent."

Idris cleared his throat and nodded, perplexity seeming to deepen.

Mzatal and I entered the tree tunnel, and the others fell in a few paces behind us.

"What was that all about?" I asked.

Mzatal smiled and squeezed my hand. "You and I are . . . different, and he must make adjustments in the ritual and support parameters."

A slow smile spread across my face as I explored the connection and merging of the two powers. Our energy signatures had changed, as if we'd exchanged a portion of our auras, bringing us into a beautiful flow of connection. "Yeah." I grinned. "We're better, stronger, faster."

"With all going as planned," Mzatal said, "we will bring a measure of stability that is sorely needed."

"Nothing ever goes as planned," I said with a grimace. I'd been on enough search warrants and other operations to know that all too well. "What's our worst-case scenario, Boss? Rhyzkahl, right? Are we ready for that?"

"Worst-case scenario would be Rhyzkahl intervening and our failure to recover the blade," Mzatal said, but then he shook his head. "No. Worse would be if he captured the blade once we had it." He gave me a look filled with confidence and reassurance. "I am prepared for Rhyzkahl this time, and we are together."

"We will kick all the ass," I told him, grinning.

Mzatal smiled back, eyes unveiled and filled with unaffected peace. "And the best case scenario is that there will be no ass to kick, and we return with Vsuhl." He stopped in the center of the grove, eyes traveling over everyone and everything, assessing and assuring that we had all we needed. He took my hand to prepare for the transfer, but then paused and gave me a questioning look.

"What is it?" I asked.

He pursed his lips in thought. "You lead. I will support for the group."

I blinked. "Me? Are you sure?"

Giving my hand a light squeeze, he nodded. "It feels right."

"Right," I echoed, then took a deep breath, soaking in the comfort of the grove to calm the sudden rush of nerves. It was here for me, ready for me when I needed it. And now I had a stronger understanding of it—its strengths and limits, and how to engage and control the semi-sentience.

"Right," I repeated with a firm nod. "I can do that." Extending, I asked the grove to take us to Szerain's palace, and within three heartbeats we were there.

I drew a deep breath, tasting the subtle difference in the air. After traveling with Helori, I knew that sharp edge, like a faint continuous flow of arcane electricity, was localized here and likely exuded from the cataclysm-born rift to the east.

Mzatal drew my arm up to link with his, tucked his free hand behind his back, and we headed out of the tree tunnel. To the north, the honey-blond stone of Szerain's palace shimmered with golden iridescence beneath a bright, cloudless morning sky. When we left nearly two months ago, Mzatal had closed and warded the double doors to the arched passage that led to the interior and the main courtyard. Now they stood open, so I had to wonder who'd visited since. The paved path rose toward the arch and, halfway there, split into three: one continuing on, and the other two branching right and left to flank the east and west wings of the palace.

"Juntihr, seek interlopers and warding," Mzatal said to the reyza I didn't know, voice focused and intense. "Idris, you know what to do, but—" He paused, frowned. "Add an additional layer. Double the pattern."

Juntihr snorted assent and leaped into the air with a bellow. Idris's brow furrowed with a quizzical look as though considering the implications. A second later he gave a sharp nod, likely having analyzed the possibilities in the time it took me simply to register the statement. With total focus suffusing his face, as if slipping into a second skin that fit better than his own, he turned and loped off down the path toward the passage. The zhurn scuttled on in Idris's wake and the kehza took flight, heading up and over the palace. Safar and Ilana paced us some distance behind.

Mzatal and I followed Idris in comfortable introspective silence, stopping only to close and ward the doors behind us. It wouldn't stop Rhyzkahl, but it would delay him or encourage him to flank the palace. Either way, it bought a little time.

We exited the passage into the overgrown tangle of the courtyard proper. Nothing had changed, yet it felt as if everything had changed. The raised circle of stone with its enigmatic eleven columns still stood among sorely neglected pathways and flower beds. The wings of the palace still angled off to the east and west. But me? I couldn't even begin to quantify the changes in me since I'd last stood here. Blatant rape of naïve innocence tended to shake things up a bit.

Letting my cop-senses assess the area, I released Mzatal's hand and headed toward the columned pavilion. I wasn't the best tactician by any stretch, but it wasn't tough to figure out that the pavilion was horribly indefensible except with the arcane.

Uneasy, I scanned the area, then looked back toward Mzatal. "Can you ask Safar to station himself on the tower there?" I asked, gesturing to a section of the palace above the arched passage that offered a good view of the grove on the other side. He nodded and turned to give the instructions while I continued on to the pavilion. Idris was already there, laying out the initial diagram. I couldn't shake the uneasy feeling, but *doing* something would help. I'd spent the last couple of weeks learning everything I needed to know about my part, and now it was show time.

"Watch out, dude," I called out to Idris, "I'm coming in."

He grinned and gave me a look of mock horror before slipping back into total focus. "Mzatal wants the patterns double-layered to amplify the resonance," Idris said without a hitch in his flow of tracing. "That doesn't change anything in the initial set-up, but when we start on the overlay, you'll have to feel into it to get the two layers to mesh."

I gave him a nod. "I can totally do that." Creating the

sigils by feel for the recovery of Gestamar last night had skyrocketed my confidence in my intuitive ability. I began to work the opposite side of the pattern from Idris, delighted at how smoothly the tracings flowed. *All that practice with Mzatal this morning*, I thought with amusement.

The main ritual pattern dominated the circle of stone, reaching almost to the columns themselves. With the double layer, it pulsed in multicolored beauty at about chest-level, quiescent sigils shifting subtly, primed and ready for ignition. Once we'd checked it over for continuity, Idris gave me a grin and thumbs up then moved out to his designated place about halfway between the pavilion and arched passage. I wasn't keen on him being exposed like that, but it was the right place for the damn support diagram.

After a brief assessment, Idris traced a compact pattern and ignited it. With an impressive burst of heat that stirred my hair even twenty yards away, he seared a neat circle in the overgrowth, efficiently clearing the ground for his patterns. Damn, the dude had skill.

I still couldn't shake the sense that I was forgetting or overlooking something. Nearby, Mzatal danced the overlays for the main ritual with such grace I couldn't help but smile. I cast my gaze out, seeking the demons. Safar perched on the roof. Juntihr flew high above. One kehza stood atop the wall of the western tower, and the other flew circles above the ruined eastern tower. I didn't see the zhurn or Ilana. *Surely we have enough eyes, and I'll feel it if Rhyzkahl comes through the grove,* I reminded myself.

Before I knew it, the diagrams were prepared, and it was time to begin. Mzatal joined me in the center of the main diagram while Idris took up his position within the support structure. Smiling, Mzatal caught my face in his hands and kissed me, tender yet with a heat beneath it that whispered hints of what he'd done to me this morning. I relaxed into the pleasure and comfort of the kiss. I could trust him utterly. I knew this deep in my essence. Yes, we were lovers now, but we were still friends and partners, and that trust would never waver.

He gently broke the kiss and gave me a radiant smile. Releasing me, he turned and lifted his hand to trace the first sigil of his shikvihr, but before he could do so I took hold of his braid and gave it a not-very-gentle tug.

Mzatal froze with a sharp intake of breath, then turned on me with demonic lord speed, catching my head between his hands in a move that should have struck fear of neck-snapping death into my heart. Instead, I smiled up at him, meeting eyes that shone with playful heat over shadowy depths. He bent and touched his forehead to mine, closed his eyes and murmured, "Dak lahn, zharkat. Thank you." I felt his gratitude far beyond the words, and encompassing so much more than this moment. He pulled me into a quick embrace, then released me, smiling. "Now, work. Vsuhl awaits."

I grinned, turned, and set about doing my part of the tracings. The potency of the ritual rose, the three of us working in a harmony that I wouldn't have thought possible until the Gestamar summoning last night. It was even better today. Beautifully unified power flowed between Mzatal and me, but Idris followed and maintained with astounding ease and adaptability. He traced sigils with a keen efficiency that would have likely left me gaping if I'd been able to spare the attention.

With a torrent of arcane power, the patterns ignited, flowing through me with sweet perfection. In a perfect dance of tracings and dispersals we wove the summoning, called to the blade named Vsuhl. I'd thought it kind of superfluous and weird before—to name a blade like it was a sentient creature—but not now that I could *sense* it. With the first touch I felt it, knew it: *Vsuhl.* Gooseflesh crawled over me, and I wanted to feel it in my hand. The blade's power began to infuse the ritual, and I smiled as I met Mzatal's eyes, seeing nothing within them but certainty that we would succeed.

The tingle of the grove reached me as a new harmony within the pattern. "Rhyzkahl comes," I calmly told Mzatal without pausing or stopping my tracing. We'd known this would likely happen, and Mzatal was prepared to hold him off until I had Vsuhl.

Mzatal's face went to the intense, unreadable mask. He nodded once and worked through the patterns to exit the diagram. "Maintain and continue. I will meet him."

The grove activated again, and I nearly fumbled my tracing in shock. "Wait! Mzatal, it's not just him." Swallowing hard, I extended toward the grove to get a better sense of what was happening. "Oh, fuck."

Mzatal reached the outer edge and turned as soon as he was fully out, already tracing new protections. "Who?"

Cold seared through me as I felt who was in the grove. "Rhyzkahl, Jesral, Amkir, and Vahl." Four! There was no way in hell we could stand against four. Maybe they'd play by their own rules and only engage one-on-one? Amkir hadn't intervened during the grove fight, so I had a measure of hope. In any case, it was far too late to shut down the ritual and make a run for it.

Mzatal's eyes narrowed, but otherwise he displayed no reaction. "Idris, lay pure defense with a support core." His voice dropped to Scary-MoFo intensity. "Kara, these chekkunden have already gone far down a dangerous path and the stakes are high. They may well dishonor our ways." Anger flared in his eyes, and I sensed it was directed at least partly at himself for not anticipating this level of treachery.

Crap. "What do we do?" I asked, doing my best to keep my cool.

He turned back to me, eyes hard on mine. "You *must* get the blade," he stated. "With Vsuhl and Khatur, we can hold against them even if they come in force. It is too close to let go now." He lifted his chin. "You know what you need to do. I will meet *all* of them."

I nodded, but worry knotted my gut. "Boss, be careful."

A whisper of a smile curved his mouth. "And you, zharkat." He turned away and took up a position about twenty feet from the edge of the main diagram, then began to lay a mobile foundation of glowing sigils around himself. The distance did nothing to diminish our bond, and I smiled in the comfortable rightness of it.

The bellows of multiple reyza sounded in the distance, and Safar took flight. The odd trumpeting call of our kehza signaled their rise to challengers. *Fuck. The game's really on.*

I spared a glance to Idris in the support diagram where he moved in a ceaseless flow of tracing. "Kick ass, Idris!" I said, giving him a wink and a smile.

He glanced over and grinned. He was pumped full of adrenaline. Probably had no idea how bad a direct combat situation could get, and I wasn't about to inform him. Then again, he was dug into a damn good defensive position with his diagram. Plus the pattern here not only mirrored the one at the nexus on the beach, it also linked fully to Idris's support diagram in the unique way developed by Mzatal and Idris. We were a kickass unit. I could only hope it would be enough.

I continued to trace and work the ritual. This was what I needed to do. The blade was close, but I knew I didn't have time to complete the next three rings and make the call before the lords could engage Mzatal. But I did have time to finish another ring before those assholes made it to the courtyard.

With the fullness of the ritual and the light merge with the grove, I felt Rhyzkahl in the tree tunnel. He moved through it and away from the grove with a speed that made me wonder if perhaps he didn't like being within those leafy walls since nearly being crushed by that power. I smiled at the thought as I continued tracing.

A few minutes later, Rhyzkahl rounded the base of the west tower, striding with arrogant confidence, badass and beautiful in full-blown potency. Behind him Jesral stalked with contained precision. Vahl trailed them, glancing around, wary and watchful. Through the connection with Mzatal, I sensed Amkir delayed by the warding on the passage door.

Why Vahl and not Kadir? I wondered. Kadir was one of the Four Mraztur, as Seretis had called them. *Maybe the other lords don't like dealing with Kadir any more than humans do*, I thought with a curl of my lip. That actually made sense. I couldn't help but feel a shimmer of disappointment that Vahl had thrown in his lot with this crowd. Then again, he didn't seem all that fired up to be here.

Rhyzkahl's eyes locked on me. I smiled and flipped him the bird while continuing to trace, and I also pulled more grove power. We were fucked. I had no doubt about that. Best I could do was keep on doing what I was doing.

Rhyzkahl bared his teeth and held up his right hand in a motion I knew would call his blade to him. His hand moved stiffly and without any of its normal fluid grace, and when he opened his fingers to receive the blade, it exposed an ugly, ropey scar.

I laughed out loud at the sight of it. I knew damn well how he'd gotten it—when Mzatal had sent potency through the blade in order to disrupt the torture ritual and save me.

"Fuck you, you worthless piece of shit!" I shouted at

him. "Guess you'll have to learn to jack off with your other hand!" What the hell, I might as well have some fun before we all died horrible deaths.

I felt Mzatal at the other end of our bond, balancing me out with deadly and silent potency as he wove sigils into a complex pattern in preparation for the lords' approach.

The blade coalesced into Rhyzkahl's hand. *Rakkuhr* wrapped itself around his fist in shimmering reds and coiling shadow, and he visibly shuddered. With blade in hand, he lowered his head, focusing fully on me with a palpable intensity.

Rowan.

I sucked in a breath as the name smothered me and slid through my essence. I faltered in the construction of a sigil, trembling to my very core. The entire ritual flickered and dimmed as I stared, stricken, at the unfinished sigil.

Kara!

My eyes snapped to Mzatal. He wasn't looking at me, but I knew that touch had come from him. The name drifted before me like a life preserver before a drowning person. In that instant I knew I had a choice. *My* choice. Slip under the sea of fear, or reach out and take what was offered, reclaim what was *mine.*

"I. Am. *KARA!*" With the proclamation, the trembling gave way to exultant determination. *I know who I am.* I bared my teeth and finished the sigil, relieved when the ritual stabilized.

"Not for much longer." Rhyzkahl didn't shout or seem to raise his voice, but the words carried to me as if he'd used a megaphone.

I flipped him off again and continued flowing through the ritual, though I did check the perimeters of the diagram to be extra super sure they were secure. Rhyzkahl advanced on Mzatal, Jesral to his right rear by only a pace. My hope that they'd engage singly evaporated. Their combined potency crashed on the verge of the ritual like storm-driven surf, and I struggled to maintain both the perimeter and my connection to the ritual itself.

Sealing the ring of sigils, I ignited it. I stood silent and unmoving for a moment as the power of the growing ritual suffused me with a tingling arcane heat. My awareness expanded with the power. I could sense where everyone was in the area—five lords, two humans, and damn near too many demons to count. I sensed Amkir moving through the passage. I saw my connection to Mzatal—not like a strand but as a constant flow and melding of energy between us. We *were* greater than the sum of our parts, and my faith deepened that we would succeed.

Breathing deeply, I began work on the next ring. Only two more. I felt the blade on the periphery of my awareness, a roiling sun of power. Fear rose. Within a heartbeat I recognized it as a remnant of Elinor, made myself breathe, and separated from the reaction. With unexpectedly gratifying recognition of the blade, I bared my teeth and breathed its name. *Vsuhl.*

"Mzatal." Rhyzkahl spoke the name with dark vehemence, words carrying clearly on the sea of power. "I give you this single opportunity to return that which is *mine*."

"Nothing here is yours, nor ever was," Mzatal said, continuing to weave and trace sigils with calm, elegant speed and precision. "We offer you this single opportunity to withdraw."

I laughed. "You don't get to keep the toys you break," I called out. "Didn't your mama ever teach you that?"

Rhyzkahl turned on me and went demon-lord still. The potency surrounding him sucked in so close and tight, I thought he would break into a billion pieces if anything touched him. I locked my gaze with his and continued to weave and trace.

His stillness shifted into dynamic motion in the blink of an eye. He gave an unnerving cry as he threw his arms wide, expanding and drawing to himself the fullness of the shadow and blood of *rakkuhr*. I'd sure as hell struck a nerve in Rhyzkahl, but I didn't have time to wonder about it right then. Shifting darkness illuminated by brilliant red arcane discharges surrounded him and lit his eyes with glowing intensity. I'd only *thought* he looked badass before.

Mzatal moved only to widen his stance, opening his left hand low and slightly out to his side, and raising his right hand open, palm toward Rhyzkahl. He gave every indication that he was acting purely in defense, but I knew from our shared connection that he had plenty of options for attack and wouldn't hesitate to use them.

Amkir emerged from the passage and headed straight

for Idris and the support diagram. *Fuck!* I knew Idris had a strong pattern, but I wasn't sure how well it would hold up if Amkir decided to truly attack it. In the sky and on the ground, demons battled. I knew that ours were sorely outnumbered, but at least for now they seemed to be holding their own. I hated that I couldn't spare any energy to try and help them, and could only hope that they would handle themselves and that none would get hurt.

Rhyzkahl's face revealed fury, certainty, and triumph as he brought his fully ignited blade in front of him and cast a heavy strike at Mzatal. In the split second before it reached him, Mzatal called Khatur to hand and lifted it high. The blade summoned the strike like an umbrella lightning rod, the *rakkuhr* channeling into it, and the residuals shedding off like rain. With his other hand, Mzatal shot forth a very sneaky left-handed strike, catching Rhyzkahl fully in the chest.

Rhyzkahl staggered back from the unexpected assault, shaking his head to clear it. Jesral strode forward two paces and sent a shimmering net of potency toward Mzatal. With practiced ease, Mzatal deflected the net, then moved in sweeping strides to fully engage in a perilous dance with both Jesral and Rhyzkahl.

On the other side of the courtyard I sensed Amkir moving closer to Idris and his diagram. The lord made a motion to strip the outer perimeter, but the well-constructed pattern thwarted his efforts. Amkir snarled, gaze traveling over the support diagram, the ritual, and then to Mzatal. Anger swept over his face as he realized that all were tied together. It had been a brilliant move on our part to link the diagrams and support together when we'd assumed that at most we'd be facing one lord. But now I worried. Four lords was an entirely different story. Mzatal currently handled Jesral and Rhyzkahl masterfully, especially with the support from Idris and his ability to draw on the grove power through me.

What the hell was Vahl doing? He hung back near the palace wall, a good thirty feet or so from either Rhyzkahl or Amkir. But Amkir, unopposed, had all the time in the world to pick apart Idris's circle, and he did so now, prowling around its perimeter, unweaving a strand at a time.

I cursed under my breath and tried to channel power

toward Idris and his diagram so that he could reinforce his defenses, but I wasn't sure it was working. I watched Amkir warily and nurtured the connection with Mzatal. Amkir's eyes were on Idris, dark and intense as he sent spikes of disruptive energy toward him.

"Dispel your perimeter, little summoner," Amkir said with a sneer. "And this will not hurt nearly as much."

Idris merely scowled, continuing to maintain the perimeter and tend the support core. His scowl seemed weirdly familiar, but I couldn't spare the focus to try to place it. I finished the ring of sigils and locked it down before igniting it. One more. The blade blazed clearly in othersight. Tears stung my eyes, surprising me with their onset and the sense of kinship that accompanied them. *Vsuhl. Once you are in my hand, all of this will be over.*

My entire circle wavered abruptly, as if in a brownout, and I hesitated in the preparations for the final ring. Mzatal still held his own against the two lords, but now Idris was deeply involved with fending off Amkir. Idris shot a quick look at me, most certainly noting that I'd set the second-to-last ring.

Amkir sent a spike through the perimeter, and Idris staggered. Then, before I could say or do anything, Idris abruptly unwound a sigil and severed the connection between my diagram and the support core.

I stared at him in shock. There was no way for me to finish the final ring without that support. But then I realized what he'd done. By severing the connection, he was protecting me and my diagram. If Idris lost control of the support core while I worked the final ring, it could jeopardize the entire ritual and would open me up to attack.

That means he knows he can't hold it, I thought in dismay. I struggled to think of something I could do, some way to help Idris, yet with the connection severed I could do nothing with the arcane. I extended through to the master ritual on the beach, felt its power, but I didn't have the skill to draw upon it. I touched the grove energy, but it flowed through and down into the patterns, feeding the ritual, feeding Mzatal.

Amkir sent another spike through the breach he'd created. Idris went to his knees, then tipped forward, barely getting his hands in front of himself in time to keep from fully collapsing. Blood dripped from his nose and mouth onto the ground beneath the patterns, sending shudders of distortion through the entire diagram. In a heart-wrenching effort he sought to stand and regain the unraveling patterns, but the strands of both the support core and ritual slipped away.

I sucked in a breath as his circle fractured completely. Idris had severed the connection just in time, but was now completely and utterly vulnerable. Having Vsuhl in hand would kick all the ass but—although I could feel the blade so close, so present—I couldn't finish the damned ritual without Idris's support. I had to do something. No way was I just going to stand there and let Idris get smeared by that fucking asshole.

Amkir had his back to me, between Idris's circle and the full ritual, and I made a quick decision. After making certain that the completed rings were stable and that the entire diagram was keyed only to me, I called grove power and tapped the connection with Mzatal. I'd never tried anything like this before, but I wasn't going to let a little thing like that stop me. All I needed was a burst. I slid out of my ritual and ran for Amkir.

The lord meticulously ripped through the circles of the diagram now that Idris could no longer hold them inviolate. He lifted a hand, and I knew it was only a matter of seconds before he called deadly potency down on Idris.

With everything I had, I pushed a barb of power before me. Lowering my head, I slammed into Amkir as hard as I could, tackling him to the ground. He let out a surprised *oof*, and in that moment of advantage, I grabbed his shoulder and turned him over. I came down hard with my knee on his groin, and at the same time punched him hard in the face—backing it all with grove power. Then I slugged him again just to be sure. "I got your *chikdah* right here, motherfucker!" In that moment, even with pain flickering in his eyes and his precious lord-blood flowing from his nose, he looked more shocked than anything. It'd been a gamble that he didn't have any physical shielding active, but apparently an attack by a human was *way* down on his list of possibilities.

I rolled off dickwad before he could recover and hurried to Idris. "Come on. Let's get your ass someplace you can hunker down." A recess in the wall of the west wing looked like a damn good choice. It had probably housed a statue at some point, but stood empty now, perfect for tight defense. I hauled Idris up and put his arm over my shoulder while I gripped him around his waist.

He staggered along with me toward the recess. He shook his head, trying to get his bearings, and spat a congealing mass of blood. "Fuck. Sorry," he mumbled.

"Don't be sorry," I said. "You kicked ass." I hurried with Idris toward the alcove. He looked gawky, but in reality he was a solid hunk of muscle and goddamn heavy. Shadows of many engaged demons flitted over us, a reminder of the conflict fought on a different level. A kehza trumpeted and careened through a high window ahead, shattering glass and crashing noisily into furnishings within. As we reached the wall, I glanced back in time to see Amkir getting to his feet. "Crap."

Idris put his back to the wall of the recess, looked beyond me and saw Amkir. "Shit . . . shit! I need to re-lay the external aspect or you won't be able to finish the final ring." The worry in his face deepened. He seemed oblivious to the blood trickling from his nose and mouth. "And Mzatal. Shit. I lost his support. Not enough time to do a new one with asslord coming."

I looked toward Mzatal. He was heavily involved, but still maintaining, at least for now. Yet without any support I didn't know how long he'd be able to hold against both lords, and I had no idea what Vahl would do. Maybe, just maybe, Vahl was honoring something of their codes and not getting directly involved? Amkir moved toward us, head lowered and nose dripping blood, radiating a mega-potency that clearly said he wanted to squash me like a bug.

"Look, you have to survive this, first and foremost," I told Idris. "I can support Mzatal. You do what you have to do to defend yourself here. Got it?"

"Survive." He gave me a bloody smile and began to trace rapidly. "Yeah, good plan. Got it."

I grinned. "Kick some ass, cuz. I'll hold off Lord Asshole." I didn't have any idea if I could really do that, but I hoped that I could at least draw Amkir away from Idris. Taking off at a run, I angled away from the alcove and toward the pavilion, checking to make sure that the lord was focused on me and not Idris.

As I'd hoped, Amkir turned to follow my movement and started on an intercept path. I felt Mzatal take a heavy dual strike from the two other lords, falling back and nearly going down. He needed me back in the ritual so I could focus and maintain our connection. I ran hard for the diagram, but Amkir quickened his pace, and I knew there was no way for me to beat him there.

"Shit." I skidded to a stop in a move like sliding into third base, pulling grove power into a shield thingy as I faced Amkir. My breath came raggedly as he approached. This was really going to suck ass.

Amkir raised his hand, blood still dripping from his nose, and murderous intent in his eyes. I tried to judge if I could make it around him, but there was no way. He advanced, and I backed. Behind him I saw Vahl skirting the perimeter of the pavilion, eyes on me. Great. From bad to worse. But I was damn glad now that I hadn't fucked him after all.

Face contorted in fury, Amkir strode forward, breathing heavily. "Insolent *cunt*," he snarled as he lifted a hand, coiling potency into his control.

I held the shield of power before me, trying to think of some sort of really witty comeback. "Oh, fuck off, you limp-dicked, piece-of-shit fuckstain," I yelled. Hey, it wasn't all that witty, but it would have to do.

His face went dark with rage as he cast the potency at me. I crouched in the utterly wild hope it would miss me. A shadow passed over, and everything exploded in motion as two reyza, locked in combat, crashed hard between Amkir and me, absorbing much of the strike in their own shielding. The rest struck them and seared past me, shattering the stone of the pathway behind and to my left. I swallowed hard. That wasn't meant to take me down. It was meant to take me *out*.

I glanced over at the two reyza still locked in combat challenge, and did a double-take. Kehlirik and Safar grappled, potency burns marring both, but the instant I looked toward them, they turned their heads in unison to me for a bare moment, eyes meeting mine. A heartbeat later, they snarled and broke into limping flight, buffeting each other and resuming their challenge in the air. *What the hell?* Had the two deliberately taken that strike to save me?

I didn't have time to think about it. Potency crackled, and Amkir gave an angry cry. My eyes snapped to him, and I blinked in surprise to see that Vahl had lassoed Amkir's wrist with a strand of potency. Amkir, holding a partially prepared strike, turned fully on Vahl.

Vahl spoke in demon to Amkir, but with the grove power running through me, I got the meaning. *No, she is not to be killed.*

Amkir ripped the lasso away. "You *dare* to interfere with me?" he growled, calling more power to hand. I didn't stick around to see how this would play out. I got my ass out of there and sprinted for the diagram. I couldn't complete the last ring without support, but I could damn well channel everything to Mzatal from there.

In my peripheral vision I saw Idris rapidly completing his defense diagram, and found myself hoping it would be enough to save his ass. A moment later I felt his patterns flare. I did a stutter step in shocked realization and glanced over to him. *You gutsy son of a bitch.* He'd danced the first seven rings of the fucking shikvihr as a foundation—not for defense but for new support. *Well, he's certainly learning how to deal with distraction*, I thought. Doing it on the column would be a walk in the park after this.

With the attention of the various lords diverted, I managed to make it back to the diagram and slide through the sigils. Already I sensed Idris rebuilding support. *But will it be enough and in time*? Mzatal was damn close to getting his ass kicked. Amkir had abandoned his retaliation against Vahl and had joined Rhyzkahl and Jesral in their attack.

I traced a pygah first and took a precious second to breathe it in, then quickly began to trace the final ring. So close. The ritual spiraled up into a perfect harmony of power. *Vsuhl*. The name resonated from and with my very essence. Mzatal, with his back against a column at the perimeter of the ritual, took a devastating triple strike that sent him to his knees. I lifted my right hand up above my head as I finished tracing the final sigil with my left. The three lords advanced upon the downed Mzatal.

"Vsuhl!" The name leapt from my throat with startling

potency. I felt the glorious heat of the blade coalesce in my hand. White-hot fire surged down my arm and through my core, filling me with intimately familiar power. Gripping the hilt tightly, I lowered the blade. My whole body vibrated from the inside out with the promise of potential, like a swarm of angry bees confined in a sack. I smiled, then sent out a burst of power that knocked the three lords back on their asses.

I breathed deeply. That was more like it. With the combined power of the grove, the culminating ritual, and Vsuhl, I was a motherfucking badass.

Like ripples in a pond, the ritual flared in rings around me. When the perimeter ignited, a sound like a massive gong reverberated, and the carvings on the surrounding columns blazed with prismatic light. Clear tones rang out one after the other around me, unique for each column. The flowering vines encasing three of them vanished in instant incineration. The tones united in a continuous low thrum that fueled me like gas on a fire. The swarm of bees in me doubled in number and furor. I didn't know how my skin held together with the intensity of the vibration, but I wouldn't have traded it for anything.

Mzatal was on his hands and knees just beyond a column. He tried to speak but coughed up blood instead. The lords got to their feet but I simply knocked them down again, laughing. I didn't feel at all helpless now. *Fuckers. You're mine now.*

Rhyzkahl and Jesral dragged Amkir up and then retreated a good distance away. I took the time to make sure that Idris and Mzatal were all right, though I kept an eye on the three lords. Mzatal struggled up to a standing position, keeping his feet in a wide stance for stability. He turned toward me, breathing heavily, bleeding from mouth and nose, with a deeply troubled expression on his face.

"Kara," he said, holding a hand up toward me. "Ease your grip."

I looked down at the blade in my hand and then back up to him. "Why would I do that?" I asked. "It's okay. It's perfect." And it was. Why wouldn't it be?

Mzatal took a staggering step toward me. I felt him extending and touching me on a level beyond the physical. "Because it is too much too soon," he said. His voice was ragged, lacking its usual strength. "Remember what happened in the grove conflict. Just ease your grip. Trust me."

I looked over at the three. They clustered together at least twenty yards away, but I couldn't tell what they were doing. I frowned, hesitating. But I trusted Mzatal. That much I knew. The power of the grove leapt within me. It wanted to fully join with the blade energy again, wanted to meld into something perfect and huge. *Again?* The eagerness of the grove lit my cells, a glorious overlay on the supercharged blade energy. More. More! There was an ancient taste to it, but I remembered how easily I'd succumbed to the lure of the power during the previous battle with Rhyzkahl.

I eased my grip on the blade, shuddering at the decrease in power. Vsuhl touched me with whisper-traces of assent. The thrum of the columns eased to barely audible, and the bees settled into a milling mass. Mzatal let out a breath as if he'd just watched a pin put back in a grenade, then began to work his way through the ritual sigils to me. "Good. Keep hold, and balance," he said. He glanced back at the three, brow furrowing. I followed his gaze and saw that all had their hands on the hilt of Rhyzkahl's blade. What the hell were they doing?

My cop-sense lit up, that vibe that had served me so well in the past of "something's wrong." Those three were up to something. They hadn't retreated. But we had the blade now. If we could get through the passage and get the hell out of here, then everything would be okay. *But they're not gonna let us just walk out.*

"My Lord!" Idris suddenly called out, alarm coloring his voice. "Kara! The perimeter. Something's happening to it!"

Even as the words left his mouth my bad vibe feeling increased about a hundredfold, and my upper chest, abdomen and right side ignited in a burning itch. *Shit!* Three of the sigils carved into my torso flared. I shot Mzatal an anxious look. He continued to work his way through the diagram to me, moving with utmost caution through the pattern so as to not leave behind any weaknesses or breaches in the protections. The ritual was over and the blade in my hand, but now we had to keep what we'd fought so hard to gain.

"Mzatal," I said as the burning itch increased. "The sigil scars—"

I didn't get a chance to finish my sentence. The three

lords lifted Rhyzkahl's blade and sent a seething mass of shadowy red *rakkuhr* arcing my way, far too familiar from my time in Rhyzkahl's ritual. Still gripping Vsuhl, I threw up my hands in pure instinct to shield. The *rakkuhr* struck the blade, sending a shudder of remembered torment through me. Scintillating strands of ruby lightning strung between the blade in my hand and the one in Rhyzkahl's, and I steeled myself for the pain that I'd been so well conditioned to expect to follow. Vsuhl leapt in my hand, dragging my arm upward, and with a single surge I felt it expand and consume the ugly potency, sucking the strands into itself with an ear-splitting whine that culminated in an ominous *crack*.

The three lords staggered back from each other. I jerked as the power slashed through the blade and into me. In the span between one heartbeat and the next every sigil on my body ignited in a sheath of pure agony. My hand spasmed tight on the hilt of the blade, and I instinctively called more grove power. I didn't even think, simply reacted to fight off the attack, to stop the agony, pushing out and away as hard as I could. I was barely aware of the wall of power I struck out with, only dimly seeing that I knocked everyone in the courtyard flat, human, demon, and lord alike.

I sucked in a burning breath. The three different potencies coiled in a fierce maelstrom within me, like a volatile chemical reaction. These were not meant to exist within one person. It never should've happened. The natural perfection of the grove could not exist with the anathema of the *rakkuhr*. Had blade energy not immersed me, had it not entwined with the grove, the grove and the dark potencies would have simply existed together but separate, like oil and water. But that third power was the catalyst, the trigger, igniting a wrenching cascade of dissonance, like the swarm of bees madly dashing themselves into one another. The unified thrum from the columns shattered into a discordant wall of sound. The prismatic light of the sigils on the columns shifted to inky blackness

Shaking, I dropped to a crouch as I tried to pull it all back in. This was bad. This was really fucking bad. Eyes wide, I breathed in shallow gasps as I carefully pulled the power back, shoved it down. Each heartbeat seemed to last minutes, pounding through me like the tolling of a bell. As

I felt the power settle within me, I slowly stood. I could do this. I could fix this. All I needed to do was let go of the grove. That would stop it.

But I wasn't holding the grove power anymore, not the way I always had before. Now it rushed like a river through me, impacting the lava of the *rakkuhr*. I couldn't let go of the river, couldn't hold it back, and the lava refused to be cooled.

My skin burned, and I looked down, shocked and at the same time not surprised to see that the sigils glowed with a fierce red-orange light. I felt as if my body could barely contain me. I trembled, hot and cold at the same, but a heartbeat later realized that it wasn't all me, that the entire courtyard shook with a deep tremor. A wind rose from nowhere, whipping my hair about my face.

Mzatal struggled up to a crouch. "Kara!" he shouted above the rising wind, shock and horror on his face. "Drop . . . the . . . blade!"

I panted for breath as if somehow that could cool the raging furnace within me. I struggled to ease my grip and drop the blade, but it was as if he'd asked me to drop my hand. "I can't!" It was a part of me—not physically, but it might as well have been.

The worry in his face deepened to distress. "Idris!" he called. "Take it down! Take it all down!"

Rhyzkahl staggered to his feet, shock written across his features, and still clutching his blade. He started to move toward me, but I flicked the fingers of my left hand and sent him sprawling again. I didn't want him anywhere near me.

"Kara!" Mzatal took a step closer to me, extending to me on all levels. He held his blade in front of him as if to shield himself from my power. "Kara, you must stop."

I was trying. Couldn't he feel that? Another tremor shook us, accompanied by the sharp crack of splitting stone. The demons had all gone to ground, huddling with wings folded close against the fierce gusts of wind. With unnatural speed, dark clouds shot through with purple lightning filled the sky. Rhyzkahl pushed himself back to his feet, teeth bared as he took a step toward me, posture bowed as if leaning into a heavy wind. The sigils burned and throbbed with the triple potency, and I knocked him back again, grinning ferally as he went tumbling.

My vision grew weird, as if everything was far too bright, but with no way to squint or shield my eyes. I felt Idris working frantically behind me, dispelling his circle and then peeling away the layers of my own diagram.

My breath hissed through my teeth. I felt and saw the power coming off me in misty tendrils. It probably looked cool as all hell, but I also knew it was seriously fucked up.

Kara!

"Here," I whispered, clinging to Mzatal's essence-touch. It felt as if the echo of our merged energies was the only thing holding me together at all. He took a step back as Idris dispelled the diagrams. Rhyzkahl stood again, blade held in front of him. As he took a step forward, the sigils on my torso flared, sending searing razors of pain through me. I felt the bindings, the wrenching of my shoulders, those ten heartbeats when he brought the pain.

Crying out, I lifted my hand. I only wanted to hold him back, but the power came from me in a heavy wave, knocking everyone flat again. Behind me, Idris let out a choked scream as he lost hold of the pattern. The diagram fractured with a whine that felt and sounded *wrong*. Light flashed over Idris in a discordant wave, and he crumpled in the grass and was still.

Gasping shallowly, I shook my head to clear it. *Idris. I hurt Idris*. Panic and terror clawed at me. I couldn't even think with the cacophony of the columns threatening to vibrate me apart.

Kara!

"Here!" I cried out. My eyes found Mzatal's. "Mzatal, help me. I can't stop it!"

Mzatal struggled to his feet again, nose streaming fresh blood. "We will stop it, Kara," he said in a calm voice that I both felt and heard. He took another step back, toward Rhyzkahl.

Amkir and Vahl both sprawled on the ground as though injured, while Jesral clawed up to his hands and knees. The black and violet clouds boiled overhead. Tremors rolled ceaselessly. The sharp bite of the air increased a hundred fold, setting hair standing on end.

Mzatal turned to face Rhyzkahl as the pale-haired lord moved up beside him. Their eyes met, antipathy and intensity literally sparking in the potency between them. The wind continued to rise to near hurricane strength. The ground heaved, and I staggered to stay upright. A massive crack of stone sounded above the clangor of the columns. Glancing left, I sought its origin, then stared in horror as the western tower lost much of its foundation to a wide crevice. The tower sheered vertically, half of its mass crumbling in a low rumble of stone on stone into the depths of the rift. Flashes of color marked furnishings, paintings, and statuary lost in the tumult. Szerain's studio. His personal chamber with its hundreds of memories captured in sculptures. All gone. Even amidst all the tumult, my heart clenched at the loss.

The two lords continued to stare at each other for a half dozen heartbeats, and then turned in unison to face me as if they'd come to a truce. Mzatal approached me with Rhyzkahl a step behind. I focused on him, vision shifting strangely. The power burned within me, completely beyond my control, but with it came an awareness of *everything*. I knew every blade of grass, every stone, every lord. Amkir struggled to stand. Jesral staggered toward the downed Vahl on the other side of the courtyard. I felt every demon, felt Idris behind me—still alive, thankfully, though who knew how long that would last if Mzatal couldn't help me stop this.

Mzatal reached and grabbed my right wrist, calling deeply to me, touching me through our shared connection.

I sucked in a breath as my blade responded to his. Vsuhl emanated a tone that soared through me, lifting, potent. Not audible, but *felt* in my essence. Mzatal's Khatur answered in a harmony that unified the energies, wound them together, and I heard them, knew them, expanded into the new joining. Everything vibrantly translucent.

Mzatal called to me, and I answered: *"Here. Here. Here."* I turned my head to look at him, looked into him. A pinpoint of blinding light in vast darkness. "Mzatal," I breathed. "So lonely."

He froze, hand on my wrist, eyes locked on mine, acknowledging. Rhyzkahl stepped forward with a scowl. My gaze shifted to him. I saw him. All of him. Crystalline leaves adrift on swirling water, far from the tree. Pushed by inexorable winds into foul depths. "Dear one," I whispered. "So lost."

He straightened, face going liquid for a brief flash before returning to the mask of determination. Vsuhl extended to Rhyzkahl's blade, to Xhan, and then recoiled violently sending a crashing wave of discord through the entwined melody of Vsuhl and Khatur. I trembled with the discordance, grateful that Vsuhl withdrew. The blade song wrapped around me, wrapped around us. Vsuhl, Khatur, Mzatal, me. I expanded. Xhan sought to join, but the *rakkuhr* dominated it, smothered it.

"All of you, so lost," I whispered. The wind ripped my words away, yet I knew they carried to all corners of the courtyard. "Foolish dear one."

A syraza appeared behind Mzatal, laid a hand on his shoulder. Ilana. Not the one I wanted. Needed. Not *my* syraza. *"Eilahn!"* My voice carried through the universe, unstoppable.

Mzatal shifted his grip so that it covered my hand over the hilt of the blade. I returned my burning gaze to him. "Take it from me."

Mzatal's mouth pressed into a hard line as he gripped Vsuhl's hilt and tried to wrest it away, backing it with potency when he found it immovable. "Ah, zharkat," he murmured such that it touched my very essence with its sorrow. Ilana stepped back, vanished.

My expanded awareness flared an instant too late as Jesral threw his dagger at my exposed back. I jerked hard as the steel buried deep, piercing my heart. Rhyzkahl gave a cry of rage and cast a powerful strike at Jesral, sending him into a tumbled heap. Pain seared through me even as deep memory stirred. Time swirled and slowed. I slid between the moments.

The gate, so perfect, has become a wild maelstrom. How? What did I do wrong? Now the ritual tears at me, tears at the world. I cannot stop it! Lord Szerain's face is cast in alternate mottled patterns of light and dark as the patterns flicker and fail. Help me. My lord, help me! He will stop this. He will save me. He steps close and wraps his arm around my waist from behind, murmurs something in demon against my ear. I don't understand what he means, but I trust him. He has me now. He will save me. Pain blossoms in my chest.

My entire body convulsed as the memory collapsed into darkness, the Elinor aspect recoiling. "No!" I screamed at everything, needing to see beyond this moment, recognizing in Elinor of then an echo of what raged within me now. Vsuhl vibrated against my palm, whispering just beyond my understanding, its tone shifting and winding through the grove energy. Whispering. *Rakkuhr* churned within me and over my skin. Molten metal dripped to the stone as the seething potencies in my body expelled Jesral's knife, healed the tissue in its wake. For all Jesral's many and terrible faults, he'd known the way to stop the breaking of the world, but had not the means.

I knew who had the answer. Knew who'd stood at the center of the destruction of the world. Knew who wouldn't look at what came with the pain. Burning, I felt Mzatal and Khatur calling to me, through me, Mzatal's hand wrapped around mine, around Vsuhl, around us. I willed time to slow. Slid between. Called up the pain, called to Elinor.

Pain blossoms in my chest, and I look down. Lord Szerain's fist is wrapped around the hilt of his blade. No. No! I don't understand. I don't understand! He bears me to the floor. Cold face. Cold stone. Cold inside. Pain. More pain. Only pain. Giovanni's face. Save me. Elinor Elinor Elinor . . . Elinor Elinor Elinor . . . forever. Pain.

I sank to my knees, this pain eclipsing the roiling power. Vsuhl whispered. *Held within. Entrapped. Rakkuhr. Pain for all. Rakkuhr entangled. Elinor.* And more that came through from the blade, beyond words. And then the pain receded to be replaced by the burning of the three potencies. Wind, cracking thunder, and shaking ground greeted my return from the time slide, and I breathed heavily.

I understood so much more, yet I had no time now to process it. I bared my teeth and climbed to my feet. Mzatal and Rhyzkahl stood before me, small, but not insignificant.

I spoke to Vsuhl. *You stopped this before. How do I do it now?*

Vsuhl whispered, its meaning flowing through me. *Two blades. I will open the way. I will hold you. Not them. I am here. Waiting.*

My gaze touched the two lords. "Both. You both must end this. Strike me with both blades. It's the only way." I understood. No normal blade could take me down now, no strike of a lord's potency. Nor could a single essence blade. Too much was in motion. Too much boiled within me. I shuddered, or perhaps it was yet another quake. The tremors grew more severe. Chaotic dances of lightning lit the near black sky. "I won't be the cause of another breaking of the world."

Mzatal touched me deeply through our connection, sharing with me his stricken resignation.

My tears burned away before they could fall. "Do it. Do what you must."

A syraza appeared two paces beyond the lords, and my heart leaped with a fierce relief and joy. Eilahn, aroused from stasis by the potency of my call and the sheer fucked-up-ness of my situation. She stretched her wings and placed her right hand on Rhyzkahl's shoulder and her left on Mzatal's. She wasn't here to save me, I knew. No one could do that. But she would be with me here, now, at the end of it all.

Rhyzkahl's free hand tightened into a fist. "There is no other way," he said through clenched teeth. As I watched, I felt him detach, his face taking on that icy look I knew so well.

Mzatal's eyes were deep wells of pain as he shifted his grip on his blade. I felt their blades, knew their blades. Like the first ignition of the columns, the Three should have resonated in harmony. But the *rakkuhr* spiked the melody, fractured it, punctuating it with bone shuddering disharmonies a hundred times worse than fingernails on a chalkboard.

Eilahn left the lords and moved behind me, took hold of my shoulders. I leaned back against her, deeply grateful for her support. I tipped my head back and looked up at the roiling sky. *I never got the chance to say goodbye to so many people.* "Please find a way to let my aunt and the others know," I said to Eilahn. Let them have closure at least. The wind screamed around us, but her chiming came to me even through the noise and discordance, and I knew she'd heard and would do as I asked.

She slid her arms around my shoulders, holding me close to her.

<<Are you sure it's the right time?>>

A cold touch wound around me, a razor coil of ice.

The two lords exchanged looks that said everything from *I fucking hate this* to *Do it now.*

The cold touch deepened, and something tugged at me through the maelstrom of power.

<<Yes, now hush and sit down. I think I have her.>>

Mzatal shifted his grip again. "*Zharkat*," he murmured, then moved in for the strike. Rhyzkahl moved barely a fraction of an instant behind him, yet before either blade could touch me, a flash of something like comprehension came over Rhyzkahl's face. With demonic lord speed he knocked Mzatal's strike wide to cut deeply into my right forearm instead of driving into my chest.

"Summoning," he hissed to Mzatal.

And then the breaking world dropped away.

Chapter 42

I knelt on smooth stone, Eilahn's wings curled protectively around me as I gasped raggedly for breath. Tremors wracked my body, as much from the shock of the summoning as from the abrupt surcease of power rushing through me. Pain lanced up my right arm, lost in the flood of churning sensations. I heard Eilahn murmuring in demon above my head as she cradled me to her, supporting me in ways far beyond the physical. Searing pain of backlash raked through my body, and a harsh cry escaped me, but before it could burn deeper, the resonant potency of Vsuhl engulfed me, easing the backlash and quieting it.

Not stone, I slowly realized as my ability to focus and think returned. I wasn't kneeling on stone, but concrete.

A hissing sound like drops of water on a hot griddle drew my attention. I stared at the deep gash in my right forearm for several heartbeats before I remembered that Mzatal's blade had bitten there rather than my heart. Blood ran in sluggish rivulets down my hand and vaporized on the long blade I gripped tightly against my thigh. *Vsuhl.* I felt its whisper still. Voices and movement around me retreated to fuzzy distance. With each hiss of blood the pain in my arm lessened. *Vsuhl,* I breathed. I felt its answering touch, knew something of its sentience after what we shared while the world broke apart. But the world no longer crumbled, and a familiar, ubiquitous and wonderful stench identified my location. Earth.

Eilahn withdrew her wings as I lifted my head, though she kept her arms around me. A chalked diagram surrounded me, looking strangely dull and crude after all I'd witnessed in the demon realm. Its sigils and protections wavered with a feeble glow, and even as I noted it, the luminescence faded to mere chalk on concrete. A few paces away was another, smaller diagram. A storage diagram much like—no, *exactly* like the one I used. *This is my summoning chamber.*

My gaze went to the summoner. Tessa. I almost didn't recognize her at first. Exhaustion and strain marred her features, and it looked as if she'd lost weight. Not that she had any to lose in the first place. But as my eyes met hers, the exhaustion dropped away to be replaced with a fierce joy and triumph that was one hundred percent Tessa.

"Welcome home, sweets," she said, voice trembling slightly in emotion and fatigue as she finished anchoring and grounding the remaining portal strands.

"I'm home," I croaked, stunned. I shook my head to clear it, then struggled to stand, only able to do so with Eilahn's help. "I'm home," I repeated, then gave a uneven laugh. "You saved me. Wow. Best aunt ever."

"Kara!"

I turned at the familiar voice. A grin spread across Ryan's face as he took a step toward the diagram. Zack was there too, giving me a fond smile.

"Ryan!" My smile began then faded. Warmth radiated into my palm from Vsuhl, and I tightened my grip in protective reflex on its hilt. Its whisper intensified. *Szerain.*

Ryan jerked to a sudden stop. He stiffened and took a long strangled intake of breath, eyes wide and intense on the blade in my hand. Zack laid a hand on Ryan's arm.

Ryan. Szerain. I staggered, dimly aware of Eilahn steadying me. "Ryan," I breathed, trembling in the wake of the power overload. "You killed her," I whispered hoarsely. "Imprisoned her for *centuries*." Elinor's essence, trapped within the blade for all that time. In pain. So much pain. Vsuhl and Elinor had shown me the horrific truth, and the sense of it ran through me in uneasy shivers. "*Centuries*." The word hissed through my teeth with a touch of my own personal potency.

Ryan's face contorted in a tangled mess of shifting features, anguish and exultation. He inhaled, a long throaty sound as if drawing breath for the first time, and shuddered, eyes on the blade. Zack gripped him by the upper arm. His regard went to Ryan, then to me, then back to Ryan, as if balancing on the razor's edge of decision.

Ryan . . . no, he was far more Szerain now. Different face. Broader of cheek. Fuller lips. Higher brow. The same as in Elinor's memories. Out of the corner of my eye I could see Tessa backed to the wall, eyes wide. I knew that the revelation of Ryan as a demonic lord had to be a *teensy* bit of a shock, but I couldn't spare any attention for her right then.

Zack tightened his grip and put a hand on Szerain's head. I knew Zack intended to submerge him again in that moment, and my stomach lurched.

"Dahn, *dahn!*" Szerain said, struggling to pull free as Zack spoke in demon. With the residuals of the power still flickering through me I understood the meaning. *Only for a moment.*

Szerain stilled, gave a single nod. Zack's brow creased with worry, as if hoping he wouldn't regret this decision. Slowly he released Szerain's head, but kept a firm grip on his upper arm.

I trembled and clenched my hand on Vsuhl's hilt. Szerain lifted his head and met my eyes, his own glistening bright as if with tears. A heartbeat later, he stared again at the blade as though inexorably drawn. Shudders ran through him every few seconds, and his head jerked to the side as though with a heavy tic.

"Slew Elinor. Created you." He took a step forward, shoulder pulled back where Zack still held his arm. He shook, shifting between an aura that radiated jubilant freedom and chaos.

I took in the differences between him and Ryan. His facial features had changed, but his build was the same and his eyes the same gold flecked with green. But even with the disturbing aura of chaotic flow—and I had to wonder if it was a touch of madness from his long confinement—he was so *alive*, so potent.

"Why did you hold her?" I asked, voice breaking, knowing—*knowing*—how much Elinor had suffered. I understood she had to die, just as I almost had to die. But entrapment?

He drew a deeper breath, straightening, though his eyes never left the blade in my hand. "I had the choice of unraveling the world or—" He hesitated. "—slaying Elinor." A shudder passed through him. "And yes, holding her," he said, with a haunted quaver in his voice. "I will not speak of why." He knew what it was like to be held, even though it was of a different nature.

A shiver of realization went through me as Detective Marco Knight's tranced words echoed, spoken to me only a few months ago during the investigation into Lida Moran's stalker.

Evil is often a matter of perception. Even the most powerful get screwed. The world was at stake, and he had to make a terrible choice. Sometimes the punishment fits the crime far too well.

Horrific entrapment for horrific entrapment? Was that what that meant? Knight had given no indication that it referred to Szerain, but that's what I'd guessed the moment I heard it. And it sure seemed to fit here. Far too well.

Gooseflesh crawled across my skin. "Is killing and trapping Elinor why you're in exile?"

He shook his head once. "Only—" He stopped as Zack tugged on his arm, as if to prevent him from saying something he shouldn't. Szerain shot Zack a look that clearly said, *I can't take this anymore*. He drew a deep breath, gathered what potency he could, gaze returning to Vsuhl. "It was most assuredly a contributing factor to everything."

Szerain lifted eyes filled with a perilous hunger to mine. "My blade," he said, voice low and fractured. He held out his hand. Twitched heavily. "Kara, give me Vsuhl."

I took a step back, chilled. Vsuhl rested cool and quiescent in my hand, telling me all I needed to know. "I don't think that's a good idea." I felt Eilahn at my back, silent and supporting, wings half-spread.

Zack's grip tightened on Szerain's arm.

"It is time it came back to me," Szerain said, baring his teeth slightly, hand still extended. "Time to end this madness." Clear in his eyes was the certainty that once the blade was in his hand everything would be *different*. And I knew that to be true.

Zack reached for Szerain's head to put him back under, but with a feral snarl, the demonic lord ducked the hand and twisted in Zack's grip, nearly freeing himself.

"Kara!" Zack shouted. "Send Vsuhl *away*!"

Sucking in a breath, I looked to the blade in confused

shock. Send it away? How? I didn't have more than a second or two to figure it out. Mzatal and Rhyzkahl seemed to simply will their blades to them and away. *Is that it?*

I did so, simply willed it to go elsewhere, felt its acquiescence, and jerked in shock when it actually did. "Holy shit."

Szerain gave a strangled cry between dismay, frustration, and fury. "*Dahn!*" He closed his extended hand into a fist, shaking more as the quiet potency of the blade departed. Zack wrapped an arm around him from behind. Szerain struggled vainly as the Elder syraza clamped his other hand over Szerain's forehead and pulled his head back.

Dismayed, I stepped forward. Stricken horror replaced the determined, haunted intensity in Szerain's eyes, as if he knew he could do nothing to stop what was about to happen. "Dahn. No. I will subside. *Jhivral,* Zakaar . . . please," Szerain gasped, voice near breaking. "I will subside."

"Please, Zack," I said, agonized, reaching a hand out toward him. I knew the torment that awaited Szerain. "Please don't."

Zack looked from him to me and back again, clearly assessing us both carefully, weighing options and determining if the risk was worth it. He slowly eased his grip. "You have a moment," he said, and only the tension in his voice betrayed how much he despised all of this.

Szerain closed his eyes and drew a deep breath. I knew without doubt that he was calling a pygah, and in a few heartbeats he visibly calmed in both features and energy. *How long has it been since he's been able to do that*? I wondered with a deep ache.

Szerain opened liquid, ancient eyes and met mine. "Dak lahn. Thank you."

I gave a slight nod in response, watching him.

His brows drew together as though he heard or smelled something he couldn't identify. His eyes shifted around, then came to rest on the exposed sigil on my chest. A muscle in his jaw leaped as his eyes traced the contours, expression shifting as if the patterns spoke to him. "Fuck," he murmured, then lifted his gaze back to my face. "Rhyzkahl?"

A chill went through me. My lip curled. "Kri."

Szerain went demonic-lord still, a deep seething anger, long submerged, perceptible behind his eyes. Without warning he ripped fully from Zack's grasp and moved toward me, eyes on what he could see of the sigils. I sucked in a breath and took a step back, but before he could reach me Zack grabbed him by the collar and seized his arm once again.

Szerain pulled against the restraint. "Release me. I must touch it. You *know* I must touch it."

Zack maintained his hold, looked from him to me. "Kara?"

"Let him," I said, feeling Eilahn's solid presence behind me.

Szerain moved in closer with Zack still holding his upper arm, intensity in his face intermittently shot with anguish and instability. He lifted a hand, laid his full palm against my upper chest, sucked in a breath.

"*Rakkuhr*. One sigil for each qaztahl, and one more to . . ." He tipped his head back, took a shuddering breath and then released it in what could only be relief. "Not completed."

"No," I said, throat dry. "Mzatal saved me."

Realization flashed across his face. "He was the one who summoned you. He is ever the wisest of the three." He shook his head. "There were times he should have listened to me. But far more when I should have listened to him." He let his hand drop from the scars. "Fuck Rhyzkahl. *Fuck* him."

I snorted. "Been there, done that. Rather not."

His mouth twitched into a smile. "And I told you it was a very poor idea."

I smiled back, seeing a shimmer of Ryan in him for the first time.

"Szerain," Zack said, a subtle strength in his voice. "It is time. You know it must be done, and it will only get harder if we delay."

An eyes-wide panic came to Szerain's face. "No. No," he said, shaking his head. "I *cannot*."

"No," I said to Zack. "Please. You can't do that to him." Numb horror rose at the memory of my own brief submersion. "It's too cruel. You can't!"

Zack didn't look at me, kept his focus fully on Szerain. "I must, Kara. He draws attention thus." He gave a hiss as Szerain backed away.

"I *cannot*," Szerain said, radiating a fear and horror that looked and felt utterly out of place on him. "And there is much I must do."

"Then we'll hide him!" I grabbed Szerain's hand. "We'll use the cuff or something. You can't submerge him again!" I shook my head. "Mzatal showed me what it was like. I can't let you do that to him."

Szerain gripped my hand firmly as he backed to the wall. Zack kept his eyes fully on Szerain. "Kara, it must be. We cannot hide him."

Szerain's eyes flicked to the stairs, clearly ready to flee. Eilahn stepped between Szerain and the exit. I looked at her, agonized.

"You can't let him do this!" I told her, keeping a tight hold on Szerain's hand. "*Please.* It's torture."

"Szerain," Zack said, speaking the lord's name clearly and with his own potency. "*You* can flee and defend and retaliate, and seek to right that which you have made wrong and that which has been made wrong in your name." He paused. "But what of Kara, and Tessa, and Jill, and," his voice dropped lower, "the one unborn." I knew he spoke of Jill's pregnancy. "What of others who might be harmed by those who would not tolerate you free on Earth?"

A deep and horrible ache went through me as I felt the keen truth of Zack's words. Time on Earth was precious to the demonic lords, and if and when the Mraztur made a play to confine an unsubmerged Szerain, they wouldn't give a shit about collateral damage. I also knew that I would willingly submerge myself to protect Jill and the baby and the others. My eyes filled with tears, but I didn't say anything to Szerain. It was a horrible and terrible thing to agree to, and I couldn't encourage it. All I could do was be here for him. Openly crying, I took both his hands in mine.

Szerain breathed through bared teeth. He saw the truth of it as well. He gave a frustrated cry as he gripped my hands hard, shaking in earnest as he looked from Zack to me. I remembered the locks of hair, the paintings in the shrine, the hundreds of statues in his chambers. To Szerain, the fate of a few humans might actually matter. Would it to another lord?

In an instant, he gathered me to him, bent his head close to mine. "I am Ryan. But I *am* Szerain." He drew a deep and shaking breath as he clung to me and I to him. "Do it," he told Zack. "Do it *now*."

Immediately, Zack put a hand to his head. I held Szerain close, fucking hating this with my entire essence.

"Kara," Szerain said with burning urgency, "tell Mzatal we were wrong." He shook harder as the submersion began, weeping against my neck. "Remember me."

Wrong? About what? I wanted to ask, but I could feel his face shift subtly where it pressed against my neck and knew it was already too late. "I'll remember you," I said, crying and sickened. "I swear."

He still shook, but now it was more a shudder of reaction than of pain. He made an *urrk* sound and lifted his head. I looked up. He was all Ryan now.

I fought to pull myself together and smile. "Hey, big guy," I said, doing my damnedest to keep my voice steady. "Glad to see me or something?"

Confusion flickered through his expression, then he gave a shaky smile. "Yeah, ya think?" He straightened, scrubbed a hand over his face self-consciously.

"Summonings do that to me too." I quickly wiped my own eyes. "Missed you." I gave him a hug, then looked around the room. Zack looked both queasy and relieved. Tessa still stood pressed against the wall, eyes on Ryan and me. I grimaced inwardly. Forgot all about her. Crap.

Yeah, Tessa and I were definitely going to have a long talk later on. About many things. I met her eyes, held my hand out while silently urging her to not ask, to not shatter this fragile Ryan.

Tessa swallowed visibly, then pushed off the wall and straightened her shoulders, settling her usual confidence and attitude about her like a mantle. She moved to me and took my hand, and I pulled her into a tight embrace.

"Thanks," I said, voice suddenly hoarse.

"Always," she murmured. "Now take care of your other business here." With that she gave me a proud smile, then turned and headed up the stairs.

I exhaled, then looked back over at Ryan. "So, did you bring donuts?" I asked, trying to restore some sense of normalcy.

He blinked, still trying to get his bearings. "Yeah, upstairs." Ryan's shaky smile spread into a grin. "You think I have a death wish? Get you back from the demon realm and not have any donuts for you?" He rolled his eyes. "You'd kill me." He lifted a hand to my face. "You're really back. God, I was so worried."

I bit my lip to keep it from trembling. "Yeah, I'm back."

"Ryan," Zack said, fully back into his easy-going surfer boy/FBI agent persona. "I need to talk to you for a few minutes after you give Kara her donuts."

Eilahn chimed softly. "And Kara has had a very long and trying day," she told both men. "She needs to bathe and to rest."

"Yes, *mom*." I rolled my eyes, yet at the same time a deep relief speared through me. I *was* exhausted, and I needed time to process everything before facing Ryan again. I also doubted that Zack truly needed to talk to Ryan. More likely he wanted to make sure that Szerain was fully locked down. My mind shuddered away from that thought as I tucked my arm around Ryan's waist.

"C'mon, bitch, gimme my donuts," I told him.

He laughed, draped an arm over my shoulder in an unsettling echo of Mzatal's gesture. "My god, you're cranky. I knew I should've had them waiting down here."

"Yeah, thought you were smarter than that," I said, then made a *tsk*ing noise. "Forgot. You're a fed."

He laughed again and gave me a squeeze as we climbed the stairs together.

Chapter 43

Eilahn bundled me upstairs and bandaged the gash on my arm, though the bleeding had long stopped, and it already looked as if it was closing on its own. Once that was done she helped me into the bathtub and kept an eye on me as well, which was a damn good thing since I ended up falling asleep. Would've been an ignominious way to die, especially considering all the shit I'd managed to survive thus far. But she got me out, dried off, and into bed, and by the time I woke up late the next morning, I felt almost coherent enough to make all the decisions I knew I needed to make.

One thing I knew for sure was that I had to get back to the demon realm as soon as possible, which meant summoning Mzatal tonight. It was only a matter of time before the hunt for me began—whether to kill or capture—especially now that I had Vsuhl. I wasn't safe here, and none of the people close to me were safe either. I needed the shikvihr and everything else I could absorb so that I could become the badass I needed to be and return here as soon as possible. I had a pretty strong feeling that Earth was where I'd be able to make the most difference with the shit coming down. Therefore, I was going to be working and studying as if the fate of the world depended on it. Which, y'know, it did.

However, a *planned* visit to the demon realm meant I could actually take some of the stuff with me that I missed while there before. I spent the next couple of hours running errands and shopping with Eilahn—now in human form—and Zack. Both stated quite firmly that I was not to be more than five feet away from either of them at any time, and I was to complete my errands as quickly as humanly possible and then get my ass back behind strong wards.

Around noon I headed home to discover that Tessa, Carl, Jill, and Ryan had taken over the place and were deep in the throes of readying a Welcome Back celebration. Eilahn and Zack didn't look the least bit surprised, which led me to believe they'd been willing accomplices.

I was surprised to find a handful of presents for me, held patiently from Christmas, a month past. The best was my lovely leather coat, which had been either thoroughly and professionally cleaned or replaced outright. I apologized for not having anything to give to anyone, and everyone lovingly teased me for my failure to do any shopping before Christmas, so it was all right.

Jill gave me a fierce hug as soon as she got me alone. "If I start bawling it's only because I'm pregnant and hormonal and has nothing to do with how worried I was about you."

I grinned and hugged her back. "Of course not!"

She pulled back, then narrowed her eyes as she searched my face. "You've been well-fucked within the last couple of days.

Mouth agape, I stared at her. "How do you *do* that?"

Jill snorted. "It's my only superpower." She leveled a frown at me, but I saw the dark worry in her eyes. "Bad shit happened to you, didn't it."

I simply nodded. I had a sweater on that hid the sigils, but Jill had a way of seeing beyond the physical.

Her jaw tightened. "Rhyzkahl?"

I nodded again.

She glowered. "Fucker. You can tell me about it later. Come on. Let's eat cookies until we burst."

After presents and cookies I went hunting for Tessa. I finally found her on the back porch, sitting in the porch swing with her boyfriend Carl, their hands entwined. As I stepped out he leaned over, kissed Tessa on the cheek and stood, then surprised the hell out of me by taking my shoulders and kissing me on the forehead before heading inside. I blinked, nonplussed at the utterly unprecedented and unexpected show of affection, then sat in Carl's spot beside Tessa.

"I'm so glad you're okay, sweets," Tessa said, then turned a piercing look on me. "You are okay, aren't you?"

I thought back to all the shit that had happened—the

escape, the betrayal, the torture. But she hadn't asked if I'd had a lovely time. She wanted to know if I was okay.

"Yeah," I said, smiling, knowing it to be true. "I'm really okay." A comfortable silence fell as we gently rocked. Snatches of voices came back to me; the voices I'd heard in the seconds before I was summoned—Ryan and Tessa.

Are you sure it's the right time?

"How'd you figure out how to do the storage diagram and get me back?" I asked. "And for that matter, how did you know *when*?" The chances of me accidentally being at a hotspot if she was trying randomly were approximately zilch.

"Would you believe me if I said it was a dream?" Tessa asked. She gave me a soft smile.

I chuckled. "Actually I think I might." I'd had enough dream sendings to know that some could be very real. I thought back to my corny wish. *I want them to know I'm safe.* Well, they sure as shit knew it now. How the hell did *that* work?

"So," she said after a brief silence. "Ryan's a demonic lord."

"Yeah." I grimaced.

Her mouth pursed. "Well that's just damn weird."

I burst out laughing. Yep, that about summed it up.

She told me that Ryan and Zack had all but moved into my house, which I'd rather suspected from the contents of the fridge. I was more than fine with it. I told her about Katashi and his treachery, and my tutelage under Mzatal. I also told her that Rhyzkahl had turned out to be a colossal dickknuckle, but I didn't go into detail, and she didn't ask. My sweater covered the sigils, but I had no doubt she'd seen them when I'd arrived.

"Aunt Tessa," I said, "I know this is going to sound like a really off-the-wall question, and I hope you don't get mad at me for asking, but . . ."

"What is it, sweetling?"

Sheesh, there was no diplomatic or easy way to ask this. "Have you ever had a baby?"

A shadow of old grief passed over her face. Her hand tightened briefly in mine. "Oh, goodness, what a question." She gave me a sad smile. "Not long before your father died I had a baby, but he was stillborn."

A weird chill stole through me. The blond hair, the grey

eyes. "I'm so sorry," I said, since that was the expected response. "Um, was Katashi . . . ?"

She let out a peal of laughter. "Oh, dear heavens, no!" She smiled, shook her head. "It was a brief fling with an American living in Japan. He left before I even knew I was pregnant, and when the baby died I saw no reason to contact him and let him know."

Something seemed off about the way she said it, as if she was reciting a story instead of drawing from memory. I was willing to bet a year's paycheck that her baby hadn't been stillborn, but I had too many questions of my own to begin to poke at her version of things.

"And now I have you," she said, patting my hand. "The daughter of my heart."

"Goddammit, Tessa," I muttered. "Now you're making me cry."

She laughed and pulled me close, and we rocked in easy silence until the others called us in for dinner.

When evening came Tessa and Carl took their leave, and Jill and Zack went to the guest bedroom to take a nap. I found Ryan doing cleanup in the kitchen, took him by the hand and tugged him out to the front porch. He followed without question, but concern darkened his eyes.

I sat down on the steps, waited for him to do likewise. The night was cool and humid, and a mosquito buzzed nearby. "I have something I need to tell you."

The worry on his face deepened. "What is it?"

I exhaled. He was *not* going to take this well. I didn't have to be a mind reader to know that. "I have to go back."

Ryan stared at me. "Are you insane?" He shook his head in denial. "Kara, you're not going back there. Really, that's crazy talk."

Yep. That was about the reaction I expected. "I'm not safe here, Ryan. Not yet." I met his eyes. "They'll come after me, and come after the people I love." The Szerain in him would understand that part. "Mzatal is training me." I paused. "We're working together."

A liquid keenness touched his eyes. He drew breath to speak, then released it. "Shit." He ran a hand through his hair and shifted. "There's so much I don't know. Tell me what happened."

There seemed to be a faint difference in him. Or was I simply imagining it? Maybe it was pure delusion on my part, but I *thought* there was a touch more Szerain to him.

I gave him a quick and dirty rundown, not going into much detail on the parts that could possibly upset him, such as the torture. Or the bit about my profound connection—and really great sex—with Mzatal. I suspected Szerain would be pleased for me and completely unthreatened, but I wasn't sure if Ryan would handle it as well, and I didn't want to say anything that could hurt him.

And, holy shit, but it was weird to think of them as two separate people. Which they weren't, I knew. Which made it even weirder.

I told him about the fight at Szerain's palace, and how everything went to complete shit, and how I damn near destroyed the world. I debated telling him that the west tower was pretty much gone, taking with it Szerain's studio, chambers, and all of his memories of humans and demons captured in sculpture—and decided against it. Nothing he could do about it submerged, and it would likely hurt like hell. "And then Tessa summoned me."

Ryan let out a low whistle. "Wow, so when you left, everything there was still falling apart?"

"It's part of why I need to return. I chalked the patterns for the ritual and fed power into the storage diagram this morning," I told him. "I'm going in a few hours."

His brow still creased with worry, but he gave a slow nod. "It's weird. When you first said it, I was like, fuck no. But now it feels like the right thing to do." Then he frowned and gave me a sharp look. "Wait. How the hell will you get there?"

"I'm going to summon Mzatal," I told him. And I knew without a doubt that I could.

I almost laughed at the shift of emotions on his face. Ryan seemed relatively nonplussed about that, but Szerain was surprised. "Summon Mzatal? On your own? As simple as that?"

I grinned. "Yeah. 'Cause I'm awesome."

Ryan laughed. "Yeah, you are." He shifted to face me. "I missed you," he said, voice suddenly rough. "I was worried sick."

"I missed you too," I said, reaching for his hand to give

it a squeeze. "I'm working out a system to send messages back and forth. I'll probably have Tessa summon a particular demon periodically who could carry mail for us." I gave him a rueful smile and shrug. "It's better than nothing, I figure."

"Wait." Comprehension flared, and his eyes narrowed. "How long are you going for?"

I hesitated, grimacing. "I don't know," I told him. "Probably not until I do the shikvihr initiation, which could be about six months." *Or more*, I added silently.

"*Six months!*" Shock and grief etched lines in his face. "Kara, you can't be gone for six months. What about your job, and Tessa and . . . and everything?"

"And you," I said quietly. Sighing, I dropped my head into my hands. "I—" My throat tightened. "I'm submitting a letter of resignation to the police department." That had been the most difficult decision, but I knew I had no choice. At least this way I stood a chance of perhaps getting my job back someday. "And I've already talked to Tessa and Jill." I didn't have to tell him that the conversation we were having right now was me saying goodbye to him. He knew that.

"Wait." I lifted my head and looked over at him, frowning. "Hasn't anybody wondered where I've *been* for the past two months?"

Ryan gave me a faint smile. "Tessa covered that. She told everyone you had a family emergency and had to be away for a while." He paused. "I also talked to your Sergeant, Cory Crawford. I filled him in since I figured it'd be easier to tie up all the loose ends with his help."

I raised an eyebrow. "That must've been an interesting discussion." Cory had found out about my arcane connections by accident, and had never really been able to wrap his head around the idea. He tolerated and accepted it, but it was damn clear he was never going to be comfortable with it.

Ryan gave a low chuckle. "He actually surprised me. He only had one pained look, and then . . ." He sobered. "He was worried about you. Like we all were."

"I tried to get a message home, but it never worked out," I said quietly. "But I promise I'll keep in contact as often as possible this time." I looked up at him. "I'm sorry. I wish I could do more. I don't want to leave you, any of you," I said, voice cracking. "But I don't have a choice. If I stay here someone will come after me." I pulled the collar of my sweater down and touched the sigils on my chest. "I'm a weaponized summoner. And they're not going to let me roam freely."

Ryan shifted to look down at my chest. He lifted a hand, touched the sigil near my throat with the tips of his fingers and went very still. For a brief instant his eyes flickered with ancient potency. Then he blinked, and they returned to normal. "Kara," he murmured, fingers still on the sigil. "I am so sorry." The words echoed in my mind, and I knew the sorrow came from Szerain.

I leaned in and kissed him. He returned the kiss with a gentle passion, lifted his hand from my chest to the side of my face. Where our other kiss had been desperate and fierce, this one was tender and spoke more to the hope of a future yet to come than a fear we might never see each other again. I slid a hand up to his neck, deepening the kiss before gently breaking it.

"I don't want to leave you," I said softly.

He held my face cradled between his hands as he looked into my eyes. "You will come back," he replied with the faintest undercurrent of potency.

"No power in the 'verse can stop me," I said, smiling.

He chuckled. "I'll make a nerd out of you yet." He stroked his thumb along my cheek, gazed at me as if trying to memorize my face. "They know not what they have done."

"They fucked with the wrong bitch," I said. I kissed him again then sighed. "I need to prepare."

Pain flickered behind his eyes, but he gave a nod. He stood, gave me a hand up, and together we headed inside. "Do you need any help?" he asked. "Packing? Anything boring like that?"

"I'm pretty much already packed," I said. I'd done most of that earlier in the day. I knew I really didn't need to bring any clothing—which felt strange—though I did pack new running shoes, a couple of sports bras, and my favorite pair of jeans. If the zrila could duplicate any of those I'd be happy. But once those were in the duffel I proceeded to fill it with more esoteric items like coffee, fashion magazines, feminine supplies, sunscreen, and more coffee. "I'm bringing an absolute buttload of coffee," I said with a wry smile.

"Good. I've been around you when you haven't had any." He gave a low laugh. "Do the entire demon realm a favor and bring *lots*."

"I'm dangerous enough, right?" Then I winced because it was true.

"Yeah, you got it going on." He still smiled but was having a harder time hiding the worry. "When's the big moment?"

"Not long. Maybe twenty minutes." I shrugged. Then I grew more serious. "You want to—" I barely stopped myself from saying "see," "—meet him, don't you?"

He shifted. "You mean Mzatal?"

"Yes, Mr. FBI suspicious guy. Mzatal."

A scowl curved his mouth. "Well, shit, Kara, you're going off for half a year or more with one of these lords." A hint of jealousy flared in his eyes that I knew was Ryan's and not Szerain's. "I don't exactly have a lot of faith in them, y'know?"

Well, now I knew I was right not to mention getting jiggy with Mzatal. "I do know." I smiled. "Which is why I'm going to let you come downstairs for the summoning if you want." This wasn't the first time I'd invited him to witness a summoning, but this time I had the ulterior motive of reassuring both Szerain and Mzatal that all was as well as could possibly be. That made the unknown risk of having the two demonic lords in the same room worth it. I hoped.

"Really?" He sounded like a kid who'd been told he was going to Disney World.

"Yeah, but this is different, Ryan." I kept my face as sober as possible. "This is a demonic lord. You have to be *totally* naked for this."

Ryan tilted his head in thought, shrugged, and then began unbuttoning his pants, grinning. I burst out laughing.

"I should totally let you meet Mzatal in the buff," I told him. "That'd teach you."

"It might intimidate him," he said with a laugh. "Best not to antagonize him."

I snorted. "With your ego perhaps." This was what I would miss the most—the camaraderie and easy banter. Would I still have that with Szerain? I didn't want to think about it.

"Okay, let me finish getting my stuff together," I said.

"Then you can carry it downstairs for me." I gave him a sidelong glance. "That's really why I'm letting you come: to carry my shit."

"At your service, Miz Gillian." He gave a mock salute. "You have anything ready yet?"

"The big duffel in my bedroom," I told him. "I just want to grab the rest of the fashion magazines I bought for the zrila."

Ryan headed off down the hall while I busied myself getting the last few things that I could think to bring.

A moment later I heard a groan. "Jesus, Kara," I heard from the bedroom. "Is your whole house in here?" He hauled the duffel out of the bedroom, staggering comically under the weight.

"If you want to head to the basement with it," I said, "I'll be down in just a few to get things started." He gave a nod and tromped down the stairs.

I grabbed a few more things and was about to head downstairs myself when Zack came out of the guest room and quietly closed the door behind him. I flicked a glance behind me to make sure that Ryan was already downstairs, then leveled a slight frown at Zack. "Are you going to let him be present for the summoning?"

He gave me a small nod. "I'm not sure it's the best idea," he said. "But then again, it just might be." He shrugged. "Better if I'm close by in any case."

I smiled in relief. "Thanks. Makes me feel better about it too." I headed to the kitchen, trusting him to follow. I grabbed the bag containing the rest of the coffee. "What happens now with your oath to not talk about Szerain's exile?"

Zack shrugged. "I won't speak directly of that which is not known to you, but it's pointless to avoid what's already clearly revealed. If I'm named *kiraknikahl* for something as asinine as that, so be it."

I snorted. "Sounds reasonable to me," I said, then took a deep breath. "I can sense Szerain more now."

Zack leaned against the kitchen doorway, folded his arms across his chest. "Kind of like putting the lug nuts back on the wheel. Sometimes you forget to tighten them all down."

"Hunh. Hate it when that happens." I gave him a slight smile, then sobered. "You're Rhyzkahl's ptarl."

He gave me a single nod. I stayed silent for several heartbeats while I tried to figure out what I wanted to say. "Has he ever done anything this—" I gestured to myself and the sigil scars, "—extreme before? Did you know he . . . ?"

"I knew Rhyzkahl had chosen that path," he replied in a voice heavy with pain. "It is part of the reason I am here, rather than there." He shook his head. "But he has travelled far along it in the years I have been on Earth."

"Did you know he had such designs on me?" I asked, eyes intent upon him.

His eyes dropped to my upper chest, and the pain in his eyes seemed to deepen. "I did not know he had come to *this*. I swear it, Kara."

My gaze stayed on Zack for a few more heartbeats, then I nodded. "Y'all need to watch out for Katashi and his people." I gave him a quick rundown of the Katashi and Gestamar summonings and our subsequent retrieval of the reyza.

His eyes went distant, troubled. "That complicates matters much,"

"Ya think?" My mouth tightened, but then I blew out my breath.

Zack's focus came back to the room, though a hint of the faraway still remained. "Jill," he said, scrubbing a hand over his face in a very human gesture. "Her risk is compounded with this."

"Jill is pretty damn special," I said, then smiled. "And I'm glad she has you."

"I would not change it," he said, echoing my smile. "And while you are gone, I will watch over Tessa and Ryan to the best of my ability."

I exhaled softly. "Thanks. I don't know how long I'll be away," I said. "I mean, it could be a long time." I shook my head. "There's bad shit going on and it's too dangerous for everyone until I have the shikvihr." I ran my hand through my hair, grimaced. "But I sure as hell need to be *here* to get a handle on what's going on with Katashi, and who—if anyone—is working Earth-side to counter or fucking help him."

"I agree. You need the shikvihr and you need to be here."

"Yeah." I sighed. "Sort of mutually exclusive."

"No need to give up so easily," he said with a sudden grin. I started to ask him what the hell he was talking about, but he spoke first. "You're near the shikvihr first ring culmination, yes?"

"Um. Yeah," I said. Damn. Did I have it tattooed on my forehead?

"Bust your ass and nail the first three. With focus, you could do it in a month," he said. "Because the third is a powerful energizer, you'll need a week or so to integrate it before beginning training on the fourth."

An ember of hope flared. "You're thinking I could spend the time between the third and the fourth here? Would it be, um, smart?"

Zack laughed. "*I* think so, but I'm biased." He laid a hand on my shoulder. "Talk to Mzatal. Tell him my opinion is that the third ring, your innate abilities, and Eilahn and me keeping tabs on you are sufficient for you and the rest of us to be reasonably secure for short periods." He shrugged again. "I mean as secure as anywhere. Everything's in flux now."

"That would be awesome," I breathed. "Best of both worlds." I knew enough to expect things to be hot both here and in the demon realm, but it would sure be nice to spend some of that time on Earth. "Thanks, Zack." I swept my gaze around the kitchen. "I guess I'd better get going."

He caught my arm and turned me to him, cradled my head in his hands and touched his forehead to mine. "Be well and be strong, Kara Gillian."

Tears pricked at my eyes. I gave him a quick hug, then gathered the last of my things and headed downstairs.

Eilahn had slipped down to the basement while I wasn't looking, and was crouched quietly by the wall with a small bundle atop a cat carrier containing Fuzzykins. I'd roused Eilahn early from stasis, and though she assured me she didn't need to return, she would need more rest than usual for a bit. Ryan sat cross-legged on the floor, not far from my storage diagram. I double checked that I had everything, all the while hoping to hell there was still a demon realm to summon Mzatal *from*.

I stepped forward and examined my chalk and blood diagram, assuring that every sigil resonated properly. *Shikvihr, here I come.* Satisfied after a few adjustments, I glanced over to Ryan. "Remember to stay away from the diagram. And it's best to just *sit.*" I dismissed a flicker of worry about whether it was a good idea to have Mzatal and a suppressed Szerain in the same room. Zakaar was a heartbeat away.

"And I might *stay* as well, but no promises," Ryan said, grinning, though there was an anticipatory tension about him.

I rolled my eyes, smiled. "That would be a really really good idea. Sit *and* stay." His only answer was a snort. I turned my full attention back to the diagram and the task at hand. Drawing power and focusing aspects, it only took a few minutes to get the portal set. My pulse quickened.

"Mzatal."

A cold wind arose, bringing with it the scent of sulphur and ozone. The diagram flared, and the air seemed to shiver and compress, as if an unheard sonic boom passed through the room. The sigils went dark, and a heartbeat later I saw a figure with a long dark braid crouched in the center of the diagram.

Mzatal drew a rasping breath, a shudder passing through him as he lifted his head. He looked like hell. That was honestly the only way to describe it: pale, disheveled, and wearing the same clothes he'd had on when I last saw him, blood and all. But the relief that flowed across his face as his eyes rested on me wiped away some of the exhaustion and strain.

"Kara."

"Hey, Boss," I said with a smile as I grounded and closed the portal, and dropped the protections. "You look like shit. Miss me?"

Mzatal drew another deep breath and stood. "Much, zharkat." His eyes went past me, and I realized Ryan had stood and taken a step forward. I looked back at him, frowning.

"Ryan?" I said, calling to that part of him.

Mzatal's gaze remained on him. "Peace, Ryan," he said, name flowing like a command. "Peace."

Ryan visibly settled, and I hoped that meant that everyone was nice and chill. Ryan looked from Mzatal to me. "You're really going," he said.

I stepped to him and pulled him into an embrace. "Yeah, it's time. I'll be back before you know it."

He wrapped his arms around me, held me close. "Don't

get yourself into too much trouble, okay?" His voice broke a bit on the last word.

"Who me?" My voice seemed to have the same unsteadiness. Must be something in the damn air. "I never get into trouble. I'm boring."

He snorted and buried his face against my neck. "Right. And I'm never moody."

I hugged him hard, then kissed him lightly before letting him go. "You'd better write. Tessa has her instructions."

He very reluctantly released me. "Yeah. Write. I will." His eyes went to Mzatal. "Don't you fucking hurt her."

Mzatal gave Ryan a sober nod. I hid a smile as Eilahn and I gathered our things, including a disgruntled Fuzzykins, and moved to the center of the diagram. I trusted Zack to take care of everyone and everything. I looked up at Mzatal. "Missed you, Boss," I murmured.

He smiled, but there was a strained and worried edge to it.

"Mzatal? What's going on?" I asked. "The destruction stopped when I was summoned, didn't it?"

"Yes," he said. "There are still residuals. But the unraveling ceased."

I didn't need my cop-vibe to know that something was seriously wrong. Unraveling of the world ceasing sure sounded like a good thing to me, but Mzatal wasn't exactly jumping up and down about it. Tension hung over him like a cloud.

"Mzatal," I said in a low, urgent voice. "Tell me what's wrong."

"They have Idris."

I felt as if I'd been doused in ice. I didn't need to ask who They were. The Four Mraztur.

I reached for Mzatal's hand and gripped it tightly. "Let's go home, Boss," I said, lip curling. "We have work to do."